A CERTAIN WIDOW

By the same author:

NO LASTING HOME

A Certain Widow

A NOVEL BY

Joseph Dever

THE BRUCE PUBLISHING COMPANY
MILWAUKEE

ACKNOWLEDGMENT

The lines from the song beginning "Give me a little kiss" are reprinted by permission of the Copyright owner, A.B.C. Music Corporation, 799 Seventh Ave., New York, N. Y.

AUTHOR'S NOTE

The characters in this book are not based on actual people, living or dead. With regard to the car-stealing escapades, once known as "looping," certain chronological liberties have been taken to unify the narrative pattern.

To both S.M.J.'s and a very
certain widow.

A CERTAIN WIDOW

Chapter 1

FAR to their left, high over the city loomed Bunker Hill monument. Inscrutable as the eternal New England hills out of which it was quarried, it looked down on the people of Charlestown, who loved it but did not know it was their sphinx, coldly benevolent, giving them a personality and a charm.

"There is no time quite like it," said pale, thin-faced Francis Ronayne. "No time like it at all."

He stood beside his older brother Martin in the crowd which had gathered around City Square on election eve, November 3, 1924. That night the stars were summer, the moon was winter, the wind was fall; the time was sweet with Now and bitter with a brevity that would too soon be Then.

In front of the Democratic "Davis for President" stand which the brothers faced, a small, spirited brass band in green capes and white garrison hats was oomping and boomping "The Wearing of the Green."

Martin Ronayne, Jr., a graduate of Ignatian College and presently a senior at Harvard Law School, seemed too immobile of jaw for his twenty-five years. He nodded his head almost imperceptibly at his younger brother's emotional words. For though he too was intrigued by the color and the gusto of election eve, though the music of the Democratic hirelings was blood-quickening, though the speeches that were to come would be searing with sarcasm and mellifluous with stock rhetorical altruisms, he could not get his mind off that other more modest and unobtrusive speaker's stand on the other side of the Square.

For there, addressing a trickle of bystanders without benefit of horn, drum, or cymbal, was a poised Republican from Beacon Hill quietly assuring a few sullen longshoremen and icily smiling old maids that notwithstanding the leather lungs of the ward bosses, Calvin Coolidge would be retained as President of these United States, and that, "you will do very well to get aboard the-uh band wagon with the rest of your countrymen."

Through the band music, Martin heard snatches of the effortless voice and wondered what James P. Hanlon would have to say about dour, drawling Cal and his chances of remaining in the White House. Wasn't John W. Davis the candidate of the Boston Democrats? Wouldn't James P. Hanlon, councilor-at-large and Demo boss of all Charlestown, swing the town to Davis?

The band burbled into silence. James P. Hanlon mounted the platform. He was a huge man with a heavy jaw and a hard face, that the Ronayne brothers knew was really not so hard. Hanlon had been a close friend of their deceased father and was still a good friend of their mother. And when he spoke out with his great coarse voice they were filled more with admiration than fright, for that was Mr. Hanlon's platform voice. They had heard his other voice in their parlor for the past few years, a voice tender and a little anguished as he pleaded hopelessly with Catherine Ronayne to marry him and become one of the first fine ladies of the ward. But there was the education of the children, she had gently insisted, and there was the weekly deadline of the *Charlestown Bulletin,* which the death of Martin Ronayne, Sr., had placed in her charge.

Now on the platform Hanlon's voice was loud with warning, raspy with sarcasm, the voice of the boss castigating Cal Coolidge and praising John W. Davis, choice of the Democratic party.

"Be remembering the Boston police strike not more than five years ago, when that lemon-faced little man was up on Beacon Hill ordering out the troops against Boston's finest, taking away the badges and the billies of our own good officers — and they forced to walk the streets looking for jobs like common criminals — and their wives and babies home without a scrap of meat or a drop of milk in the larder. The good God forgive him, is all I say. . . . "

Francis Ronayne looked up at his brother and frowned.

Martin smiled thinly. "Jim knows what he's doing."

The voice of the Republican speaker drifted across the Square.

"Give it to 'im, Jimmy!" hallooed a drunken longshoreman on the fringe of the crowd.

Hanlon inflated his chest a little and held his chin higher and firmer. He pointed across the Square.

"And there, good citizens of Charlestown, there is the likes of him that wants to run our country. Cold and slick as an eel and so terribly in love with the common people as to risk contamination by coming down to City Square to talk with them. About Cal it is, the wee, sour Yankee from Vermont, that the fine masters of the Hill would talk to us. How good entirely, how good of them to take such a sudden interest in our welfare!

"Is it our songs they like? No, for we only sing, think they, when our breath is heavy with the hard stuff. Is it the broad shoulders and the deep chests of our young bucks they admire? Oh yes, yes — if we will keep unloading their ships and bending over their looms. Is it our fair colleens they cast a likely eye upon? Yes, and those colleens bastin' turkeys in their fine kitchens, and bowin' and scrapin' for their lordships and their ladyships when the doorbell rings. And what do they want now? What is it but our votes, what but the very strength of our freedom in this good land of plenty. For this, they have the gall to come down here in our own back yard and ask us to vote for their kind, like sheep vaulting over a stile, askin' us to vote for Calvin Coolidge, a Republican, who would deliver us into the hands of Johnny Bull entirely — Johnny Bull that cannot pay his war debt to the United States because all England is too busy standing on the neck of Ireland's freedom. I tell you, good voters of Charlestown, let the Democrats stand by the Democrats, let the working people be strong for the candidate of the working people's party.

"You know his name as well as I. Vote for John W. Davis tomorrow and deliver the White House from all Yankee snobs."

The applause, the catcalls, the whistles went up raucously.

As the brothers pushed through the fraying audience toward the City Square and the office of the *Charlestown Bulletin*, they could hear the Republican speaker concluding: "Mr. Coolidge is a

Martin slipped a cigarette out of a package and lighted it. "He meant that Coolidge is going to stay in the White House and why don't we get smart and pull together, that's what he meant."

Francis started at Martin's words. They were blunt enough when uttered to him privately but here in the *Bulletin* office in the presence of his mother, they were tactless.

Catherine Ronayne rolled forward to the desk, put her elbows on the glassed-over surface and looked through a triangle which she made with the fingers of both hands.

With a screech and a squeal the cylinder press began to throb and pound again, omnivorous of the single center sheets of the *Bulletin* which would finish the night's run.

Without looking up from her fingers Catherine said: "Francis, run along and help Johnny with the inserts — he'll need some help with circulation, too. Don't be too late, though."

Francis held back the words he wanted to say to Martin.

"Yes, Mother, I . . . I . . . " He looked at Martin with helpless fury.

"Hurry along, Francis," his mother said, "Johnny will need you."

Martin blew a parachute of smoke toward his brother and flicked cigarette ashes into a wastebasket as Francis hurried into the pressroom.

"Now, my son," she began, "what is all this business about the Democrats getting smart and pulling together with the Republicans — if that's what you meant?"

Martin tossed his cigarette butt on the floor, and without unseating himself stretched a lanky leg and snuffed it out. His dark, lean, handsome face, which strikingly resembled his dead father's even as Francis' resembled his mother's, turned to the dingy-curtained window into the shuttling light and shadow of City Square. "Well, Mother — " he groped for words with dull edges. "I go to Harvard with a lot of Republicans — you sent me there, Mother, because you wanted me to get this other point of view. You felt Dad would want me to see both sides — well, Mother, gee, I'm getting that point of view, I can't see — "

"Just a minute, Martin! You're *not* to get that other point of view to the exclusion of your own, of ours. Now, go on."

"Yes, Mother, yes, I agree with you — but what I'm trying to say is that Mr. Davis, while he probably is in the best tradition of the common people, really doesn't have a chance if his success depends on lovable rabble rousers like Jim Hanlon getting up and tearing down an opponent of the character of Calvin Coolidge. Why . . . why . . . his tirades against Coolidge are absurd — "

"Enough of that, Martin." His mother laid her palms flat on the desk and looked straight at him. "Even if what you say is true, you should have more respect for Jim Hanlon than to speak against him."

"All right, Mother." Martin slipped off the desk and walked to the window. "I'm sorry if I seem disrespectful — at bottom, you know I like and admire Hanlon — but it's just that I think he's — well — unrealistic."

"Unrealistic, is it? And whatever do you mean by that?"

Martin turned from the window and looked at his mother. "My dear Mrs. Ronayne, these people I go to school with are pretty regular guys — some of their forefathers were running the state of Massachusetts, and, yes, the United States of America when Dad and James P. Hanlon didn't even exist; yet, they really haven't played the snob toward me. In fact, they've been rather cordial — one of them, Erford Parkley, has actually become a good friend of mine and has taken me into his confidence. . . . "

She looked down again at her ink-smudged hands out of which a pale grace still shone. Erford Parkley. She remembered his father well — aloof, gracious, the past-president of the City Council. Her dead husband, Martin, had debated the issues of the Spanish-American War with him on the stage of Fanueil Hall. Martin had been booed for daring to submit that the U. S. was ramming the American form of government down Cuban and Filipino throats. Erford Parkley, Sr., had denied that Teddy Roosevelt was an exhibitionist and warmonger — then he had gone on to point out the enormous mutual trade benefits which would accrue to the Americans, Cubans, and Filipinos as a result of their new "democratic association" — machinery and manufactured commodities *from* the United States, sugar, rubber, tobacco, hemp *to* the U. S. A. And he had all the statistics.

After the debate, they had attended a ball. Parkley had asked her to dance. She remembered his tallness, his Oxford gray suit, the thin, waxed mustache, the four-in-hand tie. It was not only a pleasure but it was good politics, even for a Republican, to dance with Martin Ronayne's wife. Martin Ronayne, civic-minded Democrat and editor, vigorous patron of the Democratic party and thus of the powerful if heavy-handed bossdom of James P. Hanlon. Martin Ronayne, the clear-eyed idealist who asked no political preference for his tireless journalistic and oratorical efforts, who wanted only the benevolent government he believed possible under the Democratic party.

Martin's great blind spot, she recalled, was an unawareness or ignorance of the predatory graft and venality of the spoils system which contributed to and maintained the power of the Boston Democrats. Knowing him as she did, she believed that if faced with documented evidence of political collusion on the part of Hanlon and his henchmen he would have been deeply hurt but still adamant in his conviction that the party which tried, however falteringly, to do the most good for the most people was still preferable to the cold respectability of landed gentry. The latter, he would have maintained, saw politics primarily in terms of the preservation of wealth and privilege and secondarily in terms of the welfare of every citizen, rich or poor, bank president or bricklayer.

His ideal he had lived for in the pages of the *Bulletin,* in his lectures, in his love of the Roman Church, which he passionately believed to be the refuge and champion of the poor — and his ideal of American democracy he had died for in the last great battle of the Marne. He had died in "the war to end all wars" and now his older son and namesake — although Martin, Jr., was too polite to say it — probably thought his father's idealism naïve and his death a futile waste.

Martin looked idly out the window, puffing on another cigarette. In the back room the press again screeched to a stop. John Little and Francis could be heard talking as they joggled bundles of newsprint. He glanced at his watch. His mother watched him as he jerked his left arm outward and then brought it back suavely, reading the time, a mannerism he had acquired at Harvard. It was five after nine. "I'll really have to go now, Mother," he said with what he hoped was an engaging smile. "I promised I'd meet Sis and

Alice after night school. We're double-dating — I with Alice, Rosemary with one of my school chums."

"Which school chum?" she asked.

"Well, Mother, it's Erford Parkley. I feel it will do her good to see these people step out of the pages of the *Boston Transcript*. They're really quite human, you know."

She fought back angry words. After all, she reasoned, why shouldn't Rosemary go out with one of these people — she's as well bred as any of them — and Martin would be along, too. Martin. She thought of her husband — what would he have said? He would have been angered by her intolerance. But their children's lives were their own. It hurt sometimes to admit that, especially when she disagreed with them. But of course it was true.

Her son's face crimsoned. He sensed her inner disturbance. "Don't misunderstand, Martin. I'm — I'm awfully tired. By all means, have a good time with Rosemary and Alice tonight — perhaps your new friend will be interested in a copy of the *Bulletin*. Take one along for him. And don't keep Rosemary and Alice out too late."

He stepped over and kissed her on the forehead. "No Yankee in all Boston has a mother like mine," he said.

"Now just what do you mean by *that!*" She raised her long, light eyelashes. They laughed together heartily.

"Francis!" she called. "Will you bring a few copies out here, please?"

Francis entered quickly, and without looking at his brother laid the ink-pungent papers on the desk. He stood meekly beside his mother while she unfolded a paper and spread it out before her.

Martin also snapped up a paper, glanced a little apprehensively at the front page. The scarehead read: DAVIS WILL SWEEP BOSTON. He folded the paper and placed it in the side pocket of his tweed suit coat. He winked at his mother, threw a mocking glance at Francis, which was not without a certain affection and went out.

"Don't be too late," she called after him, and turned again to the paper.

Francis moved back in the direction of the pressroom.

"Francis, may I see you a moment?" she said without looking up. He returned and stood by her, tentative, shy, his head a little averted — as he always was in her presence. She had at first thought his shyness a congenital thing, a nature-inflicted torture which he would carry as his cross through life. He had been shy, too, with his father — but his growing up and attending school had brought reports to her ears which belied the raw self-consciousness he showed whenever he was near her. At Charlestown High School, where he was now a senior, he wrote a clever, outspoken column on current events for the school paper and was also active in the dramatic society. She had heard from Martin's girl friend, Alice Stasek, that Francis had been offered a heavy role in the senior play.

"What's this I hear about the senior play? Are you going to take the part?"

"I don't think so, Mother."

"Francis," she said with a sigh, "what *is* the matter with you? Martin and Rosemary would have given anything to be in the senior play when they were at the high school. And now you — you 'don't think so.'" She sighed again. "Have you thought about the other thing at all?"

The other thing.

You could, perhaps, spell it with a capital T. It was the Thing that almost every Roman Catholic family in Charlestown, or anywhere for that matter, would like to have. It was the ordained son up on the high altar with all the gleaming vestments on him.

Catherine in trying to puzzle out the strangeness and unambition of her youngest son had constructed a pleasing logic which housed the secret desire of her heart for a priest in the family. Francis was a regular churchgoer, he showed no inclination to smoke or drink, his interest in girls was friendly, but in a selfless, undesigning way.

During the past summer she had sent him to the boys' summer camp run by the diocese down on Cape Cod. There, in affable collusion with her friend, Father Quinn, editor of the diocesan paper, who spent week ends at the camp, she had kept a mental graph-line of her son's spiritual inclinations. Father Quinn, too, had been impressed by the boy's piety and seeming indifference to a worldly calling. At the end of the summer he had given her the opinion that the boy might well have a vocation.

That was the nod of orthodoxy she had been waiting for. Now, she was determined to have Francis face up to it one way or the other. He would be graduating from Charlestown High late in the spring. If he was to enter St. Philip's Seminary, next fall would be the time.

Francis stood by her desk, his face partly averted, a little sullen, a little sad, pondering her question. In the pressroom he could hear John Little jogging the papers into bundles with lusty bumps and riffling noises.

Maybe his mother and Father Quinn were right — maybe he did have a vocation to the priesthood. He had thought it over a great deal and he had no particular ambition to become a newspaper-man like his father or a lawyer like his brother. But while the thought of withdrawing and studying the classics, philosophy, theology with groups of altruistic young men appealed to him greatly, while he loved the pageantry and solidity of the Roman Church, and most importantly, while he knew there was a sure and recurrent whisper of the Faith deep within him, he found it hard to think of leaving his family and Charlestown, John Little, the Monument, City Square, the paper on Thursday evenings and the nocturnal "loopers" screeching down Bunker Hill Street in stolen cars. He found it hard to say it, but he knew how much it meant to his mother. He knew she wanted it very much.

"Well, Mother, I think I'd like to go."

Chapter 2

SHE walked with a happy weariness across City Square, down Main Street under the El, toward the Ronayne tenement on Monument Avenue. She was happy in a habitual way because the *Bulletin* was once again thumping against tenement doors throughout the city, bringing homey weekly journalism to simple, hardworking citizens who sometimes wondered whether or not they could be much worse off under the cold, patient justice of the Republicans than they were under the sweeping half-fulfilled promises of the Democrats. And she was happy in a new and more thrilling way because now there was hope that she would hear a son of hers preaching from the altar.

It was ten o'clock. The political rallies were over and a pre-battle calm seemed to have settled in on the election campaign. Only the occasional whir of a speeding automobile, its election banner fluttering at the rear like the saucy skirt of a maiden, gave testimony to the pent-up hopes and passions of secret and noisy men who give their lives to politics up on the platform or in anonymous, smoke-filled hotel rooms. The late-night chill of early November was in the air and just a few young men in tilted wool caps were idling in front of corner drugstores. As she passed them they nodded self-consciously at her and she greeted them with a hearty and meaningful "Good night, boys!"

Knowing Catherine Ronayne, they touched their caps and shifted their feet uneasily as if the power of her words was almost enough to make them seek out their beds.

She thought about these stark young men of the night as she walked along, and her heart went out to them. Now in their late teens and early twenties, they were clear-eyed, bright, respectful to respectable ladies, and full of a restlessness which drove them into the navy, plunged them occasionally into rash and imprudent marriages, or sent them scuttling furiously down Bunker Hill Street in a stolen automobile with the sirens caterwauling behind them.

Her own little pressman and general handy man, John Little, was one of them. And she had heard through Hanlon's devious sources of information that John Little was by virtue of his skill and daring at the wheel of a "hot one," the accepted, unofficial leader of the "loopers," as they were called.

She had heard it was John who determined when and how there was to be a Saturday night junket down Bunker Hill Street and around the sharp curve at the Hill's bottom into Main Street, completing the loop.

With this information flickering in her mind she had kept John furiously busy, cleaning and oiling the presses on Saturday nights and had coupled her ruses with carefully phrased remarks to John, giving him a clear impression of her knowledge.

Finally, she had told him of her plans to help initiate a recreational program for young men which she hoped would be vital and interesting enough to harness their energies. She had asked for a year's time in which to get the thing moving. John had promised to try and persuade the gang to stop looping for at least a year.

There had not been a "loop" now for several months — the police were pleasantly bewildered — but in the poolrooms, speak-easies, on the drugstore corners of Charlestown, the intrepid young men angled their caps repeatedly, shifted their feet, chain-smoked, consumed bitter brown bottles of speak-easy beer; and since they were not in the army, navy, or going to college, longed for the chase — up, over, down the steep hill, and around the corner with brakes and sirens screeching and the thrill of living exultant in their throats.

And Catherine knew as she walked vigorously along to the tempo of a pounding elevated train overhead, that these thrill-seeking young men were criminals only in the sense that they "joy-rode" in automobiles which did not belong to them. They were, too, a menace to the peace and safety of the citizens of Charlestown, but so, in a way, were the perfectly legal aviators who skimmed over the roofs of Charlestown.

Surely, she knew, the cult of loopers must be destroyed in the name of law and order. But then, looping to young men like those she had just passed on the corner gave expression to the same lusty and wholesome energies which in other days and in other places would have found outlet in the joust, the crusade, the voyage of discovery. For their wealthier contemporaries, there were the lush variant fairyland of the country club, the Mediterranean cruise, the call of the moose in the expensive wilderness of northern Maine. The young Charlestownies could box and play basketball in the Bunker Hill Boys' Club and, too, there were periodically recurrent wars to take them out of the hair of the Charlestown police. But young men who did not have access to respectable men's clubs soon grew out of boys' clubs and the time between wars seemed longer and more tedious than it actually was.

Some kind of an attractive, constructive, recreative program of adult education, she felt, was the answer. She had been after Hanlon to pester the mayor and the city council to do something for these young men — she would continue to bother the politicians about it both with her tongue and in the columns of the *Bulletin*.

She turned off Main Street into Monument Avenue, casting a habitual glance at the illuminated column of granite which stood ever over Charlestown like some symbol of an ancient oriental culture which could know no logic whatever as a commemoration of the Battle of Bunker Hill.

She passed the fading, crumbling Yankee houses whose present Irish tenants did not suspect their olden splendor, and entered one of them, now a two-storied tenement with a brownstone front which lifted its face a little more proudly than the rest. Its wooden sills were freshly painted in dark green and there were new slats in the fence, green-painted flower boxes jaunty at the window sills.

It was to this house that Martin Ronayne had first brought her as a bride. She rarely entered it without thinking of the time he had carried her across the threshold.

She thought of how he, too, would come home on press night happily weary. She would be waiting for him on the stairs, the coffee lyrical in the kitchen, his pipe, slippers, robe, and his stuffed leather-covered armchair waiting.

The loneliness came over her for an instant as she closed the door leading into the memory-haunted parlor. She removed her hat, unbuttoned her coat, and stood there in the darkness and the momentary, sharp sadness of the room. Her imagination knifed through the curtain of blackness and she saw the room in bold outline. There near the windows and the dark red velvet drapes was her husband's chair, ponderously lonely; there against the east wall was the brocaded sofa which was her habitual knitting place. Above the sofa, dominating the richly wainscoted wall was the huge oil painting of the Crucifixion, which Martin had picked up at a Beacon Hill auction. She could look into the darkness illuminated by her imagination and see the arched compassionate eyes of the Corpus pleading out of a blood-flecked head which seemed just about to collapse inertly onto His chest.

On the wall opposite the picture was a large gold-framed painting of her husband. She visualized him seated in his chair the night before he was inducted into the army. He had looked into the face of the crucified Christ and talked to her in a low voice. She had sat on her "knitting perch," her legs folded under her, her eyes riveted on the clicking needles in her hands, her ears filled with his quietly desperate words.

"I know you'll want to understand why I'm doing this — leaving you and the children at my age — leaving Boston and the paper, going off to a war that makes sense and doesn't make sense. But even though I hate war as much as any man alive, I do not believe that young men should be asked to die by older, safer patriots of the pulpit and the press; I believe that all able men should actually participate in the fighting of our wars — all men regardless of their age or position. I have promulgated this in the *Bulletin* because I know that if all the older men who preach war or benefit by it were forced to take up arms along with the young men, there would be no wars."

With a deep sigh Catherine tossed her hat and coat on the sofa and pulled the tasseled string of a floor lamp. She switched the

"It's fine, Jim, come in."

He set down a great black derby and, as she followed him into the parlor, she detected a sag in his thick shoulders that had not been there earlier in the evening.

He crossed the room to a straight-backed mahogany chair which stood at one end of the sofa, near the coffee table. He stood by the chair until Catherine was seated on the sofa.

She waved her hand. "Sit down, Jim, sit down." She poured his coffee and filled a plate with sandwiches. She sat back watching him as he made little musical sounds with the coffee — black with a little sugar — one cup of which he always consumed before saying a word. He wiped his mouth with the back of his bearish right hand. She arched her eyebrows chidingly.

He grunted, snatched up a napkin and patted his lips with meticulous touches the way he had seen one of the Yankees do it at a Fourth of July banquet.

Catherine poured him a second cup. He was ready to talk now. He rolled a pair of greenish, protuberant eyes, conveying a look of bewilderment.

"Catherine, I think we're beaten. You're the only soul in the world I'd admit it to, but old lemon-face will be back in the White House tomorrow."

She nodded slowly without looking up from her knitting. He talked on, grateful for the hearing and the sympathy she would bring to him.

"I'm a big man in this city, and it would not do for anyone else to see me like this — sniveling like a starved whelp on the very eve of election. But I know what I know and I see what I see in the rest of the state and the country where they do not be voting against the man who broke the Boston police strike. And though our own crowd will turn out for Davis here in Boston, there is no point in fooling ourselves. It's a good lesson I'm learning. . . ."

She smiled in a wan, sympathetic way and offered him the plate of cookies. He shook his head slightly and looked up at the Corpus.

"It is yourself I hope that will pardon me for looking up at that painting the way your own Martin, God rest his soul, used to look up at it, talking, while he was in trouble.

"You know, Catherine, Davis would have done big things for me if he had been elected. There was talk even of making me Postmaster here in Boston. And me hobnobbing with all the big buckoes in Washington and maybe taking you and the children to tea at the White House sometime. And what an old fool I was to think that I could go away from Charlestown and lord it over all the ward heelers and mattress voters that made me what I am.

"But there'll be no more foolishness, I can tell you right now. Though I'll never turn my back on His Honor or the national comm-it-tee, when they needs me, and though I'll work tomorrow till the blood comes out of my hide, it is a Charlestown boss I'll stay from now on and no more pipe dreams . . . no more."

"Good, Jim!" Catherine said, "but I'm sure you've nothing to be ashamed of in trying to get Davis elected. And why shouldn't you have wanted a Washington plum? The Yankees are no different from you in that respect. It is not that they are much more honest than you and your workers — they are, perhaps, considerably more subtle. It just isn't our year, Jim, let's look at it that way."

The big, soft man, who had a reputation for being a big, hard man, sighed and nodded. "That is so, Catherine. It is just that like many a pol I don't like a beating while it is going on."

"Who does, Jim!"

The doorbell rang again.

It was a sallow bean pole of a man and a short, rectangular woman.

The man she recognized as Timmy Mackail, city councilor from Charlestown and chief henchman to Hanlon. Derby in restless hand and blinking small, shifty eyes which looked over her shoulder meaningfully, he said in swift, out-of-breath phrases: "Forgive the call at this unholy hour, Mrs. Ronayne, but I hoped Mr. Hanlon might be here. This lady is Mrs. Maggie Quigley and there seems to be some misunderstanding which has upset her very much. Could we see Mr. Hanlon for a minute please?"

"Yes, he's here, Timmy. Won't you and Mrs. Quigley step in a minute?"

The woman, whose gray-black hair straggled in wisps from under an old brown-felt hat, smiled a toothy, knowing smile. "It's nice and cozy here," she said.

Catherine flushed. She remembered that Mrs. Quigley was a poor widow on the lunatic fringe of ward politics whose one great savor in life was gossip and the smell of gossip.

Mrs. Quigley took a step toward the threshold.

"If you don't mind, Mrs. Ronayne," Mackail said, "we won't be disturbing your household. Perhaps we could talk to Mr. Hanlon for a minute right here in the hall."

"Very well, Timmy." She glanced crisply at Mrs. Quigley, turned, and went back into the apartment.

"It's Timmy Mackail and Mrs. Quigley to see you, Jim," she said resuming her place on the sofa.

"For the love of God, what do they want at this time of night?" He sensed Catherine's keen embarrassment and picking up his derby he arose heavily. "Well, I'll be going now, Catherine. It's fine medicine your coffee and your talk have been for me. I'll see the two on my way out. Good night to you, Catherine."

"Good night, Jim. Get some rest; you'll feel better in the morning."

"I will that."

On the way out he looked glumly at the two nocturnal petitioners. He closed the apartment door, motioned toward the outer hall entrance with his derby, put it on, and strode firmly out of the hall and down the stairs to the sidewalk.

Then turning to Mackail he said wearily: "Now, Timmy, just what the hell would you be wanting from me at this time of night?"

"I'm sorry, Chief, but Mrs. Quigley here has been after me all night about giving her late husband's job at the Custom House to her oldest son, Mickey. You'll remember we said something about it to her when she was running those house parties for Davis earlier in the campaign!"

"Yes, and there's been nothing but the brush-off since for me and my Mickey. What do you take me for? And my house open on several different occasions to your speakers and one of your spalpeens up to the polls tomorrow to vote in place of my Jerry, dead only these few weeks, God rest his soul."

"Come on, Maggie," Hanlon said, "we don't intend to do you

wrong, but we pull more weight in Washington only if Davis is elected. I'll say no more about our chances on the morrow. But you've been reading the papers yourself and you know that Boston alone cannot swing the nation. And you know, because of the job that your own Jerry had, that the victor gets the plums. So all I say is that your son will get a job with the Customs if we win. But if we lose — well, there be other good jobs around for strapping young bucks like Mickey and he needs no pol like myself to get one for him."

"You made us a promise, Mr. Hanlon," Mrs. Quigley said, "and I'll hold you to it, of that you can be sure. And if you don't come through, there's always the *Boston Yankee* and its high-toned readers that will go for a story about my dead Jerry coming forth from the grave like Lazarus to vote for Mr. Davis."

Hanlon shrugged his ponderous shoulders. Abortive threats and even serious ones were all part of a ward boss's daily routine. "All I can say, Maggie, is that promises don't hold when you're on the losing side. You're not the only one that could take a licking tomorrow. A very good night to you. Are you coming along, Timmy?" The Councilor tipped his derby to Mrs. Quigley and walked into the night with his chief.

"You've not heard the last of this," she muttered when she was sure he was out of earshot, "you and your high-born chippy." She glanced at the Ronayne tenement, spat swiftly on the sidewalk, and hunched along into the darkness.

Chapter 3

"WHAT's a loop like, John?" Francis asked. "What is it really like?"

They had finished their hamburgers and were dawdling over their coffee in a City Square cafeteria, after distributing the special edition of the *Bulletin*. The spacious, pungent cafeteria was humming with the talk and feeding bustle of late eaters.

John swiveled his great red head around the cafeteria before he spoke. His quick sweep of the midnight lunchers had been, for him, a meaningful one. He saw pimply, gap-toothed Mickey Quigley leave the table where he had been sitting with several teen-age girls and cross over to the table of Shiner Farrell and three other "loopers," who, John knew, were writhing under the one-year taboo laid down by mutual consent less than five months ago. Mickey Quigley had been along on the last careening ride; it had been his first and he had swaggered like a veteran ever since. It was Mickey Quigley who had been sowing the seeds of unrest among the loopers since John's intervention.

John had put it up to the boys as intelligently and as forcefully as he could. They had assented, some reluctantly, others indifferently, all with varying amounts of respect for Catherine Ronayne and their leader.

And now the swaggering restlessness of gangly Mickey Quigley, son of the widow Maggie . . .

"What's it like, John?" Francis repeated. It had not been hard

22

for him to read the story that John's look had unfolded. It would ease John a little to get him talking.

John pushed a tuft of crinkly red hair out of his eyes. "It's like skiing in Switzerland, and like shooting tigers in Sumatra. Maybe the cops and the public don't know it's like those things, but we do. It's skill and thrill. To do the whole thing right — through City Square, picking up the cops, up, over, and down Bunker Hill Street, wide open and with plenty of horn. Then the loop on Main Street, under the El, using the brake just enough to keep from tipping over; over Rutherford Avenue to Charles Street into Cambridge, or across to Mystic Avenue and Somerville, depending on the closeness and number of the cops. Then the ditching and the scattering, hotfooting it through alleys and over back-yard fences. Somebody's cellar, an empty house, maybe hopping the back end of a passing truck.

"Or — " he wrinkled the left corner of his mouth — "maybe a crack-up, a bed in the Haymarket Relief Station, a two-year stretch in the state pen. . . . "

Francis looked into his coffee. His feelings were mingled — admiration and regret. He saw his mother's point more clearly than ever — their energies needed legitimate outlets.

"And you know," John went on, "there's one big thing that is the mark of a good looper. Within the limitations he has set for himself, he always tries to return the 'borrowed' car in the same general condition in which he took it. I mean, he's chiefly out to do the loop, not to steal or damage the car."

Francis could not repress a smile.

John Little blushed and grinned. "I know, it does sound like romanticizing — but it *is* true of most of us — guys like Shiner Farrell over there; Eddie McQuestion, who's been in the pen for over a year now; my old buddy, Wally Whalen, who died in a wreck on Cambridge Street. Shiner and guys like the ones I've named are or were sportsmen — really! I've read up a great deal on the different sports of different world regions and I think that our practice of looping is fundamentally an athletic thing."

"Why don't you guys go in more for organized athletics?" Francis asked.

"A lot of the guys do play baseball, basketball, and football,"

John said. "Some of them are stars too, on the town team — but still — well, why do some men who play golf also hunt mountain lions?"

"Maybe mother's projected program will seem pretty tame to the boys — if what you say is true."

"Maybe it will — but if I know your mother at all she won't expect the boys to play ping-pong and drink cokes every evening. She talks of organizing a hunt club with bowling and billiard facilities — she'd have the city build it out in the Fellsway marshes where the boys could bang away at clay pigeons and targets to their hearts' content. She talks about organized week-end hunting trips during the fall and winter in northern Maine — she talks about cruises and deep-sea fishing. Then she believes that the boys are capable of intellectual excitement — she believes that lectures and discussion clubs can be made interesting and profitable even for guys that have only finished the eighth grade. Maybe she can do it — Hanlon will help her — it sounds like a promising experiment to me."

"What — ee-yuh say?"

John and Francis looked up. Quigley, Farrell, and the others were standing beside their table. Quigley had asked the question.

"What do *I* say?" John answered, reacting with a swift facetiousness. "What the hell do *you* say?"

"Quigley, here, thinks we ought to do one tonight in honor of the election," said Farrell, a firm, round mick in his early twenties. The roundness was also in his ruddy, friendly face on which was spread an inviting smile. He was the kind of congenitally happy person who might even smile just before the car lurched into an elevated upright. "How about it, John?"

"Yeah, how 'bout it, Little?" Quigley used John's last name with obvious defiance. "Ain't it time we stopped actin' like a lot of Sunday school kids?" Quigley's mottled, gap-toothed face was hard and arrogant almost with an adolescent anticipation of the things of life.

"What's wrong with Sunday school kids?" The words were out of Francis before he had thought to restrain them. Despite his secret attempts at understanding and feeling sorry for Mickey, he writhed before the posturing unreason of the youth and dreaded, too, that Quigley might blunderingly help to frustrate his mother's careful and patient plans.

"You oughta know that," Quigley said.

"Lay off him," Farrell said.

John said nothing and seemed absorbed in trying to get his cigarette lighter to work.

"Oh, all right," Quigley wheedled, "it's gettin' so you can't say a thing in this town about the great editor or her *friend* the great *statesman*."

Francis leaped to his feet, his thin face white, his slender fists clenched by his side. "You take that back," he said, his voice quavering a little.

"I'll take nothin' back — not for you!"

"For me you will!" John Little got to his feet, pushed Francis aside, and swung a right fist with graceful heaviness to Quigley's jaw. Quigley jerked backward and then slumped to the floor. He muttered an oath, pushed himself up on an elbow, shook his head, and began rubbing his jaw.

The teen-age girls screamed and one of them yelled for the police. All movement in the room stopped.

"If you want to finish this, Quigley," John said, "I'll meet you up by the 'Spike' in five minutes. Come on, Fran!"

Francis, chilled with the excitement of the fight, walked toward the door of the cafeteria.

John Little turned to Farrell and the others who had sat down at the table. "See you again, fellers." He knew that if they wanted to loop it tonight, nothing he could say or do would stop them. He was afraid the promise of a hunting lodge and other recreational inducements now seemed too far short of fulfillment.

"See you, John," Farrell said, smiling. He turned to Quigley who was still rotating his jaw. "Come on, you jerk," he said, "get up and have some coffee."

A police siren whined. John hurried out the revolving door after Francis. When they heard the siren, Farrell, Quigley, and the others also fled through the door.

John and Francis walked briskly down Main Street in the general direction of the Monument.

"Why don't you run along home, Fran," John said. "I'll take

a turn up by the Hill — Quigley won't show up — then I'll head home myself."

"No, I'll go with you, John, if it's all right. Then we can walk home together."

Just before reaching the neighborhood of the Monument, Francis stopped and was sick.

"Too much excitement, kid. Want to go home now?" John asked, when they had resumed their hike.

"No, I'm all right now, John."

They turned off Main Street, up Soley Street toward the Monument. High over the denizens of Charlestown, enwombed in their dank and crumbling tenements, loomed the great white picket of the night. High over all of Boston it loomed, with magnificent incongruity, symbolizing a comparatively recent American battle, the smoke of which, when measured as the years of an obelisk are measured, had hardly cleared away.

High over the Irish-Catholics who flourished so well in the Colonial atmosphere bequeathed them by the Puritan fathers, loomed the inscrutable rampart which connoted phallic symbolism to urbane Harvardians, and to the Freud-scorning Irish of Ignatian College connoted simply, clearly: Bunker Hill Day, the 17th of June.

By day a place of tourists and Charlestown urchins, by night a place of tenement-stifled young lovers, grateful for its stony, silent visage and closely shaven lawns.

"There it is," said Francis as they came into full, close view of the Hill and its towering sentinel.

"Yeh, there it is."

They climbed to Monument Square and stood for a while outside the iron-picketed fence that surrounded Monument Park. From this point they commanded a view of all the approaches from the Main Street side.

"Let's take one turn about the Spike and then head for home. He won't show up."

They entered the park, circled the Monument, and paused by a bench which two self-conscious spooners had vacated as they approached.

Francis laughed and sat down on the bench. His laughter eased the strain of the election and the special edition; it eased the tension of his decision to enter the seminary, minimized the scuffle in the cafeteria.

"Say," John began, "how come you aren't dating some little cozy from the high school? What's the matter, no moxie?"

"Yeh," Francis replied wistfully. He decided to tell John of his seminary decision. He was the only other person beside his mother and Father Quinn that would have to know until it was time to go. John was closer to him than even his brother Martin or his sister Rosemary. John would understand — he would tell him — now.

"John, I think you should know I've decided to study for the priesthood after I graduate. I've told Mother of my intentions and it's made her very happy. I'm not entirely sure of myself, but Father Quinn says I seem to have a strong enough calling to make a real try."

"Well!" John said, pulling at the narrow chin which threatened to give the dimension of length to his craggy red head, "so you're going holy on me. And I thought we'd build a pinnace some day and make that South Sea cruise. You were going to write a book of South Sea verse, remember?"

"Maybe we can do it anyway, maybe they'll make me a bishop and we can sail to Rome together."

"That would be fine," said John, "but what would a hidebound old Methodist like me be doing in Rome?"

"You could do a loop on the Appian Way."

John chuckled. "So's your old man. Seriously kid, I think it's wonderful. You really might fit into a life like that. I think — all this" — he nodded ponderously at the jagged skyline of tenements, made alabaster with moonlight — "all this embarrasses you a little, doesn't it? You know, even though you try after a fashion not to show it, some of us offend something in you, don't we?"

Francis was silent for several moments. "I don't know, John, I don't know what this restlessness in me is."

"You're a poet, after a fashion," John said. "You're built so that you see beauty in the ugliness of our things and our ways."

"It isn't hard to see beauty in people — people like you, John."

"The hell you say!" John exclaimed. "Save that line for the monthly collection. And if I don't get you home soon I'll be answering to herself, Catherine Ronayne. Let's go!"

Francis smiled wanly. If there ever was a first convert, he hoped it would be John.

"I just came up here on general principles," John said as they walked down through the park in the direction of Main Street. "As I said before, I knew Quigley wouldn't show up."

There was that phrase again: "on general principles. . . . " You could always identify John by that one and another: "after a fashion . . . " Francis reflected.

As they neared the sidewalk on the perimeter of the park they heard a distant, augmenting roar of a motor. Closer now, they heard the squeal of brakes, the squeaks of straining springs. Then the wail of a police siren.

"It's Quigley!" John snapped. "The little punk has done it!"

"I wonder if the others are with him," Francis said.

"We'll soon know — they're headed this way. Quigley's out to show me. They'll swing around the Monument up Concord to Bunker Hill Street and then down for the loop. We'll wait right here."

Headlights cut the blackness of the Adams Street curve several blocks away and blazed toward them with a screech of brakes. The pursuing squad car was not yet in sight.

On it came, hurtling through the blackness. And in these moments Francis knew something of the ecstasy, the attainment of which inspired young Charlestown males to risk death and imprisonment and brave the long, wild, tortuous way of the Loop.

The rumbling black monster with the blinding eyes bore down on them. At the corner another set of headlights screeched, sheared through the blackness, and let out a frantic whine.

As the stolen sedan swept past them, they could discern a tallish lonely figure at the wheel.

"It's Quigley, sure as hell," John said.

The car careened ominously to the right at the end of the park and swayed up Concord toward Bunker Hill Street, slowing a little.

John and Francis broke into a run heading down a side street toward Main and the Loop. The squad car bumbled swiftly around the corner after the looper.

There was little chance that they could get to the Loop intersection before Quigley or the police. But that was the place to be if Quigley cracked up. He was green and John sensed trouble.

Francis knew what John was thinking and prayed silently for Quigley as they trotted along the sidewalks and across the deserted streets past the dark, musty tenement halls. Up on the Hill there was the steady growl of a motor; up there, too, and about even with them the piercing clarion of law and order.

Francis was breathing heavily now, lagging a little behind.

John slowed down. "We'll go slower now — no sense in killing ourselves "

"Yeh, no sense in killing ourselves . . . " Francis panted. He recognized fearfully the irony of their words. "Hail Mary, full of grace," he prayed for Quigley, "the Lord is with thee. . . . "

Then the climactic shrilling of brakes. Quigley was starting his loop.

When the crash came like a clap of thunder, Francis could run no more. He heard the diabolical music of breaking glass, the hollow groan of collapsing sheet metal, punctuated by a woman's scream. The police siren grumbled into silence as if out of reverence.

John quickened his pace grimly and was soon out of sight as Francis slowed down to a stumbling walk.

"Quigley, poor Quigley," he said with dry lips.

Thus at 1:15 a.m. in the neighborhood of the crash, the lovers cooled, the miserable awakened to their misery, lights blazed, windows flew open, voices flurried anxiously through the air.

Francis Ronayne could go no farther. He turned left on Main Street toward home, his face death white, his eyes filled with tears.

High over Charlestown the great imperturbable obelisk pointed at the stars.

Chapter 4

AFTER Martin Ronayne, Jr., left the office of the *Bulletin,* earlier that fatal election eve, he walked briskly up Pleasant Street (for in Charlestown you are almost invariably walking up or down) toward the high school. He would have to hurry if he was to catch the girls as they came out of night classes at 9:15. He had mentioned the date to Rosemary that morning at the breakfast table, as she pulled on her flat-heeled shoes and then bolted down her coffee and roll. "We'll think about it," she had mocked playfully, grabbing her coat, bag, and notebook. The social agency where she did student field work had given her an early morning case over by the sugar works. She was too preoccupied with it to talk about dates.

"What do you mean, think about it?" he had retorted. "Alice will go with me, anyway. If you don't care to come along and meet Erford, we'll get someone else; you're — "

"I'm nothing," she said, kissing him coolly on the brow. "We'll be looking for you tonight after school. Bye-bye, my big, high-browed brother!"

Now, Martin saw the lights of the gray, boxy Charlestown secondary school across the street from the Monument. A melancholy blast from a Cunard liner at the near-by Chelsea docks dinned in his ears. Erford, he knew, had heard that blast in the harbors of England and France; in fact, he had heard steamboat whistles in all the important ports of the world. Someday, he,

Martin Ronayne, Jr., would stand in dark glasses and a palm beach suit on the immaculate first-class deck of a Cunard liner — someday, when he was a distinguished lawyer and could sip sherry in the salons of the Yankees.

Erford had a sister about his own age. She was strikingly attractive in a long-haired, athletic sort of way. He had seen a picture of her in *The Transcript*, on horseback wearing jodhpurs and a jaunty little derby. "Debutante Althea Parkley, just in from a brisk canter on the trails of the Cornucopia Hunt Club." He wondered if Erford would ever introduce him to her. He wondered how she would compare with Alice Stasek.

Alice. There was a girl. The soft, shy voice, the tight, yellow hank of hair, the high cheekbones, full body, the quiet, smoldering quality in her smile. Maybe he was in love with her, he wasn't sure. One thing he did know — if it weren't for the law books and his yearning to be a name on the land she would be a fire in his blood, a hammer in his brain. Maybe she was that already; he wouldn't allow himself to face it.

He stood outside the high school and puffed on a cigarette. It was fourteen past, the bell would ring in a minute. Rosemary and Alice were "culture-vulturing" an evening course in Creative Writing.

"There are forty women in the class and two men," Rosemary had told him. "Twenty-five of the women are a mixture of middle-aged spinsters and housewives. They actually write, even though they never get published. The rest of us are young chickens who can hold our chins a certain way during the lecture, giving the impression that some day, in some wonderful and inexplicable way, we are going to write novels. The two men come out of sheer boredom.

"The teacher is an Ignatian College graduate named Ambrose Callahan. He teaches English in the high school and writes occasional stories for the *Sacred Heart Messenger*. Once he won ten dollars in a short story contest conducted by the *Boston Post*. He goes to all the autograph parties over town and knows all kinds of gossip about authors. We just *love* him!"

The bell jangled, thunder rumbled on the school staircases. The central door swung outward, spilling the awakened intellects of Charlestown into their hilly world. Martin watched for the girls.

Rosemary, dark, cool, and brimming with saucy wit approached him.

"Where's Alice?"

"Really," said Rosemary, "you ought to see those old maids up here hanging on Callahan's every word. And Alice . . . " she sighed, suppressing an urge to giggle.

"What about Alice?"

"Well, it's my fault. I kept coaxing her to ask Mr. Callahan a question. We've been going to class over two months now and Alice has never said a word during the discussion periods."

"Alice is like that, Sis, that's all."

"I *know* she is, but still I thought it would be fun if she asked a question; and what do you suppose she asked him?"

"What?"

"She asked him in her very sweet, shy little voice how much the *Atlantic Monthly* pays for a short story!"

"What did the great mentor say?"

"He raised his eyebrows a little and said he didn't know offhand. He might have something in his notes on their rates, and would she please see him after class."

Martin glanced at his watch. "I told Erford we'd see him about nine forty-five."

"Oh." Rosemary wrinkled her slender nose. "Where are we meeting his majesty?"

"Now Rosemary . . . he's a regular guy. We're meeting him at the Lincolnshire. Then he's taking us to a club, a kind of high-class speak-easy, I guess."

"What's he interested in meeting me for — doesn't he realize where we're from?" she said, calmly.

"Sure he does, he's real democratic!"

"One more remark like that and you can find yourself another date!" A little squirrel track of color appeared in each cheek.

They stood waiting in the midst of a sullen, awkward silence. Finally her features softened and she turned to the immobile face of her brother.

"Marty, what's got into you since you've gone over to Harvard? Have they mixed you up a little over there? What is it, Martin?"

"I'm sorry, Sis, I really didn't mean to cast a slur on my own people. It's just . . . well . . . it's just that I'm so damned impatient to get ahead. I'm sorry, Sis, really," he said, with the rich, earnest smile, which was one of the attributes that made her fond of her older brother.

She kissed him on the check. "See that you do, you big lug! Here's Alice now! Hey, Alice, how much?"

"Hi, Al," Martin said, "how much do they pay?"

As they walked down toward the elevated station, Alice smiled her slow, sweet smile with her attractive, high cheekbones and bright blue eyes. "He couldn't find it in his notes," she said, in a hushed voice. "He's going to look it up for me."

"Why didn't you ask him what the *Sacred Heart Messenger* pays?" Martin asked.

"I never thought of that."

Alice smiled shyly and blushed, as the Ronaynes laughed.

Back in the classroom, Ambrose Callahan tightened the straps on his brief case and wondered how the *Atlantic Monthly* rates had slipped his mind. He would look them up in the *Writers' Digest* at his earliest opportunity.

At about the same time Martin and the girls walked toward the Thompson Square elevated station, where they would board a train for downtown Boston, Erford Parkley IV leaned back restfully in a small stuffed armchair which was standard equipment in the thick-carpeted Four Swans Club. He squinted quite intellectually through his glasses at his boyish younger sister, Althea. Between them at the same circular glass table sat a young student from the Midwest named Herbert Royce, thin, blank faced and almost as bored looking as Althea.

"All I'm asking, Sis, is that you say hello to these people," Parkley said. He was in his twenties, thick limbed, of average height. His hair was drastically abbreviated in what has come to be known as a "Harvard Clip."

"I don't know what you'll think of the girls he's bringing along," Erford continued, slightly contorting his bony, tight-skinned face out of which fluxed two unusually large, almost distended, hazel eyes, "but you might find Martin quite engaging.

He's really an unusual type — has remarkable discipline over the usual — ah — Irish prejudices. . . . "

"All right, all right, we'll say hello to your little pets." She toyed with the wooden paddle in her empty glass. "Where's that waiter?" she said, with an attempt at dismissing a rather annoying subject. Martin would not readily recognize her as the long-haired girl on the hunter, for her hair now was closely bobbed, which, with greenish eyes and a hint of freckles scattered over a pert nose, gave her face the appearance of a handsome boy.

"Can't say as I know the chap," Herbert Royce said nervously. "He's over at the Law?"

"Yes, he's in my class. As a matter of fact, Dad knew his father and mother quite well — the political wars, you know." He turned from Royce to Althea with a faint smile. "Althea, here, doesn't seem to realize that the Ronaynes come of very good stock. Dad could tell her things about the integrity of the parent Ronayne. Martin, Sr., crusaded for good government quite a bit in that weekly Charlestown paper, the — uh *Bulletin*. They've still managed to keep up its standards since Ronayne's death in the war. They say the old boy really martyred himself by offering to go."

He paused to light a briar pipe. Althea made a little condescending twist with her mouth. He chuckled and winked at her affectionately. "They're hopeless Democrats, of course. At least the older crowd is. Rather fond of boss Hanlon, too, although they don't cow-tow. Ver-ee solid people — really worth knowing if you're at all interested in politics."

"Daddy's little helper," Althea said tartly.

It was true. Erford Parkley, Sr., sometime state representative, state senator, and presently member of the Governor's Council, approved of his son's interest in politics. He was sharing his experience and his political responsibilities with his son, as much as he tactfully could. He had indoctrinated Erford, Jr., painstakingly with the necessity of gracefully appeasing the significant people in local politics. Such appeasement, or co-operation, if you will, was mandatory for a politically ambitious Yankee who hoped to attract support from the Irish-Catholic majority of the Boston electorate.

Erford, Sr., had singled out the Ronaynes of Charlestown as

a good example of responsible leadership among the Irish. They were the people who influenced the influencing Hanlons — they were the ones to cultivate if you wanted the crumbs of the Irish vote. The good will of the Catholic clergy was also of paramount importance. Since, by remarkable good fortune, young Martin was a classmate of Erford, there was all the more reason for him to cultivate the Ronaynes.

Parkley puffed on his pipe. "Dad's always quoting in private the statement of a political writer: 'get the principals and let them get their sheep.' "

Althea wrinkled her nose. "Gruesome! I need another drink," she said wryly. "Where *is* that waiter?"

"Maybe I'd better have a look." The morselish Royce from the Midwest excused himself, arose, and wound through the tables toward the hostess, stationed at the entrance of the lounge.

Althea glanced after him for a minute. "Really now, Erford, aren't you making Dad seem a little politically ruthless in front of our Wisconsin friend? You make him sound like a ward boss."

"Sorry if I've given the wrong impression, Sis," Parkley said. "However, I don't think Royce is offended. Politicians aren't in the 'untouchable' class out in Wisconsin. You really don't think we're less Machiavellian than the Hanlons and the Curleys do you? We wear political slippers, my dear, little flowered oriental slippers like those great-grandfather Parkley brought back from Japan. We get the same things done without offending the ladies."

"You've offended *me*, dear brother."

"You — are in the family! It is good for you to know these things. You needn't lower your defenses in the least. You can still gasp with horror over the bridge table when you read about the latest deal at the Hall. You can still be a Parkley — hurry away and dash off an indignant letter to the *Transcript*. But, I insist that you be honest with yourself. You and I would never have been where we are if it hadn't been for a long, historic series of things like 'deals at the Hall'!"

Althea's eyes focused metallically. "Tell me, philosopher, could I still be a Parkley and tell you to go to hell!"

"Quite," Erford said, through teeth and pipe.

"Go to hell!" she said.

Erford nodded gallantly and was about to speak when Royce returned with a drink-laden waiter.

"Nobody seems too excited about the election," Royce said, pulling up a chair. He had been talking to several of his classmates at the downstairs bar.

Erford shrugged his shoulders slightly. "Cal's as good as in." He shot his arm out abruptly and looked at his watch. "Say, it's time I was getting downstairs." He glanced at Althea benevolently. "Look, you two, I'll bring them over to meet you first thing. Then we'll find a table somewhere in the corner and leave you both alone. How will that be?"

Royce smiled rather unctuously, grateful for the chance to be alone with Althea. "Thanks, old man," he said.

Althea's face did not register. Secretly she thought Royce an utter bore; besides, the idea of sitting and drinking with the young Charlestownies had an element of intriguing novelty about it. She frowned, finally. She would not let Erford get the satisfaction of having her give in, however.

"See you, Sis." Erford rose and headed for the lobby.

"What is it, Althea?" Royce asked in a more intimate tone of voice. "Are you unhappy?"

"That, my friend," Althea said, patting Royce on the wrist, "is a very obvious question. My big brother is *so* realistic."

"Perhaps you could be a little more realistic yourself, Althea," Royce said, a little miffed at Althea's casual treatment of him.

"What?" Althea raised her eyes sharply.

"No offense, Althea. I was just wondering if you had decided about coming to Wisconsin for Thanksgiving?" He had invited her to spend Thanksgiving with him and his family in their palatial home on the shore of Lake Michigan.

She had avoided committing herself — not wanting to hurt his feelings, but at the same time she had little interest in going. She felt she should get it over with now.

"I've really thought about it, Herb, but I don't see at all how I could get away from the Parkley Thanksgiving dinner — it's quite a ritual in our family, you know. It's awfully nice of you to ask me. Would you like me to drop your mother a note?"

"That would be nice," Royce said flatly.

"Oh, come on, Herb, drink up. Really, you're much too serious for your age!" She lifted the Old Fashioned and drank. Then she looked in the direction of the lounge entrance, completely oblivious to Royce's presence.

Royce went white with repressed rage and frustration. He pushed back his chair abruptly, got up, and walked out of the lounge.

"There goes another one . . . " Althea said.

He was nicer, in an obvious sort of way, than most of the others who paid her court.

Her father and Erford seemed to like Royce. "He comes of good Midwestern stock," Mr. Parkley had said to her only the other evening.

"Good Midwestern stock and bonds," she would have retorted had it been anyone but her dad. But he was a sweet old guy. He worried over her gadding about and wanted her to settle down. But, damn it, she had never grown cynical about romantic love. She just hadn't ever met a man she could go for with all her being. Someone who would sweep all her pettiness and self-indulgence away with his love. So why settle for Royce or any other gilt-edge refuge for errant youth? Why settle for that at all?

"Isn't there some special ceremonial dress Alice and I should be wearing for this occasion?" Rosemary asked Martin. He smiled faintly at her with genial disdain.

"Not at all. You look fine in your halo."

They were sitting on a sofa in the lobby of the Lincolnshire, at the foot of Beacon Hill, waiting for Parkley.

Alice sat primly between brother and sister, looking a peeky look of love at all the world. Within, secure from the mocking eyes of sophisticates was the simple delight flowering out of the actuality of her presence in the Lincolnshire. Her mother, she knew, would sprinkle her with holy water and mumble thick-voiced prayers in Polish when she found out where her daughter had been and with whom. A hotel like this one, where all the Harvard and Beacon Hill swells hung out, was the kind of place you glanced into as you hurried by on your way to the Shawmut Bank on the corner. It was hard for Alice to realize that it would be perfectly permissible for simple, unpretentious people from

Charlestown to sit in the Lincolnshire lobby, dine in the dining room, sleep in a Lincolnshire bed. But there were Boston intangibles at work which were much more powerful than the Bill of Rights. If you were Alice Stasek and lived by stitching up ten-pound cotton bags of sugar at the Sugar House, you just didn't go into places like the Lincolnshire.

Bulwarked by the Ronaynes, she sat quiescently with hands in her lap and reeled with the wine of newness.

Martin blew out graceful clouds of cigarette smoke with a cool petulance as if the Hon. Henry Cabot Lodge had kept him waiting too long already. Alice felt the pulsating nearness of Martin's lithe physical being, and because of the new atmosphere that flooded her consciousness with lacquered, bony women in boyish bobs and chic, long dresses; with unconcerned men in high, starched collars and four-in-hand ties she was able to obliterate temporarily the sweet dull misery of her love for him.

Back at the Four Swans Althea Parkley, from a social and psychological position diametrically opposite to that of Alice Stasek, ordered another Old Fashioned, which would be made, as usual, from the Parkley private stock. Luxuriating a little in her elected loneliness she decided that tonight was as good a night as any for a Radcliffe graduate, '24, to get gloriously tight. . . .

"Sis, you're all alone — what happened to Herb?" Martin and the girls were twisting politely through the tables toward them.

"He had to go. . . . Where are your friends?"

"Why they're — they're right here! Alice, Alice Stasek, this is my sister Althea — and this is Rosemary Ronayne."

Alice blushed before the polite hauteur of Althea. She lowered her head a little, almost in inevitable tribute to the enormous social pressure of Yankee property and tradition.

Althea averted her puckish head casually toward Rosemary. Her inherent aplomb succored her strongly as she looked into the mirror of cold, comely darkness that was Rosemary Ronayne. "How do you do," Rosemary said.

"Here, Martin, over here," Erford called. Martin had detoured a little, making way for an exited couple. "And this is Martin. Martin, this is my sister Althea."

"Well, hello," Martin said briskly. "This is an unexpected pleasure."

"How *are* you?" Althea said, almost eagerly — eager to recoil from the colliding aristocracy of Rosemary. "Won't you all sit down — soon as I finish my drink I have to run. I've had a *gruesome* day. Rode all afternoon."

Erford and Martin each pulled up extra chairs for the girls. Erford ordered the drinks, Rosemary and Alice blandly requesting ginger ale.

Erford chatted about the election — twitting the Ronaynes good-naturedly. Althea forced a smile at the self-conscious Polish girl, who had blushed again when she reiterated Rosemary's indifferent request for ginger ale.

Behind her smile, Althea absorbed the presence of Martin. The tallness and the darkness of him — the poise and the squareness of his chin; the infectiousness of his chuckle. The storybook symbol of the prince loomed up in her consciousness.

Martin joked lightly about Hanlon's last-ditch speech earlier in the evening. To Althea his poise and good humor implied complete indifference. She found herself wanting to jar him into recognition of her.

"Oh, is he the rather gruesome man they call the Mayor of Charlestown?" she asked.

"Althea!" Erford said.

"Really, though," she continued, watching the change come over Martin's features, "aren't people like that a little pathetic?"

Rosemary lowered seething eyes to her ginger ale; Alice blushed; Erford took a strong pull on his bourbon and water.

Martin thought of his mother and her defense of Hanlon — the jollity went out of his voice. "Not as pathetic as others I've seen," he said matter-of-factly.

She pushed her drink aside. "Will you excuse me — I've got to go." She arose, weaved a little, nodded, and moved off among the tables.

"Good night, Althea," Erford said, standing, "you'll take a cab?"

"Yes, a cab."

Chapter 5

ONE dim, November morning, a week after Mickey Quigley met his untimely death in Charlestown and eight days after Calvin Coolidge hunched over the presidential desk, filled with lemony exultation over his sweeping victory at the polls, Michael Farrell, political editor of the *Boston Daily Yankee,* sat at his typewriter in the city room, scanning his morning mail.

Tall and stringy, he loomed over his machine while his owlish gray eyes roamed over the crinkly letter in his hands. There were pallid hollows in the cheeks of his long-boned face and as he read he occasionally ran a hand jerkily through a coal-black thatch of hair.

At 29, Mike Farrell, Charlestown born and bred, and graduate of the Columbia University School of Journalism, was pounding out an attractive reputation for himself as a hard-hitting journalist who reported and wrote features on Boston politics in the religiously Republican columns of the morning *Yankee.* While not a Republican himself, he did not find it difficult to ally himself with the righteous editorial policies of his paper when it came to any analysis and evaluation of the city's Democratic administration. The latter was gaudily panoplied in the person of Boston's fabulous and perennial mayor, Edward Francis O'Malley. In his daily column, "The Hill and the Hall," a commentary on events at the State House and in the City Hall, he took pot shots at the O'Malley administration wherever he could this side of libel.

"Dear Mr. Farrell," said the letter, "Our attention has been called repeatedly to remarks made in your newspaper column which seem defamatory to the character and reputation of our client E. F. O'Malley.

"May we, in a spirit of friendly advice, remind you that there are libel laws in this State which could conceivably be invoked in your disfavor if you persist in attacking the character and good name of our client in the columns of the *Boston Yankee*, or elsewhere.

"With all good wishes,

Yours very truly

P. H. O'Donnell

O'Donnell and O'Donnell

Councilors-at-law."

"Oh, brother!" Farrell muttered, running his hand nervously through his hair. He picked up a pencil from the metal typewriter table, swung around to his desk and scribbled on the margin of the letter: "Chief, here's a little love note from the boys down at the Hall. Thought you might pass it on to the legal department — don't know when I've been openly libelous in the column, do you?"

He wrote "Managing Editor" on a white slip of paper, clipped it to the letter and dropped it into the outbox. He swung again to his typewriter, on top of which several other letters lay cradled. They had already been opened and time-stamped by one of the mail girls. There were two requests for speaking engagements, a catalogue of books on political science, five books of chances from a suburban Catholic parish. The last piece of mail consisted of a gray, lined sheet, torn from a five-cent copybook on which the following was scrawled in pencil:

Dear Mr. Farrell:

I hear about your column on the pols and know it puts the fear of God in them. Despite my great grief (the loss of my son Michael in an auto-crash, that is) I still feel I should do my duty as a citizen of Charlestown.

You should see what is going on over here as well as at the Hall. There's a well-known pol across the bridge, here, who is real sweet on a widow who runs a weekly newspaper and sends her son packing off with the swells over at Harvard.

And if information is wanted about the election I know of at least one case where the dead came to life and voted for Davis — I know because the dead one happens to be in my family.

Hoping this information is of some help to you. I remember you as a little kid on Bunker Hill Street when your nose was running — you've come a long way since then.

Also this information is confidential, you understand — my name on it, that is, you understand.

                                        Margaret Quigley.

Farrell whistled softly. Margaret Quigley, Margaret Quigley. Maggie Quigley! He remembered her now. Glancing once more at the letter, he could not resist a smile. She was the loud woman from Main Street who fancied herself quite a power in Charlestown politics. Her home, he recalled, had been the scene of many a house rally for the Hanlon-sponsored candidates. Now she had the ax out for both Hanlon and Catherine Ronayne.

The Ronaynes . . . he wondered how they were. Yes, she must still be running the *Bulletin* — and one son at Harvard. That must be Martin. He wondered why Martin hadn't gone to Ignatian. Perhaps he had — yes, he would be about graduate school age now, wouldn't he? He was probably at Harvard Law.

Farrell remembered vividly the apprenticeship he had served under Martin Ronayne when he was at Charlestown High. He had worked over at the *Bulletin* office after school. Great was the patience and kindness Martin Senior had shown him. The *Bulletin's* late editor had stressed the importance of knowing the newspaper business from a news-worthy incident through typewriter, linotype, proof sheet, cylinder press, and circulation. Farrell had worked on the *Bulletin* in all the phases of its weekly production before Mr. Ronayne allowed him to concentrate on reporting and feature writing alone.

"The only place for editorials is on the editorial page," he had said upon reading Farrell's first news story — an account of a checker tournament at the Bunker Hill Boys' Club in the writing of which Farrell had pulled all the stops. Farrell chuckled, remembering those words. It had been his first important lesson in journalism — one which he applied quite handily at Columbia. It was, he recalled, at Martin Ronayne's insistence that he had applied for a journalism scholarship at Columbia, instead of attending one of the schools of journalism in the Boston area. Mr. Ronayne had also written him a strong letter of recommendation.

He had seen his patron for the last time in New York just before, as Corporal Ronayne, he had embarked with his regiment for France. Farrell was a senior then, close to graduation.

The lithe, graying Charlestown editor had had the distinguished look of a general who had mistakenly donned a doughboy uniform. Farrell had told him of an offer to work for the *Yankee*.

"Good, by all means accept it," Ronayne had urged him. "Times are changing; the *Yankee* needs the spice and the color of journalists who are the sons of immigrants if it is to get and hold the readership of the second generation. It is not enough any longer in Boston to be only a Yankee — a newer, American race is in the making. That is why the illustrious old *Transcript* will die — simply because its presses are, in a sense, geared up to a Yankee dynamo that is running out of power. That is why the *Boston Yankee* will probably continue to live and compete with the other less staid Boston dailies — by taking on new writers like yourself.

"And there's one thing, Mike, I want you to watch out for when you first go to work for a big newspaper like the *Yankee*. Just be yourself, work hard and don't say anything about the way you 'used to do things at Columbia.' "

Before he boarded the train for camp, Corporal Ronayne handed Farrell a slip of paper on which he had written the name: Lincoln Steffans. "Here's the name of a writer whose analyses of the Boston political situation you would do well to study. You probably have heard of him already as a 'muckraker.' Keep him in mind now that you're going to work in Boston. His ruthless honesty might help you see things as they really are. . . . "

Since then, deep in the labyrinth of daily deadlines that is a newspaper columnist's life, he had seen little of the Ronayne family, except for his attendance at the memorial services held for Mr. Ronayne in 1919 and an occasional meeting with Catherine or one of the children at a Bunker Hill Day banquet.

Rosemary had grown into quite the "dark Rosaleen" type of beauty, if he could judge from a recent cut of her he'd seen in the diocesan Catholic weekly, *The Beacon*. She had been awarded some kind of scholarship for social work to be done in the Charlestown area, he recalled.

He thought of the poison pen letter from Maggie Quigley. He had been about to do a piece on the looping escapades. This would be a good time to talk things over with Mrs. Ronayne. She'd know the local situation. . . . Maybe he could ask her to lunch.

He snatched up his desk phone. "Will you get me Catherine Ronayne at the office of the *Charlestown Bulletin?*"

"It won't work," Farrell said, putting down his coffee cup, dragging on a cigarette and running his hand nervously through his hair. "That clubhouse idea alone isn't enough."

Catherine frowned and stirred her coffee petulantly. They were in Rawson's Restaurant alongside City Hall, seated at a table on a narrow balcony which half-circled the restaurant walls and hovered over the diners on the main floor. Farrell's invitation to lunch had come at a very opportune time.

The death of Mickey Quigley had emphatically brought home to her the need for action if additional tragedies and jail sentences were to be forestalled. Now was the lull of horror that always followed the death or conviction of a looper. Soon, she knew, the horror would wear away and the defiant young men would be eager again for the long wild swing over the hill.

Someone had told the police that John Little had been Mickey's assailant in the cafeteria earlier that fatal night. John had been taken into custody for questioning. As always, Boss Hanlon had been approached by John's friends and, since the redhead had not been mixed up in the ride, Hanlon had been able to get him off. "One offense, yes, two offenses, no!" Hanlon always said. She knew, however, that Hanlon often broke this rule and fought to get the loopers off even after they had been convicted and sent to the state prison. They were his flock — voters and the sons of voters. Who else would protect them if he did not? And while Hanlon was honestly opposed to looping, he still knew the inevitability of his patronage — after the fact.

Who else *would* protect them? That was the question Catherine was most interested in — protection, however, before the fact. Prevention of the fact.

She had told Farrell about her plans for a hunt club out in the Middlesex Fells. She had planned a drive for funds to be publicized through the columns of the *Bulletin*. Yet she felt helpless without political support and the active sympathy of the big downtown papers. The political action she might be able to get through Hanlon. But Farrell was perhaps the outstanding political voice in the big Boston papers — thus the importance and the promise of this meeting.

"The clubhouse idea is all very fine," Farrell continued, "even though I don't believe you'd get our young roughnecks to wend their way nightly out to the Fells. It's too far away from Bunker Hill Street. Those guys will take their social service strictly in a familiar atmosphere. However, even if you could get them out there, the clubhouse isn't enough to stop them from grabbing a hot one every so often."

"What else would you suggest, Mr. — uh — *Steffans?*" Catherine asked with a smile that did not betray the hurt she knew. She had inferred from Farrell's stints in the *Yankee* that he was much taken with the political pragmatism of Lincoln Steffans. Since her own late husband had been intensely interested in the reform-by-recognition-of-human-weakness ideas of Steffans, it was not hard to recognize the muckraker's influence in Mike's columns.

Farrell's jaw dropped a little and he grinned shyly, the greenness of his years shining through the premature wisdom he had acquired. "Yeh — Steffans," he said, "but it was your husband that first got me interested in him — in case you didn't know."

She laughed. "I might have known."

"He had an engaging and perhaps even logical idea about Steffans' natural understanding of man in his fallen state — of Original Sin, as it were," said Mike.

"What did he advise you to do?"

"Oh, he suggested that I watch the guy's stuff. Said Steffans would give me a sense of things political as they really are. . . . "

"Sounds just like Martin." She looked over the balcony and down at the politicians and City Hall employees who were eating their lunches and probing with absorbed conversation the painful problems of a great, and some said, corrupt, municipality. "Quite a view from here," she added, as a preface to some less bantering thoughts which had been evoked in her mind.

"Yeh," Mike said, as a waitress refilled their coffee cups. "Now you know why I sit up here in the balcony. Who-was-with-who at lunch in this place can sometimes suggest a nice two-plus-two for my morning column. It's a little more dignified than peeking through keyholes."

"Martin and I used to sit downstairs whenever we lunched here. But let's get back to our joy riders in Charlestown. . . . What would you, and Mr. Steffans, suggest?"

"Well — we've just got to be hardheaded about the whole thing," Farrell began, watching Catherine's face. "I mean, how much effect would a good clubhouse program have on those kids if they know they can still take a stolen car over the hill, the possible legal consequence of which could be ameliorated by their political patriarch and refuge Mr. James P. You-Know-Who!"

Her face was thoughtfully calm either because of inner discipline or because of her gathering agreement with his opinion. While he believed Maggie Quigley's accusation to be the twisted suspicion of a petty mind he nonetheless was curious enough to see for himself how Catherine would look or what she would say at the mention of Hanlon's name.

It was no great surprise to Catherine that Mike Farrell understood Hanlon's key place in the looping situation. Now that she was aware of Farrell's knowledge, she felt easier about discussing the situation across the river. There was no danger now of betraying Hanlon's confidences — she was grateful for Farrell's frankness.

"Yes, Mike, I agree. We'll have to try and bring the politicians into the picture, won't we?"

Mike grinned and with relief thought of Mrs. Quigley's letter. He would tear the thing up and forget about it.

"Yes, I'm glad you feel that way. I should have known that Martin Ronayne's wife would see this line of thinking right away. But what are we gonna do — you think Hanlon would play ball with us?"

Catherine glanced over the balcony at the restaurant entrance.

"You might ask him yourself — here he comes now!"

Farrell glanced toward the door. "Holy smoke!"

Catherine smiled. "And surely you must recognize the personage just behind him."

"Well, this *is* our big day! It's Edward Francis himself, Lord Mayor of all Boston, wise and benevolent father of the commonfolk!"

All eyes in Rawson's Cafeteria focused near the entrance, where James P. Hanlon was talking softly to the waitress. Behind him, moving his lips casually, a rotund, red-faced man holding a Homburg hat, was talking to His Honor, a big, deep-chested man with curly, silvering hair and an aristocratic countenance. Wide pouches under his eyes gave the impression of dignified weariness.

The waitress smiled nervously, nodded too much, and beckoned them toward the staircase.

"They're coming up here!" Catherine said. She slipped a mirror out of her bag, glanced hastily into it, and patted her sleek gray-brown hair.

"Where else?" Farrell said gleefully.

The three plenipotentiaries followed the flustered waitress up the stairs and toward a corner table several yards behind Catherine and Mike.

Hanlon saw Catherine and grimaced with pleasure and surprise. "Your Honor," he said — the mayor had just about passed Catherine's table. "Your Honor, I wonder if you remember Mrs. Catherine Ronayne from Charlestown — you knew her late husband, Martin, fairly well in the old days, I believe."

The mayor bestowed on Catherine a rich, warm smile. Mike got to his feet.

"I remem-bah you both very well," the mayor said in a soft, resonant voice. "How are the-uh children and how is the *Charlestown Bulletin* doing? I do see it occasionally, you know." He averted his head slightly toward the dapper, rotund, little Irishman just behind Hanlon. "Brendan, please check on our office subscription to the *Bulletin* — I don't believe I've seen it for a few weeks now."

"Certainly, Your Honor," the mayor's secretary said. He knew the mayor hadn't seen the *Bulletin* in years.

"The children are fine, Your Honor," Catherine said, "and thank you for your kind interest in the *Bulletin*. We still manage to get it out every week."

"I'm sure you do, even as your husband did before you. You've undoubtedly heard this, Mrs. Ronayne, but the gallant death of your husband was a great loss to the people of Baws-dun Is-uh, this young Martin?" The mayor rolled his sad, gray eyes at Mike.

"No, Your Honor. This is Mike Farrell of the *Yankee*. I — I — thought you two were acquainted."

"I met the mayor at his last inauguration," Mike said.

"Oh yes . . . I thought I recognized you. You're the young man who writes the column. You write as though you know me quite well."

Mike's face went red. Hanlon's protuberant eyes grew even more conspicuous. Hanlon wondered what Catherine was doing here. This was the first time he had been in a position to identify this upstart of a political writer, who looked as if he were not yet dry behind the ears. He recognized him, however, from press conferences in the city-council chambers.

Brendan Kelly, the mayor's secretary, coughed meaningfully trying to catch the mayor's eye.

"We have a duty to know you well, Your Honor," Mike said evenly. "In a sense, you as mayor belong to the city of Boston."

"That's all very well, Farrell," the mayor said, "but I do wish you wouldn't imply so strongly in your column that the city of Baws-dun belongs to me!"

Mike smiled mechanically.

"Such a pleasure seeing you again, Mrs. Ronayne," the mayor said, gracefully ignoring Mike.

"Nice to have seen *you*, Your Honor," Catherine said.

The mayor and his secretary moved toward their corner table. "I'm going to be very busy, Catherine," Hanlon said, his face softening. "Will you be able to get home all right?"

"Yes, thank you, Jim, I've some shopping to do first."

Hanlon nodded and, without looking at Farrell, turned and hurried to the mayor's table.

"Well, there goes the key to the 'looping' lock," Farrell said glumly, "and I'm the one that threw it away."

"Don't be discouraged, Mike. You were merely sticking to your guns. I'll talk to Hanlon. Perhaps we can patch things up."

"You're nice!" Farrell said. "Have you got a daughter?"

"You know I have. Why don't you come over and see her some evening? You might as well get a share of the ice she's giving to all the young men who've come questing after the fair dark Rosemary."

Farrell grinned and ran his hand through his hair. "Maybe I will. If she's anything like that shot in the *Beacon,* even the ice should be an experience."

"By all means come over then." Catherine slipped into her coat which was draped over the back of the chair. "Come over some night next week after I've had a chance to talk to Hanlon. And by the way, where can I get some information on the latest ideas of this man Steffans?"

"Well, the ideas on Boston politics you'll find in his '1915 Plan' — then there's a lot of material in *Everybody's Magazine,* year 1908. You should be able to get it all in the public library."

They arose and walked down the stairs. Mike paid the check and pushed out into School Place after Mrs. Ronayne.

"Thank you so much for the food — both physical and spiritual," Catherine said.

"Mutual," Mike said, grinning.

"Well — off to the shops; see you some night next week."

Catherine waved her bag at Mike and climbed briskly up School Place past the wan face of the City Hall within whose walls seethed the dreams and schemes of the politicians and their indefatigable hireling ants — striving prodigiously to make the city of Boston the place to live in as well as the place to live on.

Mike hunched down the hill toward Washington Street, his brain humming with provocative ideas concerning his morning column and the reckless young men of Charlestown.

He stopped suddenly by the curbstone, reached into the inside pocket of his coat, and withdrew a gray, lined piece of paper. He tore the letter into confetti and flung the particles high into the air. Then he whistled happily down the hill into the omnivorous jaws of newspaper row.

Chapter 6

LATE one afternoon of the week following the meeting between Catherine and Mike Farrell, Martin leaned on the iron railing just outside Memorial Hall, reading the latest edition of the *Boston Yankee*. Beside him, Erford Parkley looked upon the benevolent, patrician world of Harvard University and found it good.

They had just emerged from their last lecture for the day and at their feet, stacked ponderously on the faded lawn were the thick tomes of law.

Thus, at this moment Martin Ronayne, Jr., and Erford Parkley III, who provided for the discerning observer a composite picture of the old and the new in Boston society, turned their hearts against the sonorous drudgery of academic law, against jurisprudence, briefs, and precedent-setting cases — Martin escaping into the news and the political acerbities of Mike Farrell, Erford drawing in exhilarating draughts of the crisp November air. He savored, too, the mellow grandeur of his father's father's school and listened for the pert, opulent toot of his sister's convertible.

"M.I.T.'s in the bucks," Martin said, snapping his paper.

"Oh?" Erford glanced over Martin's shoulder at the paper, his flattened wisp of hair, thick eyeglasses and pale, bone-tight skin making him look a little like a confounding spirit about to whisper something in Martin's ear.

"Listen to this," Martin said, " 'George Eastman, head of the Eastman Kodak Company, will give \$12,500,000 to the Massachusetts Institute of Technology, University of Rochester, Hampton Institute, and Tuskegee Institute, it was announced in Rochester today.' How much of that do you suppose Tech will get?"

"About a fourth," Erford said. "Four colleges."

Martin flipped the pages to the editorial section. "How'd you like to have a fourth of that?"

Erford Parkley smiled, knowing he probably would come into that much money one day if you included in his probable inheritance the Parkley holdings in real estate and securities. Some of that real estate was right over in Charlestown where Erford and Martin were to be driven by Althea that same afternoon. In accordance with his father's wishes to acquaint himself with problems of absentee landlord administration he was to meet the Parkley agent in City Square and inspect several blocks of tenements on Medford Street, which had belonged to the Parkley family for generations.

Althea, who was attending a Radcliffe Alumnae tea, had consented to pick Erford up. Martin would be in on the ride to Charlestown.

"A fourth," Erford said. "That would be about three million, eh? As Grandfather Parkley used to say: 'Capital, capital!' "

"Yeh," Martin quipped, "as Grandfather Ronayne might have said: 'Labor, labor!' "

"What else is new?" Erford squinted down the editorial page. "What is Farrell yipping about today?"

"It's about the Mayor — get the opening sentence: 'Edward Francis O'Malley is a nice man.' Our political oracle from Charlestown is getting quite ironical."

Erford read the column over Martin's shoulders: "Edward Francis O'Malley's private life is and always has been exemplary and above reproach. However, his very industrious and even opportunistic public life is a matter more or less of public record. And since this newspaper and this column strive to be of honest and intelligent service to the public of the city of Boston, it is our sincere objective to hold up for public examination, the *public* life of Mayor O'Malley whenever it is conducive to the best interests of the electorate which he is pledged to serve."

"Noble words!" Martin said.

"Yes, a little rhetorical banana oil goes over well every once in a while," Erford said.

"Yeh, listen to this: 'Until a more realistic approach is made in the prosecution of loopers, Charlestown will continue to be a nocturnal speedway freighted with potential death and destruction. Would our defiant young speed merchants be as apt to take a "hot one" over the hill if the teeth in the pertinent laws were as sharp and unrelenting as they were intended to be from their enactment? Can it be possible that a strange and powerful dentistry in the form of political protection has yanked out the teeth of the law whenever and however it applies in the Charlestown situation? This column will try and offer a much more definite program for the stamping out of looping in the very near future.'"

"He's talking about your good Councilor-at-large, undoubtedly."

"Undoubtedly," Martin said, reddening a little and glancing hurriedly at the large, black-bordered portrait of Harry Cain Brattle, distinguished United States senator from Massachusetts who had died less than a week before. "There was a man!" Martin said, obviously changing the subject.

"Yes." Erford peered out at the thickening late-afternoon traffic on Cambridge Street for a glimpse of Althea — she was late already. He looked petulantly down at Senator Brattle's picture. "*There* was a tragedy," he said.

"How do you mean?"

"Because he was almost great. Like Daniel Webster and William Jennings Bryan, he *might* have been president. He was what my father calls an 'inevitable' in politics. But whatever it is, bad luck, poor judgment, a woman, pride, ill-health, whatever it is that defeats a Webster, a Bryan, a Parnell, or a Harry Cain Brattle, it always seems to let them get very close to greatness before they go down."

Martin's expression was somber as he folded the newspaper and screwed it into the side pocket of his topcoat.

"What would you say was Senator Brattle's fatal flaw — more specifically that is?" he asked.

The vast, patient throat of Memorial Hall tolled for all Cambridge the hour of half-past three. The lilting chime of St. John's on the other side of the campus hurried to answer the strokes of

John Harvard with a brief flurry. All the church bells in Boston, all the bells in the mildewed sidewalk clocks of Yankee banks, engaged for a few lyrical moments in the battle of half-past three.

"I think I can give you an idea," Erford said. "Take his feud with President Wilson when Brattle was perhaps the most powerful man in the Senate. Some say that Brattle wrecked the League of Nations by his adamant opposition to Wilson's ideas."

"Yes, but wasn't Brattle being consistent with the principles of the Republican party — in his isolationism, that is?"

"I suppose he was, but still there was something monstrous about turning our back on the world the way we did — the man's inhumanity-to-man sort of thing. Brattle, I admit, probably felt, and for good reason, that he was playing his political cards well. But I think that a really great man would have looked beyond the political arena of the U.S.A. We can only wonder what would have happened if he had put aside his political differences with Wilson and fought for the League, for world peace."

"Yes, that might be what brought him up short of greatness. I might suggest, too, Erford," Martin said with a hint of the vindicative in his voice, "that Brattle's seeming provincial attitude toward world affairs is not hard to understand when you consider who he was and where he came from. . . . "

Erford laughed good-naturedly. "Really now, are you implying that Boston is provincial?"

"Yep," Martin said, glancing at his watch. "Say, are you sure the princess of the rotogravure knows we're here?"

"She'll arrive." Erford glanced with involuntary admiration at the shadowy, handsome face of Martin, who was lighting a cigarette. "There's one more point I'd like to make concerning this Brattle thing, and it concerns you."

Martin flicked away the smoldering matchstick. "Me?" he asked raising his long, inky eyelashes.

"Yes, old man, you. I think you may be what my father would call an 'inevitable' in politics. You have connections, background, ability, personality . . . and the inclination to play seriously in politics. But, I'd be inclined to warn you as early as this — don't let ambition outrun reason and ability."

"I hadn't thought about it that way," Martin said softly. "I know I'm ambitious — but a person needs the self-confidence, else you won't take chances, you won't try and break down walls, you. . . . "

"I know what you mean, Martin, but keep those walls in mind. Regardless of what you and I think about the vulnerability of the barriers that separate the Irish and the Yankees in politics, we've still got to respect those barriers which it took decades of Yankee shrewdness to erect; even though you may be able to slip through them unobserved or where they're weakest. Yet you can't get cocky about anything in politics, my father always says; you've got to keep your guard up all the time. Look at the way Brattle underestimated Coolidge, who is now president.

"My father was a delegate to the Republican convention, you know, in 1920 when Coolidge was nominated for vice-president. Senator Brattle was so sure of his power to swing the nomination his way, he was so sure of Coolidge's lackluster and political insignificance that he stayed away from the convention, lecturing to a group of fluttery clubwomen. He showed up finally in the convention hall in evening clothes and made one of his eloquent speeches. But it was too late — the shrewd little men who watch for weaknesses in proud, big men, were working quietly and efficiently for Coolidge while Brattle's personality was wowing the clubwomen. You know the rest. I got this story from my father, and I believe every word of it."

Martin nodded.

Erford continued, "And you've got to watch that you don't substitute personality for shrewdness too — the ladies and the backslappers are going to like you. But, for heaven's sake cultivate the shrewd little kingmakers — they're the ones who can give you a crown or a shroud."

"I'm cultivating *you*."

"Can it," Erford said coolly. "Here's Sis!"

The sleek, yellow car trembled gracefully to a stop in front of them. Althea waved a gloved hand and leaned far over to her right pushing open the door: "Hail, Marshall and Taney! Come, the supreme courts of Bunker Hill await!"

"I'll say they await, Sis," Erford said, stooping for the law books, a couple of which he handed to Martin. "Where the deuce have you been?"

"Oh, clucking with the girls, what else?" Althea tossed her boyish head. "What else is there in this gruesome life for women but gossip and uh — " she glanced at Martin boldly — "men!"

Since their meeting at the Four Swans several days previously, she had wondered at the vulnerability Martin had exposed in her with the sharp thrust of his tongue — a thrust which she secretly admitted had been deserved. He was the first man for a long time she had not been able to ram into mental oblivion, his face and his voice had kept coming back to her. Her decision to try and be friendly with him, since he was so clubby with her brother, had eased her. She was a little frightened inwardly at the vigor of her interest in him now.

"Hop in," Erford said.

"Perhaps you'd better," Martin said, "I'm first out when we reach City Square."

"Very well." Erford slid in beside his sister and patted her affectionately on the knee. "On to Charlestown!"

Martin clambered in and slammed the door. The chic alligator shoe bore down on the accelerator. Martin became absorbed in the dollish grace of Althea's foot. He lifted his head quickly and found himself looking into Althea's mirthful eyes. He blushed. Her eyes swung again to the windshield and the road in front of them.

The thrill of embarrassment he had felt at Erford's request that he sit next to Althea waned into a not unpleasant simmer. A wry, almost vindicative smile touched the corners of Althea's mouth.

They hummed through Somerville, over the cobblestones of Cambridge Street, and were soon winding through the elevated uprights at Sullivan Square. As they approached the intersection of Bunker Hill Street and Main, Erford nudged both Althea and Martin: "Careful, Althea, take a good look up that hill."

"Not at this time of day," Martin said, chuckling.

"You know," Althea said, "that must be quite a thrill — like taking the jump when the bar is on the top rung. I almost think I'd like to try the loop some time."

"Why not drop over some Saturday night?" Martin said facetiously. "Perhaps we can arrange a little something."

"Perhaps I will," she said, smiling slowly.

"If you knew my sister better, Martin, you wouldn't suggest things like that."

"Do you really know some of the loopers?" Althea asked.

"Does one know one's own people?" Martin asked.

"What are they *really* like?"

"They're really like everybody. You ride blooded horses; they ride potentially bloody cars."

"Gruesome!" she said, a note of sympathy in her voice.

"Sis, that's one time you used that word with some degree of accuracy."

"Please, Erford, not in front of strangers!"

They purred through Thompson Square. Althea glanced up at the obelisk as they passed Monument Avenue. "There's your precious monstrosity," she said.

"It's beautiful — to us, anyway."

"India has its Taj Mahal, Charlestown its monument," Erford said.

"A perfectly silly comparison," Althea said.

"Come and see it some night, perhaps you'll change your mind," Martin said.

They neared City Square. "Is this where you're getting out, Mr. Ronayne?"

"Yes, Miss Parkley — right over there by the police station."

"Are you actually going in there?" Erford asked.

"Yes, I'm calling on J. P. He has his office in there, you know."

"Wish I had time to go with you — I'd like to meet him," Erford said.

"Whatever for?" Althea asked. "Haven't you read about this J. P. — isn't that enough of an acquaintance?"

"Don't say that too loud, Sis. You're in Hanlon's capitol right *now*. People love him over here."

Martin was again smoldering. Just when something nice seemed to be emerging from the personality of Althea. . . .

She wheeled the roadster over to the curbing in front of the police station.

Martin pushed the door open. "See you tomorrow, Erford. Thanks for the ride, *Miss* Parkley."

"Not at all, *Mister* Ronayne. Perhaps I'll take you up on that nocturnal inspection of the Monument some time — and see for myself."

"Any time. So long."

Erford nodded and smiled, "So long, old man." As Althea pulled away from the curbing he watched Martin's tall, lithe form disappear into the granite building which housed both the police station and a block of municipal offices.

"Wish you wouldn't high-hat that boy so much, Althea — just for your own interest, that is. I'm hoping he'll do big things in Boston one day."

"Like what?"

"Like helping to run the city or the state with the friendly cooperation of both political factions in this town, that's what."

"Big order."

"I'm aware of that."

"Where are we meeting Mr. Beasley?"

"Pull up outside his office in Thompson Square. I'll run in and get him."

"Why doesn't Dad sell these filthy old houses? Aren't they really a nuisance?"

"A very profitable nuisance, my dear; you might have this property to thank for that hunter Dad gave you last spring."

"I suppose, but there must be better ways to make money."

"Name a few, Althea. Here, pull over here. I'll be right back."

She thought about Martin while Erford was in the wan, hulking bank building where Mr. Beasley occupied an office. Again she was remorseful. It would be a good lark — seeing the Monument at night with the handsome Irishman. Perhaps Erford would arrange it casually — or maybe she'd even drop Ronayne a note. She didn't suppose Erford would ever have him over to their house in the Fens — Erford wouldn't go that far. Or would he? She'd have to ask Dad about the Ronayne family. . . .

Erford and Mr. Beasley, a slight dried-up man of about sixty, emerged from the building.

"Here we are, Sis. You remember Mr. Beasley."

"Very well — I see your son, Fillmore, at an occasional club dance."

"Nice to-uh see you again, Althea — pretty as ever." Mr. Beasley spoke in a thin, dry voice that crackled harmoniously with his appearance. "Yes, yes, Fillmore is very good at that dancing business. Can't help wishing he'd show more interest in real estate."

"Where to?" Althea said, after they had climbed into the car.

"You-you go up Green Street here, across Bunker Hill Street, and down-down to the sugar works on Medford-uh Street; then you-you — well — I'll show you then," Mr. Beasley said.

Althea turned up Green Street, visualizing Fillmore Beasley, Jr., inspecting property over by the Sugar House. He might conceivably do his inspecting accompanied by a couple of chorines from the Keith Albee circuit. Late afternoon would be just about the right time for him to do the inspecting too, she mused. He'd be just about ready to stick his long aristocratic nose into the poisonous light of late afternoon.

They crossed Bunker Hill Street and rolled down Polk to the industrial, wharf, and railroad weariness of Medford Street.

"Turn left here, my dear," Mr. Beasley said.

They bumped along the cobbles of Medford Street and soon the drab, steaming mass of the Sugar House appeared on their right.

"Now into that alley on your left, Althea."

Althea swung to the left into the cobbled alley called Felicity Court. At the end of the alley were four three-storied tenement blocks forming an area known as Felicity Circle. From the Circle they could hear the strident calling of playing children.

"Felicity Court," Althea said. "Doesn't felicity mean happiness?"

"I see what you mean," Erford said, eyeing the garbage and the tin cans strewn about the alley. "Mr. Beasley will probably verify me in this — wasn't this 'street' named after one of our ancestors, a Felicity Parkley?"

"Precisely. Althea, would you park by that first tenement on the right?"

Althea nodded. "All I can say is, old Felicity would spin about in her coffin if she could see what her namesake has become."

"Can't say as she would — this is a very proper investment, very proper indeed!" said Mr. Beasley. "We shan't be too long," he added, opening the door.

"If you need any help, Sis, scream."

"You're the ones who may need help," Althea said as they walked toward the sagging front porch of the nearest tenement.

"We'll visit the tenants first — then you can have a look at the basements and premises later. These people will be preparing what they call supper about now, you know. We'd best get out of their way as soon as possible," she heard Mr. Beasley say as they walked with appraising looks toward the tenement.

Now that Mr. Beasley was out of sight, she fished into her bag for cigarettes. At the other end of the Circle the child voices were shrill.

Something black and round hurtled in the direction of the roadster's gleaming windshield. "Frump!" A soggy imitation leather football, more circular than oval, struck the creamy hood of the car and skidded off into the mud of the alley. Althea's widened eyes froze for a moment on the large, streaky smudge which violated the hitherto virginal expanse of the hood.

"Really!" she exclaimed both in panic and anger. She stabbed the dashboard ash tray furiously with her cigarette and stood up on the floor boards, looking frantically over the windshield at the smudge, the football, and the scrambling urchins — several of whom were hurrying toward her.

"Erford," she called, "Erford!" But Erford and the Yankee henchman of property were on distant safari in the dank tenement jungles of Felicity Circle.

"Who you callin', lady?" a redhead urchin asked. The wet mud from the football dripped and streaked down the creamy finish of the door.

"Eeeee!" Althea screamed, "Get off there, get off, all of you!"

She gave the urchin a push. He jumped off the running board. "Watch what yuh doin'!"

"Yeh, who do yuh think you are?" one of the little girls said.

"You stay off there, both of you. Erford," she called, "Erford!"

A window on the second story screeched open and an enormous Irish lady with forearms like a longshoreman insinuated a round, red face into the fracas. "Patrick! Agnes! In the house now, in the house this very minute or I'll warm your backsides good!"

"She pushed me, Ma," Patrick said, whining.

"Did you push my son?" the Irish lady demanded.

Althea sighed, shrugged her shoulders, and flopped back into her seat, digging involuntarily for another cigarette.

The children made leering faces at Althea. One of the girls stuck out her tongue. Patrick thumbed his nose menacingly as they backed up slowly toward the rear of the tenement.

The window closed with a dramatic slam. The children disappeared into the tenement. Althea's hand shook with frustrated rage as she lit her cigarette.

Erford and Mr. Beasley were standing in the semiblackness of a first-floor corridor which was weakly illuminated by a flickering overhead gas jet. He gripped a shaky balustrade with his right hand and worked the railing back and forth.

"Why couldn't we fix these places up?" Erford asked.

"Your father and I have discussed the matter at great length," Beasley explained. "Extensive repairs would necessitate a considerable increase in rent for these people, which they do not seem willing or-uh able to pay. It is perhaps better, Erford, to charge a moderate rent which you collect regularly than a high rent, especially in this area, which the tenants simply cannot afford to pay."

"It seems to me," Erford protested, "that a few much-needed repairs would *help* the investment rather than hurt it."

"You'd better take that up with your father. . . . Now ovah hee-uh we have an apartment which is rented to three-uh ladies. Would you like to have a look?" Mr. Beasley asked, raising his eyebrows puckishly.

Erford laughed. "Do you feel I should?"

"Since you will probably come into this property one day, you might find it of interest to hear a word or two from some of your tenants."

"Very well."

Mr. Beasley rapped firmly on the cracked, peeling door. There was no movement within the apartment. He rapped again. They heard someone yawn distantly. Feet scuffed slowly toward the door.

The knob turned, the door opened about three inches revealing the sallow empty face of a thick-set blonde-gray woman in her early forties. "What you want?" she asked in a flat, heavy voice, clutching at her kimono.

Mr. Beasley lifted his chin sternly. "I'm Mr. Beasley, representing the owner of this property."

"Oh," the woman said, her eyes narrowing a little. "The rent's paid, ain't it, Mr. Beasley?"

"Yes, yes, of course," Mr. Beasley said. "We're having a look at the property, you know. This is the owner's son, Mr. Parkley."

"Please tuh meetcha," she said, with the beginnings of a wan smile. Erford nodded restrainedly, his eyes betraying his fascination.

"Would it be possible at all for us to have a look inside?" Mr. Beasley asked.

"The other girls is still sleepin'," she said. "Can'tcha come back some other time?"

Mr. Beasley lifted his chin again, turned and looked quizzically at Erford.

"Some other time," Erford said.

"Surely, surely!" Mr. Beasley said. "Another time. A very good day to you, now."

"G'by." The sad, frayed blonde closed the door slowly.

"Say, Mr. Beasley," Erford asked with a note in his voice that was both anxious and droll, "do you suppose everything's above board in that place?"

Mr. Beasley paused a moment in the small inner porch and glanced sharply back at the door of the ladies' apartment. "Can't say I've thought about it before. Our man O'Neil collects the rents for us you know — these ladies pay promptly and in full every month — of that I'm positive. If there was any irregularity certainly the authorities would have heard about it before this."

"Yes, I suppose they would have." The authorities. Erford's thoughts ran to Hanlon and his political pull in Charlestown — this might be one of the things that was being hushed up — for a price. He was sure his father didn't suspect any of these goings on. But what if he did — what if he winked at something like this? What if Beasley was more businessman than moralist. He deter-

mined to try to get his father to sell the property. But what then?
Someone else would probably let things run on as they now were.
Yet if there was no political protection offered, vice could not
flourish, no matter how ignorant or indifferent absentee landlords
might be. But then — how could one make one's way in politics
without political preference — it seemed almost impossible, particularly in Boston.

He heard a door open on one of the upper floors. "Will you do
that for me, Mrs. Antonelli?" a vaguely familiar feminine voice
asked. "Eggnog for little Guido with every meal — the agency will
send you the eggs and the milk. I'll be in again a week from
today. Good-by, now, and don't worry. The doctor says Guido is
all right — needs a little more of the right kind of nourishment,
that's all."

"Good-ah-by and thank-ah you, Mees Ronayne." Erford heard
the door close and quick light feet thrum hollowly down the
stairs. Cool and dark and comely, almost Italian in the dark
Irish way, she rounded the first landing and stopped short when
she saw Erford smiling up at her out of his sensitive, skeletal face.

"Ah-lo, Mees Ronayne!" he mimicked. "What you do 'ere?"

"Hello!" she said, her voice doing a little ascending scale of
surprise. "I've been making a call for the agency — what *you*
do here?"

She walked slowly down the remaining steps, her notebook and
bag firmly under her arm. He held the door for her and followed
onto the porch. Mr. Beasley was standing by the creamy roadster,
shaking his head solemnly as Althea poured out her tale of horror.

"Oh, just looking around," Erford said.

"Do you mean to say you people are thinking of buying
this property?"

"We can't very well do that — you see, we've owned these
houses for years."

"Well!" Rosemary said, with little rosebuds unfolding in her
cheeks. "Don't you think it's about time you did something about
fixing these places up? These people are human beings, you know!"

Erford winced. "I'm quite aware of that, Rosemary — I intend to
speak to Father about the matter. It isn't as simple a problem as
eggs and milk, however, I assure you."

"Simple justice is always simple — even if it hurts the pocket-book," she said, descending the stairs to the walk. "Nice to have seen you again."

"Ditto. Can't we drop you somewhere?"

"Thank you, but I have a couple of calls to make."

She walked to the end of the apartment block in the direction opposite to the roadster and disappeared into an alley between the houses.

Erford kicked a tin can out of his way, sighed, and walked briskly toward the car.

When Martin, having just left Erford and Althea, entered the office of James P. Hanlon, attorney-at-law, the big man was sitting back in a hard swivel chair, his elbows on the armrests, his large jaw cradled meditatively in the cup of his hands. The greenish, protuberant eyes seemed to look into infinity.

Near his desk sat a wisp of an old lady with a kind, strong face and a sweet, misty smile.

"Perhaps I'd better come back later," Martin said. The old lady smiled through her sweet, sad mist. Hanlon lifted his hand: "It's you, Martin — sit you down, I'll be with you right away."

Martin nodded and sat down on a chair near the door.

"Mrs. Carroll," Hanlon said, "there's no more need for you to go wanderin' around the City Hall talkin' to a bunch of civil service lunkheads that will give you nothin' but a lot of rules and regulations. I've already got in touch with a gentleman at the Hall that I want you to go and see at ten o'clock tomorrow mornin'."

He hunched forward, scrawled briefly on a slip of paper, and handed her the paper with an infectious grin.

"This man will take care of you. And if you have any troubles at all with the welfare department don't hesitate to call me."

The old woman took the paper and thanked Hanlon with quiet intensity. He arose from the desk and showed her to the door, closing it softly behind her.

"There's a sweet little old lady for you!"

Martin stood up, inferring that Hanlon was ready to go. "You're coming home with me to dinner, you know, Jim."

"Yes, Catherine called about it this afternoon. She's been sayin' this newspaperman, Farrell, is to be there."

"He isn't a bad fellow, Jim. He's one of our own, you know — born and brought up right here in Charlestown. He used to work on the paper with Dad. Perhaps you'll remember him?"

The black, bushy brows rose and fell. "Is *he* the cocky, little brat that used to work for your father? Before the war it was."

"That's the guy."

"I remember him well. He was in here several times, askin' questions about politics like Lincoln Steffans himself."

"That's Mike — he's still quite an admirer of Steffans."

"It is easy to see — with all his snippy little remarks about the elimination of political pull. And it's yourself I'd like to be telling something about political preference so that you won't be getting any fool notions in your head. Come over here and sit you down for a while. I've been wantin' to talk to you about your future."

Martin sat down in the chair next to the desk. Excitement suffused through him warmly. This was the first time Hanlon had spoken directly to him about the future. He had known through his mother that Hanlon was eying him as local political timber — but in all their previous conversations Hanlon had given him the feeling that he was still not quite dry behind the ears.

"Now that you are about to graduate from law school, Martin, I believe that it is time for me to tell you that I have hopes one day of sending you along to the Hall. I am even thinking of putting you up for the School Committee from this district in a year or two. How would that strike you?"

Since Hanlon's backing would be tantamount to election, it struck him very well.

"That would be wonderful, Jim, if you think I'm capable of handling it."

"You're not entirely ready. It is to the school of the politician you need to be going. I've spoken to the District Attorney about you already. One of his assistants is going into private practice this summer. I suggest you see the D.A. as soon as you can. The job is yours if you want it. And you need the experience."

School Committee! The D.A.'s office! Martin thought. Wait until Erford hears this!

"But you've got to get certain things straight in your mind," Jim continued. "I've heard things about your friendship with the son of a well-known Yankee politician. It's none of my business and I don't intend to butt in. Yet you must remember that if we back you, you'll be representing your own people here and you must act in accordance with the wishes and the ways of those you represent. Is that clear?"

"It is and it isn't. Jim, I certainly would work my fingers to the bone for the people of this district if I was their school committeeman, believe me. Yet I still don't believe in a policy of non-co-operation with Yankees, just because they are Yankees. I don't like our inferiority complexes, Jim. I believe they debase rather than ennoble our people."

"Perhaps you've a point there," Hanlon said with reluctance, "but it's on this business of reform that I'll have to let you see our point of view."

"Yes, that is something I'd like to get straight."

"Them that screams with holy anger for reform, like the Yankees and clever young snipes like Farrell, should know something about that little old lady who was here just now as you came in. I'm tellin' you her story not to brag about myself but to show you the nicer side of our business — the side, by the way, that never gets into Farrell's column.

"The reason I am where I am, Martin, is because of the help the machine can provide to just such helpless little folks like Mrs. Carroll. That little woman's husband used to run an elevator in one of the city buildings. The poor man fell down the shaft one morning last week and that was the end of him.

"This little lady had not even the money to bury the poor soul — let alone provide for herself now that he is gone. So what does she do? In great desperation she travels over to the Hall looking for someone there that will give her some help. She talks to one of our fine civil service buckoes, she mentions the fatal elevator, between her tears and her embarrassment, and this laddy-buck, who has passed all kinds of tests, directs her to the elevators. So finally, after talking to all kinds of officious people who know how to give the most complicated directions to an old lady who has never been out of Charlestown more than ten times in her life, she gives up in despair and goes home.

"It was one of her neighbors gave Timmy Mackail a call and he, me. There'll be no blatherin' around at the Hall with her tomorrow mornin'. This time tomorrow night she'll be well on her way to a nice piece of compensation money and a pension. So there's a fine commentary for you on civil service and the need for reform!"

Martin nodded amiably. He might have raised the objection that an *efficient* City Hall would have done the same things for Mrs. Carroll without political pressure — that is to say, a reformed City Hall.

"It was nice of you to help her," Martin said, glancing at his watch. "I think we ought to get started, Jim."

"Yes, we'll go along now," Hanlon said, rising, "there's no man in the world should be late for a dinner of Catherine Ronayne's!"

Chapter 7

IN THE gleaming spacious kitchen of the Ronayne tenement, Francis and John Little, swathed in aprons, stood by a white stretch of sink scraping the skins off potatoes and carrots.

"After a fashion this is like the K.P. I used to do at the prep school," John said, slicing the green end off a carrot. "Is your mother feeding the entire Democratic party tonight?"

"Not quite. There'll be Hanlon, Father Quinn from the *Beacon*, Mike Farrell, the reporter, and the rest of the family. You and I will eat out here in the 'servant's quarters.' What's the prep school, John?"

"Oh, you know, Concord Reformatory. We did a lot of K.P. up there."

Francis scraped on a potato and said nothing. It had always bewildered him that as nice a guy as John Little could be sent to a reform school. It had happened when John was seventeen. He had been taken into custody for stealing a car. The first time, Hanlon had got him off on probation. The second offense stuck and he was sent to Concord for six months. After his release he had managed to stay out of trouble — or perhaps, he had not been caught. Now, however, he was under the benevolent and restraining influence of Catherine Ronayne.

John Little tossed the shucked carrot into a water-filled pan and looked over at the thick slabs of rich-blooded steaks laid out on wax paper on top of the stove.

"Hey, Fran? Do we get one of those?"

"You bet we do. We get everything the guests do." Francis winked. "Besides we get to dish out the ice cream."

The back door squeaked and slammed. It was Rosemary.

"Hi, boys," she said, a little short of breath. "Am I in time?"

"Hi, Sis, nobody's here yet, except Mother. She's dressing."

"That's what I've got to do — sorry I haven't time to help right now. Be in later, though," she said over her shoulder, hurrying down the long dark corridor to her room.

The kitchen door opened again. It was Alice Stasek carrying a tray of fancy Polish pastry which her mother had baked for the party. She smiled with an opulent shyness at the boys and, without a word, slipped out the door.

John Little smiled rather sheepishly. That was always his greatest act of volubility in the presence of Alice. She stood, Francis sensed, on the secret pedestal in John's odd, nonconformist life. John knew the chasms that stretched between him and Alice — her devotion to Martin, his social inadequacy; yet to admire her distantly was of no harm to anyone and was to him a precious, edifying jewel in the cluttered hock shop of his consciousness.

The front doorbell rang. It was Martin and Hanlon.

"Come in, come in," Catherine said. "Martin, will you mix some Old Fashioneds? The makings are in the kitchen."

"No Old Fashioneds for me, Catherine," Hanlon said, stripping off his heavy gray overcoat. "If ye'll give me a spot or two of this, I'll be much obliged." He dipped his hand into the bulgy inside pocket of the coat, fished out a pint of Scotch, and handed it to Martin.

Martin wrinkled his nose. "It smells of fish."

"You'd smell of fish yourself, son," Catherine said with a facetious smile, "if you came all the way down from Canada in a barrel of mackerel. Am I right, John?"

"Now, Catherine," Hanlon wheeled his eyes rheumily, "there never was no wrong in takin' a little nip to warm the throat on a cold day." He entered the parlor and took a seat under the gold-framed portrait of Martin Ronayne.

Catherine raised her hands and shook her head. "The good Lord preserve us from the Volstead Act!"

"Amen!" Martin said, heading for the kitchen, bottle in hand.
The doorbell drilled again.

"That must be Mike and Father," Catherine said.

"I'll be needin' that drink," Hanlon whispered to her as she
moved toward the door. "The forces of reform are bearing down
upon me!" He rolled his eyes philosophically and ran his index
finger along slowly between his neck and his collar.

An hour and a half later Father Quinn was saying to Hanlon:
"Jim, you've got to see it our way — you're not doing the kids or
their families any good, protecting them the way you are!"

Father Robert Quinn, slight, dark, and electric with mental
energy, toyed politely with the remains of the chocolate cake and
vanilla ice cream. The Old Fashioneds, the onion soup, the steak,
the wine, the vegetables, and the conversational pleasantries were
mellowly out of the way. Catherine, sitting at the head of the
table, had turned the conversation to the looping problem. She
had raised the question of the evening during dessert in the hope
that the subject would carry over gracefully to the parlor where
she planned on leavening the talk with some of her precious
Benedictine, a case of which her husband had shipped from France.

She was fond of retelling the story of how Martin, Sr., on leave
from his outfit, had visited a Benedictine monastery in southern
France and left an order with the monks for a case of the liqueur
to be shipped to her immediately after the war's end. Martin had
hoped to share it with his family and his friends in the ease and
refuge of his own parlor. It was ritual with her to fulfill in some
measure his intention by serving the same liqueur on occasion to
his special friends.

Hanlon pushed his empty dessert dish to one side, sighed,
fumbled in his vest pocket for a match, and lit one of the long
black cigars which Francis had served a few moments before. Then
rolling his eyes amiably at Father Quinn, he said: "I mean you
no disrespect, Father, in having to disagree with you. I've known
and respected you and your good paper for many years and there
was never a time when I wouldn't do a favor for you if it was
at all in my power."

The priest nodded.

"And while I'd like to put a stop to this looping just as much as you would, I still have certain duties to the constituents that I represent. And since there exist certain con-ditions in this town which we do not seem to be able to better, and since these same con-ditions are in some measure responsible for the tomfoolery of the sons of my constituents, I do feel called upon to give them some protection — even after the fact."

Mike broke in impetuously. "But you — "

"Just a minute now, my proud Shakespeare," Jim interrupted with deadly vitriol, "give me a chance to finish what I have to say."

"Yes, Jim," Catherine interposed quickly, mildly, "and we can listen to your remarks over the Benedictine in the parlor — shall we?"

Mike's face reddened and he ran his hand through his bushy hair. "What the hell! Let him talk," he thought. "Maybe I'll learn something I can use in the column!"

"Ah! Benedictine!" Father Quinn said. "You're sure it wasn't made by the Jesuits?"

"Father, you're impossible!" Rosemary chuckled from the china closet where she was gathering the tiny glasses.

"He's ribbing us," Catherine said. "He likes the Jesuits even though they're — " she coughed lightly, "quite as powerful as the *Boston Beacon*. Martin, you'll get the liqueur?"

"Yes," quipped Father Quinn, following Hanlon and Farrell into the parlor, "in the words of Cardinal Newman: 'I like the Jesuits. . . . ' "

Martin hurried along the hall, regaled by the wit of Father Quinn. There was beneath all the hilarity, he knew, considerable awareness on the part of the diocesan clergy of the fast-growing influence of the Jesuits and their cultural nerve center, Ignatian College. And the Yankee princes of property in Boston had learned to respect the vision and the practicality of the Jesuits who had seen in a hilly cow pasture what was to become in fifty years' time one of the choicest tracts of residential property in Boston.

"Okay, let's get on with those dishes," Martin said as he passed through the kitchen, where Francis and John were loading their plates with the considerable scrapings of two quart boxes of ice cream.

"You tend the bar, we'll tend to the dishes. Is this still like the 'prep school,' John?" Francis asked with a grin.

"Not until we start doing the dishes," John said, scooping out a hollow in the ice cream.

Rosemary poked her head fetchingly through the kitchen door. "Hey, ice-cream pusses, you've got a helper. When do we start?"

"We can handle it, Sis." Francis gulped down the last mouthful of strawberry cream. "Go in and sit down with the folks — you're a big girl now."

She snapped a dishcloth off a rack. "Nope. I've had enough serious talk over by the Sugar House all day. Let the great brains in there settle the problems of the world. We lesser mortals can chatter our little chatter in peace over the dishpan."

"Amen," John Little said, laying down his spoon.

"Amen," Francis repeated, dropping the dishpan into the sink with a clatter. "You wash, Sis, we'll dry."

Martin emerged from the cellar with the bottle of Benedictine. "All right, let's get at it!" he said grinning.

"Yes, me Lord Parnell," Rosemary said. "Did you know I saw some friends of yours this afternoon, some very hoity-toity friends."

"I know." Martin paused at the entrance to the hall. "Erford and Althea. Where'd you bump into them?"

"Well, I'll tell you, old chap. I have a client in one of their very ritzy apartments. 'Fancy meeting you here,' I said to Erford, picking my way among the cockroaches."

Francis and John laughed. Martin raised his eyes coolly and moved down the hall.

"Write a letter to the *Beacon!*" he said over his shoulder.

"Maybe I will." Rosemary sprinkled some soap flakes in the dish water and set the box down with a bang.

Francis and John were in the dining room removing the dessert dishes and coffee cups. Rosemary dipped the long pale hands that were so like her mother's into the flaky water and thought about the rudely affectionate way Mike Farrell had looked at her during dinner.

In the parlor the guests gathered in a semicircle around the Corpus under which Catherine sat with her knitting, taking, along

with the others, occasional sips from the Lilliputian goblets of Benedictine.

On the armchair to her left Hanlon sat moodily, turning the small glass around with a huge thumb and index finger. On the sofa directly across from her under the portrait of her husband, sat the restless Mike Farrell and the self-contained Father Quinn. Martin sat aloofly on the piano stool to his mother's right, his elbows nonchalantly resting on the covered keyboard. From the kitchen came the muffled clink of dishes and silverware.

"Let's hear more of your mind on the looping problem, Mr. Hanlon," Mike said. "As far as I'm concerned anything you say is strictly off the record."

"That goes for me, too, Jim," Father Quinn said, setting his glass down noiselessly on a small end table.

"You know how I feel already," Hanlon said a little impatiently. "These boys and their parents need help when the boys get in trouble. When they come calling on me — and mind you, they can't afford none of your fancy Yankee lawyers — I've no course but to try and do something for them. Now what would you suggest when two good citizens come to me in tears because their boy is in the lockup? Would you suggest that I tell them that the law is the law and please don't bother me? Tell me now, what in God's name would you do?" He gripped the midget glass in his horny hand and quaffed the libation quickly, licking his lips meticulously. "You'll never send us staggerin' home on this stuff, Catherine."

Catherine smiled and shook the folds out of the half-finished afghan. "That's the idea," she said.

Father Quinn returned to the subject. "What would *we* do? Well, Jim, we'd probably try to do what you do, namely, give these people some concrete assistance. But such assistance should go a little farther and deeper than merely getting the lads out of jail."

"With that I agree, Father," Hanlon said, "but the 'farther and deeper' is for the Church and the social workers — it is not quite the work of a politician."

"Good, Jim," Catherine said, "I'm glad you see that — that's where Father and Rosemary and people like Mike and me, who

are interested in stopping this crazy joy riding, come in. But in order to do something constructive we've got to have your word that the loopers will no longer be protected. We could provide the help you're continually asked to give through a committee of public-spirited citizens, which I'd like to see formed; but you've got to co-operate, else the people involved will go to you for help instead of to the committee."

"Committee?" Hanlon said. "What committee?"

Mike's jaw dropped a little. Catherine had obviously been reading Steffans. He caught her eye and grinned. She smiled slowly and, fishing into a knitting basket, pulled out a magazine, and turned the pages to an article by Lincoln Steffans. "The author here proposes a plan for just such a committee," she said, "a committee made up of a physician, an attorney, a businessman, a clergyman and, to use his words, 'one other, preferably someone who had done wrong enough himself to understand guilt.' Such a committee could unloop the loopers from around your neck, Jim, if you'd co-operate," she said, closing the magazine.

"It's a first-rate idea, Jim," Father Quinn said. "How about it?"

Hanlon's eyes were riveted on the parlor rug. "What do you mean by co-operate?" he asked softly, a dull ring of resignation in his voice.

"Pass the word around that you can't 'spring' any more loopers and give us your word that you'll co-operate with any committee we form to solve the looping problem," Catherine said.

Hanlon shook his head slowly. "Catherine, that might be political suicide."

"It won't be, Jim. The *Bulletin* will give you full credit if you co-operate with this committee — your stock with great numbers of good, honest folk in this town will go up, believe me."

"I'll let my readers know, if you'll help, Mr. Hanlon," Mike said.

"And I," Father Quinn said.

Hanlon sighed and raised his hands, turning his great palms outward. "All right, all right! In heaven's name, all right. You can give your committee a try and I'll not interfere. But if the committee doesn't work, the deal's off. Do you hear me now?"

"Fair enough," Catherine said.

"Who do you have in mind for the committee, Mother?"

"I thought the three newspapers represented here tonight might get together on the thing. Father Quinn would do for the clergyman."

"How about you for the businesswoman?" Mike suggested.

"I *would* like to help."

"Why not get an outstanding Republican in as attorney," Martin suggested. "Erford Parkley, Sr., might be interested. I could find out through young Erford."

"Didn't know you knew that crowd so well," Father Quinn said. "He *would* make the committee more representative."

"We should get a local physician — someone who knows the people and their problems," Farrell said, jotting down Parkley's name under those of Catherine and the priest in a small leatherbound notebook.

"Rosemary would know of someone good — she works right along with the doctors in her hardship cases. I'll ask her," Catherine said.

"There was one more," Father Quinn said smiling.

All eyes were again on Hanlon.

"Go along, now, you don't want me — and I'll tell you why. If I'm sitting there when the folks come before you, they'll be waiting to hear what I have to say rather than what you have to say. And if you do anything for them, they'll be grateful to me, not to you. I'll be helping your committee by staying out of the way, believe me!"

He was right, they knew — it would be a wonderful opportunity for him to increase the power and the prestige of the machine by revealing the committee's dependence upon him.

"It's nice of you to look at things that way," Catherine said, "but you *will* help, won't you — behind the scenes, I mean?"

"I'll do what I can," Hanlon replied.

"All right," Farrell said, "and we'll do what we can. I'll break a story on this thing in my column day after tomorrow if it's okay with you all."

"Don't be mentioning my name in connection with this," Hanlon said quickly, "at least until I've had a talk with His Honor."

"It's all right to say the heat's on the loopers though, isn't it?"

Hanlon nodded. "That is all right."

Father Quinn stood up. "Fine, the *Beacon,* too, will carry an editorial this week on the business. Now I'm afraid I'll have to be going along. It's well after eleven."

"I'll drop you in town, Father," Mike said.

Hanlon, too, arose and muttered something about going.

Catherine put aside her knitting and walked into the anteroom for their coats.

Hanlon, Farrell, and young Martin chatted in the parlor. As Catherine helped the priest into his black overcoat, he asked in a whisper, "What is the latest from the vocational front?"

"He says he wants to go, Father," she said softly. "I thought perhaps a year at Ignatian College would help him with his Latin."

The priest hunched his shoulders. "No, Catherine, no. If it's all right with you, let me tutor him this summer. I promise I'll have him ready for the sem in the fall. It would be all very fine at I.C. until he ran off to the Jesuit novitiate. We need boys like him right here in the parishes. Will you let me do it?"

Catherine laughed. "Really, Father, you're not serious!"

"I am." He tossed his head with a hint of grimness. "I could name names if you forced me to."

"All right, Father, all right." She handed him his dark felt hat. "You have my permission to tutor him, if you really want to." She chuckled. "Lord help the poor Jesuits!"

"The Lord *is* helping them," Father Quinn said. "Where's Francis? Can I speak to him a moment?"

"He might be in the kitchen." She called him.

"He went for a walk with John Little," Rosemary answered from the kitchen.

"Oh. Is there anything you'd like me to tell him, Father?"

"Well, I'd like to talk to him, now that he's made up his mind. Why not ask him to drop into the office next Saturday afternoon?"

"I'll do that. . . . We've made some progress this evening."

"Yes, I think so. Now the fun begins. Michael, are you coming?"

Farrell and Hanlon entered and slipped on their coats. "I'll try and talk to the editors first thing in the morning," Farrell said. "I really think they'll be interested in this."

"Why don't we have lunch together in about a week," Catherine suggested. "We all should have something to report by then."

"Just one more question while Mr. Hanlon is still here," Mike said. "How do we actually get these folks to come with their hats in hand to this committee we've been talking about?"

"What about that, Jim?" Catherine said. "Will you send them to us?"

"If it has anything to do with looping, yes." Hanlon fingered the brim of his hat. "Otherwise, I'll say no word either for or against you."

"All right, Jim," Father Quinn said, "if that's the way you feel. The looping people will be enough — for now."

Catherine and Martin shook hands with their guests and they were gone.

Martin closed and bolted the door for the night. "Mother," he said, "think I'll run up and say hello to Alice for a minute — then I'll hit the books for an hour before turning in."

Catherine looked at her oldest son with full concentration for the first time that evening — for the first time, perhaps, in days. "Good, but talk with me a minute," she said, as he put his hand on the balustrade which wound into the shadows of the second floor.

"Sure thing, Mother."

"You're looking more like your father every day."

Martin leaned over and kissed his mother on the cheek.

"Be stingy with those until you've passed the bar." She raised her eyes toward the second floor.

"Alice understands. We're making no plans."

"Alice is a nice, sensible girl," Catherine said. It was rather hard for her to make such an admission in front of her son. Secretly she hoped Martin would become interested in a girl with an educational background equal to his own. Some would call it snobbery, she knew; a man in professional life needed a wife who could be of intellectual as well as moral and physical assistance to him. It was better to be considered a snob than to jeopardize the happiness of husband, wife, and eventually the security of the children. She'd keep a closer eye on the two from now on — Rosemary would know how far things were going. She'd ask her — tonight.

"What did you think of tonight's business?" she asked.

"The committee business sounds like a fine idea, now that Hanlon seems to be going along with you. Do you think it will work?"

"We won't know until we've tried it out on someone."

"Maybe you won't have to try it out at all. Maybe Hanlon's tabu will be enough."

"Hope you're right — this committee thing is all very fine in theory, but in practice it will probably prove quite a headache."

"Say, Mother," Martin began, leaning over the balustrade again, "there's something I'd like to tell you. Hanlon wants to get me into the D.A.'s office this summer. I'll have graduated by then and should be through with the bar exams. How does that strike you?"

"Well, Hanlon honors my big boy! You realize the D.A.'s office is a steppingstone?"

Martin nooded. "Jim wants to put me up for School Committee in a couple of years."

"Wonderful! If you'll really work hard for the school kids, keep your nose clean, and continue wearing the same size hat."

"I'll try, Mother."

"Your father would never run for political office, you know. Therein, I think, lies the difference between you two — the big difference."

"I'm more ambitious along political lines, I guess, Mother."

"Well, there's nothing wrong in that as long as you can continue looking honest men in the eye. . . . Say hello to Alice for me, and don't stay up there too long. It's late you know."

"Okay, Mother, see you."

She entered the apartment and closed the door. Martin trudged thoughtfully up the stairs. Apart from the physical resemblance to his father, he wondered if his mother really knew how very much unlike Martin, Sr., he really was. His father had been a man to whom principle was everything, even when people, his own family, might suffer because of his adherence to it. If Martin had learned one thing at Harvard, and that mostly outside the classrooms, it was that getting along with people was often much more important than a strained consciousness of their political or religious outlook.

He reached the second floor, where a dim gray bulb in the ceiling gave a deathly pallor to the hallway. He tapped lightly on the Stasek's door. He heard a light flurry of feet. The door opened softly — she was in his arms.

When Catherine entered the kitchen Rosemary was on the kitchen stool, a magazine open in her lap, two hairpins angling out of her mouth, and her hands busily pressing and folding into bobby-pinned minutiae, the multiple locks of her sleek, raven hair.

"Hello, honey. Getting ready for bed?"

"Mmmmmm. . . . " Rosemary slipped a hairpin out of her mouth.

"Is Fran in yet?"

Rosemary shook her head slightly.

"That boy loves to wander around at night," Catherine said. She drew a glass of water from the kitchen faucet. "Sometimes I wonder if I should allow him to go around with John Little this way — but then I do trust John, and Francis is so fond of him."

"Mmmmmm!" Rosemary nodded affably.

"Colleen, I want to ask you an important question — come out from behind those hairpins."

"I'm out, Mother." Rosemary tucked away the last hairpin. "What is it you wanted to ask the oracle of the kitchen stool?"

Catherine slumped down on a chair her long, youthful-looking body inert, her face and eyes, however, animated with worry. "I'm getting a little concerned about Martin and Alice. I suspect they're getting too serious. . . . "

"Well; I suppose they are," Rosemary said after a few moments' reflection, "but they're both sensible kids. I shouldn't think they'd let it get out of hand. Alice, I know, would rather die than stand in Martin's way while he's in school."

"Yes, while he's in school . . . but what then? I think Alice is a very nice girl, Rosemary, you know I do, but it's just that I honestly feel they might have so little in common after the first torrid flare of love has waned into cold, hard facts. I honestly think it would be in the interest of their future happiness to taper off right now and think about things a while — at a distance from one another."

"One floor is not a very great distance." Rosemary wanted to add something in Alice's defense but knew her mother's stand on the matter to be a firm one. A brief for Alice now would win no point and might lead to tension and hurt in the family later. She closed the magazine, tossed it on the kitchen table, and jumped to her feet. "Good night, Mother," she said, kissing Catherine on the cheek. "Let's sleep on it, eh? Perhaps it isn't as bad as it looks this late at night."

"Good night, honey. Perhaps not."

Rosemary padded down the hall to her bedroom. Catherine leaned over the kitchen table pensively, slowly scanning and turning the pages of *Vanity Fair*. The print of the magazine communicated only the words of Rosemary which she was unable to root from her mind: "One floor is not a very great distance."

It wasn't a very great distance at all and that perhaps suggested an answer. The out-of-sight, out-of-mind solution for impetuous young lovers was as old as time. Why couldn't she persuade Martin to finish up his college year in one of the Harvard dorms? It would be much more conducive to sustained study in his final months and it would be an excellent chance for him to absorb some of the Harvard culture and make some valuable contacts. There would be the possibility, she knew, of his becoming thicker than ever with young Parkley. But one problem at a time. Besides, he couldn't marry Erford. She smiled, closed the magazine, and walked toward her room.

On the second-floor landing the lovers emerged from their embrace. "I'll see you Saturday night," Martin said. "I've two tickets to the Follies."

Alice nodded and withdrew from his arms, her face smiling but her heart anguished with love for a young man who avowed his love with embraces but inevitably retreated into a certain aloofness whenever it seemed time for some fervid commitment.

"Good night, Al," he said defensively, "got to hit the books a while."

"Good night, Martin. Don't study too hard." She watched him sink into the darkness of the lower floor. "I love you," she whispered to the walls and the darkness.

Chapter 8

EARLY one sunny Saturday morning in mid-May, 1925, after Samuel Gompers had died and Christ had been born in December, after Coolidge had been inaugurated in March, after Christ had died and been resurrected in April, after Amy Lowell had found out what patterns are for by dying in Brookline — early one sunny Saturday morning in mid-May, Francis Ronayne sat outside the railing of the *Beacon* editorial office, waiting to see the editor.

Since his decision to enter the seminary in the fall it seemed that things had happened to everyone but him. Martin had taken a room in Harvard's Kittredge Hall and had recently passed the bar exams. Rosemary was dating Mike Farrell and seemed more interested in the man than the date for the first time in her life. His mother was working furiously in behalf of the "Charlestown Community Committee" which had been formed according to plan. The committee had already arranged for the parole of several "loopers" and was now co-operating with Charlestown officials in an attempt at stamping out juvenile delinquency. Hanlon had made his word good — there had been no looping since the formation of the committee. John Little was building a telescope in the cupola of his attic room on Bunker Hill Street and looping was just about the farthest thing from his mind.

Francis wished he had a telescope with which he could look into the future. He was here today to make arrangements with Father Quinn for a summer tutoring schedule in Latin. And as he took the first steps which would lead him toward the seminary and the priesthood, the old indecision gnawed at him.

Quickly he turned his mind to the prospect of driving down to Cape Cod with Mr. Hanlon later that morning. The big man had a "golfing" appointment with the mayor at Lobster Bay Country Club and, thinking he might need a caddy, had asked Francis to come along. Hanlon would pick him up at South Station in three quarters of an hour.

Seeing him sitting there patiently, one of the typists, a gum-chewing colleen with bobbed hair arose from her desk and approached the railing. "Who did you wish to see?"

"I've an appointment with Father Quinn."

"Through the gate and right around the corner there to that glassed-in office." She assailed her gum with jouncing jaws.

Francis pushed through the gate and walked toward the editor's office.

He knocked on the door and the quick, crisp voice of Father Quinn said, "Come in" but actually seemed to convey "I'm busy, but what do you want?"

In the office the editor and another priest, hovering over his shoulder, scanned the latest edition of the *Beacon*, which had come off the presses only the night before.

"See what I mean, Will," Father Quinn said without looking up. "We're running the Cardinal's picture too much. Last week it was in the paper twice, this week three times. I've got a memo right here from him. He doesn't like it — doesn't like it at all."

"But what are we going to do, Bob? Those are news pictures the Bishop's in. You ordered them taken yourself — he's laying a cornerstone — he's presenting a check — he's accepting a check — it's news!" said assistant editor Father Will Connolly, a sad, round man with a paradoxically merry voice.

"Yes, I know it is, Will — this is no criticism of you, understand. It's just that the Cardinal doesn't like it, that's all. We'll have to find some other angles."

"It's all right with me, Bob — but you know what the girls in the women's clubs will say if the Cardinal's picture isn't in the paper."

"Yes, I know." Father Quinn looked up at Francis.

"Hello, Fran, how long have you been standing there? Father Connolly, I want you to meet Francis Ronayne. You've probably heard of his mother and late father. They're the *Charlestown Bulletin* people."

"I certainly have!" Father Connolly shook Francis' hand. "Happy to meet you, son."

"Sit down, Fran," Father Quinn said. "Be with you in a minute — now where were we?"

"The Cardinal's pictures," Father Connolly said.

"Yeh, the Cardinal's pictures. Okay, Will, only one picture next week."

"Okay."

The editor flipped the first page of the paper over. He fastened his eyes on a handsome profile picture of a Jesuit priest. "Did I see this?"

"You did," his assistant said.

"Don't remember. What's he done now?"

"He's written another novel. The review's on the editorial page."

"Favorable?"

"Very. One of his friends reviewed it."

"Oh. Any other Jesuit pictures in this issue?"

"One other."

"Where?"

"On page six — accepting a check from the Cardinal."

"I might have known!" Father Quinn said.

Father Connolly laughed heartily.

"Okay, Will, what else is bothering you?"

"What about that book-reviewing boiler plate? Do I have to keep running that slush?"

"What's the gripe — it fills a hole doesn't it?" the editor said, opening the paper to the book section.

"Yeh, that's about all," Father Connolly replied. "Why don't we kill the stuff? I know a couple of young Jesuits who'd be glad to write a literary round-up for nothing."

"What!" Father Quinn exclaimed.

"Oh, come on, Bob. How about it? I want to get rid of this page. What do you say?"

"Oh — all right, Will, all right — on one condition!" He folded up the paper, pushed it to one side of his desk, turned, and looked up at his assistant with a mock stern face. "No pictures!"

Exit the assistant editor, shaking his head solemnly.

"Pull up your chair, Fran," Father Quinn said. "Don't mind the antics of a couple of busy diocesan editors. Now, as I understand it from your mother, you're ready to start work on your Latin. How much Latin have you actually had already, Fran?"

"I've had two years of it, Father, at Charlestown High."

"Did you have Virgil?"

"No Virgil. Caesar's *Commentaries.*"

"Oh. Well, then, here's what we'll do." He opened a drawer and took out two books, a copy of Virgil's *Aeneid* and a Latin grammar. "Friday afternoon is my best time — the paper's in bed then. Can you plan on being here in my office from three to five every Friday afternoon?"

Francis nodded.

"Good, I've written out your first assignment — it's in the grammar. Every week you'll have to study some grammar, memorize some new vocabulary words, and do some translating. I think if we work hard for six weeks or so, I can get you in good shape for the exams. The sem will give you a special quiz in Latin about the first week in August, I think. After that you can relax until September. How does that sound?"

Francis nodded again.

"Okay then, Fran, I'll see you next Friday afternoon. How's your mother and the rest?"

"They're all fine."

"Good. If you want to wander around town for a while and then come back, I'll take you to lunch."

"No thanks, Father. Mr. Hanlon is taking me to the Cape with him this morning — he's playing golf down there."

"Wish I could go along. Anyway, have a good time and I'll see you next Friday."

In the elevator Francis suppressed again his inner doubts. His decision grew stronger around him now that he had further committed himself to Father Quinn. At the street floor as he left the elevator he was confronted by the inscription in gold leaf over a small, granite trimmed doorway: "Will you not watch one hour with Me?"

It was the side entrance to St. Monica's chapel, a cell of worship for businessmen, shopgirls, and stenogs — an island of quiet in the flurry and brawl of downtown Boston.

He still had twenty minutes before meeting Hanlon at the South Station, a couple of blocks away. He hurried with a feeling close to gratitude into the flickering darkness of the compact, low-ceilinged chapel and lost himself in the first pew he encountered.

There in the quiet behind a fat lady telling her beads and a raddled old man to whom this chapel might have been a front parlor from which no one would turn him away because of the smell of his clothes or the blueness of his nose, there in the candle-teased darkness he sat for several minutes asking for light and strength — even as much brave but feeble light as that of the candles, even as much strength as that of the old man who still could pray with a flicker of hope in his spent and shardy face.

He searched his heart mercilessly and found what he believed to be sincerity there. If he didn't go through with it, there would be in the minds of both himself and his mother always the lingering doubt that he should have given the calling, strong or weak, a good try. If he went to the seminary and discovered he was not suited to the priesthood, he could, by his eventual return to lay life, settle the question with finality. He experienced a measure of relief from the insecurity he had been feeling so intensely for the past several months. He lifted his eyes toward the garish painting of the Sacred Heart which served as backdrop to the altar. He thought he might have seen it once before on the cover of some Catholic magazine. The painting rolled about rudely in his consciousness. He glanced at the luminous dial of the watch his mother had given him in honor of his imminent graduation from high school. He crossed himself, stepped into the aisle, genuflected, and went out.

At about the same time Francis left the chapel, Martin and Erford sat on the edge of the Kittredge Hall swimming pool, sloshing their feet and watching Althea execute a graceful, precise one-and-a-half from the high board. When her rubber-ovaled head broke the surface confidently after the dive, they and the score of couples attending the "splash party" of the Kittredge men about to graduate from Law School, applauded strongly.

"How about that sister of mine!" Erford smiled and applauded longer and louder than the rest.

Martin nodded approval.

Althea, her slim, lithe figure even lovelier than usual because of the water-silk quality it had taken on, pulled herself vigorously up the ladder leading to the diving board.

A tanned, blond giant in tights who seemed almost incongruous out of his scull on the Charles, talked to her a moment as she paused on the ladder and turned to the graduates and their guests. "Miss Parkley will now do an over-the-shoulder swan."

Althea walked out to the edge of the board, smiled at the audience, turned her back, and went high up on her toes. She sprung from the board with surprising might for such a slight person and twisting her body fluidly, spread out her arms in the compelling symmetry of the swan. Bringing her hands together at the right moment she cut the water almost silently and was lost in an eruption of crystalline spray.

Again the applause. She swung around, eellike, under the water and with a thrust of legs, surged toward Martin and Erford. She broke the surface between their feet, panting and laughing.

"You were wonderful, Althea," Martin said.

She shook her head fetchingly and pulled herself up on the ledge of the pool between them.

"Yes, I'm afraid I must admit it, Sis."

She ripped off her rubber cap and shook the dampish tendrils of her brown hair. "If you're both so pleased with me, why not get me a cup of punch — I've heard there's something in it."

"Yes, the committee thought the fruit juices would not be adequate by themselves. I'll get you some." Erford arose and walked toward a punch bowl setting near the entrance of the pool.

"We heard about the gin over at the club," Althea said, winking at a bobbed head sitting with a crew cut near by. "Why do you suppose we're here?"

"You like to dive don't you? And look . . . men!" said Martin.

"We have our own pool over at the club — a much bigger and nicer one than this. As for the men — they're everywhere."

"Men like *us?*" Martin asked.

Althea looked full into his face. He held her look calmly, steadily. Her pertness gave way to a blush. She turned her head away — toward the diving board.

Something in Martin's chest tingled giving him the same feeling he had known when it was announced several days previously in the Boston papers that he had passed the bar exams. He had seen very little of Alice since he moved over to Kittredge. Sunday at home was a ritual to which he rigidly conformed and he usually had time to say little more than hello to Alice on those weekly visits; for either his mother had something planned for Sunday afternoon or he had been forced to leave early for Kittredge because of the increasing pressure of studies. Thus, as his mother had hoped, the intensity of his feeling for Alice had waned. But if he could judge from a passionate, pathetic letter which he had received recently from the usually reticent Alice, her interest in him had only been intensified by the period of separation.

The way his heart leaped when Althea looked at him these days was another indication of his waning interest in Alice. Somewhat conscience-stricken at his neglect of her, he had been thinking about asking Alice to the graduation hop, which was still only one week away. More powerful than his conscience was the clamor of his heart to invite Althea — she, so near and yet so far. And yet, he dreaded asking her for what he thought were two good reasons. Firstly, he didn't know quite what he'd say if she refused him; on the other hand, if she accepted, he wasn't sure how Erford would take it — for there was no mistaking that Erford's friendship, encouraging as it seemed, confined itself largely to the horizontal plane of college and politics. Martin was clear on the nature of their friendship and had adjusted himself to it accordingly — but not without the secret and powerful determination to ascend one day to social equality with the Brahmins by the sheer power of political achievement. If that was the horn upon which several talented Irishmen had already been gored, he was unaware of it and wouldn't have believed it anyway.

Althea continued to look at the diving board from which a

line of collegians was plummeting one after another into the water. Impatient for the grace and the prestige she would bring him as a prom partner, he ignored his inner objections and determined to ask her — now.

"Althea, I wonder if you'd consider going to the graduation prom with me?" he asked in casual, even tones which did not betray his strong emotion. "That is, if you haven't been asked already."

Althea lowered her eyes to the pool. She had been both afraid of and eager for some show of interest on Martin's part. Now that it had actually come, the whole drab and solemn weight of three hundred years of Parkley tradition leaded her heart. Looking at the water, wherein she could see reflected the classic features of the dark Irishman from Charlestown she answered a Parkley answer out of Parkley lips that, in a rumble seat, could have been persuaded to kiss him.

"It's real nice of you to ask me, Martin, but . . . I . . . I really couldn't go. I've already let myself in for too much social life this spring. . . ."

"Oh . . . " It was all he could say. He pushed himself to his feet, his chin trembling. "If you'll excuse me . . . I'd better dress."

Althea nodded and continued to stare into the water.

Martin scuffed into a pair of wooden clogs and clacked along bleakly toward the men's locker room.

Erford, on his way back with the punch, called to him. "Here, you big mick, where are you off to? Take one of these." Caged in his hands were three brimming glass cups of spiked punch.

"*With* pleasure," Martin said, taking one of the cups and quaffing it dry.

"S-a-a-a-y! Slow down, old man!"

Martin grimaced, then smacked his lips. "Good stuff — where do I get some more?"

"If you're going to the dressing room, you'll pass the punch bowl on your way. But why the big rush? You're lunching with Dad and me, you'll remember. It should be interesting — he's at one of those committee meetings with your mother and the others this morning."

"Okay. I'll see you upstairs," Martin's voice was toneless. Erford watched him go for a moment, wrinkled his brow, turned, and carried the drinks toward Althea.

She was still looking moodily down into the water when he approached her. "Say, what have you two been doing, Sis? Here, take a pull on this and tell me what's happened!"

Althea took the cup and drank about half the contents. Erford sat down beside her, sipping his punch.

"Martin asked me to the graduation hop."

"I rather thought it was something like that."

"Frankly, I like Martin. . . . I like him rather well. I'd like to go to the hop with him — but — oh, there's been a gruesome lot of talk about my carrying-on already. I'm simply afraid to give the girls at the club any more grist for the yammer mill."

"I suppose it couldn't be helped," Erford said. "Martin is, I'd say, quite deeply hurt. But you did the right thing."

"That's what I thought you'd say, Erford. But I don't think I did the right thing. I didn't do what I honestly wanted to do — that is, go with him — and I wonder if a feeling like that can ever be wrong."

"You still did the right thing," Erford said. "You know," he went on in a conciliatory tone of voice, "you've just jilted our next assistant District Attorney."

"How so?"

"J. P. Hanlon is arranging it. That means he's in. And if he keeps his head about him he's on his way to a promising political career."

"Rather wish he were in some office now." Althea, sighing and pushing herself to her feet. That would put him across with the girls at the dance — temporarily, at least. "Well . . . so long, big brother, I've a date for lunch with young Mr. Wisconsin."

"So long, Sis."

"You *will* try and make things easy for him, Erford."

"I'll do what I can, Sis. It might even be best to say nothing at all about the matter."

"It might," she said, moving away again. She paused at the punch bowl. She took a cup of punch and drank it all, and then still another one before entering the dressing room.

"Go with him, go with him, you little fool!" she found herself

thinking as she prepared for her shower. "What a beautiful guy. . . .
You little fool!

"I'll drop him a note . . . no that would take too long. He's
lunching with Dad and Erford at the Otis. I'll shake Royce early
and phone him there."

She slipped into the shower and as the water cascaded over her
she tried to hum a song, but no song came.

Upstairs in the cluttered suite of rooms which Martin shared
with Erford, the new assistant D.A. from Charlestown sprawled
gloomily on a red leather-covered couch, reading the letter from
Alice:

"Since you do not call me any more or answer my letters, I
suppose the only decent thing for me to do is to try and forget
you. And I have tried — believe me, Martin, I have tried to forget
you. I see now that perhaps I would only stand in your way and
that is the last thing I want to do.

"So this is my final letter to you.

"I was once under the strong impression that you loved me —
even though you never quite came out and said so. Well, I never
said so either, even though I was sure I loved you. I am still sure,
for that matter.

"I wish you all the luck in the world, and all the success, and
all the happiness. As for me, I know I will never stop loving you.

"Good-by, Martin, and God bless you.

                                        Alice"

Martin let the letter fall to the floor. There was a stinging lump
in his throat.

The humiliation in the presence of Althea and the letter from
Alice churned about in his consciousness until the commingled
rage and compassion seemed unbearable. He slipped off the couch
and walked to the French windows which gave a view over the
sparkling green-banked Charles. Across its zephyr-nibbled surface
several sculls were skimming. And on the lush lawny banks, students were loitering. A pretty girl threw a small yellow ball in the
direction of a pert fox terrier. He scuttled after the ball, and
skidded into the water, retrieving it. The sparkling young life in

and around the river slanted through the gloom of his spirit and left some brightness there.

There was, fortunately for him, an inevitable place of spiritual refuge in a moment of great stress such as this one. He fled within the graceful, thick-walled tower of his lifelong determination to one day become a name that all Boston would reckon with in awe and admiration — a man of politics so shrewd and strong that he could stand on an equal footing, in many ways, with the shrewd, strong Yankee men of property whose names had a taste to them like rare, old wine.

His heart knew one last dry constriction at the thought of the gentle, loving Alice. But give her up he would — and a hundred Alices if necessary, until he had scaled the wall between him and the Yankees.

And if it took a snob to parry with a snob, he could play that game too. For wasn't the Ronayne blood and lineage as fine as any in Boston? There were kings and warrior chieftains in the Ronayne line hundreds of years before the Mayflower. John Hancock and his sanctimonious Yankee ilk were rumrunning cutpurses by contrast with some of the Ronayne forebears, who fought at the Battle of The Boyne.

Thus did a young man of ambition dream on a gleaming day in May — out of the dormitory window and over the broad, winking purity of the Charles — the dream of a young lawyer, the long, the dauntless, the glory-beckoning dream.

Chapter 9

ON THE interminable roller coaster through the trees and beside the sea that is the highway to Plymouth and Cape Cod, big Jim Hanlon and Francis drank in the summer air of coastal New England.

J. P.'s long black sedan devoured the miles with a humming, purring servility.

". . . and she'll be waitin' there for me, in dear old Donegal!" J. P. sang, with a voice that was like grumblings of spent thunder.

He took one foot off the accelerator and tapped the floor board twice with rhythmic vigor. Then he looked at Francis and winked.

"We'll be there in an hour, Franny-boy. You'll be hobnobbing soon with His Honor the Mayor. Are you hungry, lad?"

"A little, Mr. Hanlon." Francis hadn't eaten since early morning. It was now well after twelve and he was ravenously hungry.

"We'll stop at the next decent-looking roadside stand — how about some fried clams and French fries?"

"They would be good."

"Are you feeling a little better now, boy?" Hanlon asked, bringing his black, high-topped shoe down on the accelerator again and pushing the speedometer needle up to 50. He held his face straight into the windshield, into the road, the trees, the sea, and the sky. "Let us forget about this seminary business for today."

"I feel real good, Mr. Hanlon, I really do," Francis said gratefully. "I feel more relaxed than I've been for weeks."

"'That is what I want to hear, Franny, that is what I want to hear.'"

Francis grinned and J. P. began to sing again.

More than an hour later as they bowled through the dark cool mystery of the pines surrounding the Lobster Bay Country Club, Francis remembered that two of his high school chums were caddying at Lobster Bay.

As they neared the rambling wooden monstrosity where the *nouveau riche* insulated themselves against the poor with music, lobster, and wine, Francis spotted the caddy shack nestling ignominiously behind the trim, white pro shop and the green-red festoonery of the first tee.

"Can you drop me off at the first tee, Mr. Hanlon? There are a couple of caddies from Charlestown I'd like to say hello to."

Hanlon could not repress a smile at Francis' unconcern about meeting the mayor. Thousands of patronage-seeking Bostonians would have given their eyeteeth for the chance to sit and chat intimately with His Honor over a glass of ginger ale which could be conveniently spiked with the best Canadian whisky. Francis, however, was more interested in a couple of raunchy "bag-rats" from Bunker Hill Street.

J. P. rolled his big rheumy eyes at Francis with chiding approval. "All right, Franny, if that is what you want to do. The mayor and I will be on the first tee in about half an hour — *if* you want to come along."

Hanlon smiled slowly and applied his foot to the brake.

"I sure do, Mr. Hanlon. It'll be a thrill meeting the mayor. I just thought this might be my only chance to say hello to the kids, that's all."

"All right, Franny, we'll see you later."

Francis swung open the door. The big car pulled away and he scuffed along through the crackling pine needles, up the knoll toward the caddy shack.

About twenty minutes later, Francis glanced up at the slender blue-graveled walk which wound down from the hotel to the tee. Five men were descending the short, wide staircase of the white-pillared country club veranda. Among them Francis saw J. P.

"Well, Franny," J. P. called as the group approached the door of the pro shop, "we weren't so long, after all."

The dignified, portly man with the curly, silver hair, who walked beside Hanlon fixed his merry eyes on Francis.

"This must be young Ronayne!" the mayor said with the rich resonance for which he was famous. And perhaps that was one of the secrets of his bewildering municipal success — the same charm which radiated from the speaker's platform was unstintedly directed toward caddies, porters, and apparently insignificant friends of his political associates, such as the wincing youth from Charlestown who stood in front of him.

"Yes, Your Honor, this is the youngest child of Martin and Catherine Ronayne. Francis, this is the mayor of our great city. He's been wanting to meet you, Your Honor," Hanlon fibbed.

"How are you, son?" the mayor said, placing a flabby, blue-veined arm around Francis' thin shoulders. "And-uh how is your good mother?"

"We're all fine, Mr. Mayor," Francis said, blushing.

"I knew your good father well." The mayor turned a little to the three men just behind them. "This boy's father, Martin Ronayne, was that rare thing among public servants, a man who served the people faithfully and well in an ex-officio capacity, paying no selfish heed to the personalities who happened to occupy the municipal positions of title and honor!"

One of the three men, a taciturn, black-browed giant in his twenties, winked malevolently at Francis and brought his palms together with three light, swift applauding movements, which the mayor, directly in front of him, could not see.

A grin flowered out of Francis' blushes.

"Father Splaine," the mayor continued, tossing his heavy, freckled hand in the direction of a wiry, little man with large, peeping gray eyes that seemed to project something bothersomely whimsical. "This is the youngest offspring of one of the finest couples of all Boston. Francis, this is the-uh well-known priest-poet, Father Edmund Splaine. Undoubtedly you've read his poetry in the Jesuit magazine, *A.M.D.G.*"

"You have eyes like St. Aloysius," the priest said in a painstakingly soft voice.

Francis wished he was back in the caddy shack with his friends, the "bag-rats" from Bunker Hill Street, back amid the dust and the remnants of bologna sandwiches.

"I'm sure Francis won't mind, Father, if I tell you," Hanlon said with a hint of solemnity. "The boy is entering the seminary this fall."

"I could have told you that," the elfin priest said, twisting his supple body toward Francis. "I could have told you."

"Grand, boy, grand!" the mayor said. "Behind that shy countenance, the whisper of the Lord is lurking."

Hearing the bland mixture of metaphors, the priest-poet smiled knowingly.

The mayor completed the introductions. "This is my secretary, Brendan Kelly." He nodded at the neat, alert, little man with the official smile. "And this big Turk is the novelist, Barry McQuillen, who went to Bobola College with my son, Brian."

"Hi, kid," McQuillen said gruffly. "So you're gonna be a priest, huh? Well, we sure as hell need good priests."

He rolled his eyes facetiously at Father Splaine, then winked again at Francis. "Where'd you say you were stationed, Father?" McQuillen asked.

The mayor, his secretary, and Hanlon had entered the pro shop where the clatter of golf clubs, the crunch of spiked shoes could be heard.

"I teach at your Alma Mater, my boy," the priest said with cool condescension. "Do you think we have any *good* priests there?"

"I wouldn't know," McQuillen said with impatient good humor. "Haven't been near there since I wrote my book."

"We at Bobola are rather distinctly under that impression," the priest said.

"What was the name of your book, Mr. McQuillen?" Francis asked.

"It's called *Hurly-Burly at Bobola*. You can get it in the second-hand bookstores for a dime — maybe cheaper," McQuillen replied, still with sardonic good humor.

"Oh," Francis said.

McQuillen took Francis by the shoulder with a huge, firm-muscled hand. "Come up to the tee with me. I'll stick around

until the party tees off, then I'll get the hell back to the cottage.
. . . And don't pay too much attention to clerical literary flits like
that guy in there," McQuillen went on when they were seated on a
white-enamel bench at the edge of the tee.

Before them lay a sweeping, shuttling resplendence of green: the
cropped green of the fairways and their distant border, the breathing green of the pines, deep, secret, and cool.

And on the first tee, Francis saw in the wrath of the writer,
Barry McQuillen, a reflection of the turmoil that came and went
within him. He wondered if Father Splaine might not have had
a mother who wanted him to be a priest more than anything else
in the world.

"You know why the *poet* doesn't like my book about Bobola,
don't you?" McQuillen went on in the same intemperate way that
was not without its ring of sincerity and deep conviction. "It's
because he sees himself in it. Any literary phony would see himself
in it. And you know, kid, we're all phony in one way or another.
But when you're phony in some way, or all ways, and won't admit
it — that's the unforgivable sin. That's why I wrote such a bitter
book as the *Bobola* thing. That's why I went after literary priests
in that book. The world looks at them and sees itself, not the
Church.

"There's too much evil running riot in the world — a priest just
shouldn't have time to be literary. Literary cocktail parties and
hoity-toity women's clubs don't belong in the life of a priest, as
far as I'm concerned.

"They'd tell you they're doing good by tripping around with
celebrities, drinking Martinis and chucking fat dowagers under
their double chins — but they're wrong. Lectures and autograph
parties do more for a celebrity's vanity than for the people who
attend them."

Francis sat there listening with absorption. He had never before
heard a genuine anticleric.

McQuillen fumed on, hunched over on the bench, a leaning,
lonely crag of humanity. As he talked he cracked the knuckles of
his meaty hands restlessly.

"What are too many priests famous for nowadays — tell me,
what are they getting famous for? They're getting famous in

magazines and books, they're getting famous on the lecture plat-form. But are they getting famous as holy priests of God?"

Francis was silent before the black, bitter storm of McQuillen's rhetoric. He nodded, half in agreement with, half in awe of this huge, buffeting man.

From the tee they could see Hanlon and the others emerging from the pro shop. The mayor and his secretary were carrying their golf clubs. They chatted with Father Splaine for a few moments. The cleric shook hands with them and skipped elfinly up the path toward the clubhouse.

"He's not going to play," McQuillen said. "He thinks I'm going along, so he's not going to play. He's going back to the clubhouse and recite for the ladies — he's going to lift their souls above the level of their bridge tables."

"Maybe he won't, Mr. McQuillen," Francis said. "Maybe he won't do that."

The mayor, his secretary, and Hanlon were winding up toward the tee. Two caddies, pack-laden, were scuffing slowly to their watching station near the pines, about 150 yards along the fairway. Clubless, Hanlon talked with motions of his hands to the mayor, who carried his driver carelessly in the crook of his arm. The secretary gripped his club jauntily in one hand like a cane, never for an instant relinquishing his hovering official air.

"All right, kid," McQuillen said, "all right, maybe he won't go peacocking around in there. But take some advice from a mouthy layman who still aspires to be a good Catholic. If you become a priest, be a real priest, kid."

"I will, Mr. McQuillen."

McQuillen grinned and strode vigorously down the tee hill toward the approaching trio.

"Whunk!"

The mayor's spoon shot on the seventeenth hole hooked grace-fully off the fairway and was swallowed in the black-green jungle of pines.

"There-uh goes another one," the mayor said.

"The caddies will find it, Your Honor," J. P. said. "Now about young Martin Ronayne — do you not think it would be good to bring him along through the school comm-it-tee in a couple of years? We can use young blood like his own."

Francis walked ahead with the mayor's caddy, and was soon crunching through the coolness and shadows of the forest.

On the other side of the fairway Brendan Kelly swung his midiron without luster and sent the ball bounding accurately toward the green.

"I'll fire him if he keeps that up," the mayor said with glum humor. "Yes, young Ronayne does seem like excellent caliber for us — by all means, Jim, bring him along during the next two years. If he can speak, we'll put him on the stump this fall."

"He has all the blarney of his father," said Hanlon, "and a pinch of the Harvard snobbery as well."

"I've heard somewhere that he's rather thick with young Parkley. What do you make of that, Jim?"

Hanlon raised his eyebrows a little. He was surprised to hear that Martin's chuminess with the young swell had got into the wind over at the Hall.

"It is of no serious consequence, I'm thinking, Your Honor. And doesn't he go to school with the young Yankee? His present friendship seems normal enough. I have hopes it will go no farther once the boy is working for the D.A. We'll keep him so busy he'll have little time for larking around with the swells."

"Good, Jim. . . . Have you found it, boys?" he called from the copse-thick fringe of the woods.

The caddy held the ball up for its owner to see.

"Toss it right out here, son. I'll play winter rules. I'm sure Mr. Kelly won't mind."

The mayor caught the ball, rubbed it against his tan gabardine jacket, and teed it high up on a tuft of grass. Then selecting a seven iron from the bag, he measured the ball and the distance, swung and lifted the ball in a lazy parabola onto the edge of the green.

"Excellent shot," his secretary called from across the fairway.

"A corker, Your Honor," said Hanlon.

"It *was* rather good, wasn't it," the mayor said.

Francis walked along the edge of the forest. The exhilaration of the course had swept McQuillen's jeremiads from his mind. He

had heard Martin's name mentioned by Hanlon and the mayor. . . .
Marty would have to give up some of his friends if the machine
got behind him, Francis suspected. But would he? He gave up
Alice for them, Francis reflected with bitterness. Maybe he'd sacrifice Hanlon's patronage, too. Francis knew Martin would play
along with Hanlon as long as he could, however. If only Marty
would stay out of official politics the way Dad did. . . .

The golfers chipped on and holed meticulously out; the party
safaried indolently along a path through the woods to the
eighteenth tee.

"This Charlestown Committee is a very fine thing, Jim — very
fine," said the mayor. "Tell me now — how much has the committee
had to do with the cessation of looping and-uh how much have you
had to do with it?"

"I have co-operated with Catherine Ronayne and the comm-it-tee,
wherever possible, Your Honor. I passed the word around that
there would be no more protection for the loopers."

"I suspected that, Jim. It is fortuitous indeed that Mrs. Ronayne
occupies the chair in the committee. Someone like Parkley might
be tempted to turn a searching eye to matters other than those
concerned with juvenile delinquency."

"If they do — and I don't believe they will, since Catherine sees
their task as a social instead of a political one — if they should go
snooping into the business of the people's representatives, they'll
lose any support they're getting from me. You may be sure of
that."

"Well said, Jim." The mayor wrinkled his high forehead as they
neared the tee. "You call Mrs. Ronayne by her first name. Do you
know her that well?"

Hanlon flushed. He wondered what the mayor had been hearing
about him and Catherine.

"Mrs. Ronayne is a lovely woman and a dear friend of mine,
Your Honor, but it goes no farther than that. There was but one
Martin Ronayne and though he be dead these many years he is
still very much alive in his wife's heart."

"He was a fine man, Jim," the mayor said with kind evasiveness.

Hanlon looked out on the spur 200 yards from the tee and was
grateful to see Francis standing there with the caddies.

Later, when the mayor had sunk his last shot, he slipped a five dollar bill out of his wallet and laid it on the green beside the cup. In the middle of the fairway a well-dressed foursome fretted, fumed and made nasty remarks about city government while two caddies and a boy with yellow hair putted for the greenback.

On the edge of the green the mayor steadied his golf bag with one hand and held the club heads firmly together with the other, as he watched.

Chapter 10

EARLIER that afternoon, Martin sat with Mr. Parkley and Erford in the wainscoted dining room of the Otis Club. The sting of Althea's jilt at the prelunch party had been mellowed by the drowsy opulence of lunch at the Otis.

Martin, discerning the restrained glances of polite surprise on the ruddy, lined faces of the club's ancient Irish porters and waiters, was pleasantly suffused with the knowledge that it wasn't every day a young Irishman sat down to lunch here with one of the most esteemed and traditional members of the club. Only someone with the prestige of Erford Parkley, Sr., could, in a sense, "get away with it."

The rangy, graying man who hovered over the snowy linen and glimmering silver of their corner table, twinkled his kind, blue eyes and angled his longish face a little before going on:

"Martin," he was saying, "I vividly remember dancing with your mother at the Copley many years ago. She was lovely — tall and stately — and I remember that the young belles from the Hill whispered, complimenting her beauty and wondered who she was — whether from Back Bay or Newburyport, Magnolia or Milton. Little did they dream," Parkley said with a rich, easy chuckle, "little did they dream that she was from Charlestown, just across the river, that her Hill was Breed's Hill and that her husband was that crusading Irishman who ran the *Charlestown Bulletin.*

"I saw her this morning at the committee meeting, and she was the same — the sight of her brought it all back."

"Nice that you remembered her, sir."

"How did the meeting go, Dad?" Erford asked.

"Extraordinarily well, indeed. There were no preliminaries to speak of. Mrs. Ronayne took the chair and announced that the best way to begin the committee's work was to start right in on a case."

"Where was the meeting held, Mr. Parkley?"

"Oh — it was held in one of the offices in the police station building, right there in City Square. I understand Jim Hanlon has an office thereabouts."

"That's right, Mr. Parkley."

"Well, there we were." He drew deeply on a fragrant cigar. "Right in the bailiwick of the big Boss. Mrs. Ronayne had a woman out in the anteroom who had been referred to us by the welfare department. It seems the department had gone as far as they could with her.

"She was a partially paralyzed widow, the mother of four small children and a grown boy who is now in the navy. The stroke, which has affected one side of her body, was a recent one — thus she has been unable to work and keep house and home together. So, eventually, the landlord served her an eviction notice. The city welfare department has been supplying them with enough money for food but they are not authorized to provide much more than that."

"What about the son in the navy?" Erford asked.

"I'm getting to that, son. Her grown boy, stationed in San Francisco, would be willing to come home, take a job, and undertake to support the family. What he sends her out of his pay as a seaman second class is negligible. However, it takes money to buy a boy out of the navy — and since the lad's enlistment has two years to run, buying him out seemed to be the only solution.

"Mike Farrell went out and brought the woman in. We talked to her and in her pitiful way she confirmed the things Mrs. Ronayne had told us. She went out again and suggestions were very much in order.

"Your mother said she thought she could get the sailor into

one of the printing establishments with which she's familiar. Mike Farrell said he knew the commandant of this naval district. He offered to see the officer and discuss the possibilities of getting the boy released as a hardship case. The medical member of the committee, a Dr. Applebaun, proposed to re-examine the lady and see what could be done in the way of further treatments for her paralysis. Father Quinn, from the *Beacon*, talked about the Catholic Charity Bureau."

"Then it was your turn, Dad."

"It certainly was — what could I do in this whirl of philanthropy but make some kind of suggestion? I examined the address of the petitioner and came to the conclusion that Newton Aldrich must own that property. Aldrich is a good friend of mine. In fact, he may be snoozing over the *London Illustrated News* out there in the lounge this very minute.

"I was sure he had no notion of what was involved in this particular eviction — you see, that sort of thing is handled exclusively by a local agent. I said I'd speak to the old gentleman."

"So there you have it," Parkley concluded, crinkling his brow engagingly and knocking a chunky segment of pure gray ash from his cigar end. "If every member does his job, I presume the woman will be in a reasonably good way."

"Did you discuss looping at all, Mr. Parkley?"

The older man hunched his shoulders a little, making the gesture graceful with a slight raising of his palms from the table. "What is there to discuss? There is no looping at the present time. Mr. J. P. Hanlon has apparently seen to that. I detect, too, the behind-the-scenes influence of a certain Charlestown lady of the press."

"Will you both have an Old Fashioned with me?" Mr. Parkley asked.

The two young lawyers nodded.

Mr. Parkley lifted his eyes in the direction of a waiter who was standing by the wall not far from the table. The old man, with a swift softness was at his side. "Bring us those special Old Fashioneds of yours, Pat."

"Right away, Mr. Parkley," the waiter said with just a hint of a brogue.

During the conversational lull that took place while a bus boy was clearing the table, Martin looked through the coils of cigarette and cigar smoke and noted again the marked facial resemblance between Erford and his father. Both had that longish cast of face and the hint of shrillness in their voices. The pallid complexion which Erford seemed to share in common with Althea must have come from their mother. Too, Althea seemed to have inherited her attractive, round pertness of face from her mother's side of the family.

And there was in father and son, Martin sensed, that same unmistakable, almost stodgy characteristic of moral rectitude which lent itself so well to the droll imaginations of caricaturists.

"By the way, Martin," Erford began when the bus boy had gone, "are you free to tell Dad about your plans for the fall?"

"I don't see why I couldn't," Martin said, "although I'd appreciate your taking it in confidence, Mr. Parkley. As far as I know, I'll be in the district attorney's office this fall."

"You don't say?" the elder Parkley said. "I think that's splendid!"

"As you may suspect, it's Jim Hanlon who's responsible for the appointment," Martin added.

"I thought as much. But, if I may say so, don't feel grateful about the lift you've been given. The best possible way you can show your gratitude is to go in there and work as hard and as honestly as you can for the welfare of the people."

"That's just how I happen to feel, Mr. Parkley."

"Both of you have passed the bar and will receive your law school diplomas soon," the older Parkley went on. "In many ways you represent the old and the new Boston. You both are faced with tremendous problems — problems which perhaps men from the opposite sides of the fence, like Hanlon and myself, have found virtually insoluble.

"It is unhappily true, that the fair-minded, forward-looking citizens of both parties find themselves and their city politically paralyzed by a bitter factionalism —"

"I was about to say," Martin broke in, "there is great need then of a coalition party, a party, perhaps, of the center, as they say in Europe."

lambent oblivion presided over by Emerson, Fuller, and Thoreau — all going to heaven with a Scotch and soda and the *London Illustrated News.*

He entered the lobby and was beckoned to a house phone booth by the waiter.

"Hello, this is Ronayne."

"Hello, Martin," Althea said in a shy, hesitant tone that was new to him.

"Well, well, isn't this my day! How are you, Althea?"

"Quite well," she said. "How are you among all those mummies? I hope Dad and Erford haven't asphyxiated you."

"On the contrary — they've been very nice. I think it's wonderful here — just the way I imagined it would be."

"You'll get over that. Can you see my ancestor, General Parkley? Look out the window of your booth."

"Just a minute." Martin looked across the corridor at the painting on the wall. It was an iron-visaged oil of a revolutionary general, posing in front of his troops.

"Yes, I see him now," Martin said. "He looks as though he's sniffing the body odors of the rabble-in-arms."

"That's it exactly," she said, chuckling.

They laughed for several moments. It was as if the telephones, through which they dispelled all awkwardness, were morning coffee or cocktails before dinner — such was their ease together.

"I really called to tell you how sorry I am about that dance business," she said.

"Don't be. I think I understand."

"But I am," she insisted. "I am sorry. That wasn't really I who turned you down."

"It wasn't?"

"It wasn't."

"All right, then," he said. "Will you go to the law school prom with me?"

"Yes," she said.

After he had switched off the ignition, Erford sat for several moments in the canyon coolness of the garage and reflected on the afternoon.

Martin had taken the whole thing with commendable poise and Erford knew his father had been impressed.

There was that matter of the telephone call which still nibbled at Erford's curiosity. Martin had returned to the table and said nothing about it.

Yet Erford could not help wondering who would call him at the Otis. He was quite sure Martin hadn't mentioned the engagement to anyone. His father might have said something about it to Mrs. Ronayne, but she wouldn't have called except in some emergency. If there had been an emergency Martin surely would have said something.

It might have been Althea at that. But why?

He'd speak to her — now — if she was at home. She'd best stay out of this. Any possible emotional involvements on Althea's part would simply ruin the chances of political co-operation with Ronayne.

He opened the door of his coupe and got out. He hurried across the concrete pavilion that was warm in the late afternoon sun. He ascended the stairs to the kitchen and entered.

"Good evening, Mr. Erford, you're home early."

"Good evening, Brigid. Yes, I was at the club most of the afternoon with Dad."

Brigid was sitting at the kitchen table, sewing metal clasps on a chiffon gown that was the warm, Latin color of a tangerine.

Erford paused at the entrance of the mahogany hallway leading to the front of the house.

"That looks like one of Althea's."

"It is Miss Althea's." Brigid smiled with maternal affection. "She's wearing it to a dance a week from tonight."

"Oh. . . . Is she in the house?"

"Yes, in her room."

Erford nodded and went down the hall.

She was going then, he thought. But she might be going with Royce. Of course, she might very well be going with Royce.

He climbed the stairs gently, suspecting his father might be napping in his study before dinner. He walked along the second-floor hall to the door of his room, pausing again, listening for some sound in Althea's room directly across from his.

He stepped to her door and knocked.

"Come in, Erford," she said.

She was sitting on a chaise longue, a copy of *Smart Set* open in her lap. She folded her arms somewhat aggressively and touched her features with a puckish half-smile.

In a flamboyant Japanese kimono and with her hair pinned tightly down, she looked like something out of Gilbert and Sullivan, Erford thought. She had a good idea, he sensed, of what was on his mind.

"You're home early," she said.

He sat down on a straight, early American chair at the foot of her bed.

"Yes, we were at the Otis most of the afternoon."

"Dad came in a short while ago. He must be resting now."

There was an awkward space. He had hoped she might ask about Martin in connection with the afternoon. She was too smart for that. He'd have to bring it up, betray his concern.

"Brigid is working on a lovely party gown — yours, I gather."

A flicker of irritation crossed her face.

"Yes, I asked her to sew on some clasps," she said with an off-handedness that nettled him. Her refusal to be drawn out he knew was a tactic which might be telling him to mind his own business. Well, this was his business — it was the family's business.

"I take it you're going to the dance then. Are you going with Royce?"

She shook her head. "As a matter of fact, I'm going with Martin. I told him I felt rather shabby about the way I'd treated him. He invited me again and I accepted. It's as simple as that."

"I wish it were," Erford said, rising. "And I wish, Sis, you'd taken Dad and me into consideration before you went ahead with this thing."

"What d'you mean?" she said, coloring. "It's just a date — I like Martin, but it's still just a date."

"I realize that, and I know you think I'm being rather complex. But we've established one relationship with Martin and this social sort of thing you're beginning won't fit into the scheme at all. It — it just isn't cricket, you see."

"I see, but I don't see. I like him and I'm going to the dance with him. And, really, I don't think Dad will mind. Good heavens, I'm not eloping with the guy!"

"All right, Althea, all right! Just try and leave it at that, or you *will* have Dad down on you. He's really interested in Martin's ability to do something in liberal politics. Don't spoil it! There are plenty of playmates around. What about Royce? Certainly he's asked you?"

"He has," Althea said, blinking back the tears. "It's just that I don't like Royce. He's nice but I don't like him. Do you want me to run around with someone I don't like?"

"Perhaps you haven't given him a chance to be likable. That fellow has a very attractive future. He has money, background, and he isn't an ogre to look at. Dad was telling me only the other night that Royce gave him a tip on a Midwestern investment which — "

"I've heard it all before," she said, sighing. "Royce is obviously out to impress Dad. Run along now, I've got to dress. I'm dining with some of the girls."

"Sure thing, Sis," Erford said, softening. "But try and see our position in this thing. There may be a lot at stake for all of us, Martin included. Let's keep the balance."

"Okay, okay!" Althea said, waving her hand impatiently. "Run along."

Erford rose like a parent who has recently chastised its child. "Have a good time tonight."

"Good night," said Althea.

When he closed the door she slumped down on her bed. All her life she had paid bitterly for her impulsiveness. This was one time, however, she did not mind paying. Martin was the first suitor she had known who had won her response with complete honesty and ease.

Erford and her father, she knew, were class-conscious in a more logical, less offensive way than she had ever been. She knew, guiltily, that she would not have recognized the ugliness of class superiority if she herself had not become involved.

She buried her face in the white satin spread and wept.

Chapter 11

AFTER she had put the supper dishes away, Catherine stood by the kitchen window a while drinking in the still and tender May evening. The rays of the waning sun, cooled by the lingerings of spring wind, slanted across the chipped, red bricks of the alley and spread over them a mirage of iciness.

Within, the house was as still as death. Rosemary had gone to the movies with Mike Farrell. Francis had not yet returned from Cape Cod. Outside, the small-bell voices of two twelve-year-old girls, playing hopscotch, blended with the after-supper somnolence of fading day. On just such a mystical evening as this, her husband's body had arrived from overseas. Further remembrance of things past had been interrupted, a few minutes before, by a phone call from her older son. He said he'd drop over and pick up the dress shirt she had laundered for him.

During the past week Martin had seemed evasive concerning his plans for the dance, although he had indicated he was not taking Alice. Apparently her strategy with regard to the tenement romance had worked very well. But tonight there was a sure, lightsome quality in his voice. He hadn't volunteered the identity of his dancing partner over the phone. Catherine would ask him when he arrived for the shirt.

"But it was on such an evening as this. . . . " She shook her head quickly, jarring her memory. "On such an evening as this," she whispered, "I should finish my spring cleaning."

She straightened the dish towel on a rack and walked down the hall to her bedroom. Strewn about the floor near a large clothes closet was an assortment of hat boxes, suitcases, and cardboard folios. She knelt down and added several expendable items of clothing and paper to two piles of waste. She picked up a slim portfolio and had started to untie the strings when she saw the label: "War Letters from Martin."

Her fingers stilled over the loosened bowknot. She would throw none of these away. Why open the folio?

She sighed, sitting in the museum stillness of the bedroom, self-conscious of what others would see as endless, seemingly foolish mourning — what her priest friends might call an un-Christian preoccupation with the deceased. She had thought all that through many times and had always returned, with conviction, to the evocative relics of her husband's life and days.

For she knew nothing morbid in living, to an extent, with her husband's shade. The life of loneliness since his death had been of her own choosing. The children, his paper, were the reasons she gave for avoiding remarriage. They were good reasons, too, but she knew they were reflections of the most important reason — her abiding love for her husband.

She believed intuitively and by religious training and practice that this life was the mortal phase of an eternal life. He was still in existence, waiting for her. Thus she could live with the loneliness, although it was perfectly understandable to her that most young widows could and did remarry without the slightest disrespect to their deceased.

As she had striven to aid Martin in his career while he was alive, so now she had found a new application of her devotion to him in their children. Their future achievements would reflect upon him. "They are the children of Martin Ronayne," people did and would say. "It is no great surprise that they have done well." Rosemary would marry — perhaps Mike Farrell. On Martin and Francis rested the heavier responsibility of their father's name.

She had been aware of that all along — Martin in civic life, Francis in the Church. There was still so much to do — so much planning and striving, so very much to do.

The future of the paper worried her. She did not want it to

go out of the family. Perhaps Mike and Rosemary would take it over, if they got together. Or even Martin might be able to keep an eye on it in a part-time administrative capacity.

Her eyes were on the folio. She had browsed through his war letters during spring cleaning a year ago. They were invariably calm, vivid, hopeful — poignantly so — and even though she was moved to deep emotion by them, her husband's humorous observations on his puckish or earthy buddies never failed to lighten the reading.

She debated about slipping the bowknot and opening the folio, thinking with a smile of "Stonewall" Jackson, the Louisiana private in Martin's squad whose reminiscences on possum pie were all the more pungent when the beans lay cold in the mess kits.

Then there was Private Cooney from Vermont who gave endless lessons in the technique of milking in case any member of the squad should encounter a cow. She remembered one of the phrases Martin had used: "It is almost as if Cooney were directing some invisible orchestra." She frowned, deciding against the emotional strain which a rereading of the letters might provoke.

She heard the scratching of a key in the front door. Martin. She pushed herself to her feet, smoothed down her skirt, glanced into the dresser mirror, touching the back of her hair. She hurried down the hall and greeted him as the door swung open.

"Come in," she said, as he kissed her. "You've had dinner?"

"Yes, Mother, I had lamb chops at the Oxford Grille with some guys from the dorm."

"Oh, young Parkley and all?"

She asked it lightly, but he looked at her steadily for a moment, knowing she had disclosed something deeper.

"Erford went home for dinner, I think. What have you been doing? There's dust on your chin."

"Spring cleaning, of course. Can I make you a cup of tea?"

"Yes. Then I'll have to take the shirt and run. The underclassmen are giving us a smoker. . . . "

"You're always dashing somewhere lately." She took his hand and led him into the kitchen. "This is your home, remember? We knew you long before you went to Harvard Law."

"You'll know me a long time after I leave, too, Mother." He kissed her again.

"I'm glad to hear that."

They were in the kitchen. She beckoned him to a chair at the enamel-topped table. "Tell me about the dance while I'm brewing the tea. It's next week, isn't it?"

She knew it was time to ask and he knew it was time to answer.

"Who are you taking, by the way? I don't think you've mentioned her."

"I haven't, Mother. I haven't mentioned her because it was just decided late this afternoon. I'm taking Althea Parkley."

Catherine busied herself about the stove, lighting the gas under the tea kettle, grateful for something to do with her hands.

Was this the jeopardy of which so many Irish priests had warned?

Her confessor, old Father Molloy, had clucked when she had consulted him concerning Martin's matriculation at the law school. "Send your son to Harvard," he had said, "and he'll go farther in this world than the next."

She had respected his advice but given heavier weight to what she thought might have been the mind of her husband. Martin would have seen the advantages to a young Catholic lawyer with a Harvard background. She remembered him saying: "If the religious faith of my children isn't strong enough to withstand the influences of a non-Catholic school, I would be seriously concerned about them no matter what their pursuits in later life."

This was her thinking, too, and her confidence in Martin was deep and strong. Then had come the association with young Parkley, presenting diplomatic difficulties with Hanlon — now this, another and more dangerous area, the area of the heart.

"It's only a date, Mother. She's an awfully nice girl."

"I'm sure she is." Catherine smiled and sprinkled the orange pekoe shreds into her full-bellied earthenware teapot. "I was a little surprised, I guess. I didn't know you were that well acquainted with the Parkley girl."

"She's joined us for lunch several times. She was at the splash party today."

"How does her family feel about this?"

"I don't think Erford will mind. As for her dad, he seems like a genuine sort — democratic, I mean."

"Yes, democratic." Catherine poured the tea. "I've known Erford's father much longer than you. There are levels of democracy among liberal bluebloods like Parkley."

"I suppose there are, Mother, but this is still just a dance."

"Yes . . . I'm sure you'll have a wonderful time — both of you."

Later, when he had gone, she paused at the front window watching his lank, graceful form descending the hill. She wondered about him. Was he the tractable person she had always thought him to be — the one who could always see the wisdom of living according to plan? Was he?

He disappeared around the corner at Main Street, and the cold shadow of his absence, of his disturbing growth away from her, descended. The lace curtain fell back into place.

"I must get over to the office," she thought, turning. "The man from the Sugar House will be there about his employment ad. I'll do up the tea dishes later."

She was about to cross to the hall closet for a jacket when she noticed a small square box on the sofa. She lifted the box. It bore a florist's label from Harvard Square.

She opened the box and the fragile splendor of a blue orchid filled her senses. She read the card:

> "To the beautiful lady who ironed a stuffed shirt
> for a stuffed shirt."
>
> "Love, Martin."

The love and belief soared up again, dispelling the cold of sudden doubt, up with the brief loveliness of the orchid which she cradled in front of her a moment. The dance would pass like the brief ecstasy of the orchid, she thought — he would go on in the pattern hoped for, planned — Martin Ronayne, Jr., his father's son. He would go on, he must.

Chapter 12

ON EARTH there is no heaven like the prom. No night as wondrous, sabled, star-roofed; no men as handsome, girls as April-lovely; no voices as electric; no orchestra as thrilling; no dancing as eternal; no coffee and kisses after just as dreamy; no good-night as endless; nothing, nowhere, gorgeous as the prom.

At dusk, the cab fled along the river road and Martin, rigidly handsome in dress shirt, white coat, tux pants, patent-leather shoes, knew a certain easement in the patiently breathing expanse of the Charles. He bent his watch out from under a French cuff and read the time. Twenty of nine. He would be at Althea's in about five minutes.

Across the river he could see the towers and spires of Harvard settling into a kind of preternatural shadow, a sooty gloom. Above the Harvard skyline the stars were glimmering and gaining, the moon was showing the border of its silver skirt, and a thrill of fulfillment flared in his blood.

For awaiting his coming was the Yankee girl, the precious fruit of a vine cultivated assiduously for three hundred New England years. He, the son of an immigrant Irishman taking a Parkley to a Harvard prom. And the wine of that anticipation seemed even more exciting when he thought of her as a person, a pert and lovely girl, pulled toward him, and he toward her, without consciousness of class. Indeed his dream of social ascendancy seemed ridiculous when he thought that her attraction would have been as strong had her name been Baciagalupo.

His mother had discerned his more than casual interest in Althea and he had not known what to say, except that it was a date. Just a date.

The cab turned off the drive, following the trickle tributary known as Muddy River.

He wasn't sure how Erford had taken the identity of his prom partner. When he told him about it, his answer had been a noncommittal: "I know." And when Martin had sounded him out as to double-dating he said that he and his fiancée planned to go in his coupe. "I rather think Althea would like to drive her roadster," he had added, smiling almost generously.

Well, the coolness was there, but what could you expect? Certainly Erford was a little taken aback. What was I to expect, Martin asked himself, a partnership in the firm?

The cab drew up in front of the Parkley brownstone. He paid the fare and walked across the street in the silence of a Back Bay dusk.

He could see Althea's car parked in the driveway. There was a light in the hall, dull through the long, thin, stained-glass windows on either side of the front door.

He climbed the short flight of white, granite steps and pressed a tiny, mother-of-pearl door button.

There followed the period of silence typical of a big house with servants. Martin wondered with a certain amusement if anybody could relax inside until the maid answered the door. He heard augmenting footfalls in the distance, the door swung open, the cherubic Irish face brogued him pleasantly into the music room.

He stood by one of the French windows examining the rubber plant in its wrought-iron jardiniere; he worked at appearing urbane, but the flight of the butterfly was in him and there was a tickling sensation in his throat.

He heard a door close softly in some olympian upper region. He heard the light step on the stairs, the rustle of a gown.

"Hello," she said. Framed in the black enamel doorpost of the music room, framed in a waterfall of tangerine chiffon, her pert and beckoning loveliness assailed him and he almost ran to her.

"You're much too lovely to be real," he said, walking involuntarily toward her, wanting to kiss her.

"These are too lovely to be real," she said, slowly revolving the twin black orchids which she carried.

She offered him her hand. He held it a while, letting the moment pass in which she might have accepted his kiss without awkwardness.

"You look like someone out of F. Scott," she said.

"So do you."

"Erford has gone ahead and Dad is at one of his supper clubs."

"Shall we go now?"

"If you like." He opened the door.

When they reached the sidewalk she handed him the keys to her roadster. "My horse, sir."

"You bet."

He walked up the driveway, got into the car, started it, and backed it out. She got in beside him, all in a rustle, and they drove off to the old, new life of the college prom, the old, new life of the heart.

The music of "Stardust" wailed sweetly from the bandstand at one end of the festooned boathouse. He swung her around slowly, floating with the others through the rainbow cosmos of the summer prom.

They had exchanged few words since their arrival several dances ago. The music, the atmosphere of conventional intimacy conditioned their approach to each other. They danced, laughed, gazed, and knew with rich certitude, as the night went on, that this was the way it should be — they together, this night, later, perhaps always. How, when? Ignore the when and how. Now. This night.

Looking beyond to the other dancers, in the rainbowish play of the rotating spotlights, heady with the fragrance of her bobbed, brown hair, he saw Erford's pale face for an instant, expressionless, disembodied. Erford seemed to nod, as if to remind him that he had not had that dance with his sister as yet.

Martin smiled, swung Althea away, almost with a touch of panic. Erford, for the first time, seemed a symbol of all that could stand between him and this girl — the symbol of the prim and vigilant Boston world awaiting with the cold, patient eyes of an old-maid chaperone.

"I just caught a glimpse of Erford," Martin said. He held her hand for a moment as the dancers drifted away from the center of the floor.

"Yes, I must dance with him," she said. "Be nice to Nancy Havens. Erford doesn't take her out often."

"Aren't they engaged?"

"Yes, but Erford is terribly busy, most of the time. Nancy doesn't seem to mind. She has her man."

"How does Erford feel about it?"

"Well, it's what Dad wants. The Havens and the Parkleys have been bargaining in stocks and daughters for many years." She looked at Martin with a steadiness that had in it an element of the apprehensive.

"I think we'd better stay right here and let Erford find us," Martin said, his eyes searching, but his thoughts fusing into a question.

"You know, Althea, if you don't mind my saying this, I rather thought your father was quite the modern. It's hard for me to visualize him doing something feudal — like picking out mates for his children."

"Feudal is the right word, where it concerns me, anyway. But you seem to know only the political Parkleys. Father and Erford are decidedly traditional — rock-ribbed as any — when it comes to things social *and* financial."

"I see — " Martin hesitated and then spoke, unable to keep the chagrin out of his voice. "Have they picked out your husband yet?"

"No, but they're working on it." She looked up at him and smiled. "He'd have to be at least as nice as you. And I don't know any eligible male quite like you."

"Thanks. Here come Erford and the girl friend."

Erford introduced him to Nancy with a masterful courtesy. She was a tall, pale brunette with a longish neck and cool, green eyes. The lead trumpet wept the first notes of "I'll See You Again." Althea glanced meaningfully over Erford's shoulder and was waltzed away. Martin felt Nancy stiffen under the pressure of his hand. He danced across the floor with the cool, lean beauty, sensing that behind those inanimate features an appraisal was going on.

It was an experience not to be taken lightly. These were the people he had been interested in knowing, and as his acquaintance with them grew, the boisterous Irish puritanism of his youth seemed less cold, less rigid, less clannish, because of the new social coldness and clannishness he was beginning to know.

When the waltz had ended, Erford suggested some punch. "We'll go out on the landing with it, if you like. It's getting much too warm in here."

Althea wandered out of the boathouse onto the long, wide wooden landing which sloped into the river. Overhead a swinging array of Japanese lanterns competed with the moon, the stars. The headlights of automobiles, like organized fireflies, passed and repassed each other on the other side of the Charles.

She leaned on a railing looking out over the inky distance and wished Martin was beside her. She had at first been alarmed and then warmed by the realization of her affection for Martin, the excitement and ease of being with him, the desire to be with him again.

And he had wanted to know if her father had picked out a husband for her yet. . . .

Standing there in the warm May night of the river, she knew a chill of fear that she might prove powerless before the pressures of her father and her brother — the pressures that could drive a needle into Martin's heart and return her to the misery of a wooden conformity to class.

"Here you are, Sis." Erford offered her a cup of fruit punch and a sweet cooky. "It's much cooler here."

"Much." She sipped her drink. "Where are the others — can they find us here?"

"I'll go looking for them in a minute. I wanted to speak to you alone."

"Oh?"

"I spoke to Dad at the Otis tonight before coming here."

"Was he upset — about the dance?"

"Not at all. As a matter of fact, he spoke very well of Martin. Hoped you'd enjoy this together and all."

"That was nice of Dad. . . . What else did he say?"

"Oh, yes." Erford made it clear he was coming to the point of the tête-à-tête. "He hopes you won't make any plans for Sunday evening. He's invited Herb Royce to the house for dinner."

"Royce? Dad's invited Royce?"

"Yes, he wants to chat with him about business conditions in Wisconsin. He thought you might like to see Herb, too." Erford's voice took on a more tender timbre. "You did rather let him down tonight, you know."

"Not at all. Don't I have a right to choose my own dates?"

"Of course you do, Althea," Erford insisted. "But it's just — well, it's just that you'd been seeing a good deal of Herb, that's all."

She was silent, not knowing what to say, knowing that words were quite as futile as silence.

"You'll be on hand, Sis?"

"I'll be there," she said tonelessly.

"Fine. Let's go find the others."

"I don't care to go in right now. You might tell Martin I'm here."

"I will," Erford said brightly, as if nothing could mar the destiny of Sunday evening. "Will you and Martin have coffee with us later?"

"We may see you around," she said flatly without looking at him.

"Very well."

He went up the landing and into the boathouse. The beat of the fox trot peppered her spirit with lumps of clay.

"The Monument by moonlight," Martin said, easing the roadster to the curbing alongside Monument Park. "Remember the time you said you wanted to see it by moonlight? I never thought we'd get here."

"Neither did I." Althea drew her wrap closer in the early morning air chilled by a breeze off the harbor. She peered up at the obelisk, hugely tall, spectrally-white, tirelessly indicative of the stars.

"It looks very slender when you see it from a distance — here it has a thickness that almost detracts from its appearance."

"I never thought about it that way, but you're right." Martin dropped his arm about her shoulders. "It's quite chilly."

"It really is," she said, settling back comfortably into the curve of his arm.

"Do you think Erford minded our leaving without seeing him?"

"I don't know. I just wanted to go, it was getting much too warm."

"This is much nicer. Who knows when I'll be with you like this again?"

He had said all there was to say.

He kissed her. But soon, the sun of convention would be wheeling across the harbor from the east.

Chapter 13

ON A Saturday morning in mid-November, seminarian Francis Ronayne leaned on a mop and looked out the thick, gray Gothic casement of his room in St. Philip's Hall. His roommates, Tubby Thomas and Emmet Clifton, were among the caterwauling young men playing tag rush down on the playing field.

The six sweat-shirted seminarians representing his class, the "poets" from the junior sem — Tubby and Emmet among them — were lined up defensively against the rhetoricians.

"Hey, hey, take it away!" slight, dark Emmet hallooed in his paradoxically enormous voice. He danced about in the safety man's position down by the ten-yard line.

"Block that kick!" Tubby croaked from the roving center position.

The third quarter was almost gone — the poets were losing 21–19. Francis wiped the perspiration from his brow with a hand towel, sucked in a mouthful of the stinging November air and waited nervously for the punt.

A long, calm rhetorician received the pass from center and booted a graceful spiral between Tubby and the safety man. Emmet broke into a run, fielding the oval on the first bounce. He cut sharply toward the left side of the field, catching his pursuers off balance. Tubby faded to the right, somewhat to the rear of Emmet. Just as Emmet was about to be tagged by the player who had done the kicking, he stopped abruptly and threw a long lateral to Tubby.

Francis dropped the mop and yelled joyously as Tubby waddled down the side line and over the goal.

Rhetorical heads popped out woefully from second-story windows. Francis, from the poetical third floor, leaned over and shouted: "Why don't you get a team!"

Two rhetoricians glanced up at Francis disdainfully, withdrew, and went back to their mops.

The teams were lining up for another kickoff. Francis pulled back into the room, picked up the mop, and let his eyes wander over the fading, rolling green of the seminary grounds.

Other groups of sweat-shirted seminarians were kicking and throwing footballs; cassocked Fathers were hiking about in twos and threes. It was Saturday morning and even though it was his turn to mop the floor, there was an exhilarating air of freedom about the entire sem and its environs caused by the fact that he did not have to think of books and examinations until Sunday.

He glanced at his watch — 11:05. Chapel at 11:40, chow at twelve, then maybe a long walk down by the reservoir. Coffee and a hot dog at a dog cart on the other side of the res. Vespers at five, dinner at six, spiritual conference and Benediction at seven fifteen. Then Confession, and two hours to read books or write letters.

He plied his mop dilatorily over the remaining section of varnished oak floor. As he wrung out the mop his mind went back over the two months or more that had passed since he had come here — since the *Shenandoah* buckled in a storm over Columbus in September and since October when the French said they simply could not pay their war debt — *a l'avenir, au futur, demain. . . .*

"Pal of my cradle days . . . " he hummed, remembering the farewell party his mother had held for him at home. They had gathered around the piano and sung songs like that one at the close of the evening. His mother had sat on the sofa knitting and chatting with Martin, Hanlon, and Father Quinn while they sang.

John Little, Alice Stasek, he, and Mike hovered over Rosemary, singing, as she played. John and Alice, Mike and Rosemary, theirs were two distinct life patterns taking predictable form.

Martin did not sing around the piano. That was a pattern, too. He sat in the parlor talking with that cool seriousness which had become an engaging conversational manner.

Francis knew Martin had been avoiding Alice. So he sat in the parlor, sipping coffee, telling them about his early reactions to the D.A.'s office while the piano went bonga-longa-longa, while the voices were sad and joyous, gusty or hushed in accordance with the "Silvery Moon," the "Camp-town Races," the "Rose of Tralee."

Mike turned the music for Rosemary and sang in his creaky baritone voice directly to her. He had it bad, Francis knew, and that would not be so unusual for one of Rosemary's beaux but for the fact that she seemed to reciprocate. Mike had been visiting the house on "committee business" two or three nights a week. Catherine was on to him but played her role of dutiful committee chairman until it was time for Mike to go into the kitchen for coffee with Rosemary.

At first Rosemary had taken indignantly to her room when Mike clomped into the kitchen while she was putting up her hair. But Mike, who had once got himself arrested as an alleged drunkard so that he could write candidly about unsavory conditions in the city jail, was not easily put to flight.

"You're just as pretty with your hair up," he had whispered, passing Rosemary's bedroom door on the way back to the parlor and the winking, diplomatic immunity provided by Catherine. As with Martin and Francis, Catherine knew just what she wanted for Rosemary, and Mike was it.

Rosemary had heard the pert, seductive whisper while sitting at her vanity. She flushed, slammed down her hair brush, and scowled at herself in the mirror. "That — that overbearing ink-eater! Who does he think he is — walking around the house like one of the family!"

Soon she was deftly rolling up her long hair, as black, as shiny as anthracite. The feeling of pique waned in her. The big, grinning, craggy face loomed elfishly in her mind. The enameled paleness of her features relaxed into a smile.

And there had been Alice Stasek singing at the piano with the others and telling a story just by being there with John Little.

John always seemed to be somewhere around her then. She had been dating him quite regularly. There was something thrilling about being with the reformed leader of the loopers — something exciting about his flaring red hair, his quick, crisp, erudite talk.

The things he knew and the people took her out of herself. She was grateful for his shy, yet insistent attentions since her breakup with Martin, and this gratitude had involuntarily become a certain affection. It was nothing like the old ache that was in her for Martin — but it was a warm, good thing nonetheless.

Catherine, knowing that John must either go backward or forward, as is perhaps true of all who have reformed, had appointed him managing editor of the *Bulletin*. Thus he would more than fill the vacancy left by Francis. She knew his natural brightness and the considerable, if whimsical, amount of reading he had done and was doing. He would fill the bill, with supervision, she believed.

As for John, he saw that the new white-collar position would enhance his chances with Alice.

The more John knew and loved Alice, the more awkward he felt toward Martin. It wasn't jealousy entirely — although he knew a few pangs of that. It was his bewilderment at the fact that Martin had voluntarily jilted her.

He could not know that Mrs. Ronayne had created the forces which determined the break. And, even in the parlor, as she listened, suffused with pride, to her son's reactions to his first days at the D.A.'s office, she was conscious of her part in keeping him separated from Alice and the others out in the hall. There was nothing to be gained by tearing the scab off a wound.

"What is the D.A.'s office doing about bootlegging in the South End?" Father Quinn badgered. "Are you aware, young man, that not very far from the Jesuit High School, one can get a glass of beer with a shot of ether in it for a dime? You're an assistant district attorney now. Just what do you propose to do about it?"

Catherine and Hanlon laughed.

"I'll tell him about it in the morning," Martin said wryly, "but you know as well as I do, Father, trying to stop bootlegging is like sticking one finger in a dike that has a thousand holes."

"It is true," J. P. said, proud of the observation of his protégé. "We've no course at all but to bring the hard stuff back."

"Coolidge will never do it," Catherine said. "I wonder if he ever took a nonmedicinal drink in his life."

"That's why he's President," Father Quinn said. "You know, of course, the old Yankee formula for worldly success?"

"No, what is it?" Martin asked.

"Cold water, inside and out," Father Quinn quipped.

"I'll not be much of a success," Hanlon said, popping his eyes and taking a good swig of his Scotch and soda.

Laughter all around and music all around, but only quiet resignation within for the "priest in the family."

At eleven-thirty Martin arose, pleading an early assignment in the morning. He was still rooming near the university where with the permission of the D.A., he was attending an early morning graduate course in political science.

Catherine has been disappointed that he didn't move home permanently after his graduation from law school. He had lived most of the summer at home, however, and that was a compensation. She agreed that it would be more practical for Martin to get to early classes from rooms right on the grounds. But she could not help sensing that Martin clearly preferred the social life of the university set to that offered in the Ronayne parlor.

Catherine no longer remonstrated with him concerning his social-climbing tendencies. She was proud of his scholastic achievements, and her fears of his involvements with the Parkleys were allayed by his present apprenticeship to Jim Hanlon. She saw in Martin, still, the reincarnation of her husband — although admittedly she detected differences — the pragmatism of her son, the purer idealism of the father — the ease with which he "reconnoitered" with the Parkleys — yet he was still young; he would grow out of his uncertain period.

And Francis, whose future had worried her much more, would soon be in the seminary — thank God! How happy Martin would be, if he were alive, to see his son a priest!

Before Martin left, he chatted with Francis in the bedroom they had shared from childhood through high school.

"So my little brother is leaving us tomorrow," Martin had said, dragging on a cigarette and pushing his brown Stetson back on top of his black, wavy hair. He sat on the bed, supporting himself on one elbow and surveying his brother mirthfully.

You left us long ago, Francis thought, standing at the foot of the bed. He nodded at his big brother and smiled.

"Remember the time I bought you the skis just before Christmas and you met me, carrying them, on Main Street, just after I got off the streetcar?" Martin asked, chuckling.

"Yeh, you hid them behind a fence as nonchalantly as you could. I pretended I never saw them. And remember the time you taught me to hop a truck and I was too afraid to get off while it was moving and we were stopped by a red light about ten miles later?"

"I remember. I called you a scared little weasel and you cried. Then when Mother got hold of me for keeping you out so late — I cried."

"Yeh, and the time we took Rosemary to a knothole-gang game at Braves Field," Francis said. "She kept bawling for a drink of water and there was a line of insanely thirsty kids a mile long at the drinking fountain. You bought her an orangeade and it cost a quarter inside the park."

Martin laughed heartily. "Yeh, and she was even more thirsty after drinking the orangeade, so rather than stand in line, I took her home. Wasn't she the one?"

"Yeh, the knothole gang. What medieval tortures we underwent to see the last-place Braves get deeper and deeper into the cellar."

"Say," Martin began soberly, "what's all this between Mike Farrell and Rosemary? Anything to it?"

"Three nights a week and all day Sunday."

Martin whistled. "Not our little iceberg?"

"The same."

"Say, we'll have quite a family, won't we — a priest, a writer. . . ."

"And what else?" asked Francis. "Mayor, governor, or president?" Martin pushed himself up from the bed, took off his hat, and winked blandly. "We'll see."

"I hope you do get there, Marty. But just don't forget where you came from."

"What do you mean by that?" Martin asked with an air of irritation.

"Oh, forget it." Francis held out his hand. "Drop me a line at the sem once in a while, will you?"

"Sure I will." Martin shook hands absently. "But tell me what you meant, Fran?"

"Well . . . " Francis lowered his eyes. "You might keep in mind

that there aren't enough people like the Parkleys to vote you into
office and there are, in Boston anyway, enough Hanlons, Ronaynes,
and Quinns. They're your friends . . . try and keep them that way
is what I mean."

Martin's face clouded with anger. "I certainly mean to!"

Francis shrugged his shoulders. "Okay. Let's get back to the
others."

Martin followed him out of the room without a word. He said
good night to his mother and the others quickly and was gone.

Still stinging from Francis' rebuke, Martin walked swiftly down
the hill toward the City Square elevated station. "I should have
slapped his face — the fresh little squirt. What the hell does he
know about politics! I'll show him — I'll show them all."

"Francis," Catherine whispered in the hall, after she had returned from the door, "Martin seemed upset about something.
Did you two have a quarrel?"

"Not that I know of, Mother."

One last stroll with John Little up the hill and around the
Monument in the tender midnight of early September. Francis,
standing outside the Stasek's new address farther up Monument
Avenue, could hear John creaking down the stairs.

"Wasn't long, was I?" John slipped out of the hall darkness.

"Not at all. Hope I didn't hurry you."

"Maybe you did — but for you I'll hurry. . . . Once around the
Spike?"

"Once around." Francis glanced at the luminous dial of his
watch. It was shortly before twelve. "Then I've got to get back
for coffee with Mother and Rosemary. I'm all packed and ready
to go in the morning."

"We'll miss you, Francis."

"I'll miss you, too, John. But you've got Alice now — she'll
fill your heart."

"She sure will. It's hard to believe she's going steady with a
character like me."

"No it's not."

The floodlights were out by now, but the pale September moon sent down some splendor, bringing the obelisk spectrally out of the shadows.

"Take a good look, Fran," John said. "You won't see it again for months. You get to come home summers, don't you?"

"Not for long." Francis looked up at the Monument. "They send us to a summer camp."

They crossed to the iron-picket fence and began their brisk circuit of the park. On the east side of the Monument they paused. They were just across the street from the barny, gray house, on the third story of which John's family lived.

Atop the house was an octagonal cupola, known in the days of Yankee Clippers as a "widow's watch." From the windows of the cupola on a clear day one could see most of Boston proper and a good deal of the inner harbor. It was in that cupola, just above his family's tenement that John had his bed, desk, books, and a telescope through which Francis had often watched the stars.

"Could I take one last look, John? Then I've got to scramble."

They climbed the stairs to the third floor. There was a ladder nailed to the wall of the third-floor landing. It led through a trap door to the cupola. John led the way.

In the musty, moony shadows of the "widow's watch" Francis peered out the east window, looking toward the riding lights of the harbor. John fumbled with the oil lamp on his desk.

A match sputtered and flared, giving a small, orange flower to the lamp which flickered and steadily grew until the cupola was bathed in dim dancing light.

"It works," Francis said.

"Yeh, after a fashion; needs a new wick."

There was something eerie about being high over the city at midnight in the light of the dismal little lamp. It seemed to Francis that Yankee ghosts, ghosts of minutemen, merchantmen, Puritans, and painted Indians might be hovering, mothlike, about the cupola windows.

The telescope mounted on a cast-iron stand could be raised through the ceiling so that its omnivorous eye could take in most of the heavens.

"Can I take a look?" Francis asked.

"Just a minute." John squinted through the instrument and adjusted a knob on the tube. "Now."

John had trained the instrument on the Big Dipper. It was like looking into the black-velvet showcase of an exclusive jeweler — it was cold in its hugely winking beauty.

"Swing it around," John said.

Francis moved the instrument, following slowly the stunning diamond strew of the Milky Way.

He turned away from the eyepieces with a sigh, plumped down on the cot, glancing at his watch. John devoured the stars avidly.

"What do they say, John?"

"They say you better go home or your mother will climb my frame."

John had an astrologer's chart which he couldn't quite take seriously. He would look at the chart, improvise his own whimsical commentaries.

"They say we take things too hard down here — they say if we could see life with their perspective we'd spend less time worrying and more time being happy."

Francis smiled. "Do they say I'll stay in the seminary?"

"They say maybe you will and maybe you won't." John swung the telescope around slowly. "But whatever you do, they say, it'll be for the best. So take it easy, they say — and get the hell home also."

Outside, on the brick sidewalk, they shook hands.

"So long, Frannie, be a good kid and don't work too hard. I'll drop you a line."

"Good-by, John, keep on looking at the stars."

"Keep looking at the stars," Francis repeated mentally, lifting the mop pail and carrying it out into the corridor. John would always do that.

Outside the seminary, the shouting had subsided and the clomp of cleated shoes on the boardwalk gave wearied witness that the game was over.

Francis opened the door of a mop closet, poured the muddy water into the sink, wrung out the mop, and rinsed the bucket.

Then he hurried into his room, whipped a towel off the rack above his cot, snatched up his bathrobe, and trotted toward the shower room at the end of the corridor. He knew that the "poets" would soon invade the shower room with lusty song and raucous post mortems of the game. He would listen to them from one of the ten precious shower stalls where possession was nine tenths of the law. Emmet and Tubby would be there — the stars of the game — his own roommates.

He swung into the shower room whistling and slipped into a stall. As he loosened his shoe strings, he listened for the rumble of the gang ascending the winding wooden back stairs.

Another Saturday half over — how the weeks were going by!

The two hectic months had left little or no time for Francis to question seriously whether or not he belonged. He was there, thrilled with the new things and new faces — praying, studying, and, at the appointed time, playing. Only late at night when he stirred with an involuntary chill of uncertainty, did he know the old insecurity. He had mentioned this uneasiness to his spiritual adviser, Father Carney, who had told him the feeling was not uncommon among first-year students and that he should pray hard for guidance and strength whenever he felt an "attack" coming on.

That he had done, would continue to do. . . .

He had showered and was slipping into his robe when he heard the hollow crescendo of the poets and the rhetoricians. Now the shouts and the pounding of running feet as the perspiring seminarians dashed into their rooms and out again with towels, robes, and wooden clogs. He saw Tubby lurch into the stall directly across from him. The remaining stalls were quickly filled with singing and chattering.

"Tubby, where's Emmet?" Francis called.

"Hey — hi, kid!" Tubby said, his beefy, bland face straining over the gate of the stall. "He should be right in — save your shower for him. Juh see the game?"

"Most of it. We won, eh?"

"I'll say!"

Emmet entered, running, followed closely by several others.

"Hey, Emmet, here!" Francis called.

Emmet crowded into the stall as Francis slipped out.

"Thanks, Fran," Emmet's thin, dark face creased with a smile. "We won."

"Yeh, I know it, Emmet — congratulations. You guys better hurry or you'll be late for chapel."

One of the three boys waiting glumly outside the showers nodded at Francis as he left. "Our buddy."

"Hey, Fran!" Tubby called from the showers. "Will you empty the wastebasket in the Fathers' Room for me? Everything else is tidy — I didn't have time to get the basket before the game."

"Okay." He was glad of the opportunity to get into the Fathers' Room where he could take a peek at Mike's column in the morning edition of the *Yankee.*

Later, after he set the empty basket down in its place by the magazine rack, he glanced at kindly old Father Keenan who was absorbed in the *Literary Digest;* then he lifted the *Yankee* from its perch.

The French were saying *Non* all over the front page — they were excusing themselves very profusely from their war debt. In his column Mike had written: "We ought to slap an injunction on their ocean liners. There's a sucker born every twenty years and his name is invariably Uncle Sam."

On his way to the sports section, Francis found himself idling over the society page. Althea Parkley smiled casually out of a two-column width cut. Her engagement to Herbert Royce of Harvard and Wisconsin was announced.

"There goes Martin's girl friend," Francis thought. "He won't be too happy about this."

For a moment, his heart went out to his big brother. But it was better this way. . . .

His eyes roamed down the page. Another picture. "Rosemary!" he exclaimed.

"What, what's that, son?" old Father Keenan said.

"Oh, excuse me, Father. I was emptying the wastebasket and thought I'd take a look at the paper. My sister's picture is in here — she's engaged to marry Mike Farrell, the newspaperman."

The old priest made a sympathetic throat noise and nodded.

"Well, I'll be . . ." Francis whispered, grinning. "Sis engaged to Mike!"

The sudden revelation of the engagement filled him with wonder. The Ronaynes were really in the society ink today. Rosemary rated only a column-wide picture, but she was even more attractive in her shadowy Irish way than the more stylishly groomed Althea.

Martin was on that page, too, Francis knew — his life was anyway. And maybe all of Boston was there, the old and the new.

The chapel bell drilled through the worn, creaky wood of St. Philip's Hall. Francis set the paper back on the rack and hurried off to prayer.

Chapter 14

WHILE it is undeniably true that the years go fast at Oxford, Groton, St. Mark's, and on Beacon Hill, it must be admitted, too, that the years go fast in Charlestown and even down by the Sugar House where the Mystic River stinks casually along to the sea.

And not only did the years between 1925 and 1928 go fast for the Cabots, Lodges, the Ronaynes, Hanlons, Al Smith, and F. Scott Fitzgerald, but they rocketed along for Nicola Sacco and Bartolomeo Vanzetti as well. The latter two had been nontaxpaying hosts of the state in the Charlestown pen since 1924. The latest fuse which touched off radical riots the world over was Governor Fuller's announcement on August 3, 1927, that he would not intervene further in the death sentence of either Nicola or Bartolomeo.

If, at about this same time, Calvin Coolidge had announced: "I do not choose to run. . . ." it was also oppositely true that young, upcoming Martin Ronayne, having served his apprenticeship well as an assistant district attorney, would be definitely in the autumnal running as the Hanlon-sponsored candidate for the Boston School Committee from Charlestown.

On the eve of the execution day, August 22, 1927, Catherine Ronayne sat in the unearthly quiet of the *Bulletin* office and edited news copy for the next issue. She sat at her desk in the lonely, gray light of her green-shaded, flexible desk lamp. Behind her in the darkness loomed the octopus-like bulk of the linotype, giving to the office, because of its muteness, an otherworld quality. For the slide and clatter of the linotype and the metronomic pounding of the cylinder press in the next room were, for Catherine, integral to the personality of the room.

She heard the whine of a police siren, arose, walked over to the window in time to see a patrol wagon pull out of the police station garage and swing up Rutherford Avenue toward the state prison.

"The Commies must be raising cain," she whispered. "Well," she continued with a sigh, "the poor souls will die at midnight — perhaps that will put an end to the demonstrations."

She wondered, as she had already wondered times in the past, whether or not they were guilty. They had been positively identified by eyewitnesses at the scene of the robbery and killing. The case had been renewed and reheard *ad infinitum* and still an array of circumstantial evidence pointed to their guilt. God help them, innocent or guilty. . . .

The office telephone rang. It was Rosemary — married now almost a year and the mother of a baby boy named Michael Martin. She was calling from her five-room flat in Dorchester heights.

"Mother, are you still working? It's almost eleven o'clock! For heaven's sake, Mother, please go home and get some rest — right away. . . ."

"All right, dear, I'm just about finished. How are you? How's my grandson?"

"He's fine, but I'm worried stiff. Mike's covering the execution tonight — he's going to sit right there in the death chamber when they throw the switch. Supposing the Communists throw a bomb or something. At times like this I wish Mike were a vacuum-cleaner salesman."

Catherine chuckled. "Mike could never be anything but just what he is, dear. Don't worry about the prison — the walls both inside and out are alive with big, red-faced Irish cops."

"Maybe you're right, but I'm saying my beads anyway. And please go home, Mother, this is no night to be out alone in Charlestown. I'm going to call you back in fifteen minutes and if you're not gone, I'll take little Mike in a cab and come over there after you!"

"All right, honey, I'll get along in a few minutes."

"Glory be, Mother, that paper is wearing you out. I should think after 10 years of it you'd be ready to get out. What about John Little? Alice tells me they're thinking of getting married. Why not turn it all over to him? You said yourself the last time I was home that he does everything but the editorials right now. Where is he tonight?"

"He asked if he could take Alice over by the prison to see the sights — said he'd get in early in the morning and straighten out this copy. The house was so lonely — I just thought I'd run down and do a little work for a change. With you and Francis away and Martin out pushing doorbells with Jim Hanlon or gadding about with his Harvard friend, the house is too empty. It's a year now since the Staseks moved down the hill, and I've never been able to feel chummy with that new Greek family upstairs."

"But, Mother, how many times do I have to tell you that Mike and I want you to come and stay with us? We'd love to have you and it wouldn't all be unselfish either — we spend an awful lot of money on baby sitters."

"No, dear, you know how I feel about that. I love you both for wanting me but I'll live and die in Martin Ronayne's house, please God."

"All right, Mother," Rosemary said, a little petulantly. "What do you hear from Francis? We had a postcard from that seminary camp up in the Berkshires. That was about a month ago. He said he was having a fine time."

"He is. I had a letter from him yesterday. He'll be back at the sem in a week and we'll all go and see him. Just think, Rosemary, in just a few years we'll have a priest in the family."

"It'll be swell, Mother. But, look, you sound exhausted. I'm going to cut this short and you go home, eh?"

"All right, dear. You'll all be over for dinner Sunday. Give the baby a kiss from his old grandmother. Good-by."

Catherine hung up, placed a packet of lead slugs on top of the copy and listened several moments to the whine of the returning patrol wagon before reaching for her hat.

While Catherine was locking the door of the *Bulletin* office her older son Martin stood on the rapid transit platform at Sullivan Square waiting for the train which would take him downtown, where he was to meet Erford.

Jim Hanlon had just dropped off at the entrance to the station ramp down in the square. Tonight they had finished their doorbell-pushing campaign — three weeks of ringing bells, lifting knockers, or rapping on tenement doors.

The outstanding Republican candidate for School Committee, a glib, bright young Italian lawyer out of Boston University named Mario Bartelli had spent a lot of money on fancy signs and blotters carrying his picture, the facts of his education, and the slogan: SWEEP CLEAN — No MACHINE!

Whatever that meant, it has disturbed Martin and he had asked J. P.'s advice on getting out some posters and cards.

"It's a waste of money at this time," J. P. said. "You'll come around with me and meet the people of the organization. They'll need no posters to remember you."

Then Martin had asked about Rosy Ryan, present school committeeman from Charlestown who had been, as near as Martin could tell, the machine's successful candidate for the past several terms.

"Rosy has had his time," J. P. said.

"But he's still going to run against me. He announced his candidacy in the *Bulletin* and the big dailies this week."

"It's a free country," J. P. said. "He can run if he likes. Now come over to the office at a quarter of seven tomorrow night and we'll pay a call on the right people."

So in the past three weeks, Martin had met the right people — many of them precinct leaders and influential voters. He chatted with people he had known all his life, never having realized their political significance until now — their quiet, deadly power to get the vote out.

The word had already got around that Rosy Ryan had not played ball with the machine in the matter of teacher appointments from the Charlestown precincts. Martin, having Hanlon's imprimatur, was cordially welcomed. Many of the machiners knew his mother and had known his father. This made him all the more acceptable to them.

Martin suspected that Rosy Ryan must have crossed the machine up in some way, but hesitated to ask J. P. about him. Double-crossing the machine would be the last thing he'd want to do; yet he believed that teacher appointments should be based on merit alone, as did the Parkleys; he sensed he might have trouble with Hanlon on that score.

The long black elevated train bent itself raucously around the arc of the station platform. Martin sat down across from a strikingly pretty brunette and involuntarily found himself looking into her clear blue eyes. She blushed with obvious pleasure and averted her head. Martin lifted his eyes coolly to the cigarette ad above her.

He had much more of an eye for a pretty girl these days, he reflected; that is to say, a strange pretty girl. Althea, married now and living in Milwaukee, was a dull twinge by day and something he woke up to with dry longing late at night.

But there had been no way he could have persuaded her to go against her family. He had seen her only once since the dance two years ago. It had been two weeks before her wedding and Erford and he were browsing in the Old Corner Bookstore. She entered, loaded with small parcels, a little breathless, a little wan in a lovely way, her light brown hair all massed up directly on top of her head. There was something about her that reminded him of a girl in F. Scott Fitzgerald's *This Side of Paradise*. Something that would never die, something that would, something tragic, something exquisitely gay.

He had been wondering what to send her for a wedding present and now he knew. He got hold of a new copy of F. Scott's book and asked his mother to have it rebound for him, in one of those sumptuous pigskin bindings. It said something special to her from him — he mentioned it in his inscription — something that was lost like all the goddess girls and the champagne of F. Scott's Amory Blaine — something that was lost but always around, always about to be found.

"Sis!" Erford had exclaimed when she entered the bookstore. Martin had smiled and said nothing.

They helped rest her bundles. Martin took some of them, looking at her all the while and she looking at him. "Hello," she said.

She said it in a way that he would never forget — with throaty surprise and love and excitement. That hello, he knew then and now, would have to do him a very long time because there couldn't be anyone else until he was fat and famous — until love might not enter into marriage at all.

They chatted about the nice, conventional things like Herbert Royce, her coming honeymoon in Paris, human interest at the D.A.'s office, and the swiftness with which winter follows summer in Milwaukee.

Martin offered to buy her a farewell drink in a neighboring speak-easy. That evoked the goddess smile of relief and gratitude and maybe she would have said "I'd love to" if Erford had not mentioned a tea and a time later that afternoon.

A tea and a time was the final wedge. She gave him her hand. He kissed it in a conventional way that only he and she knew was more than that. She gathered together her bundles and was gone.

So he sent her the book and with it his heart, and Herbert Royce could read what F. Scott wrote and what Martin Ronayne wrote on the flyleaf and go jump in Lake Michigan, for all he cared. . . .

For all he cared . . . his thoughts said crisply as the train clattered over the Charlestown Bridge into Boston . . . for all he cared was in Milwaukee with the big German cops and the winter that followed hard upon the summer.

There are no elevated or subway trains in Milwaukee. And if there were, the chances are extremely good that Althea Parkley Royce would not have been on one when it was 9 p.m. in Milwaukee and 10 in Boston. Yet, as she idled over her shrimp cocktail in the dining room of the Hotel Pfister, perhaps some psychic echo of *Park Street Under* reverberated in her mind. Or was it the remark of her husband concerning Sacco and Vanzetti that brought Martin to her consciousness with swift poignancy.

"The two Italians die in Charlestown tonight," was all Herbert had said, as the waiter set down the ice-cradled goblets of shrimp.

Herbert Royce, she had learned conclusively in the past thirteen months, never wasted a single word. With religious fidelity and with the ruthless logic of his high intelligence, he allotted you precisely the amount of wordage he felt you could take. Althea rather wished he wouldn't compliment his own wife so laconically, however.

"The two Italians die in Charlestown tonight" meant: you know the story a lot better than I do, being from Boston. You know where Charlestown is. "That Irish friend of Erford's comes from there, does he not?" Herbert added.

"Yes, he does," Althea answered. The string quartet at the end of the dining room struck up a Strauss waltz. Yes, I know all about Sacco and Vanzetti, she thought. Hadn't Father and Erford discussed the case at dinner a hundred times? But I don't know all about Martin Ronayne. I was much more interested in what Dad and Erford said about Martin at dinner. They wanted to talk about those two condemned Italians. I wanted to talk about Martin.

She had been married a little over a year and one really shouldn't think about being unhappily married after only a year. They had that beautiful Lannon-stone home out in Fox Point. It was on a bluff overlooking the lake and at night, after dinner, when Herbert was snoozing in the study, she'd go out there and look at the stars or the blackness — which was just as beautiful on Lake Michigan. The lights of Milwaukee shuttled with a pure diamond quality off to the right and sometimes she had the feeling it was Boston and she was home and she'd never go away. Herbert is a good guy, that's all, Herbert is a good guy. She'd say that over and over again, out there over the lake, under the stars.

Or maybe she'd say Herbert is a way of life. He belongs with me, I with him, we all belong with each other only — Father says so, Erford says so, they all say so from Fox Point to Marblehead. I say so, too. Listen, stars; listen, lake: I say so, too. That's why I'm here.

Old Milwaukee families — there was a difference between them and old Boston families — a difference of two hundred years. You didn't have to be wealthy to come from an old Milwaukee family. You didn't have to make beer or cranes or pork chops to be in an old Milwaukee family — your people just had to be around for fifty years or so. It wouldn't get you into Fox Point or the country club, however, unless you produced beer or cranes or pork chops or lived exceedingly well off the people that did.

In Boston, Althea knew, there was acknowledgment for only one kind of "old Boston family." In Milwaukee — and she found

the idea refreshing — there were old families and old families.
The waiter took the goblets away.

"How were things at the office today?" Althea asked, looking at
her rings and making a mental note to have them cleaned.

That was a question Herbert could answer in some detail. Althea
couldn't be expected to have any foreknowledge of what went on
at Royce, Royce, and Wisniewski.

The last was a Milwaukee name which one might have difficulty
spelling also. Herbert at first had urged Tom Wisniewski to change
his name, but Herbert Royce, Sr., cautioned Tom against it.
Tom's brothers were mixed up in the foundry workers' union — in
fact that was the main reason the Royces had taken him in. The
foundries were the major Royce accounts. A change of name would
mean the loss of certain advantages in having Tom around. And
besides, Tom didn't think his mother or his brothers would like it.

"The foundry contracts have been ironed out," Herbert said to
Althea with the blank, bored face, behind which went on an
appalling amount of mental activity.

"No labor trouble?" Althea asked.

"Tom doesn't seem to think so." Herbert droned on in a sleepy,
yet sympathetic voice, concerning contracts, foundries, and the
vigor and independence among labor unions. Althea listened a
while until she saw a tall, tanned young man leave the dining hall.

Martin again, she thought, sinking her knife into the filet mignon.
How utterly silly and impossible of me to be thinking of him
this way! It's gone — it really never was, it never can be.

"They're actually talking seriously about a forty-hour week,
Tom says. . . ."

Wouldn't it be nice if Martin got to be mayor or governor some
day. The way Dad and Erford used to talk, you'd think such
things were entirely possible for him. When Herbert and I go on
again I must . . . I must what?

"We may have trouble with labor if the Democrats win in
'28, Tom says. . . ."

There are no breweries on the slopes of Mt. Greylock. But
there is Camp St. Iraneus for the sons of the Irish and Italians
wealthy enough to own things like breweries, foundries, slaughter-

houses, and all their great-American-way equivalents. But also there were the sons of the fairly well-to-do who, because of influential politicians or influential priests could lug their summer duffle into St. Iraneus and rub elbows with their financial betters. And despite much tolerance and kindliness and roughhouse democracy of the baseball diamond or swimming hole it was certainly understood that some would one day go to Georgetown, the Harvard of the Jesuits, and some to Boston's Ignatian College, the poor man's Oxford. The former would have the leisure and the money to sip urbanely at Manhattans and seriously doubt whether the nun-harried girls at Trinity were as much fun as the emancipated girls at Vassar. The I.C. boys would devour their bologna sandwiches and the vile, steaming coffee served in the subterranean college cafeteria and seriously doubt whether the *ratio studiorum* would have helped them land a job if their girl friend's father had not spoken to someone who had spoken to someone else.

But it was almost 1 a.m. in the mess hall of Camp St. Iraneus and the blackness of the crisp mountain night was pestered by a single lantern that flicked on one long X-legged dining table. Around the table's end sat two young seminarians, yawning, smoking, talking easily, and sipping thick, white mugs of black, aromatic coffee. It was their turn to stand the night watch and between hourly inspections of the bungalows and the grounds they passed the time in deliciously dissecting one another.

"If you feel this way by mid-term," Emmet said to Francis, "my advice is to face up to your mother and leave the sem."

Now that the academic year was over and he was away from the strict routine of seminary life, the old, undulating indecision had again taken possession of Francis' spirit. Only for brief involuntary periods had this insecurity bothered him during the school year, for he had plunged himself unsparingly into spiritual devotions, studies, and other seminary activities.

Camp, rest, the world, a time to think again, away from routine, had convinced him the doubt was deeply seated. Tonight he had unbent completely to Emmet and told him the whole story — his mother's great desire, his own serious spiritual leanings, his honest lack of interest in a secular career. Over the coffee and the cigarettes, under the unseen but powerful spell of hoary old Greylock, he had told the whole story to Emmet.

"Maybe you'll do as I've done. If you've got a vocation it will come back to you and you'll come back — to the sem," Emmet said. "But, your big weakness lies in not facing up to your mother."

"It's just that the thing means so much to her — at least I think it does — I haven't wanted to hurt her, I suppose."

He poured Emmet and himself more coffee out of a steaming, white enamel pitcher. He made a little wincing grimace, stirred his coffee and went on: "You see, as I think I've told you before, my brother Martin is doing well in the D.A.'s office. Jim Hanlon is putting him up for the School Committee this fall and he's almost sure to get it. Mother looks at Martin, then looks at me. She wants me to make good, too, as a priest. It really would hurt her, but as you say, if I still feel this way come mid-term, I'm going to tell her and leave."

Emmet pushed his coffee aside and looked at his wrist watch, "Well — you'll talk it over with your spiritual adviser, anyway?"

Francis nodded.

"He'll probably tell you somewhat the same thing I've told you. Don't ask me how I know!" Emmet raised his eyes with amusement. "It's time to go look at the sleeping beauties again, Pal."

They picked up their flashlights and screwed down the wick of the lantern. They scuffed softly out of the building onto the sandy basketball pavilion which was a quadrangle enclosed by three long bungalows and the mess hall. With a sense of profound relief, Francis, holding his lit flashlight toward the ground, followed Emmet toward the entrance of the first bungalow.

They entered the first bungalow and moved noiselessly along the corridor at right angles to about twenty small rooms.

"All right, Mulhern, all right — give me the ball!" one of the campers was saying gruffly, deep in the exhausting athletics of a dream. They passed through the next bungalow and the next. All was well. They skirted the grounds, flashing their lights along the rutted, sandy roads, and into the shower room.

"All is well," Emmet said, as they headed back to their coffee and cigarettes.

Chapter 15

SEVERAL weeks later, at 2:15 on an astringent September afternoon, Martin puffed a cigarette near the Monument fence, just across the street from Charlestown High.

He heard the bell of dismissal jangle through the corridors and waited several minutes while the students tumbled gleefully out of the great, gray building. Then he crossed the street toward the main entrance.

That night he would give his first campaign talk in City Square and, while he had some ideas on the problems of schools and teachers already, he felt the need of talking things over with a veteran teacher. Rosemary had suggested he look up Ambrose Callahan, the evening school mentor of creative writing who was very much the plodding high school pedagogue by day.

"He has that quietly desperate look that teachers get after twenty years of ricocheting between the students and the taxpayers," Rosemary had said. "He's easy to talk to, is frank and has ideas."

Martin entered the building, sought out the school office, and inquired about Callahan.

"Mr. Callahan's home room is 207," the girl behind the office counter informed him in a flat, bored tone of voice.

"Will he still be there?" Martin asked.

"Teachers must remain in the building until three o'clock," she recited.

Martin climbed the stairs briskly. "Some flapper!"

Room 201 — 203 — 205. The door of Callahan's room was open. Inside, Martin could see three students, two boys and a girl, seated at their desks, fingering their textbooks with one hand and copying into a notebook with the other.

At his desk sat Ambrose Callahan, a sere little man with thinning, rust-colored hair. His thick-browed eyes were narrowed in semisleep and his head nodded with alternately dignified and comical jerks.

The students, noticing his ludicrous efforts to keep awake, abandoned their assignments and grinned knowingly at each other.

Martin watched a while, amused. Then he decided to walk right in and wake Callahan up. Martin wasn't sure whether such an act would save or outrage the teacher's dignity, but he had to talk to him and there wasn't too much time.

"Mr. Callahan," he said.

Callahan's head jerked up and he opened his eyes slowly, their whites still dazedly showing. He shook his head vigorously and looked at Martin, whom he mistook for a high school senior.

"*American Literary Folkways.* Outline Chapters Four and Five."

"I'm not a student, Mr. Callahan" Martin smiled. "My name is Martin Ronayne. My sister, Rosemary, used to be in your writing class at night school."

Callahan was awake. "Oh yes, yes — beg your pardon." He arose and reached out a small, damp, freckled hand which Martin shook firmly.

"It's this night school business — taught last night — all tired out. I remember your sister well — she's married now, isn't she — married that newspaper fellow — Farren, or something like that."

"Mike Farrell," Martin said.

"Yes, Mike Farrell — very good man — depth as well as cleverness. I was glad to hear she married him. That mean's she's come closer to professional writing than any of my evening school girls."

Martin smiled. He wondered now if Callahan was as naïve concerning books and authors as Rosemary had made him out to be. It began to appear that Callahan did not teach creative writing out of a pure and burning love for American letters. His sleepiness and his remark concerning it interested Martin deeply. He had heard that Callahan had a wife and five children.

Martin told him he was running for the school committee and would be interested in knowing why he taught evening school after a full, daily schedule at the high school.

"Young man," Callahan said, rubbing his eyes, "do you know how much it takes to support a wife and five children?"

"I don't believe I do."

"Just a minute." Callahan glanced at the three students who were doing more listening than outlining. "You kids can run along now — finish the outlines at home. Turn them in at class tomorrow. Vamoose!" he said with gruff affection.

The students gathered up their books and left.

"They know more about us than we do about them," Callahan said wryly when the students were gone. "They call me 'Sleepy Callahan' and they know all about me. They know I've got a wife and five kids, that I have to work nights to support them, and that I have a nostalgic fondness for literary autograph parties. So I'm sleepy, and now that you know, please don't have me fired Mr. Ronayne! That is, if you're elected," he added with a grin.

"You wouldn't have anything to fear from me," Martin said.

"You know," Callahan began, rubbing his hand over the stubble of his chin, "I always vote for the most promising young fellow who's running against Rosy Ryan. I went to school right here in this building with Rosy. He's no more interested in progressive school administration than I am in biochemistry — although I teach it at the night school — along with creative writing. They wanted someone to teach biochemistry. They couldn't get a biochemist for the money they pay. So they offer the course to an English teacher — me. I'm five pages ahead of the class."

"I'd appreciate your vote, Mr. Callahan, but I'm primarily here to get a viewpoint on your problems as a teacher. I'm already convinced that teachers should be getting more money — but on what basis should they get it? You'd probably agree that married men with children should get more money than spinsters and bachelors. But how can it be done justly? I mean, you can't give a mediocre, married teacher more than a distinguished, unmarried one. We'd lose many of our best ones that way."

"Yes, I've thought about that," Callahan said. "Maybe it's one of those unfair things that's just — necessary, that's all."

Martin sat on the edge of a desk wondering what the answer could be. "The only solution might be general raises for everyone, I guess — the amount being based on a teacher's ability and length of faithful service."

"Yes," Callahan agreed, "but there's another teacher problem to be solved which even to me is quite as pressing as the money problem. How can we get the teacher out of the social ghetto?"

"What do you mean by that?"

"I mean that the teacher is, whether he likes it or not, a special kind of social animal whose actions are always under public surveillance and who is subject to much heavier sanctions, socially, at least, any time he happens to show his humanity by erring in one way or another."

"What do you think is the solution?" Martin asked.

"I don't know that there'll ever be a complete solution for teachers dependent for their livelihood on public money." Callahan opened the drawer of his desk and put away a pencil and some notes. "Yet, I still wish a moral, competent teacher could be given the chance to live his own private life."

The three o'clock bell jangled.

"That's my whistle," Callahan said. "Home to mama and the kids."

Martin walked down the stairs with him and, later, as he descended the hill toward home he thought of Callahan with both amusement and concern.

Moon over City Square; stars over City Square. Moon and stars with cold, diamond disdain looming over the people and the politicians in City Square. And high over the square the Monument, hovering in solitary eminence, patient, oddly wise.

Mike Farrell, Jim Hanlon, and Catherine stood on the fringe of a gathering of about a hundred people, their attention fixed on the flag-bedecked wagon flat, where sat in various degrees of smugness and writhing the four candidates for the School Committee from Charlestown.

Thomas F. Reardon, a trim old man with carefully combed silver hair, was standing in the middle of the platform, about to introduce the candidates. The assembly was not to be confused with a rally for any or all of the candidates. Mr. Reardon was Grand Knight in the local Council of the Knights of Columbus and it was that fraternal organization which was presenting the School Committee candidates to the Charlestown public as a civic service. The candidates had been asked to give their qualifications and present their ideas.

"Before I introduce the candidates," Mr. Reardon began in a soft, kindly voice, "we are to be favored with a musical rendition by the Quigley twins." He nodded benignly to the steps at his right where Sheila and Teddy Quigley, age 11, were rippling in silks and nervousness.

Beside them their mother, Maggie Quigley, was bristling in a new flowered and fruited straw hat. With an admonitory hiss, she flushed the twins onto the stage and turned to the audience with a metallic smile.

"I might have known she'd have her hooks in this," Hanlon said softly.

"Somebody's got to entertain us," Mike said. "What would a political rally be without music? I'd just as soon listen to the kids play and dance as hear some of those windbags up there."

"Now, Mike, give them a chance," Catherine said.

"Sure — sure," Mike said.

While Terry burbled *The Irish Washerwoman* on his harmonica and Sheila did a jaunty Irish jig which her brother couldn't quite keep up with, Mike took a look at the candidates.

At the extreme left sat Miss Adelaide Agnew, "the last of the Charlestown Yankees," as she always described herself. She lived with several Pekingese cats in a huge, wan, old mansion on Frothingham Avenue and invariably ran for the School Committee on what she called the "return to tradition" ticket.

No one in Charlestown was ever quite sure whether she was a genuine Yankee or not. It was legend, however, that she hailed originally from Prince Edward Island, that she had worked her way up from scullery maid to governess in the old mansion in which she still lived. The rest of the legend was that the last survivor of the Cardwell Family had left her the ramshackle mansion with more relief than philanthropy.

But there she sat, long and arid, in a black, beaded gown which covered her from ankles to neck. Her stout, gold-handled umbrella leaned imperiously at her side; her slack, powdered features were rescued from vacuity by the relentless, fluxing energy of her eyes. She wore no hat and there was, Mike noticed, a courage about her that contested firmly with her ludicrousness.

Next to her, and to Mr. Reardon's right, sat bland, rotund Rosy Ryan, chewing gum and smiling his gleaming, "one-of-the-boys" smile.

Martin sat to Reardon's left, outwardly cool and contained, looking over the heads of the gathering in a way that made people think he was looking directly at them. The butterflies fluttered mercilessly in his stomach.

The twins were doing an encore now. Terry warbled "Molly Malone" on the mouth organ and Sheila sang in a thin, sweet voice about the tragic, lovely colleen who was so good at pushing all that fish around.

To Martin's left sat lean and dusky Mario Bartelli, wearing the deadly serious look which seemed to say that he had come to save the world from the tyranny of the Irish. He, like Miss Agnew, was running on the Republican ticket and that should be enough to make the old Italian Democratic ward bosses turn over in their graves.

Yet Mario had seen no opportunity for an unsponsored candidate in the local ranks of the Democratic party. After casting a jaundiced eye at Adelaide Agnew, who had been the Republican School Committee nominee for years, he estimated the number of Italian votes he might receive and decided he could give her a good fight in the primary. After that he would be swamped by the machine, anyway, but the experience would be valuable. Even Mussolini was known to have lost elections early in his career.

Mario was an intense admirer of Il Duce, whom he saw as the benevolent leader who had reclaimed the swamps of the Campagna, told the Pope off, and made the trains run on time — all for the poor, the little obscure makers of spaghetti and the buxom signorinas squashing the clusters of purple grapes with their bare feet.

The twins finished their encore, were applauded generously, and skipped happily off the stage toward the beakish kisses of their mother, who knew cunningly that they had gone over well; thus the voters would be talking about those clever Quigley children and when she went around her precinct tomorrow to say a few words for Rosy Ryan, the talent of her children would be a useful talking point.

She was for Rosy — who else? Leave him now because the Hanlon crowd was backing that Ronayne snipe? Never in the world. It was Rosy who had gone to bat for her and cinched her present job as supervisor of the owl-shift scrub women at the high school. Besides, if Rosy was defeated, and she knew with Hanlon against him, he might be, Hanlon would understand. He knew she was under obligations to Rosy — it was not so much that she was against the machine, it was just — well, she had no choice.

She sent her bespangled son and daughter wandering off after an ice-cream cone. She simpered a humble look at the audience and then turned her face up to the platform where Adelaide Agnew, who had just been introduced, was leaning on her umbrella and bringing her audience to bay.

"I've been running-ah, for school committee-ah," she began, in a crackling, high-pitched voice, "for almost, ah-ah, fifteen years."

Between all her ahs she said that the time had come for the land of our forefathers to be returned to our forefathers' sons. She also said that school conditions in Charlestown since the rise of the Irish were a source of moral turpitude to the children.

"And this moral decay, I say . . ." she brought her umbrella down vigorously on the boards and a group of young toughs cheered her lustily. " . . . these manifestations of degeneration are directly due to the short dresses, long immoral legs, and bobbed hair of the Irish hussies who stand painted and primping like Rahab on the platforms of our schools."

She thumped her umbrella again on the platform. The toughs cheered, the citizens laughed, and Adelaide thumped on righteously, invoking the sacred name of Horace Mann who founded the American public school system right here in the sovereign commonwealth of Massachusetts. She invoked, further, Emerson, Thoreau, and Margaret Fuller.

Mike leaned toward Catherine: "I wonder how she ever heard of all those people on Prince Edward Island."

"That woman may be mentally sick," Catherine said. "Why we allow her to make a spectacle of herself is beyond me. She really should be in a good home for the aged. Perhaps the committee can do something for her."

"What!" Mike exclaimed, "and deprive the Charlestown voters of a chance to bring back traditionalism!"

"Enough of your foolishness. Don't you think I'm right, Jim?"

"You are, Catherine," Hanlon answered. "But it might be said, too, that except for election time when she ruffles her feathers a bit, she leads a quiet, orderly life."

Adelaide, with one last shrill and thumping appeal for reform and regeneration, had returned to her seat.

Now that the lady candidate was safely out of the way, Thomas F. Reardon introduced the incumbent, Frederick "Rosy" Ryan, former city councilor and your present school committeeman, "who needs no introduction!"

Rosy needed no introduction. That might be a way to describe him, Mike thought.

As he stepped to the edge of the platform, fat, roseate, confident, it seemed to Mike that he was doing a tableau for all Irish politicians in America. His jaws were set restlessly — incomplete without the chewing gum which he had, with secret, casual maneuvers of the hand, plastered on the underside of his chair.

His voice seemed to have a bruise in it that made it difficult for him to talk fast and loud. He began slowly, effortlessly:

"I won't take up much of your time tonight, ladies and gentlemen, citizen voters of the ward — friends. You know me and I know you." He paused smiling.

"Only too well," J. P. muttered.

"Like any other servant of the people, I stand on my record as your school committeeman and former city councilor. Recall, if you will, how I fought to lower the price of milk and crackers in the primary schools of Charlestown. Low prices for those who could pay — free milk and crackers for those whose fathers were out of work or on the city welfare lists. . . ."

He went on for several minutes, holding out solemnly the stale, high-sounding wares of the career politician.

"I have no personal quarrel with any of the candidates on the platform here this evening. However, I offer you experience and achievement as against the forces of Yankee snobbery and the impractical idealism of crusading young men. Take your choice, good citizens of Charlestown, take your choice. . . ."

In conclusion and in conclusion, Rosy thanked the Knights of Columbus, the voters, their children, the schoolteachers, his fellow school committeemen, the gentlemen of the press, and God. Then he sauntered back to his seat amid the applause, the cat calls, and slipped another stick of gum into his mouth.

Mario Bartelli was introduced next. In shrill, rapid-fire English, which strained to slip into shrill rapid-fire Italian, he told the audience that what they needed to do was clear away the slums and build not only bigger and better houses, but bigger and better schools. "Like the ones Mussolini is building in the Campagna," he said, rolling the word Mussolini around on his tongue.

Then Mario suggested that Charlestown would do well to provide its school children with free, hot lunches. "Crackers and milk are all very fine, but they are a poor substitute for Italian spaghetti or," he added hastily, "Irish stew."

That one drew a good laugh out of his listeners and even Martin, who had been pondering with a slow, gaining simmer Rosy's phrase, "the impractical idealism of crusading young men," could not resist a chuckle.

"As for the way the previous speaker talked regarding his opponents, I have this to say," Mario continued. "It is far better to be a Yankee reactionary or a young idealist than to penalize the people by making one's political career a long round of getting elected and taking care of one's friends — getting elected and taking care of one's friends," he repeated with heavy sarcasm.

The audience applauded strongly. Mike and Catherine cheered. J. P. was sullenly silent. Martin and Adelaide arose and clapped their hands. Rosy grew rosier and accelerated the indefatigable piston of his jaw.

While Mr. Reardon was introducing him, Martin found relief in the realization that he would not have to hit out at the smug, sniping phrase of Rosy. Mario had done that one up in pretty ribbons. He could now concentrate on the remarks he had planned to make on the conditions of teachers.

The kind, mellow words of Mr. Reardon volleyed pleasantly in his ears as Martin looked off a little to the left, over the heads of the audience.

" . . . a young man, a graduate of Ignatian College and Harvard Law School . . . oldest son of an estimable Charlestown family . . . his present position is that of assistant district attorney here in Suffolk County. . . . I knew his father, God rest his noble soul, and consider it a privilege to number his mother among my friends. . . . "

The words were pleasantly embarrassing to Catherine as she looked up at her son with a pang of love and pride. She wished Francis and Rosemary were with her. But Francis was at the seminary, Rosemary home with a teething baby. It would have been good for Francis to see his brother here tonight, she felt — to see what study and determination could accomplish. But he was doing quite well at the seminary, notwithstanding . . . doing quite well.

"I want, at the outset, to thank Mr. Reardon and the Voters' Council for allowing me to present my candidacy for the School Committee to the citizens this early in the campaign," Martin began.

Mike glanced at Hanlon, whose face was relaxed into a blandness that was the beginning of a grin. "He has all of Mayor O'Malley's courtesy," Mike whispered. "All he needs now is that Oxford accent."

J. P. frowned and said nothing. He liked Farrell, now that he had come to know him better as Catherine's son-in-law, but he still thought him considerable of a smart aleck.

"No honest candidate for the School Committee," Martin continued, "could look at the Boston school system and see it other than as one of the finest in the world. I hold that it would be gross presumption on the part of myself or any other candidate to set himself up as an authority on education and take our trained, accomplished school administrators to task.

"However, like any other human institution, a school department's personnel policies may, and should, on occasion, be subject to review and correction, if necessary, by the people, through their elected representatives.

"It is my conviction that many of our teachers are too much

taken for granted, underpaid, and in some ways writhe under the restrictions of second-class citizens. I have good reason to believe that these assertions are valid ones and in the course of my campaign I will endeavor to bring before you the facts and statistics in support of my case.

"As a candidate for your School Committee from Charlestown, I am profoundly concerned about the welfare of teachers because their welfare is the welfare eventually of your children. If our teachers are maladjusted, because of financial and social hardships imposed on them all too unwittingly by the taxpayers, this maladjustment is bound to impress in one way or another the yieldy clay that are the personalities of our school children."

Catherine looked at the audience as she listened. He was holding them. Mike nodded his approval and Hanlon, too, studied with a shrewd, hard mask the effect of Martin's words on his hearers.

Martin spoke on with cool resonance and self-confidence, telling the voters about Ambrose Callahan without mentioning his name — drawing a vivid picture of an overworked, underpaid high school teacher, father of five children, struggling to live a normal life.

When he finished and sat down, the applause was vigorous and long.

Chapter 16

THE month of February, 1929, threw a mantle of clammy grayness over the seminary; and even the snow which lingered patchily about the seminary grounds seemed stale and grayly white.

It was Sunday morning and though grayness fell from the air, there was the restful interruption of academic routine and the unfailing lift of solemn High Mass to lighten the gloom which seemed to cluster about the heart of Francis Ronayne.

As he stood with the others in the seminary choir to sing the *Agnus Dei*, he fought the thoughts which wandered back to the previous evening when he had conferred with his adviser, Father Carney, telling him he had definitely made up his mind to leave the seminary in the spring.

"Agnus dei, qui tollis peccata mundi . . ." he sang with the others, sending their strong, sweet voices up through the grayness of February, gilding the grayness of February with the golden fleece of the Lamb of God who takest away the sins of the world.

"Dona nobis pacem . . ." the seminarians sang, and Francis was grateful to call out his prayer with the others. Grant us peace this afternoon when Mother comes to visit me and I tell her I'm going to leave in May; grant us peace. . . .

Later, on his way out of the refectory after brunch, Emmet flagged him down, saying there was a special delivery letter for him in the mail room.

Francis got the letter, opened it and read while climbing the stairs to his room. It was postmarked Saturday, Brattleboro, Vermont, and he immediately recognized the painstaking hand of John Little.

"Dear 'Father' Francis," the letter read, "Alice and I were married in a little town not far from here this morning. I'm going to keep on working for the *Bulletin* and, until we find a place of our own we'll live with my folks.

"Alice seems very happy and, of course, so am I. We hope you are happy, too. If not, you can always come home to Mr. and Mrs. Little. We'll write again soon. As ever, John."

Francis read the letter again, pausing on the second-story landing. He stood there a while thinking of John and Alice and the happiness they would seek together. But he could never think of Alice without thinking of Marty, too.

Tubby Thomas stomped noisily up the stairs. He saw Francis standing there absorbed, holding the letter loosely in his hand.

"What's the matter, kid — bad news?"

"Oh — hi, Tubby. No, good news. One of my friends just got married."

"Swell!" Tubby wrapped an arm around Francis' shoulders. "Coming upstairs?"

Tubby chattered, as they climbed, about the second philosophers and their basketball team. He was also worried about an exam he had just taken in Church history.

While Tubby chattered, Francis nodded and thought about the newlyweds. They clomped up the hallowed wooden stairs.

John Little was as percipient as ever. He faced the probability of Francis leaving the sem frankly, openly. And that is what Francis had finally done with Father Carney. That is what he would have to do with his mother that very afternoon.

So Alice was finally out of circulation. Francis wondered how the new school committeeman from Charlestown would react to the marriage. He'd probably accept it with the same aplomb with which he had thrown her over.

Martin had ridden the machine into office that November, trouncing Rosy Ryan soundly.

With Mike Farrell's journalistic support, he was already making a name for himself as an irrepressible, if unsuccessful advocate of teacher rights. He was looked upon by the older, conservative school-board members as a bright young man, not yet dry behind the ears. Notwithstanding, he had embarked on a series of lectures to civic and fraternal organizations entitled: "The Teacher as Second-Class Citizen."

All this Francis had read in clippings from the Boston papers, enclosed in the weekly letters from his mother. She intimated quite clearly that her elder son's accomplishments were indeed a challenge to his younger brother. "There is no reason why you, too, cannot go far in the legitimate politics of the Church," she had written recently. "Cardinal O'Garrity, you know, came out of humble circumstances similar to your own. Father Quinn thinks that if you continue to do well in your studies that a year or two of graduate theological studies might be arranged for you at the American College in Rome."

Francis had read that letter once and torn it to pieces. It had only contributed to his decision to leave.

They turned into the corridor leading to their room. Emmet was lying on his bunk daydreaming.

Francis smiled at him and headed for his cot. He lay there listening first to the hissing of the radiator and then to the snoring of Tubby who had also piled into bed. He tried to think what he would say to her, hoping it would not hurt her, knowing it would, knowing it had to be done. This time tomorrow it would be all over, this time tomorrow she would know. This time tomorrow . . . he thought, over and over again, slipping into the welcome oblivion of sleep.

That afternoon at four — his mother, Jim Hanlon, and Rosemary were coming at four forty-five — he tapped on the door of Father Carney's first-floor room. He heard the wry, musical "come in" and entered the book-strewn study where reed-thin, graying Father Carney hunched over the moral theology notes for his class the next morning.

The priest raised his head and squinted at Francis out of a thin, pale face, the spareness of which seemed at variance with his full, mischievous gray eyes. "Draw up a chair, Francis. I'll be with you in a jif."

Francis sat down on a plain wooden chair to the right of the desk. The priest pored over his notes for several moments more and Francis looked about the study. Father Carney would never be rector, he thought, with amusement. Papers were strewn about the wastebasket; on the tops of the dusty bookcases, open books were stacked pell-mell; the volumes on the shelves angled against each other with little tongues of note paper lolling from within their pages. On the knob of his bedroom door several soiled collars rocked easily in the breeze from an open window.

He would never be a bishop or a monsignor, Francis knew, but he was the best professor of "Moral" in the archdiocese, and he was the wisest, holiest priest Francis had ever met.

The seminary was Father Carney's utterly complete world. He rarely left the grounds, except to visit his relatives at Christmas and Easter. The sem was literally his cloister and all he hoped for in return for his huge, unobtrusive labors as a teacher and spiritual adviser was that the seminary should continue to be his monastery, for him as holy and immune from the world as the cells of the Trappists.

Father Quinn had been the priest Francis knew best before he entered the sem. And while he knew the *Beacon's* editor to be a sincere, good priest who did his job faithfully and well, he could not help recognizing that the reverend editor suffered by contrast with Father Carney. But then it took all kinds of priests to make a church. By no stretch of his imagination, however, could Francis visualize Father Carney sitting in his mother's parlor, sipping a Scotch and soda and wittily commenting on the world and its ways. Of course, the Jesuits might suggest that one can be in the world and not of it, but Francis wondered if there was more pragmatic rhyme than reason in that neat little epithet.

Francis winced at his recognition of the involuntary bitterness he was beginning to feel.

The priest sighed and pushed aside his notes. He rubbed his eyes with a slow, massaging movement and asked: "Well, Francis, are you ready to spill the beans?"

"I'm ready, Father, though my knees seem full of termites."

"That's normal enough." The priest leaned forward and lifted a charred briar pipe out of an ash tray. "You've lots of time yet, but have you thought about what you'd like to do when you leave?"

"Mother will probably let me go back to the paper. Yet it's

hard for me to think about picking up the same routine — after my life here, that is. I want to do something when I go back. Something more than just hanging around dreaming. The paper's my best angle, I think. There are so many things that need doing around town — and I'm wondering if I shouldn't take a more active interest."

"What sort of things?"

"Well, there's the looping situation and the political situation — they're both tied in, you know. The pols could do a lot more for the kids by way of providing jobs and recreation.

"I'm right in the middle of it all, too. My two closest friends are strong in each situation. I just might be able to do something, instead of leaving it all to Mother.

"Then there's the paper, too — I could do more there. I could write more — show Mother I'm interested. It would ease her a lot, too."

Father Carney nodded, puffing on his pipe.

"If this place has taught me nothing else, it's taught me the need for positive effort in the way of doing spiritual good. Take Jim Hanlon, my political friend, for example. He's getting old and losing his influence. He needs help now — help for himself, not for the party or anything like that. And my other friend, John Little . . . he's wonderful material for the doing of good. I want to help him if I can."

"I think you can," the priest said. "And as long as you feel disturbed this way your routine can never be quite the same as it was. The old will be a new routine if you want it to be. There is so much you can do out there, Fran. There's so much need for laymen who can be spiritual without being stuffy."

"Do you think I can be in the world and yet not of the world?" Francis asked with a wintry smile.

"I don't know, Fran," the priest said, "only God knows that. Some can and some can't. This much I do know, however — in one sense you're in a much better position as a layman than as a priest. You can reach people priests can never reach and even if you slip, you give less scandal than a man with a collar would."

"This is a tough question, I know — how can I retain some of the life I've known here — how can I keep from slipping back into — well, a kind of safe indifference?"

The priest thought about that one for several moments.

"You might join one of the third orders — the Benedictines, for example. I'm one myself, that's why I mention them. I dip into their rule along with my office daily. It's that little book over there — take a look at it."

Francis picked up the small, black book and paged through it. Matins, Prime, Compline, the day hours were there in condensed, readable form.

"Looks interesting. How does one go about joining?"

"Well, you should go to a Benedictine monastery and be invested. You'd have to go up to Rhode Island for that, though. The Cardinal has admitted no Benedictine house into the archdiocese."

"Perhaps after I leave, I could take a trip up there. Is that the English Benedictine house in Portsmouth?"

"That's the one." The priest puffed on a while in silence. "Tell you what I'll do — if you like. There'll be a Benedictine friend of mine through here in about a month or so. Read up on the rule and if you're still interested, we'll arrange for the investiture right here in our own chapel. It's a simple ceremony and the Cardinal need never know," he concluded with a wink.

Francis laughed at the thought of the Cardinal being incensed over his becoming a Benedictine oblate. "They don't have a lay Jesuit order, do they?" Francis asked, still chuckling.

"They don't need one," Father Carney said. "Anyone who has ever gone to a Jesuit school and retained his faith is a lay Jesuit forever. By the way, did you want me to speak to your mother after you've told her?"

"Would you?"

"I would."

At a little after four, the long, black Lincoln sedan eased out of the slushy cinders of the seminary driveway and turned down the macadam in the direction of Cambridge.

"We're going to dinner at that nice place along the Charles."

Catherine smiled happily at the wan young man in the dark suit and black tie who sat beside her on the rear seat.

Two pedestrians glanced admiringly at the car. Catherine touched her neckline gracefully.

"We'll take you for a bit of a drive, first, lad," Hanlon said, looking at Francis with affection through the rear-vision mirror. "It is good to see you again."

"Good to see you, too, Mister Hanlon."

"The name is Jim. You're a young man, now."

"All right, Jim, it's good to see you."

Rosemary, sitting beside Hanlon, gave a short mirthful laugh. "Has he always called you Mister Hanlon?"

"He has," J. P. said sonsorously. "He was never as sassy as you and that big-shot brother of yours."

Francis caught J. P.'s eye in the mirror and grinned.

Rosemary gave the proper laugh and changed the subject. "I wish you could see your nephew," she said. "He's as fat as butter."

"Wonderful. Who does he look like?"

"Some say Dad; others Mike."

"It all depends on which side of the family you come from," Catherine said.

Francis asked about Martin and Mike, receiving heartening reports from Rosemary and his mother. When Catherine had finished her glowing report on Martin's progress as a neophyte public official, Francis detected a slight raising of J. P.'s eyebrows in the rear-vision mirror. He determined to ask the big man about Marty later, if he could get in a word privately.

"Say!" Rosemary exclaimed. "We almost forgot to mention it. Did you know John and Alice got married?"

"Yes, John sent me a special. I think it's fine."

"It could be the making of that boy," Catherine said. "She's a lovely child."

A lovely child. Not lovely enough for Marty, though, Francis knew. Yet there was still the gleam of gladness in his heart for John. He would be good to Alice with every ounce of his being — he would try and make it up to her.

A comfortable silence in the car as Hanlon wheeled onto the Charles River Parkway. And though J. P. had turned on the heater, the sight of the river, the large, gray-blue splinters of ice and the snow-dappled banks communicated a chill to Francis. He found himself gazing moodily at the misty wastes, identifying them with the weather of his spirit.

Catherine sensed the heaviness of her son's mood and touched him on the elbow, smiling. "I want you to know how happy you're making us. Father Quinn was talking to the rector the other day. He's pleased with your progress."

Francis smiled thinly, knowing an inner panic. If only he could tell her now, get it over with. He prayed for patience. He would tell her after dinner when they were back at the sem.

He looked at her as she chatted congenially with Rosemary. She was grayer and the comely immobility of her features hinted at a slackening. But she was still a strikingly good-looking woman. His love for her buffeted up through his inner gloom.

She was talking about Martin's recent lecture to the League of Catholic Women. "He charmed them. Really, they loved it. He presented an awfully strong case for the teachers. The Cardinal was there. I watched him while Martin spoke. He didn't seem to fidget as much as he usually does when someone else has the floor. Later, Father Quinn took us up to meet His Eminence. He remembered your father and was very gracious to me. He congratulated Martin and suggested playfully that Boston had perhaps confused its public school teachers with the nuns. Nun teachers receive no pay, you know. He was charming."

The Cardinal was charming, Francis repeated mentally. Martin was charming, Mother was charming, Father Quinn was charming.

Catherine settled back against the upholstery. "If only your father could have heard him," she sighed.

They were occupying a large booth in the knotty-pine dining room of "that nice place along the Charles." Catherine and Rosemary were in the ladies' lounge.

"Marty seems to be doing fine," Francis said to J. P.

"He's going over big with the ladies, anyway," said J. P.

"How's he doing with you and the boys?"

"Well, I don't know for sure yet, Franny. Perhaps it's too early to tell. We've some friends on the school board other than Martin, you see. He's been throwing this teacher business at them and at all the old Yankees on the board as if he had been sent by the Lord."

"I like him for that, don't you? His arguments, as reported in the paper I've seen, sound pretty good."

"Marty is nobody's fool," Hanlon admitted with a nod. He slipped a cigar out of his vest, unwrapped it, and rolled it deftly around on his tongue. "But the boys at the Hall are seeing him with the Parkleys too much. They're beginning to cock an eye at him."

"Have you spoken to Marty about it?"

"I have in whatever way I could. It is not for me to choose the boy's friends. It is his business alone — for the time being, at least."

"How's he going over with the school bunch in Charlestown?"

"They like him except for the few he has been hard on."

"Who, for example?"

"Well — Rosy Ryan's little pets. There was a little girl who worked in the school office — she was a huffy little thing. The word is around that she once showed her true colors in front of Marty. He mentioned her to the principal who reprimanded her. She quit the job in a huff. It's a small loss, but sometimes those things are not good politics."

Hanlon lighted the cigar and puffed slowly on it for a few moments, relishing the smoke deeply, thoughtfully.

"Then there's our friend Maggie Quigley. It came to the attention of the school superintendent that she was sneaking a bit of sleep on her night shift at the high school. She was fired and came to me for help. I lose no love on that one, but she's better quiet than yapping. So I said I'd speak to Marty for her." Hanlon rolled his eyes with his characteristic, rheumy charm. "It was as if I asked him to assassinate the Governor. I reminded him that in order to be a statesman in this country one has first to be a politician. I mean by that, a man has to stay in office. And, sorry as it may be, it is often the likes of Maggie Quigley that keeps a man in office or, just as often, keeps him out."

"What happened to Maggie?"

"I spoke to State Senator Nealon for her. She's pushing a mop at the State House these nights."

"Does she know Martin wouldn't go to bat for her?"

"She knows. And all Charlestown will know."

"She can't do Marty much harm."

"That may be, but I'd like to see the boy more strongly established before he goes around reforming the world. I've done nothing
to slow him down yet, but that time may not be too far. They'll be
appointing some new teachers this summer, you know."

"Oh," Francis said, knowing that could bring Marty and J. P.
to grips. Hanlon would have a list of names for Marty to push at
the school board meetings. Francis suspected Marty would have
ideas of his own on that matter.

"Our boy, Marty, can go far," Hanlon said, blowing smoke
toward the ceiling, "if he does not forget his own kind."

He told her after Benediction that evening. He was alone with
her in one of those barren institutional parlors where you might
give out no gasp upon encountering a corpse. There were the dust-
laden, gray drapes, the wrought-iron jardiniere, there were the cold,
straight-backed wooden chairs, the bare mahogany table, the swoon-
ing, gilded prints of Jesus and His Mother on the walls.

". . . Father Carney thinks I ought to stay on until after spring
exams — he thinks I ought to get the credits and it's much more
graceful to leave during the bustle of term's end. I've given it a
conscientious try, Mother, and I believe the life isn't for me. Father
Carney agrees — I've talked things over with him a score of times
during the past six months and followed his every suggestion. I'm
not happy here, Mother, good as this life is for the right guys.
I want to go home."

He looked up from the table. She was staring out the window,
her face white with commingled fury and surprise, her lips trembling a little. She was making a huge effort to control herself, her
long, pale hands clasped firmly in her lap, her carriage erect in
the straight, wooden chair.

Now let me get it clearly . . . he wants to leave . . . he doesn't
want to be a priest . . . he wants to come home. He will not be
ordained. He gave it a conscientious try. Father Carney agrees,
Father Carney . . .

"Who is this Father Carney?" she asked, as though she were speaking from within a sealed cardboard container.

"He's my spiritual adviser, Mother," Francis said with a soft, mustered note of hope. "I've mentioned him in my letters. He's supposed to be the best moral theologian in the diocese."

"Does he know Father Quinn?" she asked in that same hollow, objective way.

"Not very well. He's heard of him, of course."

"Well," she began, looking at him with agonized patience and then lowering her eyes, "if you've made up your mind so definitely, I don't think you should stay here until spring."

"All right, Mother."

"Wouldn't you like to speak to Father Quinn before you leave?" she asked, sending one last needle of light through the night that had so swiftly fallen between them.

"It wouldn't be any use, Mother — please."

"Very well," she said, rising. "The others are waiting. Speak to the rector and let me know how soon you'll be home. You can call me at the office this week."

"All right, Mother." He walked before her to the door and his hand lingered on the knob a moment. "Mother, I'm sorry I've had to hurt you."

She nodded at him civilly and hurried through the door.

He followed her as she padded quickly along the hall, past the chipped statue of St. Philip and down the steps to the main entrance. He pushed the door open for her.

"You'll call," she said and turned away from him, quickly descending the stairs.

"Yes, just as soon as I've made arrangements."

She fled into the back seat of the sedan. Rosemary and J. P. waved at Francis, and Catherine looked away stonily as the sedan crunched mightily down the driveway.

"He'll make a fine priest, Catherine," Hanlon said, "a fine priest indeed."

Chapter 17

Soft in an April evening. Soft amid the clangor of the elevated trains, the shrill calls of tenement housewives, the caterwauling of drunkards, the Rabelaisian roars of laughter from the young toughs on the corner. Soft in an April evening the *Charlestown Bulletin* fell against the doorways, the darting shadows of Francis and John advanced and retreated on splintery tenement stairs.

They were working down Main Street toward City Square — up and down the tar streets between Main and Bunker Hill. John worked a few streets ahead of Francis scurrying up and down in what seemed to be a state of perpetual fright.

They would park their model-T pickup at three-street intervals. Francis would take an armful of the pungent gray newsprint and John would drive ahead, park, take another armful and hurry on — gladdening the Irish, Italians, and Polish masses with free newspapers, made possible by columns of local advertising clamoring the wares of Charlestown merchants.

Francis, perspiring happily in the gentle April dusk, rid himself of his last paper and jumped into the truck. Their evening chore was finished but for the score of papers John was delivering a few blocks away. They would do the rest of the town tomorrow.

He bumbled over the cobblestones in the truck, in the lane to the right of the elevated uprights, watching for John. He saw him disappear into a tenement with a nervous rat-gait, high on Green Street. He turned the Ford up the hill and chugged slowly after him.

One of the parish curates, young Father Doheny, was walking down the hill. Francis beeped the horn at him. The priest waved, smiling. Francis thought of Emmet and Tubby at the sem. They would be studying for their semester exams this month. Perhaps even at this moment, they were bending grimly over their textbooks while the mincing April moon trailed its skirts through their bedroom windows.

He had been away from them almost two months now. His mother had accepted his return with cool tolerance and he had taken up his duties again on the newspaper as an assistant to John. The demotion seemed to be his mother's way of expressing her disapproval of him. She was too much of a lady to bring it harshly into the open.

Francis had accepted his subservience to John philosophically and even with joy. He knew that his mother could argue that he had been away long enough to lose the feel of things around the office. He was glad for John, glad for the opportunity to help him. John was married now, more responsible, and in greater need of the additional money he earned as managing editor. Francis was happy to be back among the elevated uprights and under the soaring granite of the Monument, there on the tenement-ridden heights over the harbor where he found his peculiar happiness.

Catherine took less and less of an active hand in the paper, showing up with an editorial on press nights and taking a quick look at the page proofs before the presses started to roll. John was letting Francis do considerable of the feature writing and rewriting, saying nothing to Catherine, at her son's request. Catherine kept herself busy with the business and monthly meetings of the committee. And she had reason to be busy.

Since the melting of the snows in early March, there had been "loops" on three Saturday nights. Not one of the loopers had been apprehended — their lunatic speed, skill, and daring had made the pursuing police cars seem as plodding as oxcarts. The Boston dailies were shrilling for law and order and the police commissioner and his minions were putting their bland Irish heads together to devise new means of arresting the recurrent epidemic of joy riding.

Catherine, in behalf of the committee, had appealed to John Little and J. P. to try and stop the looping. John had shaken his craggy red head and pleaded that his influence was a thing of the past. His old gang were family men, like himself, and too busy eking out a living in the Sugar House, the navy, or on the docks, to be hanging around corners and "borrowing" high-powered cars. The loopers were the younger brothers of his old crowd and to them he was no more than a reformed has-been.

Secretly, Francis knew, John sympathized with them. What did the city expect? The kids were driven out of their rabbit-warren homes by the squalor and bitterness therein. They were the post-war waifs who found good fellowship and understanding on drug-store corners and in poolrooms, who played their polo on cobble-stone turfs at sixty-five miles an hour. For Mrs. Ronayne, he would, notwithstanding, have tried to do something. But they were strang-ers, not friends: they were none of his business.

J. P. protested to Catherine that John had been his contact man. He would, however, continue to refuse them political patronage when and if the guilty ones were arrested. "Let the police do their job and let them do it well," he had admonished. "In this time, they are better paid and better fed than most of the poor people whose taxes provide their salaries. . . ."

The committee had no recourse but to wait until the police had apprehended the guilty. Then they could take some steps toward rehabilitating the individuals involved — unless the courts chose to send the culprits to Concord Reformatory or the state pen with-out consulting the committee.

In the meantime Catherine was co-operating avidly with the Bunker Hill Boy's Club in providing more mature and attractive recreational facilities. Her progressive ideas for a clubhouse out in the marshes had gone the way of many progressive social ideas including those which receive enormous financial backing.

She had cut down on her paper's advertising space, at consider-able financial sacrifice, to make room for extensive publicity on the Boys' Club activities, pictures and news stories, which it was hoped would lure more and more young men to the club — pretty girls and free dances, basketball tournaments, billiards; pretty girls and splash parties; pretty girls, coffee, and doughnuts.

The police had finally taken drastic action. At the eastern base of Bunker Hill Street, with the co-operation of the street department, they had constructed a street-wide concrete trap, in design, not unlike the tank traps which the French were beginning to mold on the borders of Germany. Excavations at the top of the Hill and at the Sullivan Square end of the loopers' speedway were already begun.

Francis picked up John on the corner of Green and Bartlett and they drove in the direction of Bunker Hill Street, both keenly interested in taking a close look at the new trap.

"Think they'll let us drive through it — the one they just finished, I mean?" Francis said.

"I think they will," John said, mopping his brow with a handkerchief and then combing his chaotic red hair. "Alice went through there today on the streetcar. She said the streetcar whizzes through on the tracks but that the autos have to slow down to almost nothing."

"Maybe the loopers should put flanges on their tires," said Francis.

"Maybe they should. I'll bet they'll try and get through, though."

"I hate to see it," Francis said, as they turned onto Bunker Hill Street. "After we take a look, I'll drop you off home and then deliver a few copies at Hanlon's office. He's usually there until about nine. He likes to read the paper so he can see how much we know about what he already knows."

"J. P. gets more out of the paper than ever, I'll bet. He doesn't get around these days as much as he used to. They say he's grooming Timmy Mackail to take over," John said.

"I think I know what's behind that. I heard Mother telling Martin that J. P. has been seeing a doctor about his heart."

"How old *is* the guy, anyway?" John asked.

"He must be in his sixties." They were in sight of the concrete trap. "There it is," Francis said, a note of awe and anxiety in his voice.

"Yeh." John looked frozenly ahead. "Those Cossacks — they'll kill somebody, wait and see! Why can't they catch the kids the way they're paid to catch them? Now they'll sit on their spreading fannies and wait."

They rolled down to the trap, slowing as they approached it. A vicious, rectangular garden of thick concrete pyramids about two feet high covered the street from curbing to curbing. Two sets of parallel streetcar tracks cut narrow trails through the trap. The tracked corridors were separated by a slender plot of cement shark's-teeth.

They rolled slowly through the trap, wobbling on the tracks. A streetcar passed them on their left with a clattering rush.

"Pull over a minute, Franny."

Francis pulled the truck over to the curb after coming out of the hazard. John slipped out and walked slowly back through the trap, his eyes shifting shrewdly from the tracks to the shark's-teeth on both sides. A heavy Buick sedan approached and inched through, slipping from the tracks and burning its tire walls against the concrete siding. John stood among the pyramids, concentrating on the wheels and the tracks.

Kneeling on the cushions, watching, Francis knew that the old restlessness for the chase was stirring again in the former king of the loopers, once the most skillful and daring of them all. He thought of Alice and the babies that probably would be coming to the Littles. It was a relief to know that John had outgrown his looping days, even if the old gusto of horn, accelerator, and wheel was still smoldering in his blood.

John walked back to the truck, clambered into his seat, and they swung off Bunker Hill Street to the right, doubling back toward the Monument and the house of the widow's watch.

"It could be done," John said finally. "I think it could be done. . . ."

"I really need this," Martin said, raising his Scotch and soda and smiling at Erford.

Erford nodded, taking a sip of his drink. "I'm not sure whether it's you or your lectures that goes over so well with the femmes. I suspect it's the former, however."

"Where do all those flappers come from?" Martin asked, pleased at Erford's remark. "Why aren't they all married?"

"Why aren't *you* married?" Erford asked, in answer.

Martin had delivered his teacher lecture earlier that evening at the monthly meeting of the Penelope Society on Beacon Hill. Now, away from the seductive onslaught of expensively perfumed lionizers, he had fled to a quiet drink with Erford in the young men's lounge of the Otis Club.

At the supper-lecture, Erford had sat at an obscure corner table chatting with a few of Althea's unmarried friends. He had sat there seemingly unconcerned with the high-pitched drawl of Smith and Radcliffe voices. He had arranged this talk for Martin, with the approval and influence of his father. The Parkleys were interested in testing Martin's platform manner on the young Brahmin girls. If he went over well with them, the chances were that the girls would communicate their enthusiasm to their elders, preparing the way for a later, more significant lecture to one of the more staid Yankee dinner groups. Groups like the Otis Club, staid but potent with political influence — the influence of property, the deadly invisible ballot of financial holdings.

Erford knew that Martin was to see J. P. Hanlon that night and a showdown on teacher appointments was imminent. He had assured his father that Martin would not go along. The hours of Martin's apprenticeship and loyalty to the machine were ticking away. He had heard in Penelope Hall the cultivated voices spilling sweetly over the social barriers of three hundred years — rich with emancipation and feminine longing. He could be the one, Erford felt, to cut across Boston's political lines, to smash the fascism of Irish political bossdom and combine the best of the old tradition with the political virtue and maturity of the college-bred sons of immigrants. . . . If they could control him, keep his hat size stable, purge him of any sentimental attachments to the machine.

The inevitable, aged waiter brought another round of drinks.

"Here's to your meeting with Hanlon," Erford said. "Hope it comes off well."

"I hope so, too."

"May I ask what you plan to do if the big fellow insists you sponsor his list?"

Martin turned the perspiring highball glass around in his fingers. "I'll sponsor any of the applicants according to their standing in the teacher exams this summer — or if they're temporary appointees already, I'll sponsor them according to their teaching record and the grades in their original exams."

"What if he says you'll do it his way or else?"

"I've told you before, Erford, I won't do it. After giving all these high-sounding lectures, I simply couldn't live with myself. I'm no angel, you know that, but, well, there is a point of compromise beyond which I absolutely will not go." He wrinkled his forehead. "It's really a deuce of a situation to be in — Hanlon is practically one of the family, you know. I'd rather go back and face all those high-brow ladies of yours, a thousand times over, than face this thing tonight. But I will. . . ." He sighed, pulling deeply on his Scotch.

"I know you will," Erford's pale, bony face was touched with affection. "What do you plan on doing if Hanlon throws you out of the organization?"

"It will mean the end of me as school committeeman from Charlestown, that's sure," Martin began, running his hand restlessly through his hair. "I could finish out my term, I guess, then head for more neutral ground. Mike Farrell thinks I ought to send some roots down out Dorchester way — he says I'm well enough known now in the circles that count to run for the state house of representatives from several selected districts here in town."

Erford nodded.

"The thing that gripes most, though, is that I'll have to give up my job in the D.A.'s office — my income. I couldn't stay on once I broke with the big guy. I'll just have to hang out a shingle of my own, I guess."

"I think you would do all right. My dad's firm might be able to send a few things your way."

"That's swell of you, Erford. I'll need some help if I go out on my own."

"Fine. By the way, how is that young brother of yours? Did I hear you tell me he'd left the seminary?"

"Yes, he left in early March. It was really quite a shock to us all — Mother especially! We never dreamed he was cut out for anything but the altar!" Martin shook his head with a wry smile. "Such a goofy kid. He's back there with his pal, an odd redheaded little runt, getting out Mother's paper every week, as though he'd never been away. With Mother's connections among the clergy, he'd have gone ahead fast — might even have become a monsignor. I don't understand him; he's my own flesh and blood, but I simply do not understand him!"

"I don't know enough about the fellow, nor about your Catholic vocations," Erford said, "but I wonder if he's so strange. Perhaps he just likes life with your mother and the paper — your father did, it seems to me."

"Perhaps," Martin said, pushing back his gold-linked cuffs and glancing at his watch. "S-a-a-y! It's almost nine. I'll have to grab a cab and run." He gulped the remainder of his Scotch.

"Good luck," Erford said.

"Thanks," Martin said, rising and arranging his chair. "Oh, I meant to ask you. What do you hear from Althea lately?"

"They're getting along fine I guess — she doesn't see too much of Royce, except late at night. He's busy making another fortune out of his father's fortune." Erford smiled slyly. "Althea asks about you now and then."

"She does? Next time you write give her my regards."

When Martin left, Erford nodded at the waiter for another drink. He thought of Althea, Royce, and Martin. He knew from her too carefully evasive, chit-chatty letters how unhappy she was. But what point was there in telling Ronayne about it? Or what was to be gained in sending Martin's regards along. Why make a bad situation worse? Too, Althea's girl friends at the Penelope Society would mention Martin's lecture in their letters. That would be enough fuel on the fire. To be sure, Martin was going up quite nicely — better than he realized, wrapped up as he was in his difficulties with Hanlon. If he compromised with Hanlon, the machine would catapult him forward; if he rebelled, the elder Parkley, Mike Farrell, and all the self-righteous power of the *Boston Yankee* might rally behind his career. He was sure to rise politically either way. But that didn't mean he'd go up the social ladder as fast, Erford mused. Not with my sister, anyway, married or single. Not with a Parkley.

He had to admit he and his father, for political reasons, had already given Martin certain social privileges — lunching and drinking here as a guest at the Otis, lecturing to the Penelopes. But even with his friendship for Martin, based as much on good fellowship as on politics, Erford had never invited Martin to visit the Parkley winter home in the Fenway or their summer place in North Scituate.

Erford glanced moodily about in the wainscoted half-light of the bar. The bartender, another of the tribe of ancient Irishmen who gave their lives to clubs like the Otis, was polishing Martini glasses. Two students, in crew cuts and bow ties, were sipping their drinks and chatting sleepily at one end of the dark red, highly polished mahogany slab. They were the only other denizens of the lounge that had been set aside for young Otisans to learn the art of quiet dignified drinking without disturbing old Otisans who had.

And what about you, old man, Erford asked himself, gazing a little hazily into the intense, skully face, reflected in the rectangular mirror. What do you get out of all this, old man? What but the power and the personal satisfaction of the kingmakers? And here in Boston, if he could help to make the great rapprochement with Ronayne — or if Martin was not the one, someone else — that would be the thrill greater than the kisses of his fiancée, Nancy Havens, greater than the prestige of the Parkleys, greater than the stocks and bonds, the railroads and the steaming, stinking empires of tenements. If he could do what his father had failed to do, despite his efforts at honest compromise in the face of Yankee reactionaries; if he could live his father's career all over, refurbishing it with political success, laying the shattered machine of the Irish bosses before him in a huge act of love — if he could do that — Ronayne could have the honor, the tall silk hats, long state sedans. He could meet the trains, the planes, and the boats; the presidents, movie actresses, and seedy European royalty, flaunting their tarnished crowns. Ronayne could make the speeches and sign the bills, call out the national guard and pin the medals on war widows — he could have it all, once the machine lay black and gutted, once tradition, in modern trappings, ruled the city and the Commonwealth with dignity again.

He tossed off his drink, arose and left the bar, nodding amiably at the waiter as he went. He walked with unsteady reverence over the carpet through the broad, still parlor where a few septuagenarians lingered, whispered, and sipped their way back through the mellow, gracious years. He nodded congenially at old Leverett Winton, his mother's godfather. When he had passed, the old man widened his watery blue eyes, that still retained an appraising mercantile glint, and leaned over to his huddled neighbor, lost in the cavernous leather bosom of his chair, and whispered: "That-that's young Parkley — the one that brings some-some Irish political upstart in here. We-we must speak to the house committee. Heh? Brassy, heh?"

It was after nine when Francis putted through City Square and wheezed into a narrow parking space a short distance from the police building. He slammed the tinny door impatiently, wondering if Hanlon would still be around.

After the papers were distributed, John had insisted he come up to the Little apartment for coffee and some of Alice's cinnamon rolls. John's aging father and mother had moved to a smaller apartment on the other side of town, leaving the newlyweds in complete, regal custody of the three rooms and the cupola.

In the simple, clean kitchen they had sat for three quarters of an hour, talking, sipping their coffee, and eating the warm, flaky cinnamon rolls. It was as if John was still courting Alice — the way he would not let her rise and make more coffee, the way he listened with subdued excitement when she talked, the way he followed her with his eyes when she walked — it was, even after several months of marriage, as though the alarm clock would go off in the cupola, and John would awake, seeing the Monument silvered with the early morning sun, rising alone and going to work alone and coming home alone and wondering if the pretty Polish girl that once lived over the Ronayne family would ever give him a tumble at all.

But she was there in the kitchen, in the three-room flat, pretty with a pink and creamy roundness, comely with the comeliness of the peasant girls you see in newsreels. And there was a good, chuckling humor about the way she took his reverence; there was devotion and contentment and a recurrent shade of sadness in her eyes. John understood this sadness and he loved her all the more.

When she inquired about Martin in her shy, reticent way, John showed a kindly interest, too, affirming her nostalgia to be a good and sacred thing, playing the role of second best with dignity and grace. And if words were able to do what it is impossible for words to do, Francis would have castigated John for his subservience and Alice for her stubborn nostalgia, telling them that Martin was a willful stranger in a distant, irreconcilable world. But Francis knew that words give only glimmers of the way things really are — they confuse, mislead and betray us so often, and no one knows the wisdom of the mute.

Now, Francis climbed the stairs to the second floor of the police station, several copies of the *Bulletin* wadded under his arm. He turned the corner into the hall and saw the light in Hanlon's office giving sickly pallor to the frosted, lettered window.

His steps echoed hollowly through the empty offices, their windows flickering with the gas lights of the Square. Pausing at Hanlon's door he heard voices, one of them Hanlon's, the other Martin's. He knocked, heard Hanlon's gruff acknowledgment and entered.

At the other end of the small sitting room the door to Hanlon's office was open. Hanlon sat at his desk over a sheaf of papers. Puffing coolly on a cigarette, to his right, was Boston's youngest school committeeman.

"It's you, Franny," Hanlon said. "Put down the papers and stay a while, I'd like to talk to you. We'll be through here in a few minutes."

"Hi, kid," Martin said, waggling his cigarette hand. "So you've propagandized Charlestown with the Ronayne sweetness and light one more time! How about a copy?"

Francis handed him a *Bulletin* and set several others down near Hanlon. "How'd the talk go tonight?" Francis asked.

"How does it always go!" Martin said, dropping the paper flatly in his lap and turning his palms outwardly a little. "The little blue-bellies loved it. They took me to their bosoms, figuratively speaking, that is."

Hanlon laughed at Martin's unself-conscious ego and Francis, too, found himself smiling. "If you don't watch out," Hanlon said, "it will be more than figurative. From what I hear you've all the women's clubs in town fluttering like hens with a fox in the coop."

"Maybe a fox *is* in the coop," Francis said.

Martin winked appreciatively. "Maybe you've got something there, Fran."

"Did Mother and Rosemary go?" Francis asked.

"Uh-uh," Martin said. "More than one Irisher at a time the Penelope Society apparently will not allow. I'm not kidding myself. It was the Parkley drag that got me the lecture. My name isn't on the social register, you know."

"Not yet," Francis said calmly.

"Not yet is right," Martin said, taking the implication. "Now, dear brother, if you'll leave us alone a few minutes. . . ."

Francis went out, closing the door tightly behind him.

He sat down in a partially upholstered armchair and picked up a copy of *Liberty*. Behind the door he could hear the steady mumble of their voices and occasionally a word or two when one or the other raised his voice. He flipped the pages over to a serial called "The Yellow Peril." It was written under the assumption that some day Japan would attack the Philippines and Manila and even take San Francisco. There was a young American naval lieutenant in it who had fallen in love with a beautiful, almond-eyed Japanese-American schoolteacher. It was she, loyal to the Stars and Stripes, who informed him that his trusted valet, Sugi Sugiyama, was really a commodore in the Japanese navy, plotting to sabotage the Brooklyn Navy Yard.

"I'm sorry, Jim, I can't do it!" he heard Martin say. "They'll be sponsored according to their standing in the exams."

Francis concentrated hard on "The Yellow Peril." Sugi Sugiyama was constructing a wireless set in the coalbin.

He could hear Hanlon, his voice rising sonorously, angrily: "The or-*gan*-ization created you politically, and if it is to continue to push you ahead, it needs the support that can come from just the kind of people I'm asking you to do favors for. The or-gan-ization created you, lad, remember that . . . and it can undo you!"

Martin's voice lowered and what Francis heard was a mumble,

a mumble which he knew, by the tone of it, could have said: "I'm not so sure of that."

"You're not, are ye!" Hanlon roared, and with his anger, his Irish brogue was thickly resurgent. "Look here, I've never interfered with you and your snobby monkeyshines before, but I'm telling you now, Martin, once and for all, you will co-oper-ate with us in this matter or the or-*gan*-ization will back you no more!"

"I'm sorry, Jim," Martin's voice was louder now, his anger controlled. "You have my decision. While I'm school committeeman, appointments on merit are the only kind I'll recommend to the board."

"*While* you're school committeeman!" Hanlon shouted, bringing his fist down on the desk with a thump. "Believe me, laddy-buck, that won't be for long! Now a very good night to you!"

The chair scraped, the controlled voice said, "Good night, Jim."

Martin strode through the doorway, his head firm, his jaws clamped, his eyes cold. Without looking at Francis he pushed through the outer entrance, paying Hanlon a final masterful courtesy by not slamming the door.

Within the office Francis heard a profound groan like that of a mortally wounded animal. He threw the magazine aside and hurried in to Hanlon.

The big man was slumped over the desk with his head firmly in his hands. Francis had never seen the granite bulk of him so inert, so much in need of someone to lean on — he on whom so many had leaned — the pols and the people banding together, the forces of political privilege mustered against the forces of financial privilege; he, the heir of the great, coarse Irish ward bosses, makers of mayors and governors, self-appointed, stern and benevolent watchdogs of the political rights and privileges of bricklayers, longshoremen, and pushcart vendors; he, schooled as a lieutenant of Martin Lomasney, the greatest Boston boss of them all; now, aging and sick, defied by his own protégé, hunched over his desk, head in his hands, moaning with grief and what seemed to be pain — hugely pathetic and alone.

"Jim!" Francis said anxiously, rounding the desk and taking him by the shoulder. "Jim, what is it, Jim? What can I get you? Don't mind that snob, don't mind him, Jim!"

He raised his head slowly, his heavy face creamily blotched, his large eyes bewildered in their pouchy sockets. "It's all right, Franny," he said softly, smoothing his face with his hands, "if you'll get me a glass of water and the drops in the washroom there, I'll take a snifter. I shouldn't have yelled at Marty so." He tapped himself lightly over the heart. "There seems to be some kind of devilment in here. The doctor told me I've a touch of angina."

Francis entered the washroom and drew half a glass of water. He lifted a full eye dropper out of a small bottle on the shelf and squeezed several globules of the sherry-colored liquid into the glass.

He hurried back to the desk and J. P. took the glass from him, his hand shaking. He gulped the liquid down. "Arrh!" he sighed as the stimulant went to work. "To think that a few drops of medicine like a bitter banshee's brew would ever taste as good as a finger's length of bonded whiskey. Franny," he added, bracing a little, "I never would before admit it, but do you know, I'm getting old?"

"Not very, Jim."

"I'm the one that knows it, Franny, it is not my heart alone. For when a snippy young buck like Marty can afford to say he needs me no longer and go larking out the door, it is time for me to think about turning things over to Timmy Mackail. I have neither the strength nor the desire to fight Marty, but it will one day go hard with him just the same. You cannot turn your back willfully on your own."

Francis nodded sympathetically, knowing that Marty was free now to travel openly with the Yankee crowd, knowing that he would have to soar and never falter, knowing that Hanlon and his men would find it hard to take him back as long as he was politically clubby with the Parkleys. In a way, he was in Rosy Ryan's class now, the political bridges of Charlestown, at least, burning brightly behind him.

"Franny, do you have the small truck with you? I've loaned my car to Timmy — he had some business down on the Cape. Could you run me up the hill?"

"You bet, Jim." He wondered what business Mackail had down

on the Cape — monkey business maybe. He was probably running a case of bourbon into town for someone.

They walked slowly out of the office. Francis slipped his hand under Hanlon's elbow as they approached the stairs. Hanlon looked at him chidingly. He had been too strong and self-sufficient a man to accept help gracefully. "I'll hold onto the railing, Franny. I'm not an invalid entirely."

Later, in the truck, they flitted through the fluxing auto lights and elevated poles, up Chelsea to Bunker Hill Street. They wobbled through the looper hazard and Hanlon winked mischievously at Fran. "Do you think that will be stopping our boys?"

"I don't know, Jim. I wonder. Johnny Little says it can be done."

"Now if I were the President," Hanlon said, "I would build these boys a concrete speedway of their own, high over the ocean perhaps, where no one but themselves could drive — with loops and hills and sirens blowing at the curves and no one to kill or maim, but themselves."

He paused. They were at the top of the hill, where Hanlon lived in a small tenement over a second-hand furniture store.

"Right over here, Franny. Will you come up a minute? I've some nice blueberry pie in the ice chest."

Francis nodded, knowing that that was as close as Hanlon could come to saying he'd need help up the stairs.

Chapter 18

CATHERINE could not get to sleep. She lay in the big, brass-knobbed bed which she had shared with her husband and in which she had borne her children; she lay there, shifting sporadically, wondering how Martin had made out with Hanlon.

Her fingers groped involuntarily under the cool, fragrant pillow until they were in contact with the hard, glassy solace of her rosary beads. She tethered herself to the Virgin for a few minutes, telling a decade of beads. Then she glanced at the illuminated dial of the tiny clock on her dresser and pushed herself to a sitting position.

It was half-past one — surely their conference must have been long finished by now. Martin was probably asleep in his room. He had perhaps come in, seen that she had retired early, and slipped off to bed. Francis, too, must be home from the print shop, safe in bed.

Safe in bed. There was a phrase more of us ought to live by, she thought, pulling on her slippers. Not enough people go to bed any more in the long, restful way they used to. They roam about the city until all hours of the morning, especially the youngsters, constantly looking for some diversion they never seem to be able to find.

She saw in the rapid evolution of Americans as a nocturnal race of humans, a major cause of the instability of society. She wondered if enough young married couples took as much pains in the selection of their bed as they did in choosing their automobiles, clothing, liquid refreshment. While pulling on her robe she glanced affectionately at the ponderous, moon-reflecting bulk of the brass four-poster bed which her husband and she had bought twenty-five years ago. She scuffed out into the hall and peered into Rosemary's room, now taken over by Martin.

Her eyes were already accustomed to the darkness and she could see the bed was empty and had not been slept in.

"Where is that boy!" she thought. "Off drinking coffee somewhere, smoking cigarettes, and talking his political dreams into some sympathetic ear. Maybe he's at Rosemary's. Maybe I'll call — Mike's up at all hours of the night, anyway."

Late that afternoon, before starting off for Beacon Hill and his lecture, Martin had told her of his anticipated difficulties with J. P. She had sat at her desk in the office, the sliding drone and clatter of the press and linotype vying with his words. Her attitude had been one of disciplined neutrality, of sympathy for both sides. Her admiration, however, was great for Martin. He was taking a stand against Hanlon, difficult as it was, a stand on principles which did credit to him as the eldest son of Martin Ronayne. She had urged him to be a gentleman with Jim and not lose his temper if Hanlon did. She knew Hanlon too well. He would blow sky-high at what he would consider Martin's ingratitude. Martin had promised to be respectful, come what might.

It had not occurred to Catherine that while Martin's motives for defying Hanlon seemed based on principle, the stronger motivation had come out of his association with the Parkleys — his unwillingness to cowtow further to the discipline of the machine, his eagerness to try his own political wings.

For the common good of Martin Ronayne, Jr. — for the power and prestige of high governmental office, the long-sustained passion for chatting urbanely in the salons of the Brahmins. The exclusive ball after the Harvard-Yale crew race on the Charles. . . . The governor is here. He's coming in now. So very young, yet so able, so mature. Mrs. Royce, have you met Governor Ronayne? Your Excellency, this is Althea Parkley Royce. It's been a long time, Althea, a long time. . . .

Catherine shook her head. Why was she thinking such nonsense?

Was she jealous of his interest in the Parkleys — Erford, Althea? Jealous of their interest in him? She mustn't be. It was just that such an interest wasn't good for Martin — it just wouldn't work.

She turned impatiently away from the door of Francis' room. And where in heaven was *he?* He should have been in hours ago — something must be wrong. Could he be at the Littles? She'd better phone them.

She scuffed along the hall, thinking petulantly of Francis. The wound she had known when he left the seminary was scarring over — there was more throb to it now than sting. She had to admit that he had adjusted himself to the newspaper again quite nicely. She wouldn't tell him yet, but the paper would be his when and if he could measure up to it. The others were well provided for; Francis wasn't his father's son, she knew, but he seemed equipped to carry on the paper one day.

She reached for the phone and before she could get the receiver off the hook, it rang — long, shrilling, lonely, in the empty, echoing apartment.

"Hello. That you, Mother?"

"Well — ! Where are you at this time of night?"

"Mother, I'm at Hanlon's. He had a heart attack earlier tonight at the office. Martin had been there. I took him home and stayed with him a while. He seemed to be getting weaker so I phoned the doctor. He couldn't come until just a while ago."

"What did the doctor say? How is *Jim?*"

"The doctor says he'll have to stay in bed a few days and that he'll have to get out of politics or he's a goner. The doc is going to send a nurse to stay with him the next few days. But she can't get here before six this morning. I thought I'd stay here until then."

"You'll do nothing of the kind. There are more papers to go out in the morning. I'll take a cab and come over there. I can stay until the nurse comes."

"All right, Mother."

"I'll be right over. Good-by."

Erford slipped his key into the gleaming brass.

He turned, glancing across the willows and the eternally loitering Muddy River. Over the witching chiaroscuro of river, fen, and moonlight hovered that other moon, the giant, lurid electric sign in Kenmore Square, flouting its blinking tale of a wonder-working gasoline before outraged Yankee eyes.

Erford smiled and pushed against the brass handle of the door. The protests and petitions to Mayor O'Malley and the city council had been in vain — the sign was up there to stay. There had been indignation, too, some years ago on Beacon Hill when an electric sign had been erected on the roof of the Hotel Touraine, contaminating the night view from the Hill across the Common. Protests and petitions, and still the electric signs winking nightly over Boston, winking drolly at the Yankees as the old gave place to the new.

He moved noiselessly across the marble patio, at the center of which stood the slender bronze fountain nymph which Grandfather Parkley had brought back from Rome. At the top of the staircase which curved sweepingly up to the second story he could see a horizontal stave of light.

He climbed the maroon-carpeted stairs and knocked lightly on a thick, mahogany sliding door.

"Come in," the resonant voice said softly. "Is that you, son?"

"Yes, Dad." Erford eased the doors apart.

His father sat in a shiny, leather armchair, surrounded by walls of leather-bound books, one of which lay open in his lap. In the light and shadow above the bookcases hung several prints of colonial and revolutionary scenes — Cotton Mather denouncing a witch in Salem, General Washington accepting the command of the American army on Cambridge Common.

In a long, glass case fitted into the bookshelf area was a collection of the Parkley walking canes that had come down through several generations. A half-dozen silver yachting cups, a few diplomas, and a ponderous mahogany flat-top desk were other eye-catching appointments in the study.

On the combination mahogany lamp and table stood a large silver coffee tray bearing a slender, steaming coffee pot and two eggshell-thin cups and saucers.

"Sit down, son," the elder Parkley said, smiling and removing his heavy tortoise-shell glasses. "I thought you might get home in time for coffee. How did the lecture go?"

Erford pulled up a chair and took the clinking cup of coffee offered him almost ritualistically by his father. "Martin seemed to go over very well with the girls. His lecture was sound, poised, forthright, but I venture to say his sex appeal took priority over the lecture."

Mr. Parkley chuckled and took a sip of black coffee. "That phrase 'sex appeal' which you young people got indirectly from Freud, I'm afraid Grandfather Parkley would have considered an obscenity, but now it seems perfectly harmless. . . . So young Ronayne did tolerably well, eh?"

"First rate, Dad. The fellow has everything. I hope he can do lots more with his talents. He anticipates trouble with Hanlon on that teacher-appointment business, you know. I think I mentioned it to you already."

"Yes, you did. I imagine it will go hard with him if he won't co-operate."

"It will," Erford said. "He's seeing Hanlon tonight — probably has already."

He glanced at his watch, it was close to eleven. "I said I'd speak to you if he loses his job at the D.A.'s office."

"I'm sure we could throw some work his way. Have him come into State Street if he's interested."

"That's sporting of you, Dad. He'll really be in need of a hand. Mike Farrell thinks he could run for the State Legislature from Dorchester. How does that strike you?"

Mr. Parkley set his cup and saucer down on the table, his brow furrowed, his lips pursed in thought. "He might, he very well might. It won't be an easy road for him if Hanlon and the O'Malley crowd are down on him. We may be able to give him a hand, however, if his zeal for the public good is as nonpartisan as it seems.

"You know," Mr. Parkley ruminated, cocking his long graceful head reflectively, "I've been reading the letters of Daniel Webster this evening." He brought a slim, pale hand down on the open book with feathery emphasis. "His was the tragedy of so many brilliant politicians and statesmen — all of them 'might-have-beens.' He took a stand against the States' rights boys and it cost him the Presidency. Henry Cain Brattle gored himself on the horn of the League of Nations. Al Smith has his Catholicism to blame — although I do not believe he would ever put it that way. "And you know, son, thinking about this young Ronayne gives me a little twinge."

Erford lowered his eyes, knowing his father was going to shop a little in the market of nostalgic regret.

"When I was Ronayne's age I was elected to the State House of Representatives. Big things were predicted for me and there was even talk of running me for Lieutenant Governor. However, I fancied myself as a liberal in those days — and still do for that matter. Twenty-five and thirty years ago Boston conservatives were supreme and it was political suicide to acknowledge publicly the growing power and maturity of the Irish.

"On one occasion, I supported in the assembly several Irish representatives who objected to the construction of Back Bay Station — seeing it as a social affront to their constituents, which perhaps it was. From then on despite your grandfather's attempts to smooth things over, I was labeled as a rebel.

"My final demise as a future candidate for major Republican office occurred when I was invited to deliver the Bunker Hill Day address at the Hibernian Society banquet in Charlestown. I accepted quite rashly and in my address expressed the opinion that the Irish were politically coming of age.

"You know the rest of the story — Parkley the liberal. Valued committee member, arbiter, Governor's councilor. As they say, always a bridesmaid. . . ."

"But really, Dad, you know you've wielded more power at times than the actual custodians of high office."

"That is true." Parkley nodded. "But sometimes there is not enough in that to feed a man. Let us hope, however, that young Ronayne will not have to tread such a road."

"I believe he'll make out, Dad. Hanlon would probably block him only in Charlestown. J. P.'s too much of a friend of his family to hurt him all over the city. I think I'll turn in now, Dad."

"Very well, son — a good rest to you."

When Erford had gone his father sat and looked into the shadows. He hesitated to encourage his son to enter the political lists. There was too much heartbreak in it, he knew from his own experience, and not enough of the glory that disturbed the dreams of Webster, Brattle, Al Smith — that disturbed his own dreams, too, in the long and melancholy watches of the night. Erford would do well to play along with someone as promising as young Ronayne. But he did not want him to suffer as he had suffered. The Brahmin liberal, he was convinced, should work behind the scenes, putting the right words into the mouths of the conservatives so that they seemed liberally conservative — if you could put it that way — and, thus, acceptable to a wider number of citizens. Young Ronayne was perhaps already too liberal for the purposes of hard and practical politics. The successful art of American politics, Parkley believed, lay in the efficacy with which one seemed, at the right moment, liberal to the liberals and conservative to the conservatives.

Liberal to the liberals. . . .

He had the glimmering notion that he should get up and go to bed. His head nodded again and sunk gently against his chest. . . .

He was standing on the steps of the State House addressing a mob of restless, angry Irishmen who carried torches, longshoremen hooks, pickets, and those sawed-off hockey sticks that the Irish use in the game of "hurl." Around him was a ring of grim, steel-helmeted National Guardsmen, their Springfields leveled toward the mob. He set his chin, motioned for the guardsmen to lower their rifles, and began to speak:

"Fellow citizens! As Governor and protector of the Commonwealth, I command you to return to your homes. I promise that your voices will be heeded in the governance of this great state as will the voices of the Italians, the Poles, the Greeks, the Armenians, and all the other races which have given riches and vitality to the Commonwealth."

A great brogued cheer reverberated throughout the mall under the golden dome. He stood there wondering what the members of the Otis Club would say, wondering what they would say over their creamed oysters and coffee, when they heard he had given Massachusetts back to the people.

"Let the hitherto all-powerful minority fall back on the rights of the minority. Let the minority relinquish the rights of the majority, to the majority.

"Put out your torches and go home to your families in peace, my fellow citizens. I will talk it all over with His Eminence, Cardinal O'Garrity, in the morning. . . ."

In a shining, enameled kitchen, Mike Farrell poured his brother-in-law another drink. "Here, put another one into you!" he said in his rude, good-natured way. "It'll shorten that long face. You shouldn't be busted up about what happened tonight. You're free now, man, don't you understand? Free!"

"Yeh, free," Martin said glumly. He lifted his glass, nodded at Mike and said dourly: "Here's to political freedom and necessary ingratitude. Here's to a great guy, Jim Hanlon. May my political career rest in peace."

"Rest in peace, my eye!" Mike's puckish face glowed defiance. "We're just beginning now, you hear me, just beginning!"

"My-ike!" the sweet, irritated voice of Rosemary called from some pillowed depth in the middle of the house. "Will you close the kitchen door? I'm afraid you'll wake the baby."

"Okay, Rosemary." Mike winked at Marty, arose, and closed the door. "All right, now." He poured another drink. "You'll run for the Legislature right from this ward. You can establish your residence here — after all, this is your sister's house, right?"

"Right."

"I told you as much even before you spoke to Hanlon. I can't come right out and handle your campaign — the paper wouldn't like it — but I can do just as much for you from the side lines."

"The Parkley's would help us."

"The hell with the Parkleys! This is Dorchester — we don't need their help. Keep on the good side of them, sure. After you get elected they might come in handy."

"Okay. What's our first move? I don't know this town."

"Don't worry about it. We'll get you set up nicely. People around here have been wanting me to run for years — but I don't want it. I think they'll be interested if I back you, though. Also you're already known to them — the courageous young liberal on the School Committee, that's you! They know you and they'll continue to know you, unless I lose all my friends on newspaper row!"

"Good, old boy." Martin smiled a little stupidly from the effects of the whisky.

"And another thing," Mike said in that mildly snarling way he had of talking which you knew was without malice. "Put the soft pedal on all this 'old boy' stuff when you're in Dorchester. This isn't the Penelope Club. These snotty Irish kids that go to Ignatian College would be mimicking you all over the place. Talk to them the way you talk to the Charlestown crowd, that's all. . . .

"We won't mention your candidacy until midsummer. In the meantime I'll get you a series of speaking dates here in town. I think maybe you better tone down that teacher business, too — I mean I think you ought to harp on problems of wider, more sympathetic interest. And when you talk about your college years, stress those up on University Heights. Most of the Dorchester Irish send their sons to Ignatian College. And don't mention your years at Harvard unless you have to!"

Martin sat back in his chair, pleasantly mulled, his thoughts clear in the way that fish are seen through the aquarium glass. The heaviness and misery were replaced by that sense of release Mike had been talking about. "I've had enough for a while, Mike," he said, as Mike moved the bottle toward him.

"Okay. Here, sip on this." Mike poured him a glass of cold ginger ale. "What about big Jim? Do you think he'll try and put the blocks to you?"

"No, I don't think he'll bother me unless I run for office in Charlestown. Is the present incumbent here an O'Malley man?"

"Yeh, I think he is. A good-natured old tad named Terence O'Neil. Hasn't had any worth-while opposition for years. I think we can beat him. If not, look at all the fun and experience you'll have had."

"What about the Republican candidate?" Martin asked.

Mike grinned and ran his hand through his black mass of hair. "This is Dorchester, remember? . . . 'Sure, a little bit of heaven . . .' " Mike sang in a loud, mimicking Irish tenor.

He sang on, the pleasure of midnight wassail sweeping away his awareness of the slumbering baby near by.

He finished the song amid Martin's laughter and applause.

Another sweet singer took up another more anxious refrain. The baby's thin, piercing wail stilled the father and the uncle. They looked at each other with awe, a sudden pride, a sudden mutual smile.

Mike arose and hurried sheepishly down the hall.

Catherine Ronayne, dozing by the window in Hanlon's bedroom, heard the "clock" of hooves, the jingle of milk bottles, and opened her eyes. Below her the gas lamps still flickered, but up above the black, still tenement cliffs, she could see the Monument emerging with cold whiteness, garbed in the first pale rags of morning. She glanced at her watch. It was five-thirty; the nurse would be here in half an hour.

She pulled the shamrocked afghan, which she had once knitted for J. P., closer about her and looked at his bed. His eyes were wide open, tender, grateful.

"It is you, Catherine?" His voice was husky. "I did not know you were here."

"I've been here since about two, Jim. The doctor gave you something to make you sleep. Did you get some good rest?"

"I did. I feel much better now. Will you not run along home now and get some sleep yourself?"

"When the nurse comes, Jim."

She got up and went over to his bed, putting her hand on his brow. "You don't seem to have any fever." She tucked the blankets around him.

Hanlon smiled, thinking he had come almost to death's door before he could know the touch of that cool hand.

"Now, will I be needing a nurse?"

"You will, Jim, the doctor says you'll have to stay in bed about three days."

"He does!" . . . Three days, three whole days in this room, and the work piling up at the office. The people coming in with their troubles and only Timmy to handle them. "I'm in a bad way." He sighed.

"Not so bad if you do what the doctor tells you. Is there something I can get for you now?"

"I don't suppose I could have a small drop? There's a bottle of rye in the kitchen cupboard."

"I'm sorry, Jim, the doctor says . . ."

"The doctor says too damned much, my girl. I'll be up and around this afternoon."

"Jim! You won't."

Hanlon sank deeper into the pillow with a deep sigh. "I'm afraid not, Catherine — I'll stay here, just as he said. I'll settle for a glass of water."

She went into the kitchen for the water.

"Arrp!" He smacked his lips after drinking the water. "It is good even to be able to drink a glass of water."

Catherine placed the glass on the small table.

"Do you suppose the nurse will be as pretty as you are, Catherine?"

Catherine colored. "You're getting better, Jim." She looked shyly out the window.

"Did you see Marty tonight?" Hanlon asked.

"He wasn't home when I left. Francis told me things didn't go so well. I hope Martin wasn't impertinent to you."

"He was not. Just stubborn and young and a bit foolish, that is all. I got a bit out of temper with him — but it was for his own good. I bear him no grudge."

"What will it mean, Jim? Will it mean he'll lose the support of the organization?"

"It will." Hanlon cleared his throat. "We cannot put up with insubordination. We would have no power left if we did. We did things for him and he must do things in return or get out."

"Will he lose his job with the District Attorney?"

"I'm afraid so, Catherine. But he will have no trouble finding another nice position. He has a good record now and good experience."

Catherine nodded. "If I know Martin, he won't stay out of politics long."

"I'll raise no hand against him if he should run for office outside Charlestown. It is up to O'Malley to decide whether or not he'll be opposed elsewhere. But there will be no question of that if he keeps on with his blue-bellied playmates."

"He's young, Jim. The Parkleys represent something he thinks he wants. He'll have to find his wisdom the only way young people seem to want to find it — the hard way."

They sat in silence a while. Produce trucks and bakery wagons were racketing along Bunker Hill Street. The eastern sky was a vast explosion of silver lances.

"I've had a long, hard, and, I think, happy time of it, Catherine," Hanlon began. "Another year or two and I'll turn things completely over to Timmy."

"The doctor thinks you won't last that long if you keep on working," she said, alarmed.

"The doctor again! While I'm alive, my life's my own, and within the law, I'll run it my own way. When I die, now or later, I hope my life will be the Lord's."

"I hope it will, too, Jim."

"That Franny of yours is a good boy. He took me home, you know; gentle as a lamb he is."

Catherine sighed. "Yes, I suppose he is quite a good boy. He gives me some anxious moments, however."

"You've no cause to be anxious about him, Catherine, if I may say it. He's better off here at home with you and the paper than to be up on the altar and never at home at all. It is none of my business, but I sometimes wonder if you really know the gold you have in that boy."

"I wish he would show more of it to me. His brother's example doesn't seem to bestir him much."

"He's as different from Martin as night and day," Jim said. He wanted to add that he was a damn site finer, too, but knew that would be going too far.

There was a knock on the door.

"It's the nurse." Catherine arose. "I'll talk to her a while and then go. I'll look in on you again tonight, Jim. Please rest now."

"I will, Catherine. It was good of you to come."

Later, on the long staircase leading to the street, she pondered Hanlon's remarks about Francis.

Perhaps she had been too hard on him. There was a streak of rebelliousness in both her sons which may have been inherited from the fierce independence of their father. In Martin it seemed

securely geared to reason, but in Francis to whim. It was easy for
Hanlon to talk — he was not responsible for the boy and saw him
from an entirely different perspective. Still, he was quite a good
and dutiful boy. Yes, she'd go easier on him.

She opened the door and went out into the chill, sterile morning air. She pulled the door behind her, yanking for a moment on
the glass knob. The streetcar spit and clattered to a stop in front
of her. Two older women descended.

Catherine turned and looked into the lifted eyes of Maggie
Quigley and another woman, home from their washerwomen
chores at the State House.

"Good morning," Catherine said shyly. She looked the role,
caught off guard as she was, with which the accusing eyes of Mrs.
Quigley invested her.

"Humph!" Mrs. Quigley tossed her head sharply, grabbing her
companion by the elbow and walking her swiftly down the hill.

Catherine stood there a moment, embarrassed, wanting to call
after her that J. P. was ill and all that. Then she made a little
face of resignation and started up the hill.

She was more worried about the mercurial career of Martin
Ronayne, Jr., than she was about the gossip that would be about
the hill that very morning. But news of Hanlon's illness would
soon be abroad and the gossip would be stillborn. . . .

But what would Martin do now, what would he do?

Chapter 19

It was mid-September. The stock market had recovered temporarily. "Black Tuesday" was still over a month away.

In the dinnertime emptiness of the Dorchester subway train Francis perused the final edition of that day's *World*. Beside him, holding a carton of political cards, sat John Little, his eyes swinging every few moments from Francis' newspaper to the sooty blackness of the subway walls.

"Doesn't look like there'll be a crash. Stocks are climbing again, it says." Francis squinted with amateurish aplomb at the Wall Street page.

"It'll crash," John said glumly. "Alice has a cousin that chauffeurs for a broker on Broad Street and cocks an ear as he drives. He's the dumbest Polack I ever saw but already he's worth twenty thousand bucks in stock. When chauffeurs and chambermaids can speculate like that on their meager earnings, there's something phony about the market."

"Mother won't have anything to do with the stock market. She thinks it's phony, too."

"After the nose dive things took during March and May, she's smart. Where do we meet Mike?"

"He said he'd pick us up at Field's Corner."

"Is Marty speaking tonight?"

"Yeh. But one of us will have to stay with Mike. Marty's talking on the other side of town and Mike wants to distribute cards during a speech our worthy opponent, Terence O'Neil, is giving. I'll stay with Mike if it's all the same to you."

"Sure. In fact, I'd like to hear Marty speak. What are his chances, anyway?"

"Mike says they're good. O'Neil's not a very good speaker and he hasn't had any serious opposition for years. Mike thinks Marty's talks to the civic clubs here last spring went over big."

The train ascended a long grade and clacketed out of the tunnel into the Dorchester night. The crispness of September was made even more pungent by the sharp seaweedy aroma of the running tide.

They rattled along briskly between the tenements and the sea. The train slowed, pulling into Field's Corner.

They climbed the stairs to the street and stood on the bridge waiting for Mike and Marty.

"Shall we divvy up the cards now?"

"Let's wait till they come. Maybe we can do it in the back of Mike's car."

A blocky, red-faced mick in overalls and a railroad engineer's cap went by, carrying a lunch pail under his arm. He went down the stairs to the station.

"Looks like Hanlon," John said.

"He does," Francis said.

Hanlon. The big man was on his feet quite steadily now; following about half the doctor's orders, he went to his office only a few hours each day.

Francis had seen him a short while ago at lunchtime in the Waldorf cafeteria. J. P. had inquired eagerly of Martin's progress in his Dorchester campaign for state representative:

"O'Malley tells me that Representative O'Neil has been wailing about the favor our boy Martin is winning in his district. That omadhaun O'Neil! Don't tell Marty I said so, but I think our brave rebel will be up on the Hill come November. O'Malley loses no great love on O'Neil, between you and me. If Martin is elected, I may have another little talk with him. O'Malley could use his support in the 1932 elections. We have great hopes, you know. If the depression comes, it will kill the chances of a

Republican victory. On the tail of a Democratic sweep, Martin could go far."

Francis wondered if Marty would settle for the tail. Yet J. P. had the huge optimism and the conveniently short memory of the professional politician. And even more significant than the latter was Hanlon's lingering feeling of responsibility for what happened to Martin politically. He wanted him to make the right moves, even though he no longer controlled him.

"He's getting on well in his own practice, you say?" J. P. had further inquired.

"I only know what Mother occasionally drops around the house. Marty doesn't tell me a thing when he's home. And these days he's not home. He's living with Sis and Mike for political reasons — Dorchester's his official residence now."

"I thought as much! Your mother's so busy with the Boy's Club program, I don't see as much of her these days. Do you think the concrete traps have as much to do with the falling off of looping as the lemonade, the doughnuts, and the pretty girls?"

Francis thought so. Since Bunker Hill Day, the past seventeenth of June, there had not been a "loop." In the dark, predawn hours of that festive day, tragedy had struck. Two young loopers had defied the police and the traps only to be stilled in the twisted, blood-flecked wreckage of their stolen sedan. It was a topic one did not discuss with John Little, who clung almost perversely to the conviction that the traps constituted municipally countenanced murder. . . .

But now on the bridge at Field's Corner Francis heard the blast of Mike Farrell's horn and walked with John to the curbing.

The gray sedan lurched to a stop. Mike grinned and thumbed abruptly toward the back seat. Martin was seated beside him, trim in an Oxford gray suit.

"I don't believe you've met Erford, Franny," Martin said.

Francis opened the door and looked into the creased paleness of the younger Parkley's face. "Hello there," Erford said, "I've been looking forward to this for some time. Your brother has told me a good deal about you."

"He's told me a lot about you, too." Francis shook Erford's

long, bony hand and climbed in beside him. "This is John Little."
John passed in the carton of cards.

"This little guy," Martin said, "is the managing editor of
Mother's paper. These two are never happy unless they're together."

"Damon and Pythias," Erford said.

"What happens now?" Martin asked Mike.

"It's still pretty early. I thought we'd have a powwow over a
cup of coffee. Have you guys eaten?" He looked in the mirror at
Francis and John.

"Yeh, we grabbed something in City Square before we left,"
Francis said.

Erford thought about Francis. There was perhaps a shyness and
depth about him in marked contrast to the easy charm and urbane
glibness of Martin. Not that there wasn't depth to Martin, whenever he would take the time to sound it. Francis had "grabbed"
something in City Square. The studious former seminarian did
not have to talk that way. Erford wondered if that was not a
dominant trait of the educated, second-generation Irish — the inner,
formal resources of the trained, even cultured mind — the outer
manifestations of the low-born. And there was Mike Farrell, one
of the keenest journalistic minds in Boston, an honor graduate
of Columbia, yet still, in manner and speech, "one of the boys."
It looked fine in the neighborhood — the rigid preservation of the
"it hasn't gone to his head" attitude — yet it seemed absurd, Erford
knew, to people in whose families higher education went back
several generations.

Mike pulled up in front of a one-arm lunch cart on Dorchester Street.

"Here we are, Parkley," Mike said. "It's not the Otis Club,
but it'll have to do."

"I'm sure it will be delightful," Erford said.

They got out of the car and entered the restaurant.

In the crowd of lady shoppers, old men, teen-age corner lizards
who wander about Uphams Corner at seven o'clock on a moon-
bleached September night, Francis stood beside Mike, waiting for
State Representative Terence O'Neil to speak his piece.

Under his arm Francis held a block of Martin's political cards, which he would distribute whenever Mike gave him the sign. Martin, Erford, and John were over in the Savin Hill area where the ex-school committeeman from Charlestown was to address a group of Dorchester club women gathered in a private home. "The women's votes are every bit as good as the men's," Mike had said over the coffee. "In fact, if they like you well enough, they'll get their husbands and older children to vote for you. Franny and I will go see if we can make life miserable for Terry."

A short, natty, middle-aged man in a gray Homberg jumped onto the platform which had been erected on the trunk rack of an old black sedan. He removed his hat and began to speak in brisk, broad A's and R's. "Before I introduce our representative, we are to be favored with a rendition of a campaign song written especially for Terence O'Neil by Georgey Teagin, well-known accordionist and singer, formerly featured at the Seaside Gardens. Take it away, Georgey."

A tall, round-shouldered man with a red nose struggled onto the platform carrying a piano accordion.

He spoke in a birdy voice: "I wrote this song for Terry's campaign because he's a grand fellow and deserves the continued support of every last man of you. Copies of this song, I *unner*-stand, will be printed up and distributed at the rally for Mr. O'Neil in Codman Square next Saturday night. The tune is one with which you're all familiar — 'Sweet Rosie O'Grady.' "

"This guy sings for drinks in a 'speak' on Dorchester Avenue," Mike whispered.

They listened to the tuneful trials of Georgey's accordion. Then he began to maneuver the accordion rhythmically and sing in that same birdy voice:

> "Faithful Terry Oh-nee-heel
> Is our man 'neath the dome.
> There he fights for Dor-chester,
> Church, fam-lee, and home.
>
> Soon, he'll be elected,
> Without much of a fuss.
> We love our Terry Oh-nee-heel,
> And Terry Oh-nee-heel loves us."

A flurry of handclaps and a few teen-age whistles were acknowledged by Georgey Teagin, who nodded his head to the north and south with the proper mien of theatrical humility.

"If I were O'Neil, I'd shoot Teagin for writing those lyrics," Mike said.

The natty man stepped up and introduced Honorable Terence O'Neil, State Representative from Dorchester for the past ten years. "Representative Terence O'Neil needs no introduction from me or anyone in Dorchester — he is one of our own and has been for many years. There can be little doubt about the integrity and ability of a candidate on whom the voters have put their stamp of approval by keeping him in the State Legislature for ten consecutive years. I give you, then, your present and future state representative, the Honorable Terence O'Neil."

"Faithful Terry Oh-nee-heel," assisted by the master of ceremonies, clambered up on the platform and looked, with searching intensity, into the neutral eyes of his constituents, who, knowing Terry, were ready for just about anything.

Terry, Francis noticed, was a man who had probably once been stocky in the bullish way of J. P. Hanlon. But now there was something shriveled about the man — his clothes hung loosely on him and the big, protruding bones of his body seemed to minimize the flesh. His cheeks were hollow, his nose, blue-veined. Several thin strands of gray-black hair were carefully plastered over his baldness. His green, fishy eyes fluxed with something that was a composite of fear and anger as he assaulted the ears of his audience in a hoarse, rapid-fire voice which was not without traces of brogue.

"Thank-yuh, Jimmy; thank-yuh, Georgey; it is good of you to compliment my record so. And it is good of you people to come and hear me this night, for I have an important message for you."

Mike touched Francis on the shoulder. "Start passing out the cards," he said.

Francis nodded and moved among the listeners, handing them the record and the Bachrach portrait of Martin Ronayne, all on one neatly printed pasteboard.

Some of the people ignored his offerings, others took and read. The total effect was a creation of restlessness among the onlookers.

Francis repressed his initial embarrassment and pushed among them as Terry paused, glaring.

"I have," he began again, "an important message for you concerning the background and activities of my smart-alecky young opponent who has been delivering such flowery oratory against me around the town. . . ."

Mike put his hand to the side of his mouth. *"Why were you thrown out of the longshoremen's union in 1921?"* he demanded in a loud, challenging voice.

The gaunt face slackened and the speaker's mouth worked a little, but no words were immediately forthcoming. The audience laughed heartily, and Mike slinked off to the right.

Francis, chuckling at Mike's antics, continued to distribute the cards to people who now seemed more amenable to looking at them. Finally, O'Neil found his tongue.

"What happened on the docks of South Boston in '21 is of no importance now. There *was* a little trouble, over which I had no control," he said with nervous nonchalance. "But to get back to the present assault that is being made on my record of service to the people. It has come to my attention that this young Ronayne . . ."

"You haven't answered my question!" Mike bellowed from his new position on O'Neil's left. *"Why were you kicked out of the longshoremen's union in 1921?"*

O'Neil stood on the platform, his face purple. The audience continued laughing and glancing alternately at Mike and Terry.

Mike nodded to Francis, raising his eyes toward his car, parked across the street. Francis, with only a few cards left, walked toward the car.

Several feminine listeners picked up their shopping bags, giggled, and went their way. O'Neil was sputtering into coherence again when Mike climbed into the front seat beside Francis.

"He'll go after Marty and the Harvard angle now, for sure," Francis said.

"Let him," Mike said, chuckling and shifting into first. "He's lost his audience. They won't remember anything but this longshore business once they get home."

"Was he really mixed up in something like that?"

"He sure was. I'd heard he used to be a longshoreman in the early twenties. I figured if he was mixed up in deals at the State House, as he is, he might have been mixed up in some shady longshore politics. I went through our old newspaper files, covering the early twenties. Sure enough — he was kicked out of the union for selling union secrets to the officials of the steamship lines."

"Does Marty know about it?"

"Sure. He's trying it out on the clubwomen tonight."

As they wheeled along toward the sea and the Savin Hill section of town, Francis had the unmistakable feeling that Marty had acted more brilliantly than rashly in forsaking Hanlon's powerful patronage for the clever, aggressive tactics of Mike. Mike made up for what he lacked in the way of a well-tooled organization in honesty, an understanding of human nature, and a fearlessness in the execution of his ideas. Could Hanlon have known of Mike's clever campaign tactics when he prophesied Martin's election? Francis doubted it. Thus there was all the more reason to feel optimistic about the campaign.

"That was a helluva lot of fun, wasn't it?" Mike said, grinning into the windshield.

Chapter 20

SEPTEMBER and October went, November came, the nation plunged
to the proportionate depth decreed by proportionate lust and
imprudence; bankers and chauffeurs, chambermaids and dowagers
were ruined and only the courageous, hold-the-line optimism of
Rockefeller and Henry Ford matched the eager, rising political
optimism of a certain Bostonian named Martin Ronayne. Herbert
Hoover whistled in the dark of his nation with heartening hopes
for the future, but the solid gold and silver hip flasks of F. Scott
Fitzgerald's gods and goddesses collected dust in the windows of
pawn shops, sere with a quenchless thirst; the Stutz roadsters were
jacked up ignominiously for the long winters of American dis-
content that were to come before a new man in the White House
would sit by his fireside and coax away fear with a mellifluous voice.

And on election night in Boston, those who had not run with
the financial hounds to their inevitable destruction, namely the
Yankees who knew how to preserve their moderate wealth, and
the immigrant Irish, Italians, Portuguese, Greeks, and Armenians
who knew how to preserve their moderate poverty, were thrilled
again by the running of the political hounds — a race that would
not end in financial ruin and suicide but in the exhilarating
continuum of the American idea.

At 8:30 that night, in the waiting room of Doctor Herbert
McDonald, obstetrician, Alice Little awaited her turn and avidly
perused the Dorchester election returns in the *Daily Camera's*

special election edition. Her face brightened when she saw the figures: Martin was leading O'Neil by five thousand votes. The reportorial roundup of election news predicted his certain election as most of the returns were in when the paper went to press.

Her heart was happy for him. He had done it again. And defeated a well-intrenched incumbent, too. John would be probably calling her at home. He and Francis were over at Martin's headquarters with Mike, Rosemary, and Mrs. Ronayne.

John had wanted her to come over and wait with them — but she had pleaded a visit to her parents. She hadn't wanted to tell him about this until she was sure.

The excitement she felt on reading the news somewhat allayed the fear that was rooted in her. Had she not been told by her old family doctor that she was incapable of having babies? Had he not implied that it would be, in any case, dangerous for her to have them. John wanted a son so much — and so did she. Tonight would tell. If God wanted her to have a baby, she'd have it, no matter what.

A buxom woman of thirty-five or so smiled at her from the sofa on the other side of the room. "Your first?" she asked, waiving all presumption with the friendliness of her question.

"Well — maybe," Alice smiled and then blushed.

Later, as she walked along Main Street listening to the newsboys shrilling the inevitable tidings of Mayor O'Malley's re-election, she fought the terror aroused in her by the doctor's kind yet firm words concerning the danger involved in the carrying and birth of her child. She fled almost feverishly to glad thoughts of Marty's election, the joy that would be his mother's and Francis' and John's.

John's joy would be greater by far at her news. She knew she must tell him, too, of the danger involved for her — she would tell him that as gently and as optimistically as she could.

She walked along among the ugly, pondrous, black legs of the endless steel insect that crawled down Main Street.

The newsboys caterwauled "O'Malley!" whose political star, however tarnished, seemed firmly fixed over Boston. She thought of how another rising political star, new and bright, lay buried in the tabulations of some back page. She spoke silently to the new life within her of how exciting it was to be alive in the world

at such a time. She whispered a prayer that the new life would
come to earth in strength and purity.

So Alice, however inarticulately, made a little Advent in her
heart, saying other words with her mind but singing clearly and
purely with her heart: "Be it done unto me according to Thy
Word."

The Wisconsin night was filled with frigid blackness, the sick-
cow moan of fog-bound lake steamers and the brisk, hag-riding
whistle of milk trains. Althea Royce stood on the patio of her
lake-shore home trying hard to discern the aura of the moon or
even a solitary star. It was a routine rich with reminiscent loneliness, this, her after-dinner devoir paid to the lake, the sky,
the cinema of memory, sweet with nostalgia and vain regret. Herbert was in the study snoozing over *The Milwaukee Journal*. In
an hour or two he would be ready for a drink and another sym-
posium about the vicissitudes of meat and steel, dairy products and
near beer.

She would tell him tonight. She shuddered a little in the chill
of the swirling, spectral November night. The chill, she knew, was
of her spirit as well. She knew how outraged her father and Erford
would be when she told them she wanted a divorce. But she would
face them soon — at Thanksgiving. She would go to Boston alone.
Herbert would be in Eau Claire on business. She would stay in
Boston until arrangements for the divorce could be made.

The indignation of her family and the conventional coventry
which would be her lot at the hands of many of her Boston friends
was altogether preferable to this fool world of matrimony wherein
it seemed the marriage couch had been removed to make room for
a battery of ticker tapes.

The greatest happiness she had known since coming to Wisconsin
were the morning canters she took on her sleek brown hunter about
the woodland bridle paths. Riding at breakneck speed beside the
lake, her hair streaming in the wind and Daystar galloping surely,
evenly, as if he could sustain the pace all the way to Boston —
pausing with him on a spur overlooking the lake — seeing and
hearing the mallards honking poignantly northward in the spring
and south in the fall. But no profoundly unhappy vicissitude, she

knew, is without its seed of wisdom, one which has within it the ultimate flower of happiness.

She saw her marriage now, after two years of its minimum conventions, as something of an expiation for the wild "debutramp" life she had led in her late teens and early twenties. There had been enough of the Parkley acumen of moral stability in her to motivate her marriage to Royce as a graceful flight to stability. That she knew had been in the mind of her father and brother. Althea then thought of the safe, secure haven of a financial and marital stability, consonant with her background and her breeding. But she had tasted too deeply of the emotional life, good and bad, to settle for security alone.

So in Milwaukee in the year of near beer, 1929, she was paying for the apparent wisdom of her father and Erford; they would pay for their presumption later when she told them of her decision to call it quits. And it was not that she wanted to flee back to the devil-may-care ways — she had had enough of champagne out of slippers in New York penthouses and hilarious football week ends at Dartmouth, Harvard, and Yale. But she would not concede that, young and pretty still, she should be denied the happiness of a mature and abiding love.

The telephone in her sewing room, just off the patio, buzzed insistently, needling an impulse of excitement into the painful inertia of her lonely lakeside world.

That must be Erford, she thought, hurrying across the patio, through the French door to the sewing room. She had phoned him in Boston earlier that evening to discuss her Thanksgiving plans. He was not at home, but the maid had promised to try and locate him. "It's election night, Miss Althea, you know," the maid had said.

Election night in Boston. Althea had forgotten. She had wanted to ask Brigid if she knew how things had gone for Mr. Ronayne, but that would have been tactless.

She picked up the phone, spoke to the Milwaukee operator for a moment, and then listened to the brisk, self-confident twang of the Boston operator putting through the call. She gathered from the dialogue of the connection that they had located Erford at the Hotel Touraine. What would he be doing at the Touraine?

Then she heard the crisp, high-pitched voice of Erford coming out of a background of hilarious voices, the clink of glasses, and the ragtime beat of a piano.

"Sis!" Erford said. "What is it, dear — anything wrong? Emily tells me you've been trying to get me all evening. . . ."

"I can't say much about it over the phone, Erford, but I want to come home for a few weeks — alone. That will mean I'll be home for Thanksgiving and Christmas. I feel Herb and I need a vacation from each other. Don't tell Dad that, however. I'll tell him myself, later. Simply say Herbert's going to be away on business Thanksgiving — which he is — and I'll be home. Give him my love, won't you? How is the old dear?"

"He's fine, Sis, all hopped up about the election. You'd think Martin was a Republican, Dad's so pleased about it all."

"Martin? Did he — did he get in?"

"Did he! He beat O'Neil by three thousand votes. He's on his way!"

"Wonderful!" Althea whispered, blinking sudden tears through her eyelashes. "Give him my . . . my congratulations."

"Why not give them to him yourself — he's right here. I'm at his victory party here in the Touraine."

"Marty! Marty!" she could hear him calling before she had time to protest. She knew that Erford must have had several drinks — it wasn't like him to be so puckishly informal. She thought frantically of hanging up — but that wouldn't do. Why should she?

"It ain't gonna rain no more, . . ." they were singing happily at the piano. . . .

"Hello, Althea," Martin said with a warm excitement that sent the blood rushing to her head. "Is it really you?"

"Yes, Martin, it is. How *are* you? How happy you must be tonight!"

"Yes, it is a great night for me. And you — how are things with you?"

"Oh — all right. I do a lot of riding these days. It's wonderful riding country."

"I knew you would be. I can just see your picture on a hunter in the Sunday supplements. That was the way I first saw you, you know."

"Did you?" She seemed to be pulling away from the brink of something in her voice, something in his. "Well, you'll want to be getting back to your party. Congratulations again and best of luck. This is the beginning of big things."

"Maybe it is," he said. She heard Erford's voice whispering in the background. "Erford tells me you'll be in Boston for the holidays. Perhaps I'll get to say hello."

"Perhaps."

"Here's Erford again. It's been swell hearing your voice again, Althea."

She could not say the cool thing nor the warm thing. She said a lot with silence, though, and soon she was discussing home-coming arrangements with Erford again.

A few minutes later, as she hung up, she heard Herbert rustling the newspaper in the study.

"Are you there, Althea?" he called.

"Yes," she said softly and walked into the study.

Back in the suite on the seventh floor of the Touraine, Francis leaned on the piano sipping a beer. On a sofa, near by, his mother was talking quietly amid all the singing and tippling to old, but spirited Mrs. Farrell, a well-known Catholic clubwoman in Dorchester who had helped no little in getting out the vote for Martin.

Francis had noticed the little vignette at the telephone; and while he hadn't been able to hear what was said, he surmised that the call had been a long-distance one. The tenderness that had swept over Marty's face as he talked hinted at the identity of the party on the other end of the line.

At the piano Rosemary, wearing a huge, blue orchid that was beginning to get tired of symbolizing victory, banged out another favorite while Mike and John Little roared away.

"Give me a little kiss, will yuh, huh?
And I'll give it right back to you-oo!"

When they finished the song, Mike took a swig out of his glass, before leaning down and whispering a kiss that was a question into his wife's fragrant black hair.

"Can you play 'Rosy O'Grady' from memory?"

"Maybe."

"Okay," he said softly. Then he brought himself erect, turned, and faced the gathering. "I wanna sing a little song," he began nasally, "in honor of our new Representative, a ditty, no doubt, with which you're all familiar. Take it, Rosemary."

"Faithful Terry Oh-nee-heel," he sang in huge, shrill mimicry, "is our man 'neath the Dome. . . ."

Martin, chuckling at Mike's take-off on O'Neil's campaign song, saw Erford to the elevator, down the hall from the suite.

"You know, of course, that you're going to be wooed by the O'Malley crowd stronger than ever," Erford said as they walked.

"I suppose that's so. But there's really no way of accepting their support without pledging loyalty to their politics. On those terms I don't believe I'd be interested."

Erford pressed the elevator button. "Well, I'll see you at the office sometime within the next week or so, eh? This is no time to talk about it — you're flushed with success and I with good bootleg whisky. But you will have to make a decision soon regarding the support and security of an organization. You can't go it alone — that is, if you're to go anywhere."

"I wonder about that. How far do you suppose an Irishman turned Republican would get?"

"That would depend largely on the ability and personality of the candidate."

"Maybe so," Martin said. "I'd sure hate to hear the gossips in Charlestown if I ever turned Republican."

"Gossips do not elect good politicians — intelligent voters do." The elevator door clanked open. "Have a good rest — see you later in the week."

"Yes, I'm going up to the Berkshires for a few days. See you Thursday."

The elevator door slammed. Martin stood there a minute reflectively. "Republican," he mumbled, tasting the word slowly and wrinkling his forehead petulantly. "Ridiculous." He walked toward the fraying ragtime and the last, lingering dregs of victory in Dorchester.

Chapter 21

IN THE front seat of the taxicab which nibbled swiftly at the down-town traffic, Francis wondered why Jim Hanlon had not phoned Marty or even dropped in at the victory party. Marty said he and Mike had tried to get in touch with Hanlon, once the returns were in. They had called his apartment in vain, then rung him at his headquarters, where one of his boys took the message. But no Hanlon.

Francis had assured Marty that Hanlon wasn't nursing any grudge. In fact, it was entirely the other way around, he told the new officeholder — Hanlon still liked and admired him immensely. "The guy is probably sick in bed, so don't go thinking he's giving you the freeze!"

Now, on the way back to Charlestown, Francis decided to stop off at Hanlon's and check up on the old war horse. Beside him sat John Little, fast asleep.

In the rear sat his mother, electrically awake, her eyes peering restlessly into the shifting pillars of the fog. The woman who had been in many ways the architect of this day — who had excavated even the fair Alice out of the foundation pit of her son's career. This was her day as well as Martin's, and it was Martin, Sr.'s, too. She would never leave him out of any of her triumphs. His son Martin was showing the stuff that had been bequeathed to him.

Despite her affection for Hanlon, she was deeply grateful that Martin had conducted and won his campaign without the preordination of the O'Malley machine. She knew, as did her late husband, that every so often there comes along, in American politics, men so percipient of the heart and the will of the people that they are able to rise above the trammels of party machinations and bring their ability directly to the attention of the voters. John Quincy Adams had been such a man and Theodore Roosevelt.

Martin, she knew, must go ahead now — his record would be subject to the scrutiny of the entire state electorate and there would be no standing still. How he would progress without the sponsorship of the machine she could not say. Certainly he couldn't turn Republican — she had faith in his common sense and his natural gift of appealing to the voters. He would find a middle ground.

Soon, too, he should be thinking of finding a good wife. It would not do for a bachelor to aspire to the highest office in the state. It takes a family man to understand the problems of families.

Certainly he was not without admirers. The fluttery young ladies at the Sunday teas of the Catholic Junior League often inquired about him whenever Catherine stood in the reception line. It was interesting that Martin had not had a girl friend at tonight's party. He simply wasn't interested in anyone, Catherine gathered. "You're my best girl," he had said to her.

It was nice of him to say that, but she suspected differently. Rosemary had dropped a few hints to her concerning his lingering interest in Althea Parkley. Catherine had rightly suspected that the prom had been more than "just a date." It was a good thing for all concerned that the flighty young thing had married when she did. It wouldn't have worked, of course.

Francis followed, with his eyes, an ambulance that clanged eerily along the river road in the early morning mists. He found himself looking into the keen, wide-awake face of his mother.

"Someone's in trouble," he said shyly, turning his eyes toward the windshield again.

"God help us!" Catherine said. The shy, thin, white face of Francis glowed in her consciousness momentarily, then faded.

What of this other son? What was he doing for himself? What had she done? How full would be her cup if it had been God's will for him to stay on at the seminary. How his family could have used the graces and consolations he would have brought to them as a holy priest of God. The old wound of disappointment twinged within her. She sighed. She had come to terms with her disappointment and, besides, he seemed to be doing very well over at the paper. It was about time he, too, thought about settling down with some nice girl. But, even more than his brother who seemed to have quite definite reasons for not taking up seriously with some young lady, Francis had no amorous interest in the girls.

There were times when Catherine simply could not understand what manner of creature he was — there was something unstable, something of the drifter in his make-up that she could not account for. She knew that much of his world was an interior one, and she was irritated by her inability to penetrate the masquerade with which his exterior actions seemed to obscure another self.

They clattered over the viaduct, past the gray, buttressed bulk of the state prison into Charlestown, and up Rutherford Avenue to City Square.

"I'm a little worried about Jim Hanlon, Mother," Francis said. "Something must have happened or I'm sure he would have called to congratulate Marty. Would you mind if I jumped out here and walked up to check on him a minute? I have a key to his place — if he's resting well, I won't disturb him."

"Surely. There's no need to walk up there through the fog, however. I'll have the driver run you up — try not to be too late. It's two-thirty already."

"Thanks, Mother. But I don't want you to wait. I may have to do a few things for Jim."

"Very well."

They flapped along Chelsea Street and turned up Bunker Hill Street. Outside Hanlon's place, Francis said good night to his mother, tousled John's head, calling forth a fudgy mumble, and slipped out of the cab.

He heard them drive away as he slipped the key into the lock. He tiptoed up the stairs and opened the door leading into the small carpeted hallway in Hanlon's apartment.

In the bedroom to the right a small light was burning. He could hear the rustle of a newspaper and smell the pungent smoke of a good cigar.

"Is that you, Franny?" the familiar, hearty voice called.

"It is, Jim." Francis opened the bedroom door.

Hanlon lay under the blankets, his huge body swathed in a faded, flannel nightgown, his head propped up by two obese pillows. The cigar was nowhere to be seen although a blue aura curled guiltily about his head.

"Jim, you've been smoking."

Hanlon rolled his eyes. "Well, Franny, I — I — it was election night. I heard about our boy doing so fine — and O'Malley walked into office again. I just thought I'd . . ."

"Okay, Jim." Francis could not suppress a smile. "I know . . . it's just that the doctor says . . ."

"The doctor be damned!" Hanlon punched the pillow with his big fist. "If I'd-uh done everything he told me to do I'd be dead and gone six months now entirely."

"Maybe." Francis sat down.

"Will you be mad, Franny, if I take a few more puffs? His Honor himself gave me this Havana only this morning. Surely the damage is already done."

"It's your funeral, Jim." Francis reached for the cigar in an ash tray under the bed.

"It's a good thing Catherine is not here. The cigar would be out of the window and me after it for not following the doctor's orders. But it isn't every day we send a Ronayne to the State House."

"We?" Francis raised his eyebrows.

Hanlon struck a match and took a long pull on the cigar, blowing out the smoke with a long, satisfied sigh. "Sure. Didn't I say a word in the right places for the boy? You did not think I would stand idly by and let that omadhaun humiliate our Martin, did you?"

"Wait a minute, Jim. Marty and Mike did pretty well for *themselves*."

"That is so." Hanlon nodded. "But there are them that would have voted for O'Neil if he was the divvil himself, did they not get the word through O'Malley that old Terry had outlived his usefulness."

"You'd have a hard time convincing Marty of that. By the way, where were you tonight? The new Representative was quite upset when you didn't drop around or phone. Did you get his message?"

"I did. It is over there on that little table. I got it about eleven
when I came home from the polls more dead than alive. I was hardly
able to take my few drops and cart myself in here. I woke a half
hour ago, feeling like a new man indeed and wanting to read my
paper and have a few puffs. I'm itching to call the boy in the
respectable hours of the morning. It is that proud I am of him."

"That's what I thought. I told him you were probably flat on
your back. When are you going to give in, Jim; turn things completely over to Timmy and take things easy?"

"Give in?" Hanlon held his cigar close to his chest as if he had
just been told that O'Malley was in jail and the sheriff was on
his way to arrest the political boss of all Charlestown. "Give in?"
He looked glassily out the window into the fog-bound street. "I'd
be dead in a month, Franny. I'd much rather pass along while I'm
still on the job. The very thought of lying up here all alone, day
and night, with the life I've known and loved flowing by me down
there on the Hill is enough, Jesus forgive me, to make me want to
take the gas pipe."

"Don't say that, Jim. We wouldn't leave you all alone up here."

"I know you wouldn't, Franny, you and your mother. But there
is the cold finger of the Old Nick on my heart whenever I think
of retiring."

Francis nodded sympathetically and glanced at his watch. It was
after three. He could say *Lauds* now — perhaps it would be of some
consolation to Hanlon. He patted the right side of his chest. The
book was in his inside pocket.

"I could say the office of *Lauds* about now. You know — the little
book. Would you like to join me?"

Hanlon pushed aside the newspaper. It slithered off to the floor
on the other side of the bed.

"I'd like that fine, Franny. Then you're still at this monk business
you told me about some while ago."

Francis grinned. "It isn't that it's so monkish, Jim, it's just that
it's a good way of praying, I guess."

"And what does Catherine say about it all?"

"She doesn't know about it, Jim."

Hanlon's face went from red to purple and the cords stood out on his short, bullish neck. "Damn and blast it, man! Why don't you tell her these things! It's no wonder she has no more understanding of you than she has of a Chinese!"

"I thought it might upset her, Jim. Half a loaf isn't necessarily better than none where Mother is concerned."

"Well . . . well, all right, boy. Read your prayers. My old soul is sore with sin and pride. It is a lot of prayers I could stand. God help us all!" Hanlon blessed himself with swift economy.

Francis could not resist a smile at Hanlon's sudden and furious fervor. "Okay, Jim, I'll read the Latin first and then the English. You can say the English after me if you like."

"*Deus in adjutorium meum intende,*" Francis began. "Incline unto mine aid, O God."

"Incline unto mine aid, O God," Hanlon said.

Francis read on, pausing for J. P.'s repetitions. On through the canticle of David: " . . . Thine, O Lord, is magnificence, and power, and glory, and victory. And to Thee is praise, for all that is in heaven, and in earth, is Thine. . . . "

More praise than is given to the Democratic National Committee, to Mayor O'Malley in all of Boston, and to James Patrick Hanlon in all of Charlestown, Francis thought, listening to Hanlon repeat the phrase with increased fluency.

"Thine is the kingdom, O Lord, and Thou art above all princes." Above President Hoover, John D. Rockefeller, Henry Ford, and King George of England. Above Martin Lomasney, Erford Parkley, Sr., the DuPonts, and Metro-Goldwyn-Mayer.

". . . Thou hast dominion over all."

"*Sana animam meam,*" Francis chanted in the short responsory, "*quia peccavi tibi.* Heal my soul for I have sinned against Thee," he translated.

"Heal my soul for I have sinned against Thee," Hanlon repeated, making another lightning-like sign of the Cross as a tear bowled swiftly down his ruddy check.

He thought of the municipal building contracts he had once raffled to the highest bidders and of the time he had spent a champagne week end at Nantasket Beach with Maggie Quigley when she was saucy Peggy Norton, the girl with the prettiest ankles in the ward.

"*Sana animam meam, quia peccavi tibi,*" repeated Francis, seeing Hanlon's tears and thinking he must bring Father Carney over to see him soon.

"Heal my soul, for I have sinned against Thee," Hanlon intoned.

"We are filled in the morning with Thy mercy. We have rejoiced and are delighted."

Hanlon's head sank back in the pillow. He nodded, listening to Francis read the singing Latin of the Canticle of Zachary. "*Benedictus Dominus Deus Israel, quia visitavit, et fecit redemptionem plebis suae.* Blessed be the Lord God of Israel, because He hath visited and wrought the redemption of His people."

Hanlon mumbled sleepily. Francis read the rest of the prayers in silence. When he had finished, Hanlon was fast asleep, abandoned to peace like an infant.

He reached over, pulled the cord on the bed lamp, and tiptoed out of the room.

despite her father's cold disfavor. Erford, Martin gathered, seemed to take a conciliatory attitude toward the matter, but secretly, perhaps, sided with his sister. He was too fond of her not to sympathize with her profound unhappiness, Martin knew.

He had seen her once, around Thanksgiving time. Erford had invited him to join them in a drink at the Otis and, again, they had talked with each other in what they did not say. More than once during the time she was home he had been on the verge of calling her. Two prudential factors had restrained him: Erford, and the fact that she was still a married woman.

But soon she would be a divorced woman. Yet where would he come into the picture even then? It would be political suicide for an Irish Catholic to be seen stepping out with a divorcee — and she a Brahmin also. It would be hard if and when she returned to Boston to keep her out of his consciousness. Erford had said she would go to Bermuda for several months after the divorce. The Parkleys owned a plantation there and she would be well received. But she would come back eventually.

He would have to try and forget her, he would have to forget her as quickly and as completely as possible. It just wouldn't do. There was the chic, little school principal he had taken once to a School Committee reception — what was her name? — it was an odd one — Edwina Fanchon, that was it. She had gone to Vassar and was tingling with all the latest *avant-garde* ideas on education.

He swung around, picked up the phone, and asked the operator to get him Miss Fanchon at the "Margaret Fuller Girls' High School."

He got hold of her right away and he said the nice things about secondary education he knew she'd like to hear and she said the nice things about the state government she knew he'd like to hear. Then he asked her if she'd have dinner with him at the Copley on Saturday night and she said she'd love to.

He said good-by and listened to the phone make a hollow, mocking sound as he dropped it into its cradle.

He swung around again and faced the snow, the roofs, and the clouds. They all made one terrifying picture, cold and lovely in the blinding, winter morning sun; they all formed one lovely picture and its name was Althea.

So again he fled himself, fled into the outer self, the Honorable
Martin Ronayne who had a session of the House to attend that
afternoon. There would be a great to-do about new highways and
he would have to cast his vote on P.L. 742, as it was called.

He would have to rise and vote one way or the other — and since
he was a Democrat he would be expected to vote with the party so
that the roads along the coast and west to the Berkshires would not
be so bumpy next summer. He would be voting for contractors
Hogan and Bunelli so that they would have nice new cars to drive
along those nice new roads. But then, somebody had to build the
roads and the Republican contractors, given the opportunity, would
charge the state almost as much as the Democratic contractors. It
was just that the Democratic contractors were in and the Republican contractors were out.

Maybe O'Malley would think he was coming around and the
Parkleys would think he was drifting away, but the voters of Dorchester would read his name among those who had voted for im-
proved highways and simply conclude he was doing the job they
sent him to do.

He had delivered his maiden speech two weeks ago. It was full
of blood and thunder about "our duties to the people" and he had
received a tremendous round of applause from his colleagues of
both parties. But later at the cocktail party held in private rooms
at the Parker House for the new legislators, Mike had told him
they always give a big hand to the maiden speech and not to let it
bother him. Since no one had mentioned the speech, other than
Mike and his family, he concluded Mike's observation must have
been true. "They make you feel good your first time up," Mike
had said.

But they could all go to hell. He'd still pop off when the time
was right. And he *had,* just last week when they wanted to keep a
Socialist off the next gubernatorial ballot.

A Republican member had read some clause in the state con-
stitution which could be twisted into a slammed door for Socialists.
Martin got the floor and asked the gentleman from Westfield if he
had ever read the Bill of Rights in the national constitution. The
Socialist candidate under discussion happened to be a native-born
American citizen of good character and responsibility.

"Socialism, in its elevation of the rights of the State over the rights of the individual, runs contrary to the Christian ethical tradition upon which our form of government is built," Martin had declared, aware of the sensitive ears of the clergy and faithful of the archdiocese. "But until constitutional laws are passed in this country and this state outlawing Socialism, clearly and definitely, we would endanger the rights of every legitimate minority in this country by infringing upon the rights of a single citizen — Socialism notwithstanding."

There was a scattering of applause among the representatives and a big burst of it up in the gallery where several men in need of haircuts were holding up a crudely lettered sign which read: "DOWN WITH MONOPOLY CAPITALISM!"

They kept the Socialist off the ballot anyway, but the papers carried a story next morning on the courageous liberalism of the new representative from Dorchester. Mike, not at all self-conscious about his brother-in-law, belabored the point a little further in his column *The Hill and the Hall*, pointing out that Socialist threats to take the case to the Supreme Court must be considered quite seriously. "Representative Ronayne is to be commended for his forthright stand on civil rights."

The Parkleys, too, were pleased at the liberal twist Martin had given to an issue that was normally a political hot potato — especially in a community so conservative. Mr. Parkley had mentioned the matter to the Governor and there was a letter on Martin's desk inviting him to lunch with His Excellency, Foster S. Dahlwood, Governor of the Commonwealth.

Dahlwood, a somewhat progressive Republican, was confronted by a predominantly Democratic legislature which had him at its legislative mercy. He was attracted by the story of a green, young representative who had defied both parties in taking a brilliant stand for minority rights. He had heard that young Ronayne had come to the House without any strings attached to the O'Malley machine. Usually, in due course of time, such a solo Democrat left the House and organized politics without strings attached to anything. It would be interesting, as Parkley had pointed out, to hear what this young man had to say over a disarming bowl of oyster stew.

The buzzer on his desk "zitted" sharply. He clicked a switch. "Mister Hanlon and another gentleman are here, sir," Miss Modglin said.

"Fine, Miss Modglin, show them right in."

With a thumping bull rush of affection, Hanlon rushed through the doorway and threw an arm around Martin's shoulders. "How *are* you, boy? It did my black, old heart good to see your name on the door and you in this fine little office, looking as important as the governor himself."

"Thanks, Jim." Martin smiled, and arranged a chair next to his own. "How have you been feeling? Mother tells me you still get those spells."

"Oh, I get them all the time, now; it is the Lord's way of punishing me for my sins. I'd have been in to see you long before this if I'd had better legs under me." Hanlon turned to the neat, little man who lingered politely just inside the office door. "You've met the mayor's secretary, Brendan Kelly, have you not? Surely you two know each other by now."

"How are you?" Kelly offered a meticulously manicured hand. "I've heard a lot about you, Ronayne, but I don't believe I've ever had the pleasure."

"Same here," Martin said politely, shaking his hand. "Won't you sit down?"

He drew up a chair for the mayor's secretary. He sat, opened the leather cigarette case, and proffered it to both. Hanlon shook his head, and Kelly selected one with gracious ease.

After he gave Kelly a light, Martin said: "You see, Jim, I've put that swell leather set you sent me to good use. You got my note, did you?"

"I did. It was nothing at all — and the least I could do to let you know how much I respect the way you've gone on under your own power. Besides, it was the kind of set I've always wanted myself — there's a certain crazy satisfaction in giving that kind of thing to another."

Kelly chuckled. "We'll have to remember that, Jim."

"Never you mind," Hanlon said gruffly. "The day when I liked to sit behind a fancy desk is by me now. It is young bucks like you and Marty that need the fineries."

"As you say, Jim," Kelly said, unrebuffed. He took another puff on his cigarette, looked intently through the smoke at Martin who, he sensed, was a little impatient to get down to the real business of the visit. "Well, Ronayne, how are things in the House? P.L. 742 comes up today, I understand."

"Yes, it does." Martin was laconic, performing an easy noncommitment with several long drags on his cigarette.

Hanlon sat back in his chair with an attitude of friendly neutrality, making a knowing obtrusion with his thick, faintly bluish lips.

Kelly flickered his eyelashes in the smoke of his cigarette and continued: "Of course, you realize that Mayor O'Malley and your Democratic colleagues will be interested in the kind of a stand you'll be taking. We sure would like to feel you're one of us — in this."

"It's no great secret." Martin wrinkled his brow. "I don't see how any intelligent representative or senator, Republican or Democrat, could vote any way but 'yes' on the highway bill. No matter who gets the gravy — we've still got to have good highways."

"I'm happy to hear that," the mayor's secretary said. "We were wondering, you know. You usually take such an independent line — uh — Martin." He paused, showing his first sign of self-consciousness.

"We're surely glad to hear you're lining up with us on this, Marty," Hanlon said. "There's been talk you might throw your vote to the Governor. You know," he continued, turning over his gnarled right hand, "your friendship for the Parkleys and all."

Martin reddened.

Hanlon knew he had said the wrong thing almost before he finished saying it.

"If it's all the same to you, Jim," Martin said crisply, "the Parkleys have nothing to do with the way I vote — nor, with all due respects," he nodded at Kelly, "has Ed O'Malley."

"Forgive me, Marty-boy," Hanlon said intensely. "You've no need to tell me that. It is no secret that you stand on your own two feet. Your father was the same. Didn't you drive a knife into the heart of me by being your own honest self? It is just that there is a lot of blather going on — it's the talk I meant, not you."

"That's okay, Jim. Talk is cheap."

"Yes," Kelly said, bringing his words shrewdly to bear on Martin, "and promising young public servants like yourself are too rare to be hurt by it. We want to help you stay right out in the open, Martin, we really do. I know what you'll say — we want to help ourselves, too. Well, it's true, only 'ourselves' are the people, Martin. We represent the Democratic party, never forget that."

"I haven't forgotten it. Although I'm of the conviction that democrats are where you find them."

Kelly was unrebuffed. He was ready with the big pitch. "What would you say if I told you that the Mayor is going to run for governor next fall?"

"I'd say the rumors we've been hearing around the Hill are well founded."

"Hear him out, Marty," Hanlon said with a note of almost desperate kindliness.

"And what would you say if Jim and I told you we thought O'Malley might be persuaded to take you along as attorney general?" Kelly said, fixing his soft, gray eyes on Martin.

Martin chilled and his mouth itched with dryness. So this was it. Attorney General . . . a steppingstone to the governorship itself. This was the most tempting political bait ever cast before him. He savored it eagerly, his heart beating quicker, lighter. But it had the opium of O'Malley in it, the bittersweet soporific of the machine.

"It's very attractive," he said. He was silent for several moments. "It's *extremely* attractive, but — well — I just couldn't accept. I'm sorry."

"Oh," Kelly said, cooling. He had gone as far as he was empowered to go. He had made the big pitch . . . this kid was a waste of time. They'd have to break him at the polls . . . he'd have trouble lecturing to the Sunday schools when they got through with him.

"Marty, Marty-boy!" Hanlon said. "Holy Jay-zuz, man, it's the chance of a lifetime and you're kicking it away."

"I'm sorry, Jim. You know as well as I do what's involved. I wouldn't fit in the organization — it just wouldn't work — we might as well avoid all that right now."

"Well, it's been nice seeing you, anyway," Kelly said coolly.

"Yes, it was good of you to come in," Martin said.

Big Jim shook hands slowly with Martin, covering their grip with his other hand. "I'll say no more, Marty — you've a mind of your own. Perhaps I'll see you at your mother's one of these days."

"Sure thing, Jim, and thanks so much for dropping in. Take care of yourself."

"My old pump has more kick in it than the sawbones will concede. You should hear it thumping after I've had a nip or two."

Laughter and exit. The swivel chair again, the snow, the roofs, the sky and lunch with the Governor looming. "Representative Ronayne had no sooner turned down a chance at the attorney-generalship than it was time to lunch with the Governor," he thought, chuckling a little feverishly. He glanced at his watch — 11:15 — he'd just have time to duck out for a haircut before meeting the Governor and Mr. Parkley at the Bellevue.

As he snapped his hat off the rack and walked out of his office, he thought of how O'Malley's face would look when Kelly told him he had turned down the offer. Maybe the benign, patrician face would redden and the rolling, Ciceronian tongue would utter a lusty string of Anglo-Saxon epithets.

He walked briskly through the resounding halls of the State House feeling the warm excitement of his decision, yet not quite sure which was stronger in him — the feeling of conquest or the urge to run and hide. But the Governor had summoned him to the Bellevue and he would go over there without traces trailing or traces to kick over.

But what now, he asked himself, walking the floors that Calvin Coolidge had walked, mingling his footfalls with the ghostly echoes of Henry Cain Brattle. He had thought long and conscientiously about Erford's repeated implications that he go over to the Republican Party and ally himself with its more liberal elements. Governor Dahlwood was such a Republican liberal, a democratic Republican, you might say. He came from the western part of the state where the normal, town-meeting democracy of rural Republicans seemed at variance with the stiff-necked economic royalism of the Bostonian.

Such a Republican candidate, Martin knew, was always certain of winning a good percentage of the votes of Democrats dissatisfied with machine politics. On the other hand, Martin believed that a liberal, unfettered Democrat stood a fairly good chance of garnering votes from the rural and small-town areas where many Republicans were down-to-earth people, unconcerned with the financial importunities of the State Street and Wall Street Republicans.

Yet as Boston went, so went the governorship. Thus, O'Malley, unassailably secure in his appeal to the Boston Irish-Catholic electorate, would only have to poll a moderate amount of votes in the larger cities of western Massachusetts in order to be elected.

And Irish-Catholic Boston, the key to state-wide electoral success, would inevitably deal a lethal political blow to any Catholic candidate who ran on the Republican ticket. The pioneering urgency of the Parkleys notwithstanding, Martin valued the mind of his parents on this matter far above anyone else. You could change political parties in a state like Wisconsin with an impunity commensurate with diplomacy and your personal integrity, but in Boston, where democracy was perilously close to theocracy, you had better keep mindful of the clergy and the faithful.

The Governor and Mister Parkley would probably tell him the same thing as Hanlon had — that he had better ally himself with a faction if he was to survive politically— and since he seemed unalterably opposed to the O'Malley machine, why not come over to them?

Why not? Why not? His thoughts metronomed as he descended the broad, stone stairs and crunched along the snow of Beacon Street, toward the Lincolnshire's barber shop. Tell them why not, Mother. Tell them why not, Jim Hanlon and Father Quinn. Why not, Monsignor? Why not, Bishop? Why not, Your Eminence? Tell the Governor why not. Yes, Your Eminence, tell the Governor what His Honor knows profoundly. . . .

Chapter 23

IF YOU were a Charlestownite, you could not blame Hoover for the depression on Bunker Hill Day, the 17th of June — there would be too much seeing, too much jubilation on that day. You could blame him for the bread lines and the men idling on the corners during the slate-gray weariness of February and March, during the mud and the wind and the rain of April, amid the chill, fish-redolent breezes of Easter Sunday; you could be nostalgic about Al Smith in May as the urchins were skipping rope on the sidewalks and some Harvard student had had the nerve to take the first illegal dive off the Lars Anderson Bridge — you could blame Hoover in May in that nostalgic way, wondering, if you were a Demo, when the Demos would give the country back to the people again.

But on the flat tar roof of Hanlon's tenement, standing in the tar that was soft and pungent, kneaded by the hot hand of the maturing sun, Francis and John were not in a blameful mood. They leaned on the wooden parapet, watching and listening, as the sonorous brass of endless high school bands thumped and winked hugely beneath them.

This was Charlestown's big day. What the Fourth of July was to the rest of the country, the Seventeenth of June was to Charlestown.

Francis nudged John as a helmeted, khaki-clad platoon swung around the corner at the bottom of the hill. "The Guards."

"Yeh. Shiner O'Neil and some more of the gang are marching — that's about the only way they'll get to go through the trap."

Before the construction of the barriers, there had been few
Bunker Hill Day eves in recent years on which a "commemorative"
loop had not taken place, bringing in the holiday with whooping
horn and screaming brakes.

They watched the Guards trudging through the traps while the
band up ahead broke into the strains of the field artillery song,
"Over hill, over dale . . ." Francis hummed, his blood quickening
with the music.

"Come on, John, snap out of it," Francis said. "Charlestown's
finest are down there — schooled in danger and daring at seventy-
five miles an hour."

John nodded and the small, wise map on the hairy, red globe
wrinkled amiably, letting the sun into its darker corners.

The Guards were down there — the mudguards, they were called
with a certain sarcastic affection. With the depression there were
more of them now than ever — drill once a month — six weeks of
maneuvers in the summer — march all day, drink all night. Strike-
breakers, riot quellers, paraders, and inevitably among the first to
go and make the world safe for democracy, Great Britain, and
Standard Oil.

Above them, where a lone cloud loitered, like some exquisite
snowy corsage on a great gown of blue, several rickety National
Guard planes droned about, zooming and spinning above the
marchers and the crowd.

Francis looked across the roofs to the busy habor, the ships and
small boats making their green, foamy furrows, the Navy Yard,
alive with bunting, its gray, sharklike vessels bobbing patiently at
their moorings.

The brass, the banners, and the uniforms bobbled tunefully
around the corner, up and over the Hill, flaunting their kaleido-
scopic vitality in the face of the cold, crunching death symbolized by
the jaws of the traps.

Francis thought of the two young loopers who had impaled
themselves challengingly on those municipal reefs. Their death
seemed all the more lamentable because of the singing summer life,
throbbing all about him. He breathed a prayer for them, and
danger-minded, found himself thinking of Alice Little and the
impending birth of her child.

"Just what I was about to suggest. I'd like to call Alice, too."

"Say, you can call from Hanlon's place, right downstairs. I've got a key."

They went down through the skylight to the hall outside Hanlon's apartment.

While John made the call in Hanlon's bedroom, Francis ran his eyes over the dreary, repetitious catalogue of clerical and club-women names in the latest copy of the *Beacon*. The Cardinal was attacking Hollywood again this week and several doe-faced young men were leaving for the seminary.

The sem. Father Quinn had run his picture, he remembered, just like these kids. He had had the same, scared look, too. He wondered how Emmet Callahan and Tubby Thomas were getting along. They were hectically busy — he rarely heard from them, and it seemed their world and his were separated by a universe of space and time. They would be ordained in a year.

He looked up from the paper, sensing John's return. He stood in the bedroom doorway, his eyes lowered, his large head carried a little to the right.

"I think I better be getting back to the house. Alice doesn't answer the phone — she must have gone out to the store or something, but I think I'd better go home anyway."

"Sure, John — I'll go with you. She must have gone to the store."

They went down the stairway, out to the seethingly joyous sidewalk. The paraders were taking a break. They pushed and jostled their way through to the street. A beefy cop brogued out some kind of an order. They ignored him and trotted across the street, pushing again into the roisterous depths of the onlookers, drunk and sober, jobbed and jobless, making their carnival fearlessly in the face of tomorrow's empty cupboards and tomorrow's rent collectors.

They hurried up Lexington Avenue toward the Monument and John's house. There were flurries of people on the roofs, the porches. But the knot of older women standing and talking with taut faces outside the Little tenement conveyed that which they had not quite allowed themselves to believe.

John exchanged a few strained words with Mrs. Piatrek, the

plump, compassionate housewife, who lived across the hall. Alice had fallen down the back stairs while emptying the garbage and had been seized with abdominal pains. Mr. Piatrek, with the kindest of cruelty, had racketed her across the bridge to the Chelsea Hospital in his old Chevrolet.

"Anyone call Doctor McDonald?" John asked woodenly, knowing it was the right question, filled with a frenzy to run wildly in some direction that would get him quickly to Alice.

"Yes," Mrs. Piatrek said, "your wife asked me to call. The doctor's on his way to the hospital."

"Let's go, Fran." There was a crazy note in John's voice. Let's go before she is gone, he seemed to say, before all my life is gone, before the world dies and laughter dies and love and hope and joy.

They broke into a run down the hill toward City Square and a taxicab. They trotted briskly, with a kind of marathonic desperation, through the gay streets and past the porches and windows festooned with immigrant peoples who were celebrating with a curious patriotism, the brawling of farmers and redcoats on Breed's Hill over a century and a half before.

At the square they scrambled into a cab and soon were winding with maddening slowness through the traffic jam which had congealed at the tail end of the parade.

"Maybe we ought to get out and run for it," John said.

"It's too far for that, John. He'll get moving."

When they had crawled past Bunker Hill Street, the traffic lightened and the driver wheeled faster over the Chelsea Bridge.

While Alice writhed between eternity and earth, while the taxi played a squeaking symphony on its scores of tired body bolts, there was feasting and gaiety in the apartment of Catherine Ronayne. For there the present was ever fraught with evocation of the mellow if elusive past.

Tinkling their glasses and their wit at each other in the parlor, before sitting down to Catherine's traditional Bunker Hill Day lunch of baked ham and potato salad were Father Quinn, Mike Farrell, and the rising young state representative from Dorchester. Catherine and Rosemary were in the kitchen.

"You know the proof for the absence of human life on the planet Mars, don't you?" Father Quinn asked dryly, pecking at his Scotch.

Mike winced and Martin smiled that politic smile for which he was becoming well known.

"Okay, let's have it, Father," Mike said. "It can't be much worse than some of the others I've heard you get off."

Father Quinn was not to be wounded out of his little joke.

"The Jesuit missions don't have anybody up there on their mailing list."

Martin intended his laugh to be a polite one but it came out of him quite involuntarily. Father Quinn was ribbing the Jebbies again. Mike Farrell made another pert face and finished his highball. "I really need another one after that — join me?" He got up from the sofa.

"I'll stay," Father Quinn said, making an amiable little motion with his glass. "I don't usually have a refresher this early in the day. This is an occasion, however — I haven't missed one of your mother's Bunker Hill Day lunches in fifteen years."

"When Dad was alive, I remember, we used to hold open house, all day," Martin said. He nodded at Mike and handed him his glass. Mike thumped down the hall with the glasses, humming a warm, indistinguishable song.

"Yes," the priest said, as though Martin had almost given the right answer in a history exam. "Charlestown was more like Back Bay then in an Irish social way, that is — there were more of the high-Irish like your mother around. Now they've all moved away to Dorchester and Belmont and Newton, away from the elevated trains, the Sugar House and the aromatic Mystic River."

"They're all gone now," Martin said, practicing a mellow phrase he would be able to use with much greater sincerity in ten years.

"Yes." The priest took another sip. "But you needn't be so nostalgic. It was our world — Catherine, your father, Hanlon, myself. Your world is all about you and you seem to have quite a chunk of it in your grasp already. How are things up on the Hill? What are your plans for the fall, if any?"

That was a big question coming from the clerical editor of a powerful diocesan weekly — it was a big question even when posed informally over a glass by an old and trusted friend of his mother. He heard the glasses tinkling in the hall and was glad Mike would be around when he attempted to answer it.

"Here I am again — stoutly fortified against any and all clerical jokes," Mike said, handing Marty his drink.

"Father wants to know my plans for the fall."

"Tell him," Mike said with the choleric impatience that could be mistaken for anger. "We're going to break it in the papers after the first of July, anyway. This is strictly off the record until then, Father."

"Mike has persuaded me to take out papers for attorney general this fall," Martin began. "He says he'll ask for a three months' leave of absence and manage my campaign. Mike argues that if O'Malley thinks I could be elected, we should feel the same way."

"Does O'Malley?" Father Quinn raised his eyebrows coolly.

Mike took a swig of his highball. "You're practically one of the family. Tell him, Marty."

Catherine and Rosemary entered the dining room, their hands heavy with steaming platters of sliced ham and potato salad. In the kitchen young Mike could be heard, pounding a spoon on the tray of his high chair.

"We'll be ready for you in just a few moments," Catherine said. "Has Francis come in?"

"Not yet, Mother," Martin said.

There was a crash and the mocking tinkle of broken crockery in the kitchen. Rosemary sped out of the dining room.

"Gracious!" Catherine said, hurrying after her.

"Your son grows impatient with convention already," Father Quinn said, chuckling.

"A good sign in a child of the new Boston," Mike said.

The new Boston, Martin thought. That was a phrase — that was a dream. The old Boston, as a phrase, suggested almost exclusively, he felt, the mercantile oligarchy, the Boston of the Brahmins. Theocratic Boston was old, yet only recently had it come into power. What would the Boston of the priests and the hierarchy — symbolized right here in this parlor by its leading clerical propagandist — what would theocratic Boston have to say about his imminent state-wide defiance of the O'Malley machine? For, no matter what could be said against the ethics of the machine, it was certainly good to the Church. While the Church could never countenance many of the machine's methods, it nonetheless was the recipient of much financial patronage, directly or indirectly attributable to the social consciences or the guilty consciences, or both, of powerful Catholic politicians.

It was no great secret in Boston that one of the heaviest contributors to diocesan fund drives was none other than His Honor. Jim Hanlon, himself, could kneel in his parish church and see about him the stained-glass windows which were the result of his philanthropy.

Martin knew that no matter what Father Quinn's personal feelings were, he could be expected to make a diplomatic reaction to the news that the mayor's own choice for attorney general would run for the office with an independence that unmistakably implied defiance.

"Where were we?" the priest asked.

"I was about to say that last winter I was approached by two of O'Malley's lieutenants — one of whom you know very well — and was told that the big boss would like to have me on the gubernatorial ticket as a candidate for attorney general."

The priest made a little bird cage of his fingers. "You refused?"

"I did."

"Sure he did!" Mike said. "What else could he do, after the way he's gone it on his own?"

"You needn't burst a blood vessel, Michael," Father Quinn said. "I think it all very laudable. However," he added meaningfully, "I wouldn't care to wager any money on your chances of being nominated in a state-wide contest. You have neither the money nor the organization for a state-wide campaign, you realize."

"We're well aware of it, Father. The *Beacon* wouldn't want to subsidize good government for twenty grand or so, would it?" Mike asked, smiling slyly.

"Really, Michael," Father Quinn said with more of his amiable impatience. "Even you would admit that the *Beacon* does not dabble in politics. That is not to say, however —" he raised his eyes in Martin's direction — "that we would be editorially unsympathetic to a young man who seems to have the courage and ability to stand up and fight the old guard in the name of what he believes to be more honest and more progressive government."

"Thanks, Father," Martin said, surprised. "It's nice of you to take that attitude."

"I'm not taking any stand on the matter at all — nor could I, until your actions or O'Malley's appeared to jeopardize in any way the spiritual welfare of the faithful."

"Could I quote that in my column?" Mike asked facetiously.

"You'll do nothing of the kind."

"Oh, you don't want to be in my column, eh?"

"No, thank you," the priest said, rising. "Are you fellows as hungry as I am?"

"Not me," Mike said. "I'm saving my appetite for tonight."

"If you mean the Bunker Hill Day banquet at the armory," the priest said, walking toward the hall, "I much prefer what comes off the skillet of Cathcrine Ronayne."

As his self-assured footsteps echoed down the hall, they looked at each other smiling.

"Well, Martin, the diocesan press won't hurt you."

"He took it nicely," Martin said absently, thinking about the banquet, which he planned to attend.

Hanlon had sent him an invitation, scrawling a note beneath the formal engraving: "Charlestown is proud of you, even though we did not put you in office. Try and be there, Marty. It will do you no harm."

"You're going to the banquet, eh?" Martin asked Mike.

"Yeh. The Gov will be there, I guess. He may give me an idea or two for the column."

"The Gov will not be there," Martin said. "I was talking to Erford on the phone this morning. His Excellency is upstate on personal business. The Honorable Erford Parkley Senior will represent him."

"Oh. I see where Rosemary and I will be dining at home then. We won't want to sit through all that just to hear a canned message from old Parkley — I can get what I need from one of the boys."

Old Parkley, Martin thought, as a pall of silence settled over the parlor, broken only by the clink of dishes and the hum of voices in the kitchen.

Old Parkley. Old Parkley's daughter.

He had not seen her since her return from Bermuda. He had wanted to get in touch with her, but decided it would be best to wait. Wait, that was integral in the art of living on all levels — wait until the right moment to eat or run for office or love — wait.

Then he felt upon his spirit, heavy, prudent, and wise, the strong and ancient hand of his Church and sensed with a chill that Althea, a non-Catholic and a divorcee, could not be for him. He knew that the love he bore for Althea was the one ungovernable force in his being — he knew if he flung open the door of that love, the flame would roar up and reduce to ashes the carefully engineered structure of his life.

If he had been a praying man, he would have prayed at that moment. And perhaps he did, perhaps, in a way, he did — knowing that he might have to choose one or the other, knowing that either way there lay ahead for him suffering and loneliness, with or without the woman of his heart.

Mike pushed himself to his feet. "I'm going to see just what they're doing out there."

After he had gone the phone rang.

"I'll get it," Martin called. "It's probably my itinerant brother."

"Hello — hello, Marty." It was Francis. "Tell Mother I'm at the Chelsea Hospital. Alice is here, they rushed her here, the baby is coming. . . ."

"Well, how is she?"

"We don't know yet. She's on her way to the delivery room. Tell Mother I won't be home for lunch. I'll grab a bite here maybe."

"All right. But let us know how Alice and the baby are as soon as you can. Do you want to speak to Mother? She's out in the kitchen."

"Never mind. I want to get back to John."

"All right. I'll tell Mother. Let us know."

"I will. So long."

For several moments, Martin stood by the phone after hanging up. He came to sharply, turned, and strode down the hall calling: "Mother, Mother. . . ."

Chapter 24

THE clock on the wall in the maternity ward waiting room is the only face therein that does not change. It does not change, come life or death, come hope, despair, or topmost joy; it ticks in the silence, amid the whispers, the strangled cries of joy and pride, amid the striking of matches, the crinkling of magazines and newspapers, the pad and click of furtive and official feet; and occasionally it ticks indifferently away amid the sobs of men from whom a little life has been taken or a big life — it ticks and ticks, the metronome of patience, measuring the length of dread and hope, of small, evasive talk, of wild elation, and sometimes the mouth dryness and speechlessness of death that is more of yourself than yourself.

Through the window of the door opening into the Fathers' Room, Francis, returning from the hall phone booth, could see the bland face of the clock, like some imperturbable, white-faced cow, chewing with patient, invariable rhythm, the endless cud of time.

It was one-fifteen as he opened the door, entered, and sat down beside John on a soughing leather cushion. John, pretending to read a *Collier's* story, did not look up.

"Heard anything more?" Francis asked, picking up a copy of the *Daily World* and glancing at a small apple-shaped Italian of middle age who sat primly on a metal chair directly across from them.

"The nurse was in a minute ago," John said tonelessly. "They're still holding Alice outside the delivery room."

"Oh! I called Mother."

"You're going home, aren't you?"

"I told them I'd be late, John. We can get a bite later on, huh?"

"Yeh, later on."

The little Italian across the way smiled at them — a smile that went from hesitancy almost to amusement.

John was again looking at the magazine, but Francis winged a glance at the little man which almost said: "What the hell's so funny?"

The little man flushed and looked at the floor for a few moments. Then he raised his head and smiled a broad, even smile.

"I smile because I remember my first time," he said softly and in a slow, rich way, giving the cold English words a Latin warmth they do not quite deserve. "Now I am here five times," he added, smiling again and nodding his head with sad, wide eyes. "That is a good wife in there — I can tell by him." He motioned at John. "She will do her best for him and the small one."

A wrinkle of easement touched John's features. He did not look up from the magazine.

Now it was Francis who nodded amiably, taking the tender pinch of unsolicited love on behalf of John. He thought of that line from Keats he had once puzzled over in a seminary English exam. You had to tell what kind of figure of speech it was. The little Italian had taught him its real meaning forever. "O, for a beaker of the warm south . . . " would never be merely a figure of speech again.

O, for a beaker of the warm south to fill the icy pit of loneliness in John Little; O, for a beaker of the warm Alice and the new baby Little to fill the cistern of loneliness in John.

Francis offered John a cigarette, which he refused. He lighted one for himself.

"Have you been waiting long?" Francis asked the man, trying to make up for his initial rudeness.

"From ten o'clock," said the father of almost-five. "The wife, she's in there now."

There was silence again, the silence of impending birth so eloquent with dammed-up joy and that tenuous, over-the-shoulder icy breath of tragedy.

John read on. Francis stabbed out his cigarette. The Italian sat in his kind, philosophical halo, waiting for the certainty of lusty, yowling number five and Maria, bouncing buxomly, writhing to be at the washing machine again.

Francis glanced at the clock; it was close to two.

"Think I'll get a drink," he said. He touched John on the shoulder. John looked up and projected some softness out of the set hardness of his features. He returned to the magazine.

Francis went out into the corridor. He walked to the drinking fountain and swallowed a mouthful of the stinging ice water.

He heard the door of the delivery room open in the distance; there were the cushy squeak of wheels, the padding, whispery movement of nurses, the thin, muted whimper of a newborn child. Another door squeaked in the waiting room. He heard the ritualistic congratulations from the obstetrician and then the short, sharp yip of the little Italian's joy.

The door squeaked again, the eager feet shuffled, and Francis' ears were teased briefly, liquidly, with a sibilant flutter of Italian sounds. The only word he could discern in the poetry that the Latin uttered as he walked was "Maria." It was said with music and with love, whispered with wine-like warmth and zephyr-touched with tenderness.

It made Francis think all the more sharply of Alice and John — Alice drawing agonizingly close to her time; John in the waiting room, knowing in the exuberant joy of the little Italian, his own potential joy and his own potential sorrow.

He hurried back.

In the barny, flag-festooned armory at nine-thirty that same evening, Martin sat at the right wing of the head table, toying with a coffee spoon and listening abstractedly to Jim Hanlon. He could see Althea at the center of the head table, dressed in impeccable white linen, a little shy and more than a little lovely.

J. P. was telling him that things looked good for O'Malley in the gubernatorial the coming fall. "And if I know you at all, boy, you might be in there running for something yourself, with or without O'Malley's backing."

Martin smiled without averting his gaze. Hanlon was too nice to come right out and ask him his plans.

"I may be in there somewhere, Jim — I can't tell you any more than that right now. But what I said to you and Kelly still goes. With all due respects, I prefer to go it without O'Malley's patronage."

"I understand that, Marty." Hanlon lifted his ginger-ale glass and reached under the table for the half-pint bottle of rye he had secreted there. He splashed a good measure into the ginger ale.

"Say, I thought that stuff wasn't good for your heart condition," Martin said.

"That is what the doctor is saying. But I'd be gone to my rest long ago was it not for the little taste I take now and again. Would you like a little in your coffee?"

The banqueters were smoking, munching their pie and ice cream, sipping their coffee. Their center of focus was the head table, where O'Malley sat in a palm-beach suit. There, too, at the right of the master of ceremonies — a kindly looking, old gentleman attired almost incongruously in the brassy and braidy trappings of the Ancient and Honorable Artillery — sat the Governor's representative and his wan, attractive daughter.

The speakers would be introduced soon. It would be good to have a little something to make all the oratory bearable, Martin thought with amusement. Batteries of electric fans, elevated at both ends of the hall were attempting vainly to sustain a comfortable temperature. But the heat and humidity of a June night in Boston were relentless. Collars wilted and handkerchiefs were soggy. The speeches would be an ordeal.

"Don't mind if I do," Martin said. "I don't want it in the coffee, though. I'll flag down a girl and get some ginger ale."

"That is the good boy," Hanlon said, "a little taste will help you ride out all the wind that is soon to come our way."

Martin looked again in the direction of Althea. He had watched her all during dinner, hoping to catch her eye. But her glances had performed a little, exclusive periphery made up of her father, the unfamiliar official who sat at her right, and the tables directly in front of her. She looked with definiteness, neither to the right nor left wings of the head table. It was almost as if she knew he might be there.

He could not be sure whether her seeming timidity indicated

fear or propriety. There would be dancing after the speeches —
a great, humid rhythm of sweltering people going through the
tuneful calisthenics that they might become more congenially hot.
He would approach her then, pay his respects to Mr. Parkley and
ask her to dance.

But the Parkleys might leave right after the speeches. He could
not chance it. He would send her a note.

Hanlon was mumbling thickly to the man on his left when the
waitress returned with the ginger ale. Martin slipped out his card
case and scrawled a few words on one of the tiny white
rectangles. "Would you give this to Miss Parkley, please — she's the
young woman at the head table."

Hanlon poured a good-sized dollop into Martin's glass. "I'll take
a little more myself, while I'm at it," he added.

"Here's how," Martin said, drinking.

"A short life to the divvil," Hanlon said.

The toastmaster was pushing back his chair when the waitress
slipped up behind Althea. Martin watched her tautly.

The toastmaster clamored against a glass pitcher with the heavy
end of a steak knife. The talking and laughter subsided, lost in
the sporadic creaking and scraping of chairs.

The waitress whispered at Althea's shoulder. She received the
card, glanced at it, almost as if she had expected it and knew
what it would say.

"Fellow citizens of Charlestown . . . " began the kindly old
man in the uniform reminiscent of a South American dictator.

Erford Parkley, Sr., took his eyes off his notes long enough to
smile at his daughter. She returned his smile and he went back to
his notes after a confident look at his audience. He had noticed
two unusual patches of white in her cheeks. But her smile re-
assured him.

The toastmaster made the usual jingoistic remarks about
the Battle of Bunker Hill and Charlestown's glorious role in
the building and preservation of the nation. But no matter what
he said or how he said it, to Althea, her eyes fixed on the table,
he was repeating Martin's message over and over again.

Martin had written: "Hello. Might I see you in the lobby for
a moment after the speeches?"

"The same Charlestown spirit of freedom is still abroad *in the lobby for a moment after the speeches . . .* " the toastmaster seemed to be saying.

She slipped her hand into the pocket of her white linen jacket and gripped the hard, thin coolness of the card. "See him! See him!" her heart said wildly. She crumpled the card until it was a cracked little ball.

She lifted her head and sought his eyes. She looked to the left vainly; she swung her eyes eagerly across the audience to the right, making the visual arc that might eventually describe a rainbow of ruin over the conventional pattern of their lives.

Finally, she saw him. They caught each other's eyes. They smiled at each other through the rosy glow of the patriotic platitudes.

"So without further introduction, I give you the Honorable Erford Parkley, representing His Excellency, the Governor of the Commonwealth, who will speak to us *in the lobby for a moment after the speeches. . . .* "

The speeches were over. Erford Parkley, His Honor, and several others had said their patriotic say. The orchestra was tuning up and Martin puffed on a cigarette in the lobby. He stood by a glass trophy case awaiting her coming. The strength seemed to have drained from his legs, reminding him of the morning he made his maiden speech in the state assembly. He would have to make a kind of speech to her, he knew, and it would perhaps be taken much more seriously than the boys on Beacon Hill had taken his first offering.

There was an exodus of young couples. Many of them were lingering about the lobby now, sipping cold drinks and waiting for the music to begin.

Outside, through the open doors, he could see a cool, diamond mosaic of stars. The sight of them, high in the ebony distance, seemed to make the oppressive heat slightly more bearable. He wished now he'd borrowed Mike's car — it would be good to take Althea for a drive, that is, if she'd want to leave her dad.

Then he saw her moving along slowly, searchingly, through the clusters of soggy, mutually commiserating people.

"There you are!" she said, her face, her lips, her eyes quickening with relief. "Can we please get out of this place?"

"Just what I was thinking." He took her by the elbow and walked her toward the exit. They stepped from the heat of the armory into the heat of the outside world.

He noticed her calm, unruffled appearance. Her hair, suit, make-up were still quite presentable. It must be some trick they teach them at exclusive finishing schools, he thought — some way to keep their noses powdered even when the ship is going down.

They descended the staircase and stood in the humid darkness looking at each other.

He took her hand. "I'd rather despaired of getting to see you at all."

"And I, Martin. You've been doing well, I know."

"I don't seem to have done too well with you, Althea."

An elevated train made its brief, brawling clangor near by. Althea followed the train with her eyes, sensing in the lusty chaos of its passing a kinship with the feelings Martin had aroused within her.

Then there followed silence within her and without, broken only by that which does not seriously violate silence — the sound of neighborhood voices and laughter, the lone honk of a horn, the fall of feet against the pavements, the sweet, high-pitched singing of tenement children.

"I — I haven't given you much chance, Martin. And besides, I'm not the fresh young thing I used to be, you know. Then there are your people, your career. Perhaps it's best . . . "

"Perhaps it's best that we go for a ride and talk things over. I can hail a cab. We might go down to the North Shore — there'd be a breeze of some kind."

"I have my roadster," she said, almost too quickly, as though she was afraid to reason about it any further. "Dad was chatting with Mister Beasley who has his car with him. I'm sure he'd take him home. I'll drop back and see Dad for a moment."

He watched her spring up the steps, lithe and lovely, fresh among the wilting. He watched her go, knowing his heart went with her, away from all the gnawing and ecstatic longing for public greatness. . . .

"Paper, mister?"

A redheaded newsboy with a pure, impish face was holding up a copy of the *Daily Camera.*

"Sure, kid." He gave the newsboy a dime and glanced at the mammoth pictures of the parade.

"Ain't you Representative Ronayne?" the newsboy asked.

Martin nodded amiably.

"I seen your picture in the *Camera* once," he said a little shyly and then walked away.

The newsboy's acknowledgment added a note of poignancy to his inner debate. He concentrated on the paper.

The troops, the bands, the flags and floats seemed images without meaning. He couldn't get the idea of renouncement out of his head. Why am I so wrapped up in all this? Maybe Althea won't have me, or maybe we could work things out if I am elected.

If I am elected. . . .

Then he saw her coming down the steps. She was smiling and there was an air of excitement about her that lightened his heart and made his fears seem stupid and ugly. They fell away from him like sodden cerements of the grave as he hurried to greet her.

They rolled smoothly through the tropical oppressiveness of the night. They left the elevated uprights at Sullivan Square and purred down Middlesex Avenue toward the Fellsway and the North Shore.

They talked about everything but themselves, knowing, no matter what they said or how they said it, they really meant: "We are together."

They shot over the cobblestones past the mammoth plant of International Grocery.

"I worked in there when I was at Ignatian College. I worked in the beverage department. They have a great, frigid tank of crystal-clear water in there. I used to pause sometimes and look at my face in it. It was the purity of the water that attracted me."

"Like Narcissus," she said smiling into the windshield and handling the wheel in a firm, graceful way that told you she had been driving her own car since she was sixteen.

"Like who?"

"Like Narcissus, the ancient Greek who fell in love with his image. I saw your face in a pool once."

"Where?"

"In Wisconsin."

"Did you like it?"

"That's telling," she said. "I was reading that lovely, singing F. Scott book you gave me. I was out in the woods reading by a little pool. There was some way the shadows of the branches came together that reminded me of you."

"Wisconsin," he said cryptically.

They sped by the Ford plant where people were looking through the windows at the bluish artificial daylight and the relentless, giant erector set that is an assembly line.

"It's beautiful in the summer and fall out there if you can keep your mind on it," she said.

The breezes were cooler now, sifting in from the sea. He talked of his plans for the fall, how he would run for attorney general independently. "If I get the nomination, he'll have to support me anyway — unless he wants a Republican in there. I figure, too, I may pick up a few Republican votes."

"I'm sure you will — once it gets around that you're not geared up to the machine. I know a few people that will vote for you already. I'm sure of at least one," she said, smiling.

He reached over to the wheel and covered one of her hands. "That's a vote I thought I'd never get."

She smiled again and they drove swiftly on in silence, streaking along beside the astringent marshes and the wide, thin sheets of coolness spread out by the flooding tide.

Now they could see the lights of the amusement center along Revere Beach. They saw the Ferris wheel making its tawdry bright circle against the summer night; they heard the piquant pipings of a merry-go-round, and above them, in the winking distance, on its crazy trestle, the rattle and roar of the roller coaster.

"It must be thrilling," she said.

The car was caught now in a long, toiling jam of drivers, seeking what they were seeking, the drinklike succor of an ocean breeze.

The lights of the roller coaster were no longer pinpoints above a black mass of wooden stilts. The great, spidery bulk loomed over them now as the traffic moved slowly along. Again there was the chilling rush of the clattering, swaying carriages and, again, the screams of women charging the night for an instant with an ecstasy of fright.

"Have you ever been on it?" Martin asked.

"No." She looked up at the big drop, the long, steep plane that evoked all those screams.

"There's always a first time. What do you say?"

"It would be wonderful!"

"There's a parking space over there," he said. "What are we waiting for?"

As they walked up the boardwalk he told her how he used to come here after the high school dances in the early summer and early fall. "It was a way you could get a girl in your arms without all the awkward preliminaries," he said, chuckling. "She'd get frightened and there she'd be in your arms with the long, slow climb through the tunnel coming up. I'll bet they still have the tunnel."

"I'll bet they do," Althea said, laughing. "But I don't frighten easily. Ever do any jumping with a hunter?"

"I've never been on a horse, except for a pony picture as a kid. Somebody, probably my father, held the pony while I was on him. You can see the hand in the picture."

She laughed again as they rounded the corner onto the midway. On the other side of the street the tide was ebbing a little from the endless strip of beach.

"I'll wager that pause at the top just before the cars dip downward gives you the feeling you get as the hunter gets set for the jump!"

"Could be," Martin said. "I don't think of hunters at that moment, however. The old Irish takes over in me and I say a prayer."

"I've never been able to pray much," Althea said, as they neared the roller-coaster entrance. "I've always been too close to palpable things I guess — I can understand horses, music, the need for a drink, some men, some women. I've — oh — I've just never had much patience with anything I couldn't understand, I guess."

Martin bought the tickets and they joined a line that was waiting for an empty carriage.

"Maybe you've been closer to prayer than you think," Martin mused. "My brother Fran, who used to be in the seminary, told me something interesting about prayer once. He said that people who know great unhappiness and bear it with patience and dignity, are very close to prayer."

Althea's eyes were shining when she looked up at Martin. "That was a nice thing to say. No wonder I kind of go for you."

"Kind of?" Martin asked with mock petulance.

"What more can a divorced Yankee female say to a young Catholic gentleman with a promising political future?"

A uniformed attendant unhooked a chain, letting the people into an empty carriage which had just rattled to its berth alongside the platform.

Her features were immobile, until he touched her elbow, urging her toward seats in the middle of the coaster.

"Let's do it the hard way," she said, nodding toward the front seat, which was still vacant.

"Okay." He took her firmly by the arm.

They had to hurry to beat a weaving sailor and his bulgy, blonde girl friend.

"It's all yours, mate," the sailor said genially. He stooped over to pick up a kewpie doll which his companion had dropped.

"He sounded too acquiescent," Althea said, as Martin snapped the lock on her safety belt.

They settled back and the attendant released the brake which started them forward. The coaster rumbled slowly down an incline which led into a tunnel.

"Is this the one?" Althea asked facetiously.

"No, this is just a short one, if I remember correctly. The long one comes near the end of the ride. This will do, though." He dropped an arm around her shoulders.

"Don't you dare, Martin Ronayne," she said, tolerating his arm. "I'll make a statement to the *Boston Yankee*. 'State Representative Assaults Divorcee on Roller Coaster.' You'll be ruined."

"We just discussed that a while back." He withdrew his arm. "And I wish you wouldn't keep calling yourself a divorcee."

She was silent before the tender, yet stinging chastisement he had given her. They shot down into the tunnel.

"You can put your arm back there, if you want to." She whispered out of the cool, clanking abyss.

He took her in his arms and kissed her. Her face grew moist with tears.

They veered out of the tunnel, out of the cool void of blackness into the sultry, light-speckled night. They began the long, jerky climb.

He held her closely as they looked out on the roofs, the sea, the sky. The pedestrians and automobiles moved far below them like some confused migration of insects.

"This is a glorious experience for me," she said.

"Look at all you missed by not going to Charlestown High," he said, laughing.

She laughed in return, slowly, richly, flickering her eyes. "You wouldn't have noticed me. You'd have thought I was dull and fallen in love with some unconventional Yankee debutante."

"I'd have spotted you anywhere. . . . We're almost there."

"Yes, I have the feeling of the jump I was telling you about. Say those prayers of yours."

"I will. May St. Malachy and St. Brigid and all the Irish saints preserve us from the abyss of the devil, and may St. Patrick be at our bedside when we die at one hundred and nine."

"Amen," she said, as the front truck of their carriage gained the summit and seemed to linger there for a moment; there, in majestic eminence among the stars, before they plunged downward with a shrilling clatter of wheels, down, down, and down at ninety miles an hour with the women screaming and the screams of men beating importunately against the inside of vise-tight lips.

He held her tight with one arm and gripped the front railing with the other. They blinked into the wind and the blackness below them, their bodies straining tautly against the safety belts. Down, down they plunged, together, into the abyss of the big drop and into the abyss that wildly followed the long, tortuous climb of their love.

Chapter 25

"BOTH?" John asked hoarsely, standing in the middle of the waiting room, his hands lolling limply by his sides. "Both?" he pleaded again in the same harsh whisper, his face white as whey against the red of his hair.

Doctor McDonald, a tall, cropped blond, stood there in his wilted white coat looking more like a football captain than like the man who had manipulated frantically by the shore of the darkest sea as Alice slipped steadily away.

He wrinkled his sharply chiseled features, resisted a temptation to lower his eyes; he looked directly at John.

"Both of them." He glanced at Francis, sitting starkly on the sofa by the wall. He put his lean, sun-tanned arm around John's shoulder. "Come into my office, old man."

John moved dumbly along with him. They left the waiting room and disappeared down the corridor.

When they had gone, Francis continued to sit there staring at the wall. He could have been standing, lying down, or floating in the air, for all the physical feeling he had.

"Both dead," his mind tolled over and over again. "Both dead."

It was 12:18 a.m. The nurse had been in half an hour before to tell them a baby girl had been born and that Alice was hemorrhaging badly. "We're doing everything we possibly can, Mister Little — everything. . . . "

But even when you know someone you love is dying, you do not

believe it, and when he or she is dead you do not believe it —
at the wake, at the funeral, after the funeral, you do not believe it.
Months later, at breakfast, a saucer clinks and you believe it,
a letter comes for the deceased and you believe it, an old friend
from out of town phones, asking for the dead and you believe it.

When the nurse slipped out into the corridor, Francis had
followed her.

"Will you get her a priest?" he had asked. "Her and the baby."

"We've already called the priest," she said with something of
a sweet weariness. "That's routine around here if the patient
is a Catholic."

He had stood there looking at her fixedly. She could have been
a wall, a clock, anything to fix his eyes on.

In her large, brassy bed Catherine lay propped up on two pillows
in the darkness, her rosary beads partially spread out on her bosom,
partially entwined in her hand. Her other hand dangled toward
the floor; her lips moved rapidly, making a sustained, whisking
sound.

Before retiring, an hour ago, she had phoned the hospital, talked
to Francis, and learned of Alice's worsening condition. This was
the third rosary she had said, since that time, for the little Polish
girl who used to live upstairs. When she finished this one she
would call the hospital again.

That child should never have married, she thought. She'd have
made the purest, sweetest nun to have come out of St. Mary's
parish. That little odd John running off with a precious little
thing like her. She wasn't cut out for marriage at all, God help us,
though I know the little redhead kisses the ground she walks on.

She sighed heavily. On the wall a luminous crucifix glowed with
a certain tawdriness that could not confound the old-country piety
with which Catherine looked upon it. You could almost dress the
Corpus in the habiliments of Rudolph Valentino and still not
confound the X-ray devoutness of old-country religion.

She looked at the crucifix intently and called down the Lord's
mercy upon Alice Little and her child. She blessed herself with
her rosary crucifix, tunneled it under her pillow, and settled back
with another heavy sigh.

She dozed a while, determined to rouse herself in a few minutes and call the hospital. It had been a tiring day — what Bunker Hill Day wasn't? The festive luncheon, the old friends, old talk, the bands playing in the distance, the people thronging to and from the parade, outside her parlor window.

The Alice thing had taken the savor out of it, however; her holiday fatigue was not the happy weariness she had known in other years. Perhaps she should be grateful, God forgive her, that Martin had not gone ahead and married Alice against her will. A tragedy like that could tear the heart and the ambition out of a man. It would do something to little John, she feared — she would have to do something extra for him if Alice passed along — God forbid.

But it was always something in this life. Martin's path was certainly not one upon which he could skate to fame, although there had been no suction caps on his shoes thus far. She had heard something late that very evening that bothered her much. It was only the stunning news of Alice's extremity that had pushed it farther back in her mind.

Jim Hanlon had come in for a cup of coffee after the banquet. Coffee, indeed! He wanted a nightcap, but she wouldn't give it to him because of his heart. "You won't go staggering home from Martin Ronayne's house," she had reminded him. "I've enough on my soul without sending one of my best friends to the Lord unshriven. By the way," she had added, "when was it you were to the sacraments last?"

"The past Sunday," Hanlon had said, pouring his black coffee into a saucer, lifting it drippingly to his lips. A seminary friend of Franny's was saying Mass at St. Mary's. I was having one of my spells. Franny brought him over to the house — Communion and all."

"It wasn't that Father Carney who used to teach Francis out there?"

"It was. And a fine, scholarly priest he is."

"As Father Quinn tells it, he's rather an odd duck," Catherine had reflected. "All mixed up with the Benedictines and filling the seminarians with a lot of notions about the liturgy and those social action ideas. I'm as liberal as the next one in this town, but I think

I know what these young priests face when they go into the parishes — pastors that keep the young ones so busy with the routine of the parish that they have little time for the liturgy and all these change-the-world-overnight ideas on capital and labor. Such seminary teaching makes for future parish malcontents. Father Carney may be right, by the books, but he's a little ahead of his time."

"He's all right any time if it is me that has the say," said Hanlon. "I don't understand this lit-turg-ee business at all. . . . But I did see something tonight that made a little story in my head."

"What was that?"

"Your oldest boy, it was. And he walking off with the belle of the ball."

"And who was she?"

"The little Parkley divorcee herself — sweet and fresh as the first robin — and our boy Martin looking at her all through dinner with the softness of a baby in his eyes."

"Well!" Catherine had exclaimed. "Well," she repeated in a softer, more restrained tone. "Did he dance with her right there in the armory, in front of all those people?"

"You know Marty better than that, Catherine. They went out separately, after all the official blather at the head table was no more. She talked to her father a while, I noticed. One of my boys saw them drive away together later. They were in need of a little fresh air — and weren't we all this long, hard day?" He smiled a sad, haunted smile at Catherine and mopped his brow with a soggy handkerchief. . . .

Now, lying in bed, she thought of Martin again, and her head began to spin with fatigue. As if Alice's condition was not enough for one day — now this. Hanlon said it might all be a little lark on Marty's part, but he had said it with a hint of fear in his eye. Surely to God Marty wouldn't get himself involved with that high-toned little baggage. . . . He couldn't, he simply couldn't, not after coming this far. She'd speak to him soon. She wished now he'd stayed home, but he was elected from Dorchester and she had to admit it was better for him to stay there with Mike and Rosemary.

She had seen in her husband's untimely death the annihilation of a fine career. But there remained over the whole memory of his life a glow of honor and accomplishment and the irrepressible nostalgia of future promise.

That glow would not hover over Martin's life, she knew, if he became involved with this girl. If only his father were around to tell him some of these things — and that strangeling, Francis, he needed his father's help. Lord knows, I've tried and tried, but there's no substitute for a good father's strong words.

"Martin, Martin . . . " she said, burrowing her eyes into the pillow. It was still as if he had gone away only a day or so before. In all those years she had lived the totality of her moments, however, secretly, as though he would come walking into the kitchen one evening and sniff the fine aromas of her cooking before gathering her in his arms. In the world of the spirit he had never gone from her and would never go.

Chapter 26

THE afternoon of the funeral was sparkling, zephyric, but the sun was forbiddingly high above them; there was none of it in their hearts. John and Francis pushed out of the Waldorf Cafeteria where they had lingered over hamburgers trying to eat a little.

Alice and the stillborn infant were in the ground. They had been buried that morning at Holy Cross Cemetery. John's people had been there, the Ronaynes, Hanlon, Mike, the women weeping, the men solemn, tight lipped.

John had stood by coldly, saying no prayers, looming over the rich, warm earth of summer which received all that was richest and warmest in his life.

Martin had put his arm around his sobbing mother — statuesque, the tears tentative in his eyes, his face pinched with tension and, perhaps, remorse. Father Quinn read his breviary, in silent duet with the parish priest. Beside the former, Hanlon had stood, his gnarled hands folded around his black derby, his eyes oily as those of a fish.

They had all been there by the rich, warm earth, their bodies crying out against the impossible fact of death, their spirits struggling up and worrying the mercies of their God, their hearts calling ceaselessly with the priest as the casket swung gently over the ultimate mine shaft of man's remains: *"Miserere nobis, miserere nobis. . . . "*

"They're in heaven, John," Francis said, as they turned up Chelsea Street.

"Yeh, heaven."

"They *are* in heaven, John. They really are."

"Okay, kid, okay," John said with a wintry smile. "Let's take a walk, huh?" He sighed deeply, making an attempt to throw off the heavy weather of his mood. "Let's take a walk up to Shiner O'Neil's. I could stand a hooker or two."

They turned up Bunker Hill Street toward Shiner's place. The speak-easy was in a thickly walled enclosure to the rear of Shiner's Pool Hall. The first of the concrete traps covered the width of Bunker Hill Street directly in front of Shiner's.

John paused, looking at the hazard intently. Francis was half-way up the short flight of steps leading to Shiner's. He waited for John, apprehensively. "Come on, John!"

"I still think it could be done."

"Come on!" Francis repeated.

"Okay, Fran." John turned. His voice seemed to strike an odd, new note of elation. He turned and followed Francis into the pool hall.

They walked through the poolroom and the voices of the players subsided. The lone, hollow sock of ball against ball was unaccompanied by profanity or the triumphant thumping of cue sticks against the floor.

John rapped twice on the sheet-metal door at the end of the poolroom. A panel slid back, a bloodshot eye ogled, the door opened.

Two old men sipped their beer, standing at a small, scarred mahogany bar. Behind the bar Shiner O'Neil leaned on his elbows fingering a wet circle and talking in a low, firm voice. When he saw John, he straightened up, wiped his freckled paw on his apron, and reached across the bar.

"John," he said, "I'm terribly sorry."

"Thanks, Shiner." John moved close to the bar. "Pour me a stiff one."

"That I'll do — how about the young feller? Aren't you the little Ronayne kid?"

Francis nodded, noticing the furry tangle of orange hair on Shiner's great forearms. There were similar tufts in his ears.

"I'll have a glass of beer."

The old tads to their left whispered their recognition of John. Francis could hear the hollow "klock" of the pool balls in the other room as he sipped his beer and watched John toss off two straight shots.

"The only thing that bothers me about those traps," John began, turning his beer chaser slowly, "is that the cops probably think we couldn't take one through there with the accelerator flattened. Just because those young kids cracked up they think it's impossible. Shiner and I and the gang pulled stunts every bit as tough as that in the old days — right, Shiner?"

"Yeh, and walked away from them," Shiner said, stretching for the glasses of the two elderly tosspots.

"We could do it, Fran," John said, pushing his empty whisky glass toward Shiner. "We really could."

"I know you could, John." Francis wanted to tell John to slow down, but how could he? John wasn't talking about the traps or the cops or looping. He was really talking about Alice and the little baby — his love and longing for them was coming out in hatred for the empty world which he must now face alone. John tossed off the drink and another beer. "That's enough for me," Francis said.

Francis finished his beer and slipped off the stool.

John tried to pay for the drinks but Shiner waved him away.

On the sidewalk John paused, his eyes again searching the concrete trap. He looked up and down the hill; there were no streetcars or automobiles approaching. He stepped into the trap and walked through it, along one of the narrow streetcar lanes, pausing and measuring the distance with his eyes. Francis waited on the sidewalk.

A streetcar clanged in the distance. John walked slowly out of the hazard and returned to the sidewalk.

"Where you heading now, Fran?"

"I'm going with you."

"The hell you are!"

"The hell I'm not!"

They walked along briskly, down a side street in the direction of the Sugar House on Medford Street.

"Don't do it, John. Don't do it; it isn't worth it."

John walked steadily on down the Hill. There was a flush of
excitement in his face and his small, blue eyes were touched with
a wild light. "Why don't you head on home, Fran," he said with
steely quietude, "or go up the Hill, if you want, and watch the
show."

"I'm staying with you." Francis trotted to keep up with him.

They turned into a parking lot near the Sugar House. John's
roving eyes picked out a new Ford sedan with a window half
open at the driver's seat. He walked over to the car, reached inside, opened the door. He climbed in and fumbled with the wires
under the dashboard. Francis stood vigilant at the entrance to the
lot, alternately glancing at John and at the street approaches to
the area.

John yanked two of the wires out from under the dashboard
and spliced them deftly with his fingers. He stepped on the starter,
the motor came to life with an eager roar.

Francis leaped on the running board as the car rolled out of
the area onto Medford Street. He pulled anxiously at the door
handle as the car gathered speed; it was locked. He pleaded with
John. John shook his head. Then he jammed on the brakes and
lunged at the door. It snapped open, hurling Francis to the street.

He picked himself off the cobbles quickly, but John was already
away from him, moaning swiftly south.

As he stood in the middle of the street, his eyes filled with
tears of frustration. He saw, through the rear window of the
speeding car, John's right hand waving slowly, gallantly.

"Hey, you dirty . . . hey!"

The infuriated voice and a staccato of pounding feet filled his
ears. Francis glanced apprehensively over his shoulder. A husky
longshoreman was running toward him.

Francis bolted into the alley at his right. It wound up the
Hill among the rickety back porches. He loped up the alley twenty
yards or so, then ducked into a tenement doorway and down the
cellar. He lurked in the dampness and darkness until he heard the
heavy scuff of feet approaching and dwindling. Then he groped
through the cellar toward the front of the tenement and climbed
the stairs to the hall. He hurried out onto the street, crossed it
into another parallel alley, and chuffed again up the Hill.

He emerged on Bunker Hill Street at a point between the trap at the bottom of the Hill and the one just at the Hill's crest. He stood there panting, chilled with fear, and heard the first unmistakable summons of the police siren.

John had apparently picked up the cops down in the City Square area. The calling of the siren charged the entire Hill with a familiar electricity. Shiner and the denizens of the pool hall were out on the steps straining their eyes toward Chelsea Street. In tenement windows up and down the Hill housewives were framed and wriggling children. Pedestrians paused on the curbing, awed, almost reverent, as if they were about to witness a public execution.

Francis, too, stood there in an impotent chill, waiting for the guttural roar of the motor, the eek of punished tires, that would signal John's entrance into the cobbled raceway of Bunker Hill Street.

The municipal whining was louder now. John was coming. Not another. Not he and John watching some other guy. He tried to pray but could not find the words.

Now John came in the awesome, illicit majesty of the chase, screeching around the turn and veering into the straightaway incline that led to the first trap. His path was clear but for a lone streetcar in the other lane, which had loitered to a stop, its conductor having heard the shrill manifesto of the police siren.

Francis focused his eyes on the little red blur behind the wheel of the onrushing Ford. He looked like a fused metal figure in a toy racer. He came on toward the first great concrete crocodile, whose saw-toothed jaws lay directly in the furious current of his course.

Francis saw a method in the career of the oncoming car, which careened about the streetcar tracks at first, then wobbled, then seemed to ride them smoothly. John would test his theory of getting through the hazard with unaltered speed by holding steadily to the tracks. It was the only way.

He held the car on the tracks steadily now, approaching the hazard with unabated speed. The police car rounded the corner behind him and slowed in anticipation of the trap.

The Ford entered the trap, holding the tracks securely. Francis saw with eyes that did not want to see.

He was through. As he approached Francis swiftly on the long, uphill stretch, between the first and second hazards, he sounded a long, triumphant blast on his horn. From the steps of Shiner O'Neil's there went up a yell and a series of whistles.

Francis' face relaxed and then quickly stiffened as John approached the second hazard at the Hill's crest.

Below, the squad car inched ignominiously through the trap.

He roared past Francis, still holding the tracks. Francis called and waved involuntarily; then broke into a run toward the top of the Hill. He saw John enter the second trap and traverse it smoothly, heard again the two long blasts on his horn as John dipped down the Hill.

"Lord, just one more," Francis prayed, loping to the top of the Hill.

From the summit he could see the gleaming sedan scooting along the tracks into the final hazard. Immediately to Francis' left the police car bumbled slowly through the second hilltop barrier.

Below, the sedan lanced into the trap and, for an instance, skidded against one of the concrete curbings. The front, left wheel grazed one of the pyramidal stanchions, the car lurched to the right, then regained its equilibrium, squealing. Francis closed his eyes.

Three long blasts of a horn assaulted his ears and brought stinging tears of joy to his eyes as John, with raucous brakes, jolted into the straightaway, approaching the turn into Main Street.

The car shot around the corner, completing the loop. Then he heard a maniacal screaming of brakes, the frump of collapsing steel, the mocking tinkle and clatter of exploded glass.

Francis ran again, down the rest of the Hill and around the corner.

The right, front end of the sedan was embedded in the side of a red furniture van. It had been either the van or an elevated upright. John had chosen the more resilient, if quite as deadly, obstacle.

The driver's door of the sedan lolled foolishly on its hinges.

John lay on the cobblestones beside the sedan, his face masked with a gauze of fresh, augmenting blood. Two policemen were pushing back the onlookers, another dabbed at John's face with a blood-stippled handkerchief.

Francis pushed through the bystanders. "Let me through!" he said to a huge policeman whose face was a study in bland, red meat. "Let me through, please."

Francis was past him before the officer could make up his mind. He knelt down beside the unconscious John, stripped off his jacket, and, with the aid of the policeman, folded it under John's head.

"The ambulance should be here any minute," the policeman said. "Are you related to this boy?"

Francis shook his head slowly and watched the unstanched blood well out of John's forehead and ebb down over his face and eyes.

"John," Francis said, kneeling there helplessly beside him. "John!"

The police ambulance coughed around the corner. Two of the cops lifted him onto a stretcher. Francis tried to follow the stretcher into the ambulance but was detained by one of the police. "You stay here," he said, "there's a few things maybe you can tell us." The cop put a hand to his mouth and called after the ambulance driver: "I'll phone the information into the station, Jack, as soon as I get. . . ."

"Now," the policeman said, poised with pad and pencil like some elephantine stenographer, "what is your name and what is his name?"

"Hey! That's the guy right there, officer!" The hoarse voice of the longshoreman buffeted against Francis' bewilderment and misery. "That's the guy was with him."

"Is he now?" the policeman said, lifting his hat and dropping therein his pad and pencil. "Come along, young feller, come along."

He juggled the pad and pencil into a flat position, donned his cap, and grabbed Francis by the elbow.

The two policemen, Francis, and the longshoreman entered the prowl car and drove down Main Street toward headquarters.

Francis looked emptily out the window — he could not weep, he could not pray.

Chapter 27

AMONG the fragrant, branchy shadows of the bridle path, Martin loped on a plump, gray gelding and saw the fused, silken chestnut mass of her and the hunter streak around a sharp bend twenty yards ahead. The wind sifted through his hair, tossing it wildly. He wished he'd gone back after his hat. The gelding had plunged after Althea near the stable and the hat sailed from Martin's head. The stable manager, standing near by, had retrieved it — waving at Martin as he sped away.

If at this same moment in the late afternoon an ambulance in Charlestown insisted its jangling throughout the hillside, here on the sylvan horse trail that skirted Jamaica Pond only the heavy chuff-chuff of the gelding's pace and the hollow rhythmic tattoo of the chestnut stallion's steady gallop violated the stillness of the woods.

She had wanted him to come riding with her in the morning. The morning was the time — the air was crisp and cool then, and you could almost drink the dew as your mount swept you along past the trees and the flowers. There was nothing like it in all living — the morning sweet and crystalline, beckoning you on forever until you and your horse were weary.

When she talked to him over the phone the other night, that is what the singing in her voice had said.

He had to get a lot out of her voice over the phone. For in a sense, since the beach trip after the banquet, there had been no way in which they could make certain that the night at the beach had not been a dream.

They had agreed to see each other at an interval of several days under the most discreet circumstances. Although morning was really the time for riding, she had pointed out that there would probably be no one on the trail late in the afternoon, no one that would recognize them and put a succulent story on the deadly news syndicate that is the human tongue.

So, jogging along, always a little behind her, he told her the story of his foundered romance with Alice and the twinge of remorse he had known at her death.

She had nodded sympathetically in time with the easy rhythm of the horse's gait, while he, unused to the saddle, slid about in the leather slowly, uncomfortably, thinking confusedly about Sloan's Liniment and also about the way he would remember her riding forever. . . .

But what should they do? They couldn't work out their love in terms of late-afternoon horseback rides. Where could they go together, where and when would it be all right for them to be together?

Anywhere, he had insisted, any time.

She had shaken her head soberly. As for herself, she would be willing to face her family and her friends. "What does it matter?" she had said. "I'm already established as a misfit. You are the one, Martin, that would pay the price. You'd be ruined if people saw us together, no matter how sincere our love, how good our intentions. The Irish and the Yankees, too, would have no part of you politically. You've too much to lose, Martin."

She leaned over, whispered something to the hunter, brushed his gleaming flanks with her heels, and bolted down the trail and around the bend. He slapped the gelding and jogged after her.

"Althea — wait — wait, Althea."

She was far ahead now pounding through the woods in the wild, easing purgation of flight. It was thus that she had fled another kind of unhappiness down the mystic green shadows of a Wisconsin trail. Then she had galloped away from a kind of hatred, now she was running away from love. But you always had to face it, she knew, even with the wind in her face, the good masculine smell of the limber animal in her nostrils. "You always have to face it, Daystar," she whispered into the hunter's mane. "You can run as far as you like from hatred or love but you always have to face them eventually." She tugged on the reins a little. He slowed to a trot with the grace and self-control of a thoroughbred.

She would do anything for Martin — love him, live with him, marry him — give him up? Yes, even that. That was so easy to say: "Give him up. . . ."

As the horse slowed now to a brisk walk, she turned in the saddle. She could see him loping along, a hundred yards or so behind. She brought her mount to a halt near a sheltered inlet of the lake that was speckled richly with water lilies. She dismounted and walked him up and down the trail.

When Martin arrived she was sitting on an ancient crone of a tree which lifted its gnarled old arms out over the water. She heard his step behind her, a lush rustle in the mildewed loam and the endless echelons of buttercups. She arose quickly and turned to him; then she was in his arms, knowing that the afternoon at least was theirs, if not the morning, if not the days and the years.

Later, after she had dropped him in front of the Common on Tremont Street, he walked through the park toward the State House in the mothy tenderness of the early June evening.

A lock of his hair slipped down over his forehead and he pushed it back involuntarily. His hat. They'd send it out to him in the morning. The riding master had been out on a lesson when they got back to the stables; the hat was locked in his office. The stable boy took his name and promised to have it sent over to the State House.

He left the Common, crossing Beacon Street toward the capitol mall. It was after six, he'd have to use a rear entrance — there were some letters to sign and he should call his mother and Mike.

He walked up Beacon and, glancing at the main entrance, he noticed a familiar figure coming down the walk. The graceful, reedy figure with the skeletal head moved toward him in an attitude of absorption.

"Erford!" Martin called genially, knowing nonetheless a chill of foreboding.

"Hello, there," Erford said. It was the kind of casualness that could be attributed to either breeding or displeasure. Now it was perhaps both.

"Got time for a drink?" Martin asked. "I've a little phoning to do and a few letters to sign, then I'll be free."

"I really couldn't," he said, smiling with his face muscles. "I'm dining at home this evening — be a little late as it is."

"Oh! Some other time then," Martin said. She would be there. She would be there, brighter than the linen and the silver, lovelier than the cut-glass goblets, more exciting than the wine.

Erford nodded politely. "By the way, I just had a phone call from the Pondway Stables. The riding master said he was sorry to be out when you got back. He said to tell you he'd surely send your hat over in the morning."

"Fine," Martin said, blenching. "How come the riding master called you?"

"I can explain that," Erford said. "He had your name all right, but didn't seem to connect you with the State House — he's probably not from Dorchester."

Martin's face was whiter now.

"I still don't know why he called you."

"Very simple — he's known Althea and me since childhood. He knows I'm about Dad's office a good deal. I left a message with the night porter for you."

"Thanks."

Erford's features softened. "I was rather surprised to discover that you and Althea have been seeing each other, Martin. . . . Both of you have too much at stake."

Martin was silent several moments. "We do see each other occasionally, and I guess we want to continue. Maybe you noticed our interest in each other long ago?"

"I did, a long time ago, but the whole thing seemed to be solved."

"Yes, it seemed to be."

"All I know is," Erford said, sighing, "you'll hurt yourself with Dad if you keep on seeing Althea. You may as well face it now — the fall elections are very important to you."

"Yes," Martin said somberly, "I suppose it would hurt your dad if Althea and I. . . ."

"It'll hurt more than my dad. It's impossible, Martin, just impossible!"

"We've thought about that and talked about it a good deal. Maybe we'll have to make a fight of it."

Erford shook his head slowly. "It can't be done — you won't have a chance; not in Boston, Marty."

Martin sighed and turned his palms slowly outward. "What about you? Where would you stand if we went ahead with all this?"

"You know where I'd stand," Erford said. "You know where I'd have to stand."

"Okay," Martin said. "You've been a good friend, but I can't give her up."

"Maybe she'll give you up," Erford said.

"We'll see," Martin said. He looked at Erford steadily, his jowls tightening.

Erford turned and walked briskly north.

Martin watched him go for several moments, then continued on toward his office.

As he opened the door of the anteroom, he could hear the phone ringing with a mournful insistence that communicated unmistakably the six o'clock desolation of the surrounding offices.

He hurried in and picked up the phone.

"Hello."

"Hello, that you, Marty. I've been trying to get you for hours," Mike said.

"I was out horseback riding. What's up?"

"I'm over here at the City Square cop house. Fran's been pinched."

"Pinched? What the hell for?"

"He got mixed up in a looping deal with John Little."

"Holy . . . "

"Yeh. He wasn't in the loop, though. They're holding him 'before the fact.' "

"What about John? They holding him?"

"He's a goner — cracked up just around the corner from Main."

"No!"

"Yes. Come on over here — your mother's a nervous wreck."

"Okay, Mike, I'll be right over. What about the papers?"

"They're giving John the play. I talked to some of the boys. I don't think they've got much on Fran, anyway."

"Can we get him out?"

"They won't let him out till morning. Look, I'm taking Mother Ronayne back to the house. Join us there."

"Okay, Mike, I'll grab a cab right over there."

"Yeh, make it fast; so long now."

"So long."

So when he had taken the cab down Beacon Hill, across the river, and up the interminable hill that is all of Charlestown, when he had thought with great irritation about his brother, about the hurt to his mother and the possible embarrassment to him politically, it was time for him to pay the cab fare and run up the short flight of stairs to the Ronayne apartment.

She was there in the parlor in her familiar place, knitting, her face white and strained after tears. Mike was with her and Rosemary.

She arose and came toward him, embracing him.

"It's all right, Mother, it's all right, we'll have him out first thing in the morning."

"Martin, Martin," she said. "It's good you're here — you're like your father — you make things seem better just by walking in."

Martin's face tightened. His arms went limp on her shoulders. "Like your father. . . ." Her words echoed in some forgotten hallway of his mind, leaving him a little dizzy.

If only he could have been like his father. But that was nonsense for him. He was different, he told himself, different. If only his mother could see all that in some flash of insight — without the bewilderment, the pain of the endless labyrinth that is complete human understanding. If only she could know all about his love for Althea and Althea's love for him — his powerlessness before this love, the accepted challenge to his career and his religion. In this instant of lashing conscience he saw his burden of impossible explanations — and for her, the eventual bewilderment, the pain. But she would have to face it — even as he was facing things. One had to be ruthless about matters like these, even with a mother. It was *his* life, *his* life. . . .

"I hope this won't hurt your chances in the fall, Martin,"

He thought of the holy people who had been in prison under far more harrowing circumstances than his own. Somebody holy and with a gift of phrase could write a wonderful litany of the saints who had been in prison. It would be good, Francis mused, to say such a litany if you were yourself a prisoner: Joan, prisoner of the English captains, pray for us; Edmund, prisoner of Queen Elizabeth, pray for us.

If he could have become the priest his mother had wanted him to be, perhaps he might have written a litany. There was nothing which said a layman couldn't compose prayers; yet, always the world seemed to get in his way — there was always the imposition of the world even in the midst of his deepest spiritual impulses. It was a kind of sloth he could never quite get rid of and it would probably keep him mediocre always.

Mediocrity was his cross — although his mother thought his mediocrity was her cross. Still it was good to recognize that one was mediocre and be bothered by it — perhaps there was a way to salvation in that.

And he had wanted to be a journalist somewhat in the way he wanted to be a priest; a great welling up of inspiration which would not eventually conform to regimen. It was a most helpless and frustrating condition if you didn't have some great writer to turn to, like St. Paul, who understood, who had managed to say it all out, but who still understood how impossible it is fully to express profound emotion in words.

His eyes fell again on the Second Epistle of Paul to the Corinthians: "Thrice was I beaten with rods, once I was stoned, thrice I suffered shipwreck, a night and a day I was in the depth of the sea. In journeying often, in perils of waters, in perils of robbers, in perils from my own nation, in perils from the Gentiles, in perils in the city, in perils in the wilderness, in perils in the sea, in perils from false brethren. In labor and painfulness, in much watchings, in hunger and thirst, in fastings often, in cold and nakedness. . . . Who is weak, and I am not weak? Who is scandalized and I am not on fire?"

If he could only say it, now, if he could utter poetry, with what lyrical ecstasy would he pour forth his love and grief for little John. How weird and insubstantial seemed the lives of Alice, John, and the infant now that all the testimony of sense and reason decreed that they were gone from this life, never to return.

If she would let him remain with the paper and attempt to fill John's shoes, he would get the chance at least to say some of this in print. Perhaps she would accept it if he offered a series of articles as a project in co-operation with her committee work. He could tell John's story without mentioning names. "The Life and Death of a Looper" he could call it. Maybe he could say out these things he was feeling now. He would try hard, if she'd give him a shot at the paper again.

He leaned toward the bars and called to the attendant. He asked for the little black book in his leather jacket. He received it, thanked him, and slumped into a sitting position on the bunk. He read the words of *Compline* that were written for him and for all inarticulate men of good will: "Keep us, O Lord, as the apple of Thine eye — protect us under the shadow of Thy wings. . . ."

He read the psalms, canticles, and prayers of the abridged service. Then he lay on the tickly woolen blankets a while before slipping into a sleep not untroubled by the things of earth and the things of heaven.

Chapter 28

THERE was the potted fern in the wrought-iron stand near the entrance to the music room and she had been looking at it sporadically through the rose-gloom mist of Chopin, playing there in the morning sunshine and wondering where Martin was and how he was.

It had been a week now since she had seen him on the bridle path. There had been long and furtive phone calls late at night when most people were sleeping and their talk could be warm.

Erford knew, Erford knew. Martin hardly had to tell her of the meeting in front of the dome — it was in Erford's smile and Erford's eyebrows and in the way he talked of Martin's chances in the fall.

Chopin, Chopin in the slanting morning sunshine, nocturne in the morning, and the moth wings of his music brushing gently, swiftly against the singing wires.

And that young brother of Martin's — the one that had been in the seminary — an odd little fellow. Helped someone steal a car — looping they called it. Something they'd interpret in terms of Freud at Radcliffe. It was good they kept it out of the papers — the Ronayne name, that is. There'd be some kind of a sociological hearing this morning and his mother would be there as a member of the board, sitting in on her own son. There was stalwart stuff for you — principle and all that.

She lifted her hands from the piano at the thought and buried her face in them. She pulled away her hands abruptly and looked at them fixedly.

"Althea," a voice called.

She looked up at the fern and saw her father smiling at her from behind it.

"Althea, pet, will you stop reading your palms and drive me over to Charlestown. I've got to make that hearing this morning. Would you?"

"Dad! You footpad! Have you been there long?"

"Long enough to know there's something bothering my little girl. Come along now, we can chat a bit on the way."

Erford must have told him. But Erford had failed to communicate his coldness and unsympathy, for there was warmth and maybe understanding in her father's eyes — and in his speech and in the way he lifted his fingers, beckoning.

They walked along the cool, dark, wainscoted hallway to the kitchen and out the back door to the garage. They walked saying nothing and saying a lot in the mustering of what they were to say.

Edward was puttering around underneath the Lincoln when they approached the barnlike structure which despite its refurbishings of steel and concrete still looked like a place of creaking carriage wheels and hay and stamping horses.

Edward wheeled quickly out from under the car on one of those little carriages mechanics writhe upon.

"Glorious morning, Edward," Mr. Parkley said. "Having a look at the springs?"

"Yessir. Did you and Miss Althea want the roadster?"

"If you will, Edward," Althea said. "How is Mrs. Walsh?"

"They're all well. Terry wants to enter the Little Sisters of the Poor in the fall."

"How nice!" Althea said. "How does your wife feel about it?"

"It's the will of God, she says."

"How about you, Edward?" Mr. Parkley said. "How do you feel?"

Edward ran his bumpy red hand through his gray-streaked red hair. "It's a hard life for such a young girl, begging food and money from door to door. She could have a much better time in one of these orders that teaches flouncy young things in a high-toned private school. I've told her the same, but she'll have none of the easy way at all."

"You may have a little saint in the family," Mr. Parkley said, glancing at his watch.

"That I may." Edward scrunched into the roadster, kicking the engine over, and rolling out onto the concrete pavilion in front of the garage.

When they were coasting down the driveway Mr. Parkley wrinkled his forehead and asked: "We mustn't forget little Terry in the fall — whatever do you give a girl entering the convent, anyway?"

"I wish I knew, Dad," Althea said. "You'll be seeing Mrs. Ronayne won't you? She should be able to tell you."

"So I will. She should indeed."

They wheeled along through the tree-sifted sunshine of the Fenway toward Massachusetts Avenue and the West Boston Bridge. They were at first quiet as the morning, the muted, throaty music of the roadster blending with the drowsiness of the Muddy River which meandered along beside them.

"Erford tells me you've been seeing something of young Ronayne," he said.

"Yes, Dad, I have." She spoke softly, tentatively.

"He's a fine young man."

She nodded.

They turned onto the bridge and far ahead of them, sparkling in the astringence of the morning sun, like some virginal vista of the capitol of the Republic, loomed the symmetrical buildings of M.I.T.

"Do you remember the one about the West Boston Bridge?" he asked with a patience more pungent than maddening.

"Yes, I do," Althea said with mock petulance. "How to get to the Midwest: drive across the West Boston Bridge and turn left."

"You have a good memory."

"I should have. You told that one to my late Wisconsin husband at least a dozen times."

"Did I really!" He chuckled a while and after another opulent stretch of silence said: "Do you think it's good to see young Ronayne so much — at — uh — this time, that is to say?"

She shook her head slowly. "It isn't good, Daddy, I know it isn't good — for him, for his future, anyway. We're, well, we're. . . ."

"Don't try to explain," he said, "I think I understand."

Her grandfather would have understood in a different way, he reflected. In the ancient way of the upper classes — the way of appealing rigorously to tradition and aristocratic heritage — the way of getting her and a maiden aunt on a boat to Paris as soon as possible. But unless you entered into the by-now illusory world of blooded aristocracy and made yourself a corny old fool in the eyes of your daughter you could not get noble and turn her out if she would not run sobbing off to Europe.

Underneath all his realism he still felt that his world and the world of the maturing Irish had not and could not quite come together. Yet there was the fact of his daughter's early marital tragedy because she had conformed and there was his very satisfactory acquaintance with young Ronayne and his folks — fine people, as fine as many of his own class.

If her mother were alive — and she had been a rigorist of the Yankee hothouse world — there could have been no question about his course of action. And, in a sense, her mother *was* alive in Erford who was angry and adamant about this disturbing romantic tangent which his "political" friend had taken into their family life.

Now in silence again they were rolling lightly, swiftly along the north side of the river. To their right loomed Beacon Hill with old, cold, brooding majesty, and almost beside them, the cat boats dipped and flickered in the brisk, westering wind.

"Althea, dear," he began with a sweetness that was painfully slow, "do you think you could do something for me, something all the more difficult, because you're no longer the little girl or the collegiate madcap you used to be?"

"Maybe I could, Dad," she said a little grimly.

"If Mother were alive, she'd want to send you off to Europe or to our place in Bermuda — you'd always be a little defenseless girl to her, you know. I know that's not quite the treatment for you now — you've suffered as much at the hands of life — perhaps more — than your good mother ever did. But I — I do think it might be wise to run up to Aunt Maude's place in the White Mountains and think things over for a month or so. I'm not think-

ing of you alone; I'm thinking, too, of that bright young man and
his future here in the state. The citizens need young men like
him in the government, perhaps as much — perhaps as much, I
say — as you need him, my dear."

She gripped the wheel tightly now, as they jolted over the
high viaduct past the state penitentiary into Charlestown. It was
before her now, the renunciation of her love, even as in Wisconsin
she had had to face the renunciation of her hatred. The feeling
way down in the heart was the same in both cases — there deep
down where the cold steel bar insisted, the feeling was the same.

"Would you go up there, very soon, dear?" he asked offhandedly.
"I could write Maude this evening — "

"Yes, Dad, I will," she said, blinking at the street ahead. "I will!"

After Jim Hanlon had grinned reassuringly and entered the
darkly paneled committee room where Catherine Ronayne and the
others were chatting quietly and making little official rustling
noises with their papers, Francis continued to sit on the lumpy
leather sofa of the anteroom, his eyes taking in the framed historical
map of Charlestown that hung on the opposite wall.

It was the kind of pictorial souvenir that tourists bought up, and
in the buying it gave them the sense of knowing the history of the
town, particularly the Revolutionary history, without being sub-
jected to the pain or embarrassment of recalling lectures on the
subject.

But to Francis the map's evocation was a most contemporaneous
one. "The spot where Warren fell . . . " was to him the spot where
he and John waited tensely for the onrush and the death whine of
Mickey Quigley's fatal sedan. And the "Widow's Walk," from
which Tory spies once signaled nocturnally to British frigates
anchored in the harbor, was Alice Little's honeymoon flat and
John's observatory and a score of other minute yet poignant
meanings.

The door from the hall opened; he turned and saw a tall,
graying man in his early fifties. Following him was a girl with a
body slender and strong as a lance and an attractive, mobile face
which communicated hauteur and a certain melancholia.

The man, whom he immediately took to be Mr. Parkley, was the last of the committee members to arrive. The girl he surmised must be Parkley's daughter Althea, the divorcee, the one Marty had a crush on once. Francis recalled Jim Hanlon telling him that Marty had met her at the Bunker Hill Day dinner and taken her home afterward. So she was the one. . . .

Mr. Parkley gave him a polite, appraising smile, paused and spoke softly, measuredly to his daughter.

"We shan't be in there much longer than an hour. Would you want to take a drive — have some coffee somewhere perhaps —"

"Whatever you say, Dad." Her eyes were impatient to get back to the young man — Marty's brother — the odd ex-seminarian who didn't seem to fit into a pattern.

"Very well," Parkley said, "I'll be looking for you."

He glanced again at Francis and walked past him into the committee room and closed the door behind him.

She looked at him full on now, the touch of haughtiness gone from her face. She looked at him with almost a gaze, as warmth and compassion involuntarily flooded her features.

"You're Martin's brother!"

"Yes." He smiled slowly, feeling the same embarrassment he had known when he had been forced into a dark room with a pretty girl at a high school house party. He remembered that the girl had been almost as embarrassed as he was — and they had talked nervously until people investigated and mockingly set them free.

"You're Althea — Marty's . . ." he blushed and strained for the more graceful word, glancing painfully away. "You know, Marty, don't you?" he asked finally.

"Yes, and I met your sister Rosemary once, a long time ago. How is she getting on? She must have a family by now."

"Yes, two little babies."

"That's wonderful. Do you mind if I sit down?" She nodded at the sofa beside him and plumped down after fishing in her bag for a pack of cigarettes, She offered him one.

"Not right now — I'm nervous enough, I guess, as it is."

"It might ease the tension," she said, lighting her own.

Through the walls they could hear a sporadic hum of voices. She blew out a bluish parachute of smoke and smiled at him.

"All right, I will have one!" he said, grinning. "I don't know what I'm so nervous about. I haven't done anything tremendously wrong."

"So I gather," she said almost casually. "It's something about pleasing your mother, isn't it? Nice of you to go through with the thing so well."

"Yeh, nice," he said, thinking that she and Marty must be getting close — if she had that much information.

"Martin is at the State House, today, I imagine," she said.

You imagine, he thought. He knew they were in love. It was the way she said "Martin," the tentative way, damming up a lot of love and enthusiasm for him. So Martin was in love — and with society stuff. It might signal the fulfillment of Marty's lifelong dream — or would it, would it fit the dream at all?

"Go to hell; but marry well," Father Carney had once quipped about overambitious young people who married largely for money or social prestige. But maybe this was the real thing — it wouldn't be too hard to disassociate her from ancestor worship and aspidistra plants — she was regular and fresh and lovely.

"Mike, my brother-in-law, is in there — he's on the committee, you know, and has already told me he'll take my part. Mr. Hanlon is sitting in, too."

"There's nobody against you at all, I'd wager," Althea said, "not even your mother if you come right down to it. . . . It seems to me, if I may say so, she's more interested in saving face."

Francis nodded, warming to the girl's discernment. "With Mother it goes a little deeper than saving face. It's a matter, I guess, of family pride and a kind of intellectual honesty. She started this committee thing and she'll see it through."

"Yes, it is admirable in its way, but awfully hard on both of you privately, I should imagine."

"I can stick it out all right," Francis said. "It's Mother I'm bothered about. She'll take the thing very hard — and all on the inside."

Althea took another puff of her cigarette and thought about the seemingly overdone rectitude of Catherine Ronayne. She's as righteous as any of my people in her way, Althea thought.

"I'd be glad to give you a lift somewhere after the business is over," Althea said. "I could leave a message for Dad. Maybe you'll need a brisk ride and a milk shake."

"I might take you up on that," Francis said.

The door opened and Mike stood there inclining his shaggy head toward the committee room.

"Here I go," Francis said, rising. "Nice to have run into you anyway."

"Same here," Althea said.

"Go in and face 'em," Mike said. Then he looked Althea up and down with swift skepticism, before following Francis into the room.

When he entered the room he noticed right away that his mother was not sitting in the chairman's place. Mr. Parkley was there, wearing a pince-nez, fingering an ivory letter opener and looking very much like a picture of a horsy Puritan captain he had once seen on a wall at the Old South Meeting House.

His mother sat to his right. She looked at him as he entered with a cool detachment that was quite admirable because he knew how things must have been thrashing about in her mind. It was a good show she was putting on for what she thought were good reasons.

So he was determined to play the part too, for her.

Jim Hanlon was sitting near the door. He scraped his chair a little and cleared his throat almost boisterously as if to say there was really nothing to it and it would be all over soon.

"Have a seat, young man!" Mr. Parkley said. "We're going to ask you a few questions and we wish you'd think out your answers carefully, giving us the information we'd like as accurately as possible."

Francis nodded and sat down in a chair beside Mike Farrell. He looked around the table while Mr. Parkley made a tense, scholarly face at some notes he had in front of him. Before lowering his eyes with the meekness which he knew he really did not possess, but which one always affected at a time like this, he had noticed the bright young doctor, Morris Applebaum, peering at him through his tortoise-shell glasses.

It was as if something Doctor Applebaum had read in Freud suddenly tied in with Francis and his situation. The doctor, who

had once sold chickens at the A & P in Thompson Square on Saturday nights, while he was at Harvard medical, glanced owlishly at
Mrs. Ronayne, then back at Francis, then at the ceiling wisely and
with restraint. Even though he was kept busy snipping at vericose
veins and delivering babies over on Medford Street, he still knew
something of what a psychiatrist knows about the way a mother
and son can get all tangled up psychologically.

Francis winced, sensing Doc Applebaum's percipience, and waited
for the release Mr. Parkley's questions would bring to him and the
entire gathering.

"Well, now, Francis, we'd like to hear your version of the
story — uh from your own lips," Mr. Parkley began, taking off his
pince-nez and going into an attitude of sweet reasonableness that
had in it an unmistakable element of shrewd reserve. "Tell us
what happened to you and the late John Little after the funeral
of his wife?"

"When we got back from the funeral we went and got something
to eat at the Waldorf in City Square," Francis began.

His mother sat there tall and motionless, her attractive, youngish
face arguing cogently against the splashes of gray in her tightly-
bunned brown hair. There was age in her eyes, however, as she
looked upon her willful younger son; there was sadness there, too,
and a hint of bewilderment.

"We walked up Bunker Hill Street toward the looping traps. . . ."

"May I ask a question?" Mike Farrell said.

"Surely," Mr. Parkley said.

"Francis, had you any reason to believe when you started out
on this walk that John Little intended to do a loop?"

"None."

"Did you ever have any desire yourself to do one of these loops?"

"I've often wondered what it would be like. But who could live
in Charlestown and not wonder about looping?"

"That's all," Mike said.

"May I ask," the doctor said, leaning forward almost as if this
were a congressional committee and the newsreel cameras were
grinding. "Did John Little ever discuss with you the-uh, what
shall I say, the kind of ecstasy, the physical kick a looper gets
out of such a ride?"

An electricity of awkwardness charged the room as Francis shifted in his chair and cleared his throat with a slight, nervous rasp. Catherine Ronayne lowered her eyes but not before a touch of mirth had shot through their melancholy. Hanlon glared at Applebaum. Father Quinn, who sat to the right of Catherine, shook his head faintly, before returning his eyes placidly to the ceiling.

Mr. Parkley crinkled the corners of his mouth for an instant, sobered, and was about to make some comment when Mike cleared the air.

"What the hell has sex got to do with this investigation? Is the boy criminally involved in the looping incident or not? That's what we're here to determine. Let's stick to the point!"

"Yes, Doctor Applebaum," Mr. Parkley interjected quietly. "Your question is undoubtedly of interest from the clinical point of view, but it is rather beside the point of this inquiry."

The doctor blinked a few times behind the transparent bastion of his thick eyeglasses. "Sorry . . . my apologies to you, son, and to all of you. Too many babies over on River Street this week."

"Okay, Doctor," Mike said with friendly impatience.

"Yes, yes, of course," Mr. Parkley said, squinting at Francis and wrinkling his brow. "Francis, tell us, did John Little say anything of pertinence to this hearing while he was examining the traps?"

Francis reflected for a while. "Yes. He said he thought the traps could be crossed without slowing down — he seemed resentful of the tragedy the traps had brought to the green kids who tried to maneuver them in the spring. He seemed determined to show it could be done."

"And, of course, he did show exactly that," Mr. Parkley mused. "But what attitude did you take toward all this, what did you say to him?"

"Later, after leaving O'Neil's tavern I tried to dissuade him — but it was no use."

"Might I ask Francis a question?" Father Quinn said.

"Certainly."

"Just how much did John Little have to drink?"

Enter the moral theologian, Francis thought. He saw the quickening of interest on the part of his mother.

He pondered the question, his eyes on the table, yet seeing, nonetheless, the sleek, sure cleric looming — the molder of parishional thought and action, decrier of Communism and free love, he whom Francis had betrayed in the act of betraying his mother — betrayed the oiled machinery of the seminary, the editorial post on the *Beacon*, and once he had been ordained, the prestige and influence of his mother grading him on and up to the purple empyrean of the monsignori — Church and State: a son in the Church, a son in the State — and now the grand design half shattered; Father Carney, shambling, obscure, and holy, could not be denied — John Little could not be denied — dead John, gone John, wild-hill flight to Alice and the small one stilly — *miserere nobis.*

"He had several whiskys chased with beer." Francis looked with firmness at Father Quinn.

"How many whiskys would you say?" the priest asked.

"About four or five."

"The boy couldn't have been in full possession of his faculties, then," Father Quinn said.

"I don't see how he could drive as well as he did if he wasn't," Mike said.

Then Francis heard her voice, soft and steady, with the hurt hinting from its deeps:

"'Tell the board whether or not you had anything to drink."

There was in the ring and the root of her question the endless history of his failure. The traditional Irish feminine prejudices against the "hard stuff" had never been present in their family; but that was the point, it was a family matter. He could have beer or even whisky at home if he wanted it; but to drink under the criminal circumstances of John's escapade fitted the stubborn, defiant pattern of his nonconformity and confirmed his basic waywardness further in her mind.

"I had a beer while I was waiting there with John."

"What happened then?" Mr. Parkley asked.

"John and the bartender talked about the traps and felt the members of the old gang could go through them. Then we went outside and John headed for the parking space down on Medford Street, where he picked up the car."

"Did you try to dissuade him?" Mike asked.

"Yes. I think I told you that already."

He related the rest of the story as he knew it. How he watched at the parking lot while John got into the car. How he attempted to get into the moving car and was hurled to the street.

"Why did you try to go with him?" his mother asked, her lips taut with inner control.

He was silent a while, not knowing quite how to put it. "I — I just wanted to be with him, I guess; he was determined to go and I just couldn't let him go alone."

"Tell us, Franny," Jim Hanlon said in a booming, confident tone of voice, "did you have any desire to go larking down the Hill at this or any time?"

"None. Never," Francis answered.

There was a silence following his answer, a subscription, it seemed, to the finality with which it was expressed.

He got, at that moment, the feeling that they would probably clear him. But what would that avail? Guilty or innocent, the sincerity of his mother's committee activities would have been demonstrated. But he had to find some basis on which to live and work with his mother, after this was over. He had to declare himself to her in some way — let her know, however indirectly, that he wanted to help with the paper more than ever now, no matter what had happened to her best laid plans.

He had solidified his resolution made that night in jail — to stick by the paper — he still wanted to do some articles on looping from the preventive point of view.

But simply walking out of here cleared wouldn't be enough. He had to make some gesture to his mother and the rest of the committee — here, now.

Mr. Parkley cleared his throat carefully.

"Very well," he said, "if there are no more questions, I suggest we ask Mr. Ronayne to step into the anteroom for several minutes."

Parkley glanced around the table politely. There were no questions. He nodded at Mike, who stood and walked over to Francis.

Francis arose, half turned to follow Mike toward the door, paused, and again faced Mr. Parkley.

"Would it be possible for me to make a further statement?"

A flicker of interest crossed the faces of the committee. His mother looked at him oddly, almost as if amused at this unexpected show of vigor.

"I don't see why not," Mr. Parkley said, "unless there is some objection."

There was no objection. Mr. Parkley nodded at Francis.

"Thank you. In fairness to my mother's position on the committee and to the good work that she and all of you are trying to do, I think it's necessary for me to admit my legal, if not my personal, guilt in this case. I mean if I can be held up as an object lesson to other kids in Charlestown who might be deterred from looping, I'd like to co-operate. I'll do anything in my power, from here on, to help the committee — in jail or out."

"There is no question of jail!" Hanlon said, purpling.

"Mr. Hanlon," Parkley broke in firmly, "this is not the time for committee decision."

"Don't Mister Hanlon me!" the big man said, bringing his fist down on the table. "This — this — hearing is only a damn farce and yez all know it!"

"Jim!" Catherine called, her eyes filling with tears. "Please, Jim!"

"Come on, Fran," Mike said, grinning and taking Francis by the elbow.

"It is not a farce, Mister Hanlon," Parkley said calmly as the door closed behind them. "Judge Donahue of the Juvenile Court has authorized us. . . . "

While Erford Parkley, Sr., was graciously putting Jim Hanlon in his place, Catherine blinked away the tears and absorbed the dampness around her eyes with a handkerchief. The self-humiliation of Francis followed by the explosion of Hanlon had given her a double jolt. Knowing how close Francis and big Jim had become she had immediately identified their outbursts with the long and weary pattern of her struggle to give steadiness and direction to her younger son's life.

Hanlon's violent protest, she knew, was not so much directed at Parkley as it was at her. It was almost as if Jim had said, following her son's submission: "See here, Catherine, you silly fool. See what your son Francis is really like!"

Well, it was courageous of the boy to speak out that way. Martin would not have done it — he was much too — yes — too guileful for that. She sighed while Parkley summed up the testimony. . . . She had compared Martin unfavorably with Francis. Why? Martin was achieving everything she had hoped he would, but in what manner? Playing a dangerous game of political tag with both political factions. How long would that succeed? And the little divorcee! She could never think of her now without a twinge of anger. Martin never mentioned her, yet he was probably seeing a good deal of her.

Francis, on the other hand, had fulfilled none of her major wishes. Yet, bewilderingly, something fine kept shining out of him, something she would not at first concede was there. But it was there, she had seen it today more powerfully than ever. It fitted into a pattern she had never before recognized — his basic honesty, his unfailing humility before her displeasure. She fought back a maudlin urge to rise and go to him.

The voices were buzzing about her, she grew faint, shook her head.

"Mrs. Ronayne," she heard Parkley ask, "are you ill?"

Hanlon watched her out of sullen eyes, sensing her inward storm. Mike sat fascinated as the castle of feminism tottered for the first time in his acquaintance with her. The others reacted with polite reticence, knowing her travail largely in terms of upset emotions: Doctor Applebaum opened a window; Father Quinn breathed a prayer.

"I'll be fine in a minute," Catherine said. "Please continue."

"We're about finished," Mr. Parkley said. "I take it the mind of the meeting is that we recommend complete clemency to Judge Donahue. We respect your position with regard to the defendant, Mrs. Ronayne, and you needn't give an opinion, unless you feel you ought to."

"I would like to say something," Catherine said. "No parent is without blame for any of the unhappy involvements of its child. I will appreciate the chance to try and help Francis stay out of serious difficulty in the future."

She almost said more, but something in the features of Doctor Applebaum, a greater intentness, prevented her. It would do neither

her nor Francis any good to make a confessional of the committee hearing. She would give him a free and confident role in
the editing of the paper, if he would take it; she would try to stop
meddling — yes, that was the word — in his life.

"Splendid, Catherine!" Parkley said.

"There is one more thing," she said. "I want to offer my
resignation as chairman of this committee. I would, however, like
to stay on as a member and continue to work with you all."

"Very well," Parkley said. "Are there any objections."

There was silence.

"Would you care to advise your son of our decision, Catherine?"
Parkley asked. "You can do it now or later — whichever you prefer?"

"Thank you. I'll do it now."

She excused herself, smiling, and walked out of the room.

Chapter 29

HIGH noon was blazing when Francis stepped out of the building into the exhilarating racket of City Square. The sea was in the air, giving its pungency to the dust of the city; the long, gray, sharklike ships of the navy were moored near by, calling him seaward — a call he must continue to deny.

His life was stable again with the weight of a linotype machine and a cylinder press. She had come into the waiting room and told him of the committee's decision and asked him if he would like to take over John Little's position as managing editor.

Sensing a frailty in her that he had never before known, he accepted eagerly.

"I'll see you at dinner and we'll go into more detail." She had kissed him on the cheek.

He stood on the concrete porch of the police building a moment, blinking his eyes. He'd have a bite at a lunch counter and decide where to go — it would be a good time to call on Father Carney at the sem — a time of fresh decision. . . .

"Your car is ready, sir," he heard Althea say.

She was leaning on the railing to his left, her tanned skin dark against a bright yellow frock, smiling and nodding her pert, brown head, as if she knew all that was churning within him. "I left a message for Dad. He'll understand — he always does. Where can I take you?"

"I was going to eat something," he said, quietly, unsurely, as if she had been talking to someone behind him.

"Fine!" She straightened up and jingled her car keys. "Where did you want to go after that? We could drive in that direction and eat some place along the way."

Since she was offering him the ride, he thought again of Father Carney. He'd been putting off the visit for too long. And the sedentary priest-professor was really the only one he felt like talking to that afternoon.

"I think I'd like to go out to St. Philip's seminary and visit with an old prof. You wouldn't have to take me all the way — you could drop me off downtown perhaps."

"Your car is ready, sir," she repeated with an engaging petulance.

He laughed and followed her toward the roadster.

He left the booth to get some cigarettes, and she could see the river from the snack bar. The Charles was never blue even if you were in love, but in its curving, slow-flowing symmetry it was quite as attractive as the Danube.

She watched him at the cigarette counter, blond, thin, graceful — almost like a girl, she thought, but with a toughness to him that was pronouncedly masculine.

He seemed so different from Martin — his was the black-Irish attractiveness — the smoother, more calculated manner. She thought she was attracted to Francis because he was Martin's brother in considerable difficulty. But now she knew it was the boy himself that had drawn her.

He came back to the booth, and they smoked over a second cup of coffee. He had told her of the committee's decision and his mother's invitation to edit the paper.

He looked up from his coffee and found her holding him with her eyes. He felt the color rising in his face.

"You're an odd one," she said with tenderness.

"So are you."

"Now I think I know why Martin hasn't told me much about you. I'm not sure he could."

"He could tell you a lot of things from my mother's point of view."

"That's very possible," she said. "But I wonder, too, if you completely understand him."

"I'm not sure I do. He knows what he wants, he has the ability to get it, and he seems to be well on his way."

"Does he want too much?"

"That all depends."

"On what?" She put down her cigarette.

He hesitated. He had struck flint inadvertently. He recoiled from pursuing the matter further. But the thing could wreck Martin's career, his religious and family stability. Looking at her, proud and warm and vibrant, he knew Martin's conflict.

"Perhaps we're not talking about the same thing," he said.

"I think we are. What does it depend on, Martin's future, that is?"

"You."

The wax of her pride began to soften. She lowered her head and there was a sudden wetness in her eyes.

They were silent a moment. She fished for a handkerchief in vain. Francis slipped out his, flat and fresh from the pocket of his polo shirt. He handed it to her, smiling.

"Have a good blow."

"I love him so much." She opened the handkerchief and dabbed at her eyes. "I just don't want to face it — but we have to, both of us."

"I knew you loved him. I guess I knew it when I talked to you this morning. But he can't have both — you and the Irish Free State of Massachusetts. It's one or the other. . . . Besides —"

"I know — Dad knows too, and Erford."

"We're all in on this," Francis said.

"What would you say if I told you I was going away — immediately."

"It's probably a wise move," he said. "Not that I know too much about it. Maybe it's hard to say what's wiser than love. It's just — well, it's just that circumstances are hopelessly against both of you."

"I know." She was calmer now.

"Does Marty know?"

"I think he does. But as you suggested he wants too much. And he's headstrong enough to try and get it. He's much stronger willed than I am — I'm afraid I might give in if I stayed around any longer."

"That's his genius — making people see his vision or his point of view. But this is different; the Church will be involved. . . ."

"We have our taboos also, but I guess I've shattered a few of them already," she said with a hint of bitterness. "I mean it wouldn't be so much of a wrench for me as it would be for Martin."

Francis nodded. "All the more reason for going away." He glanced at his watch. It was close to two.

She picked up her compact and the check, and smiled bravely. "Well, I'm grateful for this chat. You're a lot older than you look. You'll be wanting to see your priest friend before it gets too late. I'll go powder my nose."

He watched her go toward the ladies' lounge, knowing a gratitude for her honesty and good will, but wondering how far away she would be going. How far is far from love? he wondered. Maybe New Zealand or the Belgian Congo, but even that is not far.

She left him standing in the shadow of St. Philip's. She waved as her roadster lurched forward; crunching against the cinders and conveying a sense of plunging, equestrian flight which was, he sensed, articulate of the frantic pattern of her life.

He turned and thought about her a few moments more, cool in the shadow of the huge gray bulk which Patrick Cardinal O'Garrity had reared up with the pennies of the poor. A strange and lovely girl! For an instant he envied Marty the love of her, but the shadows looming over that love were much deeper and colder than the long jagged shade of St. Philip's — longer, deeper, colder.

He walked toward the main entrance of the Hall in the clandestine stillness of midsummer afternoon — a hush which was broken only by the intermittent stitching of a cricket somewhere in the foliage surrounding the main building. There was that fragrance and sultry lushness about the trees, the bushes, the flowers, which made one remotely grateful that the seminarians did not have to frown over their philosophy and theology books at such a time. It might be more difficult to refute the fallacies of pantheism while all the senses were assaulted by the languid summer beauty of New England.

They were away now, many of them proctoring at summer camps. He thought of his old roommates, Tubby and Emmet. They would be ordained soon. He had lost contact with them, after an exchange of one or two letters. But now, standing on the great granite staircase leading into the Hall, his old intimacy with them came flooding back. He could hear the roaring locker-room laughter of Tubby, the quiet, scholarly talk of Emmet. He saw their faces, in elation and chagrin, or transformed by prayer. He knew a twinge of regret.

But all was silence and his footfalls echoed hollowly in the cool, wooden hallway, as he moved toward Father Carney's room. He passed the professors' recreation room and in it, snoozing with a droll opulence, his eyeglasses awry over his nose, was an ancient, rubicund priest with shaggy white hair. The vivid glimpse of him, slumped over his newspaper in a mothering leather armchair, sent a chill of timelessness through Francis. For the old curate was the same he had once encountered in the Father's Room as he snatched a quick look at the morning papers long ago. He recalled seeing the fresh, winsome faces of both Rosemary and the Parkley girl shining out of the society page. The swift and fickle labyrinth of the years had led them all into strange places and strange ways.

It was comforting, however, in a world of treacherous change to know that there existed a place and a group of people which had about them an unmistakable air of changelessness. Such was St. Philip's and such the witness given by an old priest, hobbling to heaven with his glasses dangling over his nose.

The door to Father Carney's room was ajar. He was lying, T-shirted, on a horsehair couch beside his desk, his eyes on the ceiling, his black-stockinged feet twinkling out of a pair of gray, cotton trousers.

It was as though Francis had come upon him sleeping. He paused and turned softly to go.

"I see you there," Father Carney said, without taking his eyes off the ceiling. "I wondered if it might be you coming softly along the corridor. You show a little too much consideration to be mistaken for one of our own Indians."

"Sorry if I interrupted your rest, Father."

"Come in, come in." The priest arose and swiveled his legs to the floor. Francis noticed a book yawning on the floor next to the couch.

"I rather thought you'd come to see me eventually. How is it with you?"

"Better, I guess. Mother seems to be coming around. She's been quite irked at me up until this morning."

The priest reached for his pipe and pouch which lay on the edge of the desk. "What had you done to get her dander up this time — joined the Republican party?"

Francis sat down and told the story of the looping incident, the hearing, and the aftermath. Father Carney listened reflectively, his gray eyes resting on the trees outside the window.

When Francis had finished, the priest puffed silently on his pipe for a while. The stillness of the seminary and its lush environs was bewitching. "Let's take a walk," Father Carney said abruptly. "I'll get a cassock on." He took another puff on his pipe and punctuated his remark with a swift, blue billow of smoke.

He went into his bedroom, and Francis stooped over to examine the book he had been reading. It was a treatise on the Holy Trinity and one could tell by the penciled notes along the margins and the well-thumbed appearance of the cover that the priest had been through the book many times.

Francis browsed through the section to which the work was open. His eyes were arrested by a passage which was enclosed in double pencil brackets. It read: "Our nature, as Pascal said, has perfections in order to show that it is the image of God, and defects in order to show that it is only His image."

"What do you make of that?"

He started a little and looked up at Father Carney who was standing behind him.

"It says it."

"I'm glad you think so. Come along and we'll talk about it some more."

They climbed Cemetery Hill in the center of the seminary grounds. It was a height bounded by the athletic field on the east and by the seminary buildings and the reservoir on the west.

"How's the Benedictine oblate these days? Are you still with us?" Father Carney asked, setting himself on a bench and lighting his pipe.

"I still read my little breviary," Francis said. "Matins and Compline, at least."

They were silent for several moments, drinking in the vista of water, trees, and sky, which they could see from the hilltop.

"Did you ever think about coming back to us?" Father Carney asked offhandedly.

"I suppose I have — not too seriously though, I mean. I've got to pitch in on the paper and help Mother out. There's so much that I can do now that she offered me the chance."

"I'd say you've made the right decision. I'm glad you didn't get cynical about your family troubles. Remember that paragraph you read in my room? We're all imperfect images of God, but still His images. We're all brothers in ugliness as well as in grandeur."

"If I'm not too presumptuous, I wish my mother fully realized what you just said."

"She will, she will," the priest said, taking one last puff and knocking out the ashes on the side of the bench. "Pray for her and be patient. She seems to be coming around."

"Yes, she does. I've a lot to be thankful for. And, anyway, no matter how she treats me, I can't get away from my love for her."

"There's a certain nourishment in that, which will see you through," the priest said. "I'm sure she still loves you, too."

"It's awfully hard to believe sometimes — although today she was fine. But I suppose you're right. Mother has a personal as well as a religious regimen which she lives by faithfully and she expects her family to do so also. My big sin has been nonconformity."

"It is a sin, if you want to call it that, which in your circumstances might well get you into heaven," the priest said. He glanced at his watch.

"I've a convert coming in about five minutes. I do wish we had more time to just sit here and chat. You'll keep in touch with me, though; let me know how this newspaper business comes out and all?"

They walked down the grassy path slowly — involuntarily postponing the return to the sultriness of the world below them. An automobile horn sounded lengthily across the silver stillness of the reservoir. In the late afternoon somnolence, the sound was like the cry of some lonely, winging mallard, soaring into the first roseate rags of a bright, pure day.

Chapter 30

Francis was passing out cards in the fall again. This time they read "Ronayne for Attorney General," and there was a greater excitement about it all.

They were in a little town near the New Hampshire border — he, Marty, and Mike. They were north of Lowell, north of Boston. But they were north, east, south, and west of everything as far as Francis was concerned; because this was the place to be at that moment when the first hint of crispness is in the Indian summer air and it is election time forever in the fall.

Marty was up on the platform that had been erected on the rear of his secondhand roadster. He was telling a handful of villagers why he had come up here so early in the campaign. Yes, he was a Democrat, but an independent one; he wanted the democratic nomination, but he wasn't working with the machine; he had a good record in the School Committee and at the State House; it was all in the record, and they could read it on the back of the cards the young man was passing out.

He told them that, next to the governorship, there wasn't a better place for an independent than the attorney general's office; and all he asked right now was that they consider his candidacy on the basis of his record and his educational background. He'd be back later in the fall to talk to them about the issues of the campaign; but right now he just wanted to come up here and introduce himself. And thank you very much.

Francis finished distributing the cards to a group of about twenty-five villagers and farmers. The faces of the men, most of them die-hard Republicans, were noncommittal. But in the features of their womenfolk he detected a kind of filing-card sympathy for the lean, good-looking legislator. He circled around the disintegrating group and headed for the car. He was beginning to be impressed by Marty's astuteness in persuading Mike to help him begin the campaign out here in the sticks.

"This is worth trying," Mike said as they got into the car. "You might have to settle for an even break with the machine in Boston. The votes that could put you in are the ones you'll pick up way out of town. Sure they're Republicans, or Democrats who vote against O'Malley, but remember one thing, most of them have wives and daughters; wives and daughters have a way of voting for a clean-cut young man with shining ideals and a mellifluous voice. Or so I notice tonight."

Marty had nodded as if he had already thought of that and was thinking of something else, something more important.

He was thinking of a girl named Althea and she was still as bright to his soul, to his life as the golden dome of the State House. He was thinking of how he had put through a long-distance call, from Boston to Gracklewood, that morning, after getting no answer to his letters during the past several weeks.

Over the phone he had told her he was near the New Hampshire line and he wanted to drive over and see her later that night. He could be in Concord by midnight. Could she be there to meet him?

No, she had said, no darling, no, no, no. But what she had meant and what she had finally said was yes. Yes, darling, yes, yes, yes.

They would meet in front of the post office around midnight. She would find some plausible excuse for taking the late-afternoon train down from the mountains. Jinny Stover, one of her Radcliffe chums, lived in Concord. She could visit her — Aunt Maude would approve of that — a day in the city, the city far away from Boston.

"But is it all right for you, dear, is it all right for you? Yes, it's all right for me, but is it all right for you? Yes, midnight in front of the post office. Yes, I do, darling, I do. Aunt Maude is coming in from the garden. Good-by for now."

She slipped the ponderous receiver onto its hook by the windup phone on the wall. She glanced through the wide, sun-rich windows of the dining room and saw Aunt Maude scuffing lightly along the flagstones, spade in gloved hand.

What to tell her? What else but a lie? Jinny Stover called from Boston where she had gone on a shopping trip. No. Jinny Stover called from Boston to say there was a special meeting of the New Hampshire alumnae in Concord that evening. Could she come in early enough for dinner at the Stovers?

It would not be easy to lie to Aunt Maude, but it would be harder still to continue to lie to herself and Martin.

Short, sere, head high in the warm splash of the morning sun that scattered the mountain cool of the valley, Aunt Maude turned off the path into the garden shed.

Althea, her tension relieved by the detour, looked beyond the garden and the neighboring colonial dwelling of the Widow Powell to the mountains.

Heavy with majesty they weighed upon her. Looming high and hazy, snow-capped, purple-ringed. Always there, heavy, lovely, seen through sun or haze, cloaked in night or skies of storm, always the sense of heavy thereness, always the weight of them on you.

She had fled to Concord and Jinny Stover before — movies, shopping, cocktails, riding — but always the mountains and the loneliness waiting, the longing for Martin strong and vivid, never waning.

Aunt Maude came out of the tool shed, the bright, eternal lark of the Parkley family. As she approached, Althea saw a possible prefiguration of herself. She could become Aunt Maude. She had heard the story of Maude's love for a British naval officer whom she had met at the Parkley plantation in Bermuda many years ago. Grandfather Parkley had been called back to Boston on emergency business about that time and took Maude with him.

Why not tell her the truth — she would understand. Yes, understand, but not betray her brother's trust.

The screen door creaked, followed by the sweeter, gentler creak of Aunt Maude's voice.

"Did I hear the telephone, pet?"

"Yes, dear," Althea said, walking toward the kitchen. "It was Jinny Stover calling from Boston. She's on her way home and wants me to . . ."

They were in the car and driving fast through the branchy night toward the next border town.

Mike was talking about Rosy Ryan, the machine's choice as candidate for attorney general. "You can beat that bum in Charlestown or anywhere. Hell, the intelligent voters will laugh at him."

"Sure they will. But are there enough intelligent voters?"

Francis wondered at the odd new note in Martin's answer — there was something of cynicism in his voice and something of doubt.

"How'd they look back there, Fran?" Mike continued, angling his jaw toward the rumble seat where Francis sat.

"The men were dead pan — but the women! My brother should be in the movies!"

"Just what we wanted," Mike said. "If we get you around enough all the women will vote for you."

"Maybe," Martin said.

"No maybe about it! You've got to play that sex appeal for all it's worth or you won't make it. We need those extra votes."

"Okay, Mike," Martin said.

They were silent, responding to the mood of quiet which pervaded the car for several minutes as it droned along the country road.

Francis was convinced, by now, there was something weighing heavily on Marty's mind. I'll bet it's the girl friend. She must have gone away like she said she would. He'll snap out of it — he'd better.

"By the way, Fran," Mike said, "your mother likes those articles you're doing for the paper. Has she told you?"

"She said she likes them."

"She said more than that to me."

"What articles are those?" Martin asked.

"The kid here is doing a series called 'The Life and Death of a Looper.' He points out that the citizens of Boston and, particularly, Charlestown, are guilty, in a way, of murder. Better read them, Marty. People will be asking you about them."

"Yeh, I guess so."

The car bore steadily into the tunnel-like blackness of the treed-over night. Marty slowed approaching a curve, and hummed into it with the plodding security of a heavy old car. Making the southwesterly turn, his headlights picked up a sign which gleamed out ghoulishly: NEW HAMPSHIRE STATE LINE.

"Say, there's the state line!" Martin said.

"We've been playing tag with it all evening," Mike said. "What's so exciting about that?"

"Oh, nothing, I guess," Martin said. "What's the nearest big city. Nashua?"

"Yeh, Nashua."

"How far is Concord from there?"

"I don't know for sure — maybe an hour's drive. Got a pal up there?"

"Maybe. . . ."

Concord, Francis thought. Could she be there?

They rolled into the town of Tewkston, their third and last call that night. It was close to nine-thirty as they parked the car under a gas lamp near the greening bronze statue of an obscure, mounted Civil War colonel, who was by no means obscure in Tewkston.

Francis wound up the phonograph in the rumble seat beside him, maneuvered its large horn until it yawned out the window. He flicked the switch, dropped the needle. The tinny strains of "Stars and Stripes Forever" broke the rustic quietude of Tewkston Mall.

Then he got out of the car dragging behind him a framed, oilcloth sign which he erected on the hood.

"State Representative Ronayne For Attorney General!" the sign read, *"The people are my party machine!"*

"Drink it up," Mike said, an hour later, swinging around on the stool and thudding his feet against the floor. "We've a lot of ground to cover tomorrow."

Francis gulped down the rest of his malted milk and joined

Mike at the cigarette counter. They pushed through the revolving door into the quiet of Tewkston Square and turned left toward the hotel.

Behind them they could hear the druggist locking up for the night, his lights shuttling out and giving a flashing caress to the main street.

All about them was the ancient peace of a small New England town. The gas lamps flickered in the square, playing their shadows over the old wooden buildings and the paneled windows of the store fronts. On the corner outside the hotel the constable looked up and down the square, and then, as if scenting their strangeness, surveyed them coolly as they approached.

"Bank robbers," Mike whispered, as they turned into the gloomy stair bottom that passed for a lobby. They climbed the wooden stairs to their double room.

They shut the door behind them and they were enclosed in the two bare rooms with the spindly white iron bedsteads and the porcelain washbowl. "The toilet is down the hall," the desk clerk had twanged earlier. "Ye'll need a flashlight."

In the flicker of the street lamp they could see the flashlight on Martin's bed. He had declined a malt earlier and gone to the car for the light.

On the bed, under the flashlight, was a sheet of paper. Mike flicked the button and read. Francis groped for the wall switch and threw on the dim ceiling light.

"You'll have a bed all to yourself." Mike handed Francis the note.

"I've got to see somebody in Concord." The note read. "It's better I slip off this way. I'll contact you later."

"Better this way, he says."

Mike sank down on the bed. "Yeh. As if he'd listen to us anyway. Who's up there, this Parkley broad?"

"Probably."

"What the hell's the matter with him?" Mike snapped.

"It's simple enough, Mike. They're hopelessly in love."

"Love," Mike said. "If O'Malley and his boys find out about this, they'll crucify him."

"He shouldn't see her now. You'll have to talk to him, Mike."

"Sure, I'll talk to him. Either he stays away from her until after the election or we're through. God almighty! What's gotten into him?"

Francis shrugged his shoulders.

"Oh, well . . . nothing we can do but wait. Run along to bed, kid."

After Francis had said his prayers he lay on the white bed in the moonlight, thinking. Marty was rushing through New Hampshire toward her. Mother would not believe this of him — or would she? There was nothing to do but wait for the morning to come, wait for a message, and see what love had decided concerning politics and religion.

There was a red light ahead. Martin took his foot off the accelerator for the first time since he had left Tewkston. He pumped methodically on the brake. The red light loomed up in front of him faster than he expected it. He pressed hard on the brake and lurched to a stop at the crossroad.

Behind him in the rumble seat, he heard the phonograph shift abruptly. He heard the click of the needle against graphite and the shrill music of "Stars and Stripes Forever" filled the car and sifted across the lone midnight of the crossroad.

He listened to it, stunned for several moments, even after the stoplight had turned green. The raucous music in the serenity of the night was utterly incongruous — like a fire siren wailing in a cathedral.

His next reaction was laughter, loud, mounting laughter, relieving the tension he had known all evening. He turned and shut the phonograph off, removing the record.

He resumed his seat, and accelerated along the state road to Nashua, the road that led to her, away from the golden dome, away from his mother and Father Quinn.

There was something about the tinny martial music that reminded him of the futile feeling he had that afternoon when he stood on the Common looking up at the dome thinking of the same choice he was facing tonight.

They could try and keep things quiet until after the election.

Then they should be able to make some sort of graceful public announcement.

Now he had that same feeling of choice in a much more powerful way — a feeling about which he was going to do something. The dream of fame, all the striving, all the ironclad urbanity, the devious conformity to his mother's wishes reared up within him again.

Maybe Mother could get Althea's marriage fixed up — her priest friend — Father Quinn's connections at the Chancery. How did it go? Baptism — yeh — Baptism. Maybe she hadn't been baptized. Yeh, she'd be the first Yankee in history that hadn't been baptized.

Her husband is alive, sure he's alive, very much alive.

Martin took his foot off the accelerator — the old car coughed, slowing.

No, no, none of it would work — her, just her, be with her, be with her always.

He jammed his foot on the accelerator. His hands were clammy on the wheel. The back of his neck tingled — coldly, warmly. . . . The life and death of a looper — the life and death of a lover. . . .

The outlying street lamps of Nashua were in his windshield. The old car coughed through the late-night streets that were desolate with silence. He accelerated out into the country again, toward Concord, and the lady of the mountains. She, the first lady of the land where love is blindly elected.

Chapter 31

THE telephone continued to ring, long and insistently. Erford blinked his eyes, glanced at his watch. It was 2 a.m. He must have fallen asleep over that last Scotch and soda.

He pushed himself out of the black leather armchair, rubbed his eyes again and moved toward the hall. It might be Dad calling from Osterville where he was attending a Harvard class reunion. Perhaps something had happened. . . .

He hurried to the phone and lifted the receiver.

"Hello."

"Hello, for heaven's sake hello!" Aunt Maude said. "Is that you, Erford? Where's your father? I want to speak to him immediately. Oh dear, dear, dear!"

"He's not here, Aunt Maude. He's down on the Cape with his classmates. But what is it? Is Althea ill? What is it?"

"Oh dear!" Aunt Maude went on in a singsong of bewilderment. "He would be away now. Oh, my dear!"

"What is it, Aunt Maude! You must tell me!"

"Yes, yes, of course! You'll have to handle this for your father. It's Althea. She's gone off somewhere — maybe with that young Irish boy. She left for Jinny Stover's this afternoon and never returned. I called Jinny shortly before one. Althea hadn't been there and, what's more, she wasn't even expected.

"She's done something rash, I fear, Erford, something extremely rash. Oh, my dear, what will your father say!"

He was fully awake now, electrically awake. Ronayne again.

Ronayne upsetting the balance again. Independent in politics, independent in love. Ronayne again, smearing the lines of the pattern — Ronayne. The Parkley temper, that grows colder as other tempers grow warmer, chilled steadily within him.

"Come now, Aunt Maude, settle down and tell me exactly what happened today? Did Althea receive a letter from Boston? A call?"

"Yes, yes. There was a call from Boston. Jinny Stover called. . . . No, she told me she didn't call. It must have been from that young man. I was in the garden with my gladioli. I was in the garden when he called."

"Very well. Now, please give me the Stover girl's phone number."

He wrote the number down on a pad. "Yes, Aunt Maude. I'll call you in the morning. Yes. I'll get in touch with father as soon as I know for certain. Yes, Aunt Maude. Good night."

He stood by the phone several moments staring into the shadows of the long, wainscoted hall. If it were true, this would be the end of Ronayne in politics. He'd see to that. But Althea, Sis? If it was true, she at least had what she wanted — the silly little ass! Love, love, love. And what about the suave young man from across the river? What about him? He seemed to want Althea more than political success, family — religion.

Well, they'd better be satisfied with each other.

He lifted the receiver and asked for long distance. He spoke the Stover name and number, waiting.

There's nothing else for them, he thought, nothing else. That fool, that blind, pigheaded fool. And my sister, my own sister. . . .

He stood in a black void, cold with rage, for what seemed like hours.

"Here's your party."

"Hello, Jinny. Forgive me for calling at such an hour.

"Yes, I've just talked to Aunt Maude. Where would they be likely to go? Isn't there some sort of quick-marriage place up your way?

"Yes, Belleview, that's the place. I'll call there.

"Yes, I'll ask Aunt Maude to relay the news. Thank you so much. Good night."

Belleview. Do you take this woman out of her world and does she take you out of yours until death do you part?

"Hello, operator, will you connect me with Belleview, New Hampshire? I want to talk to the justice of the peace up there, or to any number of them if necessary."

There was only one justice of the peace in Belleview. His name was Willard Standring and at one o'clock he had issued a license and performed the ceremony for a man named Ronayne and a woman named Parkley.

"Thank you very much. Good night."

He put the phone down, walked back into the study, and splashed a large measure of Scotch into a glass. He drank it, grimaced, and returned to the phone. Then he called the city desk of the *Daily Yankee*.

"I have some news for you. The candidate for attorney general, State Representative Martin Ronayne, has just eloped with Althea Parkley Royce of Back Bay. They were married at one o'clock this morning by the Justice of the Peace in Belleview, New Hampshire. . . . No, I do not care to give my name. You may call Belleview and check this information if you like. . . . That's quite all right. Good night."

He set down the phone and went back to the study. He poured himself another dollop of Scotch, quaffed it, grimaced again, and poured still another.

At Scituate by the sea, by the beautiful sea, the morning is cooler than morning is cool; the trees are deeper, darker, than trees are deep and dark. And that is the New England coast — the trees all around you, rich, dark, and green — then, suddenly, as you avert your eyes from the west, the mighty diamond sparkle of the sand, the sky, and the sea under the sun's relentless encroachment.

As Catherine opened her eyes in the cliff bungalow of her son-in-law she could not know by the sighing serenity of the sea that back in her Charlestown apartment the telephone was ringing hysterically, a reporter was chinning himself on her bedroom window sill, and already the morning papers were on the streets emblazoned with black shame for Mr. and Mrs. Ronayne.

She could tell by the sweet order of their breathing that Rosemary and the babies were asleep in the next room. But there was a great restlessness upon her and she decided to rise and put on the coffee.

In the kitchen, after the kerosene had sputtered into a smoky, blue glow under the coffee pot, she sat at the table smoothing her eyebrows and wondering about her boys. Mike and Francis were due back at the beach in the afternoon and she was anxious to hear how Martin had been received.

Martin would not come on to Scituate with them. He had business at the State House. But then he always had business somewhere these days.

Perhaps he had always got on without her, although he used to be tactful enough to conceal his independence. She hadn't known for a long time about his continued interest in the Parkley girl, for example. Nor could she ever remain quite at rest concerning his deftness at playing both Hanlon and the Parkleys.

Jim Hanlon. She fumbled around in her kimono pocket for his latest letter which she had read before retiring. She took it out and read parts of it again, trying to recapture the solace and amusement it had given her originally.

The letter was written in broad-lined pencil, the characters large and erect against the white, pseudolinen stationery:

"You've asked me how I got into the naval hospital with a suite of my own and all. Well, didn't I up and join the naval reserve the time Martin, God rest his soul, went off to the war? And haven't I done a few favors for the Navy Yard in my time. Where is your memory, girl?

"Colopini, the building contractor who wants to buy your paper came around to see me yesterday. It was nice of you to refer him to me because you know I am against such a business.

"He offers a pretty price — twelve thousand, and half in cash to hold the deal. His money is good, I well know. He got it all from the city and we supervised his every move.

"He wants the paper as a plaything for his son who will soon graduate from journalism college. But my opinion is still *no*. I told him I'd talk it over with you and would take no money now.

"Francis is doing a fine job for you — admit it now. And the thought of Martin's paper being in the hands of the ginnies is no consolation. That paper should go to your family and to no one else — to Francis, in particular, since the others seem to be well taken care of."

She looked up from the letter at the first perk of the coffee. Jim was right. She had never seriously considered selling the paper, anyway. And Francis *was* applying himself. She finished the letter:

"So young Marty is campaigning upstate — and doing things without the organization. Well, he's much to be admired. But sooner or later he will have to combine with someone or something. He cannot go on forever alone.

"Drop over to Chelsea and see me when you get home. I'll shout you to a dinner in my rooms, with a Filipino waiter and all, as nice as you please."

She frowned, then smiled slowly, putting the letter down. Jim Hanlon would never change. Like most people the good in him had always to be accepted along with the dubious.

She was sure Hanlon recognized his weakness in playing politics for his own selfish ends even as she recognized her own weaknesses — frailties which she found difficult if not impossible to strengthen. It had taken her many years to realize that her family and friends probably found her devotion to her dead husband unreasonable and even a nuisance. Her attempt to influence the lives of her sons, she knew, was rooted in that devotion to Martin.

"Let them live their own lives." She brought her hand down firmly on the kitchen table, sighed, and reached for the coffeepot. Then she remembered her sleeping daughter and grandchildren. She poured the coffee into a cup with meticulous care.

"Is that you, Mother?" Rosemary called softly from the bedroom.

"Yes, dear."

She listened for the children and heard nothing except the scuffing of Rosemary into her slippers.

"You're up early, Mother," Rosemary closed the kitchen door behind her. "Feeling okay?"

"Fine dear. Come have some coffee."

They heard the whir of bicycle wheels up the gravel walk from the road that wound down the cliff. The paper boy rolled by them, tossing the packet of news.

Rosemary opened the screen door, picked up the paper.

"I wonder how the Braves made out," she said, spreading the front page out on the kitchen table.

Their watches read nine o'clock when Mike and Francis descended to the tiny, musty hotel lobby that morning. Martin had not returned so they called at the desk, assuming there would be a message.

"Do you have a telegram for Ronayne or Farrell?" Mike asked the ancient, sad-eyed clerk who looked upon them patiently.

Without a word the clerk turned, selected a yellow envelope from a pigeonhole and handed it to Mike.

"Thanks," Mike said, ripping it open, reading, and handing it to Francis.

HEADING NORTH TILL STORM ENDS. READ THE MORNING PAPERS AND YOU'LL KNOW WHY. THANKS FOR EVERYTHING.

MARTIN AND ALTHEA

The telegram was addressed to Ronayne-Farrell, and had been sent from Manchester, New Hampshire, at 8 a.m.

"I'll bet they were on their way here when they saw the papers. Now they're running away," Francis said. He had a hard time swallowing.

"Might as well." Mike sighed. "He's finished. Let's get the papers and see if we have any appetite left for breakfast."

"This is no surprise to me, Mike," Francis said when they were on the sidewalk. "Marty's been gone on that girl for a long time — and she on him."

"Yeh, gone," Mike said. "What do I do now — run for attorney general myself?"

"You'd do better than Marty."

"Right now *you* could beat him," Mike said. "What are you doing next fall?"

They went into the drugstore, and over their coffee and rolls they read the papers. They read what had disturbed their dreams the night before, they read what they had refused to read in their minds.

REP. RONAYNE ELOPES WITH DIVORCEE
Is Candidate for Attorney General

"Is Candidate for Attorney General," Mike said. "*Was* candidate for Attorney General."

In front of Francis on the sooty day coach creaking toward the South Shore, there was a fat man puffing and complaining to the soldier beside him about how "hot it is for September!"

Mike had stayed behind in Boston to call on his newspaper friends and do what he could to tone down further scandal-sheet interest in the elopement.

Francis blinked out the open window of the coach and took an allotment of soot along with his mouthful of fresh, warm air.

The soldier did not feel like talking and nodded glumly. Francis shared his mood and was glad there would be no chatter about the weather. He found sufficient conversation in the cool green of the trees that thickened about them as the suburbs thinned, a green that in a few short weeks would go yellow and red.

Now the local slowed where the highway curved like a scimitar beside the track, the heat waves giving a mirage of silver wetness to the steaming tar.

Set back twenty yards from the turn was a large billboard announcing the annual Labor Day clambake of "The Sons of Irish Freedom"!

GAMES!   FRIED CLAMS!
3.2 BEER
GUEST SPEAKERS:
YOUR NEXT GOVERNOR
EDWARD P. O'MALLEY
YOUR NEXT ATTORNEY GENERAL
JOHN "ROSY" RYAN

Attorney General Ryan, Francis thought. And what of "Attorney General Ronayne"? To whom would *he* speak from now on? To his wife, to his pillow, to the depths of that third or fourth Scotch and soda?

The fat man and the soldier got off at consecutive back-yard stops. It would be another half hour into Scituate. The air was cooler, the trees deeper, darker, as the train approached the sea. His mother would have to be faced and he did not thrill at the prospect of telling her his side of the story. Very likely she had already heard about the elopement through the papers or over the radio.

He could not control his old bitterness upon thinking that she might go on and on like she used to. On and on about the seminary and their father and the way that both he and Martin had failed her and themselves. He tried to think about something else — about Rosemary and the children, Mike coming up tomorrow, the sea, the sand, the long Labor Day week end.

But Martin would not be there, nor — and it sounded odd to call Althea that — his wife. He thought of the two of them, comely, bright, and courageous; she, cut off from her traditional roots, he, from his religion as well. They'd attempt to carve out a new life somewhere maybe, but no matter how much courage was theirs they still would know the midnight dryness in the throat, the sharp, momentary wave of bewilderment, the longing for the familiar voice, the yearning for the sheen of the sun on the Charles in April, or the long shadow of the Monument over the sooted snow.

"We all choose our own kind of crucifixion — good or bad," Father Carney had once said. They had chosen theirs.

He looked out the window at the hugely breathing contour of ocean. The astringent vitality of the wind and sky were a ballet of natural gladness. Yet a grayness weathered up in him at the thought of Martin's absence and he could not respond to joy.

To Catherine's right was that same sea, heaving with emerald immensity into an ultimate water promontory which seemed higher than the cliff from which she viewed it. To her left a ribbon of fine, white dust wound down along the edge of the cliff toward the town.

Faintly from the strip of beach at the foot of the cliff she could hear the squeals of her grandchildren as they cavorted with Rosemary in the frothy edges of the surf.

The breeze crinkled the newspaper in her lap. It was good of Rosemary to leave her alone, to pack a lunch and keep the children at the beach since early morning.

The first stunning blow of Martin's act had waned into a dull ache. And she had wept as she had not wept since her husband's death.

With tear-reddened eyes she glanced again at the afternoon edition of the *World,* which she had reread several times, almost as if there must appear some additional explanation which she had missed in her earlier readings. "The newlyweds checked out of a Manchester hotel about eight this morning and left no forwarding address. Employees at the hotel last saw their car heading north. . . . " She started to weep again and lowered her head into her hands.

Above her a gull keened and wheeled, flashing against the pure-blue sky.

She dropped the paper on the lawn. I could have helped him, she thought, knowing that she was as much to blame for this as anyone, knowing that she had, over the years, been more interested in what *she* wanted, than in what her children wanted.

And Francis. With what dignity he had endured her willfulness! How she had pushed his life around. Francis. . . . He would not have ignored his religion. He would not have run away without facing her. He had faced her always — raw with embarrassment, but unflinching — in the seminary, after the looping escapade. He had submitted to her, proud and arbitrary though she had been.

Well, she would have to try and make it up to him. But would he let her after the arctic breath she had continually blown over his life? She raised her head.

Beneath her the road dipped away from the cliff and the sea into the highway and the trees. She saw a young man emerging from the trees. It was Francis.

She pushed herself to her feet and called his name, hurrying toward him. Above the sea and the cliff the gulls wheeled and whimpered, adding their largess to the billowy glee of the day.